INDULGE IN JOANNE FLUKE'S CRIMINALLY DELICIOUS HANNAH SWENSEN MYSTERIES!

WEDDING CAKE MURDER

"There are plenty of Fluke's trademark recipes on view here, and the New York trip and reality-show frame give the episode a fresh twist."
—*Booklist*

DOUBLE FUDGE BROWNIE MURDER

"Lively . . . Add the big surprise ending, and fans will be more than satisfied."
—*Publishers Weekly*

BLACKBERRY PIE MURDER

"Lake Eden's favorite baker, Hannah Swensen, finds herself on the wrong end of a police investigation . . . in Fluke's good-natured 19th [installment]."
—*Kirkus Reviews*

RED VELVET CUPCAKE MURDER

"Culinary cozies don't get any tastier than this winning series."
—*Library Journal*

"If your reading habits alternate between curling up with a good mystery or with a good cookbook, you ought to know about Joanne Fluke."
—*The Charlotte Observer*

CINNAMON ROLL MURDER

"Fans of this wildly popular series will not be disappointed. Fluke has kept this series strong for a long time, and there is still plenty to enjoy for foodie crime fans."
—*Booklist*

Books by Joanne Fluke

Hannah Swensen Mysteries

CHOCOLATE CHIP COOKIE MURDER
STRAWBERRY SHORTCAKE MURDER
BLUEBERRY MUFFIN MURDER
LEMON MERINGUE PIE MURDER
FUDGE CUPCAKE MURDER
SUGAR COOKIE MURDER
PEACH COBBLER MURDER
CHERRY CHEESECAKE MURDER
KEY LIME PIE MURDER
CANDY CANE MURDER
CARROT CAKE MURDER
CREAM PUFF MURDER
PLUM PUDDING MURDER
APPLE TURNOVER MURDER
DEVIL'S FOOD CAKE MURDER
GINGERBREAD COOKIE MURDER
CINNAMON ROLL MURDER
RED VELVET CUPCAKE MURDER
BLACKBERRY PIE MURDER
DOUBLE FUDGE BROWNIE MURDER
WEDDING CAKE MURDER
CHRISTMAS CARAMEL MURDER
BANANA CREAM PIE MURDER
JOANNE FLUKE'S LAKE EDEN COOKBOOK

Suspense Novels

VIDEO KILL
WINTER CHILL
DEAD GIVEAWAY
THE OTHER CHILD
COLD JUDGMENT
FATAL IDENTITY
FINAL APPEAL
VENGEANCE IS MINE
EYES
WICKED
DEADLY MEMORIES
THE STEPCHILD

Published by Kensington Publishing Corporation

JOANNE FLUKE

Lemon Meringue Pie Murder

KENSINGTON BOOKS
http://www.kensingtonbooks.com

KENSINGTON BOOKS are published by

Kensington Publishing Corp.
119 W. 40th Street
New York, NY 10018

All Kensington titles, imprints and distributed lines are available at special quantity discounts for bulk purchases for sales promotion, premiums, fund-raising, educational or institutional use.

Special book excerpts or customized printings can also be created to fit specific needs. For details, write or phone the office of the Kensington Sales Manager: Kensington Publishing Corp., 119 W. 40th Street, New York, NY 10018, Attn. Sales Department. Phone: 1-800-221-2647.

Kensington and the K logo Reg. U.S. Pat. & TM Off.

First Kensington Hardcover Printing: March 2003

First Kensington Mass Market Printing: February 2004

ISBN-13: 978-1-4967-1402-2
ISBN-10: 1-4967-1402-4
First Kensington Trade Paperback Printing: October 2004

10 9 8 7 6 5 4 3 2

Printed in the United States of America

This book is for The Great Nicky Borzoi.
We miss you, boy.

ACKNOWLEDGMENTS

Thank you to Ruel, who stops the trucks from
getting through.
Thanks to our kids, who know that the cookie jar
is bottomless.
Thank you to our friends and neighbors:
Mel & Kurt (our gardening angels), Lyn & Bill, Gina, Jay,
Bob M., Amanda, John B. & Walt, Dr. Bob & Sue, and
everyone who asked for that fifth cookie.
A huge thank-you to my editor, John Scognamiglio, for his
talent, his constant support, and his encouragement.
And thanks to all the good folks at Kensington who help
Hannah Swensen bake up a storm.
Thank you to Hiro Kimura for his delightful cover art.
Lemon pie never looked so good . . . or so menacing.
A big hug for Terry Sommers and her Wisconsin family for
critiquing my recipes. (I may have to forgive you for
preferring the Packers.)
My thanks to Nicole, who tests my cookies in Illinois, and
to Mom and Betty Jacobson, for their lemon pie tips.
Kudos to Jamie Wallace for making MurderSheBaked.com
a great web site.
And a big thank-you to all my e-mail friends who share
their thoughts, their baking tips, and their love for
Hannah Swensen and Lake Eden, with me.
I've included an extra cookie recipe for you.

Lemon Meringue Pie Murder

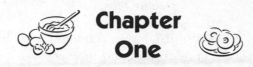

Hannah Swensen was startled awake at four forty-seven in the morning. Two feral eyes were staring down at her. She batted out at them and they vanished, leaving an accusatory yowl floating in their wake.

"This is my pillow, not yours!" Hannah muttered, retrieving it and settling it in, under her head. But before she could close her eyes for the few precious minutes of sleep that remained until her alarm clock blared, guilt set in. She'd never slapped out at Moishe before. Her orange and white tomcat had taken enough abuse while he was living on the streets. His left ear was torn and he was blind in one eye, a reminder of how he'd once fought to survive. In the time since Hannah had invited him in to share her condo, they'd become friends. Now that friendship was in jeopardy. If worse came to worst, Moishe might never trust her again.

"I'm sorry, Moishe. Come here and I'll scratch your ears." Hannah patted the sheets, hoping for feline forgiveness. "I'd never really hurt you. You should know that by now. You just scared me, that's all."

There was another yowl, a bit less irate this time, coming from the floor by the foot of her bed. Hannah patted the sheets again and she felt a thump as Moishe landed on the mattress. All was forgiven and that made her feel good, but now that she was wide awake, her neck began to twinge with a vengeance. Moishe must have commandeered her pillow shortly after she'd gone to bed and now she was paying the price of his comfort. The only cure for her sore neck would be a long hot shower before she went to work.

"Fine. I'm up," Hannah grumbled, reaching out to flick off her alarm. "I'll get your breakfast. Then I'll shower."

Once she'd found her slippers, Hannah padded down the hallway to the kitchen. She flicked on the light and opened the window to catch any early morning breezes that might be lurking outside her condo complex, but only warm, muggy air greeted her. Lake Eden, Minnesota, was in the middle of an unseasonable heat wave, unusual weather for the tail end of June, and the nights were almost as hot as the days.

Moishe took up a position by his food bowl and gazed at her expectantly. His tail was flicking back and forth like a metronome, and Hannah wondered idly whether she could attach a fan and harness all that energy.

"Patience is a virtue," Hannah muttered, quoting her mother. Then she remembered that the admonition hadn't worked on her, either. "I'm getting your breakfast right now, even before my first cup of coffee. If that isn't an apology, I don't know what is!"

Moishe's tail continued swishing as Hannah went to the broom closet and opened the padlock she'd installed on the door. Some people might think that the padlock was overkill, but Moishe got insecure every time he could see a bare patch at the bottom of his food and he wasn't shy about helping himself from the mother lode. Tired of sweeping up spilled kitty crunchies, Hannah had attempted to secure her stock by several unsuccessful methods. Moishe had conquered a bungee cord, a new heavy-duty latch, and a hook-and-eye fastener. When her determined feline roommate wanted food, he turned into a regular Houdini. No lock could stop him for long.

Once Moishe was crunching contentedly, Hannah poured

herself a cup of coffee and headed off to the shower. Today was Friday and it promised to be a busy day. Not only was Friday Pie Day at The Cookie Jar, Hannah's bakery and coffee shop, she had to fill an order for five batches of Old-Fashioned Sugar Cookies. The order had come from a Minneapolis caterer and the cookies were for a wedding reception.

Hannah and her partner, Lisa Herman, had mixed up the cookie dough before they'd locked up the previous night. Hannah would bake the cookies and then the pies, Lemon Meringue this week, before Lisa came in at seven-thirty. It was Lisa's job to decorate the cookies with the initials of the bride and groom, "PP" for Pamela Pollack and "TH" for Toby Heller.

After a few minutes under the steaming spray, Hannah's neck pain had faded into a dull ache. Since the KCOW weatherman had predicted that today could be one of the hottest days of the summer, she decided to wear her lightest-weight slacks, the ones she'd chosen last summer on a rare shopping trip with her sister, Andrea. Hannah stepped into the slacks and struggled as she attempted to pull them up. Even with the zipper wide open, she couldn't get them past her hips. They hadn't been this tight when she'd tried them on in the dressing room!

Hannah eyed her straining slacks balefully. She'd gained weight, a lot of it. It was bad enough being the tallest one in her petite family and the only daughter who'd inherited her father's unruly red hair. Now she was also overweight. It was time to go on a diet whether she liked it or not.

Visions of an endless stream of salads with low-cal dressing danced through Hannah's head as she peeled off the slacks and rummaged in the closet for a pair with an elastic waistband. Jogging was out. She hated it and she didn't have the time anyway. Joining a gym wasn't possible, either. The nearest gym was out at the mall and she'd never drive out there to use it. As much as the prospect sickened, she'd just have to limit her intake of food. It was the only possible way for her to shed the weight she'd gained.

Hannah turned to glance at the bathroom scale. She knew it was only her imagination, but it looked coiled and ready, like a rattlesnake set to strike. She told herself the sensible thing would be to weigh herself now, to see how much she needed to lose. She even took a step toward the scale, but she stopped when her heart began to pound and her palms grew damp. When was the last time she'd stepped on the scale? It had to have been at least six months ago. Perhaps she should diet for a week and then weigh in. That way the shock wouldn't be so severe. At least coffee didn't have calories. She'd have another cup and decide later about when she should weigh herself.

The hands of her apple-shaped kitchen clock were approaching five-twenty by the time Hannah finished her third cup of coffee. She refilled Moishe's food bowl and poured the rest of her coffee into the car carrier Bill Todd, her brother-in-law, had given her two Christmases ago.

" 'Bye, Moishe. Be good while I'm gone," Hannah said, giving him a scratch under the chin and then slinging her saddlebag-sized purse over her shoulder. "I may be condemned to lettuce for supper, but I promise that you'll get a big bowl of . . ."

Hannah broke off in mid-sentence as the kitchen wall phone rang. It had to be her mother. No one but Delores would call her this early. For a fleeting second, Hannah thought about letting the answer machine pick up, but her mother would just track her down later, perhaps at an even more inconvenient time. There was no sense in delaying the inevitable.

The phone pealed a second time and Moishe turned his back on it, sticking his haunches in the air and flicking his tail. Hannah laughed, amused at his antics. Delores was not one of Moishe's favorite people. She was still laughing as she grabbed the phone and answered, "Hello, Mother."

There was silence on the other end of the line and then Hannah heard a chuckle, a *male* chuckle. "I'm not your mother."

"Norman?" Hannah plopped her purse on the kitchen table and sat down in a chair. Norman Rhodes was one of her favorite people and she dated him occasionally. "What are you doing up this early?"

"I always get up this early. I wanted to catch you before you left. Hannah, I need a favor."

"What is it?" Hannah asked, smiling as she pictured Norman. She could hear water running and she knew he was making coffee in his mother's kitchen. Norman wasn't what most people would call handsome, but Hannah liked his looks. He had the kind of face people instinctively trusted.

"Will you reserve a big table at the rear of The Cookie Jar for me at nine-thirty this morning?"

"I can't," Hannah said with a grin.

"Why not?"

Hannah laughed outright. "Because I don't have any *big* tables. They're all the same size. How about if I push two together for you?"

"That'd be fine. I've got some exciting news, Hannah."

"Really?" Hannah glanced up at the clock. She was running late, but that was all right. The pies wouldn't take long. She'd baked the crusts before she'd left work yesterday, and all she had to do was cook the filling and put on the meringue. She wanted to talk to Norman. She'd just work a little faster when she got to her cookie shop.

"I made an offer on a house and it's been accepted."

"You bought a *house?*" Hannah hadn't had an inkling that Norman was in the market for a house.

"That's right, and I want to sign the papers this morning before the seller changes her mind. I got a really good deal on the Voelker place."

"That's wonderful," Hannah said, hoping that Norman knew what he was getting into. The Voelker place was a wreck. It was on a nice piece of land overlooking Eden Lake, the body of water that was within Lake Eden's city limits, but the house hadn't been modernized in over six decades. "Are you going to remodel it?"

"It needs too many improvements for that. I just bought it for the land. I'm going to tear it down and build our dream house."

Hannah wondered if she'd heard him correctly. "Did you say *our* dream house?"

"That's exactly what I said. I'm talking about the one we designed for that contest we won. Those plans were perfect, Hannah. It's a great house and it'll be a real showplace."

Hannah was speechless, a real rarity for her. She'd helped Norman design the plans and she'd been ecstatic when they'd won the contest. They'd split the prize money and she now had a window air conditioner in her kitchen at The Cookie Jar, eight new ceiling fans that had been mounted in the coffee shop, and new shelving that was being installed in her pantry. Their dream house *was* a great house, but Hannah had never in her wildest imaginings thought that Norman would actually build it! What was he going to do rattling around in a four-bedroom, three-bath, split-level home anyway?

A frown appeared on Hannah's brow. Certainly Norman wasn't planning on living there alone. Had he assumed that she was going to marry him without bothering to ask? And if he wasn't about to propose to her, did he have someone else in mind?

"I guess I must have shocked you," Norman said with a chuckle. "You've never been quiet for this long before."

Hannah nodded, even though she knew that Norman couldn't see it. "You shocked me, all right. I can't believe you're actually going to build it."

"Well, I am. Living with Mother is a real pain. Every time I leave the house, she asks me where I'm going and what time I'll be back. I know she means well, but she can't seem to accept that I'm an adult."

"I know *that* feeling," Hannah sympathized. Carrie Rhodes had been attempting to control Norman's life ever since he'd come back to Lake Eden to take over the family dental business. "Was your mother upset when you told her that you were moving out?"

"She doesn't know yet. I'm going to tell her at breakfast this morning. She's been complaining about how they need more storage space for Granny's Attic and I'm sure she'll be glad to get all of my stuff out of her garage."

Hannah clamped her lips firmly shut. Why shatter Norman's illusions? It was true that Granny's Attic, the antique shop their mothers had opened, needed more off-site storage space, but that wouldn't keep Carrie from being upset. Hannah was sure she'd be fit to be tied that Norman had made a decision without consulting her.

"I still can't believe how I lucked into the house. You knew that Rhonda Scharf inherited it, didn't you?"

"I knew," Hannah said. Rhonda was a regular on the Lake Eden gossip hotline and everyone in town knew about her inheritance. The day after her great-aunt's will had been read, Rhonda had come into Lake Eden Realty and listed the house with Hannah's sister, Andrea. "Does Andrea know that you bought the house?"

"Of course. Rhonda called her last night and Andrea advised her to accept my offer."

"Well . . . that's good," Hannah said, wondering why Andrea hadn't called to tell her. What were sisters for if they didn't share news like that?

"I told everyone to meet me at The Cookie Jar. There'll be four of us, and I thought you could be a witness. You will, won't you?"

"Of course I will."

"Good. I'll see you at nine-thirty then. This is a big step for me, Hannah."

"I know it is. Congratulations, Norman." Hannah was frowning as she hung up the phone. Of course she was happy for Norman, but she was royally miffed at her younger sister. Andrea liked to sleep in until seven, but Hannah picked up the phone and started to punch in her sister's number. Even though Hannah had been out late last night, catering coffee and cookies at a bridal shower, Andrea could have left a message!

Just as the call was about to connect, Hannah glanced over at her answer machine. The little red light for incoming messages was blinking frantically. Andrea *had* called, several times by the looks of it. Hannah slammed the phone back in the cradle before it could ring and retrieved her messages. There were six and every one of them was from Andrea. When Hannah had come home from her catering job, she'd been too tired to check for messages. And she'd forgotten all about it this morning.

Hannah had just finished erasing Andrea's messages when the phone rang again. Delores? Andrea? Hannah grabbed it on the second ring, wondering if she'd ever get the chance to skin out the door.

"Hannah?" It was Norman again. "Sorry to bother you twice in one morning, but do you still have that pen I gave you for Christmas?"

Hannah's eyebrows shot up. How quickly they forgot! "You didn't give me a pen. You gave me a silk scarf and a gold circle pin."

"I know. That was your real gift for under the tree. I'm talking about the giveaway pens from the Rhodes Dental Clinic. You didn't throw yours away, did you?"

"Of course I didn't. I thought it was cute. I've never had a pen shaped like a toothbrush before. It's right here . . . somewhere."

"Could you look? I saved some, but they're in a box in Mother's garage and I don't have time to look for them. I thought it would be a nice touch if I used one to sign the papers. It's not critical or anything, but the pens were my dad's design, and since he can't be here, I . . ."

"I'll look right now," Hannah interrupted him. "Hold on a second."

Hannah put down the phone, upended her purse, and dumped the contents on the surface of the kitchen table. There were at least two dozen pens and pencils, but the one from the Rhodes Dental Clinic wasn't among them. She stuffed everything back inside her purse and checked the cracked coffee mug on the table that served as her penholder. No Rhodes Dental pen there, either.

"Sorry, Norman," Hannah said, getting back on the phone to report. "I checked my purse and the pen jar on the table, but it's not there."

"How about your bed table? You told me you always keep a pen and steno pad handy in case you get an inspiration for a recipe in the middle of the night."

Hannah was surprised. She didn't recall mentioning that to Norman. "I'll check before I leave. If I find it, I'll bring it down to the shop with me."

Hannah hung up the phone and headed back to her bedroom. It was clear that Norman was nervous about buying his first house. Becoming a homeowner was a big step. When she'd signed the papers for her condo, she'd found herself missing her father, wishing that he'd lived long enough to see her take this step into adulthood. If signing the papers with a Rhodes Dental Clinic pen that his father had designed would make Norman feel more comfortable, she'd spend the next hour looking for it.

And there it was! Hannah's eyes locked on the pen the moment she stepped inside her bedroom. She grabbed it, stuffed it inside her purse, and was just preparing to step outside her condo door when the phone rang again. It was probably Norman, wondering if she'd found the pen. Hannah rushed back into the kitchen, almost tripping over Moishe in her haste, and snatched up the phone before it could ring a second time.

"Hi, Norman. Your pen was in my bedroom, right where you said it would be. I'll bring it to work with me."

Hannah heard a startled gasp, followed by a lengthy silence. The person on the other end of the line was so quiet, Hannah could hear a clock ticking in the background.

"Oh-oh," Hannah breathed, recalling the exact words she'd spoken when she'd answered the phone. For someone who hadn't been a party to her earlier conversations with Norman, the fact that his pen had been in her bedroom would be food for some juicy gossip. She was about to say hello again, hoping that the call had been a wrong number, when the ticking clock began to chime and she recognized the strains of "Edelweiss."

Hannah groaned. She'd really stuck her foot in it now. The only person in Lake Eden who had a clock that chimed "Edelweiss" was her mother!

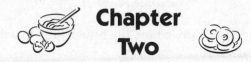

Chapter Two

"This is your mother, Hannah," Delores Swensen said at last. "How did Norman's pen get into your *bedroom?*"

Hannah started to laugh. She couldn't help it. She'd never heard her mother sound so shocked before.

"Stop that laughing and tell me! I'm your mother. I have a right to know!"

Hannah wasn't about to argue that point, not when her mother sounded capable of going into cardiac arrest any second. "Relax, Mother. Norman wanted me to find the Rhodes Dental Clinic pen he gave out at Christmas. I told him I always keep a pen on my bed table and he suggested that I look for it there."

"Oh. That's different. For a minute there, I thought . . . never mind. Why does Norman need that particular pen?"

"He's signing some papers this morning and he wants to use it for sentimental reasons. He just bought a house."

"Norman bought a *house?* Which house? Where?"

"It's the Voelker place. He's going to tear it down and build our dream house on the land."

"*What* dream house?"

"The one we designed for that contest we won. You remember, don't you?"

"Of course. You showed me the blueprints. But that house was huge, wasn't it?"

"Four-bedroom, three-bath."

"But a house like that is much too big for . . ." Delores stopped speaking and gasped. "Is there something you're not telling me, Hannah?"

"Not a thing."

"Then you're not considering any life-altering changes?"

Hannah glanced at the clock and frowned. "The only life-altering change I'm considering is ripping the phone off the wall so I can make it to work on time."

"Oh. All right then, dear. I'll make it short. I called because I have some wonderful news. Michelle is coming home."

"She is?" Hannah started to smile. Her youngest sister had just finished her freshman year at Macalester College and Hannah hadn't seen her since Christmas. "When is she coming?"

"On Tuesday night. She doesn't have to go back until Sunday. The Drama Department is moving to a new building and all the student workers have the week off. She's coming in on the midnight bus and she wants to stay out at the lake cottage."

"But I thought you had it rented out for the entire summer."

"I did, but Andrea worked something out with the renters. I'm staying out there with Michelle, of course. A girl her age still needs supervision."

Hannah grinned, imagining Michelle's reaction to that bit of news. She wouldn't be happy that her idyllic lake vacation would be graced by her mother's presence.

"I was hoping you could pick her up at the Quick Stop and bring her out to the lake. I have an important decorator coming in that night and Carrie can't handle her alone. And after that, I have to run straight out to the cottage to get things ready. I'll barely have time to make up the beds and hang the towels before Michelle's bus comes in."

"No problem," Hannah reassured her. "I'll meet the bus."

"Thank you, Hannah. I knew I could count on you. I've got to run. Carrie's picking me up in five minutes and I still have to fix my hair. We're doing the front window display this morning."

Hannah was smiling as she hung up the phone, not her usual expression after a conversation with her mother. It would be good to have Michelle home again.

By seven-thirty, Hannah had accomplished a lot. There were a dozen Lemon Meringue Pies in the ovens and she'd baked all the Old-Fashioned Sugar Cookies for Pamela and Toby's wedding reception. She poured the last cup of coffee from her travel carafe, sat down on a stool at the stainless-steel workstation, and reached out to grab one of the Old-Fashioned Sugar Cookies she'd designated as seconds. The cookie was slightly off round and she wanted the wedding cookies to be perfect. She was about to taste it when reality set in. She couldn't have cookies. She was on a diet. In her heart of hearts, she knew she had at least twenty pounds to lose, maybe even more. And come to think of it, perhaps that was why Norman hadn't asked her to marry him.

Sighing a bit, Hannah placed the cookie back on the plate. She had to exercise willpower. She had to be strong. She'd just convince herself that she loved low-fat cottage cheese and salads until she could get back into her summer slacks. Once she got down to the perfect weight, Norman would take one look at her new, svelte figure and pop the question. And she'd say . . . What would she say? Did she really want to marry a man who hadn't proposed to her because she was twenty pounds overweight?

Hannah reached for the cookie again. She wanted a man who would accept her just the way she was. If twenty pounds or so stood between spinsterhood and wedded bliss, there was something wrong with the system. Besides, marrying Norman would mean that she'd have to give up Mike Kingston.

A sigh escaped Hannah's lips as she thought about Mike. He was the handsome and sexy head detective with the Winnetka County Sheriff's Department. He was also her brother-in-law's partner and Bill hadn't been shy about telling Hannah that he hoped she'd marry Mike. Andrea also liked Mike, but she'd adopted their mother's view. As long as the candidate was male and single, any old groom would do in a pinch.

Thoughts of her mother caused Hannah to withdraw her hand without taking the cookie. If she got thinner and Norman proposed, Delores would have to stop playing matchmaker and fixing her up with every eligible man who stepped inside the Lake Eden city limits.

But did she really want to get married at this point in her life? Hannah reached for the cookie again. It might serve her better to stay a little heavy, delay any proposals of marriage, and date both Norman and Mike into perpetuity.

The back door opened and Hannah pulled her hand back from the cookie plate. It was a guilty reaction, pure and simple, and she gave her partner, Lisa Herman, an embarrassed smile. "Good morning, Lisa."

"Hi, Hannah." Lisa hung her purse on a hook, grabbed her apron, and walked over to stare at Hannah curiously as she put it on. Since she was petite, she had to roll it up around the middle and wind the strings around her waist twice. "I saw you put that cookie back. Is there something wrong with them?"

"No. I'm sure they're delicious."

"Then why didn't you take one?"

"Because I'm on a diet. No desserts until I lose twenty pounds. If you see me reaching for another cookie, slap my hand."

"Okay. But what brought this on?"

"My favorite pair of summer slacks. I bought them on a shopping trip with Andrea last summer and now I can't even zip them up."

"That's strange. You don't look like you've gained weight to me."

"Not to *you* maybe, but . . ." Hannah stopped speaking and sighed. "Norman bought a house."

"He did?" Lisa looked startled.

"It's the house Rhonda Scharf inherited from her great-aunt. He's coming here to sign the papers this morning."

"Then Norman's moving?"

"Not yet. He's going to bulldoze the old house and start building the dream house we designed for the contest."

"That's wonderful," Lisa said, walking over to the sink to wash her hands, "but what does it have to do with you losing weight?"

"He called to tell me about it this morning, but he didn't ask me to marry him."

Lisa turned to give Hannah a stern look. "And you really believe that the only reason Norman didn't ask you to marry him is because you're twenty pounds overweight?"

"Well . . . no. But . . ."

"Don't get me wrong," Lisa interrupted her. "Go on a diet if you want to, but don't use Norman for an excuse. He's crazy about you. Anybody can see that. I think he'll ask you one of these days."

Hannah felt her spirits rise. "Do you really think so?"

"Absolutely. It takes some men a while to work up the nerve. I've been dating Herb for as long as you've been dating Norman, and Herb hasn't proposed yet."

"Do you wish he would?" The moment the words were out of her mouth, Hannah regretted them. Lisa's relationship with Herb was none of her business. But Lisa didn't seem to mind the question and she smiled slightly as she dried her hands.

"Sometimes I wish he'd ask me. How about you? Do you want Norman to ask you?"

"I don't know. But I do know I don't want him to ask anyone else."

Lisa laughed. "I don't think there's any danger of that. So how about the diet? Is it still on?"

Hannah thought about it for a moment. "It's on. I can't afford to buy a whole new wardrobe."

"Now *that's* a good reason for a diet," Lisa said, heading for the door to the coffee shop. "I'll go start the coffee so you can fill up on something that doesn't have any calories."

The stove timer sounded and Hannah rose to take her pies out of the ovens. By the time she'd set them all out on racks to cool, Lisa was back with a fresh hot cup of coffee.

"Here you go." Lisa handed her a white mug with THE COOKIE JAR printed in red block letters on the side. "This'll get you going. And once you increase your energy level, you'll burn more calories. Gorgeous, as always."

Hannah, who had been about to take her first sip of coffee, looked up at the apparent non sequitor and found Lisa eyeing the row of baked pies.

"I think lemon is your prettiest pie. Of course your cherry pies are nice, too. They look yummy with all that bright red juice bubbling up through the latticework crusts. And your apple pies are gorgeous, golden brown on top and they smell so good. And your blueberry pies are just . . ."

"Stop!" Hannah interrupted her, holding up her hands in surrender. "I'm on a diet, remember?"

Lisa looked embarrassed. "Sorry, Hannah. Forget what I said about your pies. Are the wedding cookies cool enough to decorate?"

"They should be."

Lisa went to the counter and began to sift confectioner's sugar into a bowl. "I'll mix up the frosting and do the initials first."

"Good planning. They should be dry before you draw the purple hearts around them."

"Violet," Lisa corrected her, measuring the sugar into another bowl. "The bride wants the initials to be the same light blue as a summer sky just after daybreak. And the hearts are supposed to match the color of the first wild violets of spring."

Hannah's eyebrows shot up. "That's positively poetic, but it all boils down to light blue and light purple, doesn't it?"

"You're right," Lisa said with a grin, stirring in the butter and then reaching for the heavy cream.

While Hannah mixed up another batch of cookies and began to bake them, Lisa finished the frosting and filled a pastry bag. Hannah glanced over at her several times as she piped the light blue initials on the face of the cookies. At first Lisa had been noticeably shaky in her attempt to decorate cookies, but she had practiced with a perseverance that Hannah envied. Lisa was now an expert and that meant The Cookie Jar could offer personalized cookies for any event they catered.

They completed their work at the same time and Hannah walked over to admire Lisa's handiwork. "They're perfect," she said, smiling at her young partner. "Follow me. I think we deserve a coffee break."

The first thing Hannah did when she stepped into the coffee shop was to turn on their new ceiling fans. They created a slight breeze as their blades revolved lazily, stirring the air and the red, white, and blue streamers that Lisa had hung from the ceiling in honor of the Fourth of July.

"Go sit down. I'll get our coffee," Lisa said, heading for the big urn behind the counter.

Hannah chose her favorite table. It was in the rear of the shop, but it still had a nice view of the street through the front plate-glass window. Sitting at a table in the rear had one big advantage. The shop looked empty unless someone approached and pressed a nose to the window. And if the customers couldn't see them, they wouldn't knock on the door and expect them to open early.

Lisa's streamers looked nice and Hannah was glad she'd decorated. Lake Eden residents took their patriotism seriously and the Fourth of July was one of their small town's biggest holidays. There would be a parade in the morning, political speeches and events throughout the day, a huge potluck picnic and barbecue on the shores of Eden Lake, and a fireworks display at night.

"What's wrong with that fan?" Lisa asked, setting their mugs of coffee on the table.

"Which fan?"

"The one directly over your head."

Hannah glanced up and saw that the blades weren't turning on the fan in question. "I don't know, but Freddy and Jed are coming in this morning to install the new shelves in the pantry. I'll point it out to them."

"Freddy looks good," Lisa remarked, sitting down next to Hannah. "He told me that Jed makes him take a shower every morning and dress in clean clothes."

"That's a plus. I can remember a couple of times when I had to stand upwind."

As they sipped their coffee, Hannah thought about Freddy Sawyer. He was mildly retarded and he did odd jobs around town, supplementing the income from the small trust fund his mother had set up for him before she died. Freddy had to be in his early thirties, but his naïve manner and boyish grin made him seem much younger than that. He lived just outside the Lake Eden town limits on Old Bailey Road in the house his mother had owned for years. His cousin, Jed, had moved in with him last month, and it seemed Jed had been a good influence on Freddy.

"People underestimate Freddy," Lisa said, looking rather fierce. "They think he can't learn new things, but they're wrong. Janice Cox told me that she taught him to tell time."

"That's good," Hannah said, turning to look as a car drove up and parked in front of the shop. "There's Andrea and she's early. She isn't supposed to meet Norman here until nine-thirty."

Lisa jumped up from her chair. "I'll go let her in. Just sit there and relax. I know you were up late last night catering that bridal shower."

Hannah sat. She *was* tired. The shower had been a big event, over forty guests. Andrea had been invited, but she'd stayed only long enough to deliver her gift, congratulate the bride-to-be, and give Hannah a message from Mike. Mike was out of town, attending a five-day conference in Des Moines on intervention techniques for youthful offenders. When he hadn't been able to reach Hannah on the phone, he'd called Andrea to say he was staying over on Sunday night, but he'd be back in Lake Eden at noon on Monday and he'd drop by The Cookie Jar to see her.

The two sisters hadn't had time to exchange more than a few words before Andrea had to leave. She'd told Hannah that Bill had turned into a regular mother hen now that she was pregnant. He urged her to rest when she wasn't tired, he was forever bringing her afghans and pillows she didn't need, and just recently he'd taken to making her high-energy snacks that played havoc with her prenatal diet.

"Hi, Hannah." Andrea breezed in through the door, the picture of chic. She was wearing a light green skirt that swirled gracefully when she walked and a matching hip-length top. There was a turquoise scarf around her waist, a color combination Hannah would never have thought to attempt, and a silver and turquoise pendant around her neck. Andrea's light blond hair was pulled up in a complicated twist. She could have stepped from the pages of a glossy magazine.

"You're looking gorgeous this morning," Hannah said with only a small stab of envy. Andrea always looked fashionable and Hannah often felt like a frump beside her.

"Mother called you about Michelle, didn't she?"

"Yes, I'm meeting her bus. It's going to be great having her home."

"I know. We haven't seen her in ages." Andrea pulled out a chair and sat down. "Why didn't you call me last night? I left a zillion messages on your answer machine."

"I forgot to check it. I didn't know about Norman's new house until he called me this morning."

Andrea looked disgruntled. "Well, don't blame me for not telling you. You really need a cell phone, Hannah."

"I don't want a cell phone."

"Everyone who's anyone has one."

"Then I guess I'm not anyone. I know it's the age of technology, but I don't like the idea of being on an electronic leash."

"It's not like a leash. Anytime you don't want to answer it, you can just turn it off."

"That would be all the time." Hannah began to grin. The end of the argument was in sight. "And if I never answer my cell phone, why have one in the first place?"

"Coffee, Andrea?" Lisa called out, holding up an empty mug.

"No, thanks. Doc Knight limited me to one cup a day and I've already had it."

"How about a glass of orange juice?"

"That sounds good." Andrea smiled at Lisa, then turned back to Hannah. "I had to get up at the crack of dawn. The only time Doc Knight could see me was at seven-thirty."

"Seven-thirty isn't exactly the crack of dawn."

"For me it is. I'm fine, by the way. I turned down the ultrasound. We don't want to know the baby's sex until he's born."

"Until *he's* born?"

"I'm just saying *he* as a concession to Mother. She's positive it's a boy this time."

Hannah was amused. "What makes her so sure?"

"She says if you carry the baby in front and your stomach sticks out, it's a boy. If you're big all over, it's a girl."

"That sounds like an old wives' tale to me. Besides, your stomach is still as flat as a board."

"No, it's not. I've been dressing to hide it, but nothing fits me right anymore. I'm going to start wearing maternity clothes the minute Claire's shipment comes in."

"You asked Claire to order maternity clothes for you?" Hannah was surprised. Claire Rodgers owned Beau Monde, the dress shop next door to The Cookie Jar, and her clothes were expensive.

"I know it'll probably cost an arm and a leg, but Bill wants me to have the best. He says it might even be tax deductible. After all, I'm a real estate agent and I have to be well dressed for my job."

"You'd better check with Stan about that." Hannah curbed her impulse to laugh. Stan Kramer was the best tax man in Lake Eden. He was pretty liberal about what was and what wasn't a tax deduction, but Hannah didn't think he'd go quite that far.

Andrea looked up as Lisa brought over a plate of cookies. "Thanks, Lisa. These look wonderful and I didn't have time for breakfast. What are they?"

"We call them Apricot Drops and they're Hannah's invention. They're Oatmeal Raisin Crisps made with chopped dried apricots instead of raisins."

The phone rang and Lisa rushed off to answer it. Hannah watched as Andrea took a bite of her newest cookie and she relaxed as her sister started to smile. "You like them?"

"These cookies are winners, Hannah." Andrea took one more bite, then leaned forward. "So? What do you think about Norman's plans?"

"They're great. I can hardly wait to see our dream house."

"Then you said yes?"

Hannah bit back a grin, knowing full well what her sister was asking. "Yes to what?"

"To marrying Norman, of course!"

"No."

"Then you said no?"

Hannah shook her head. "I didn't say anything. Norman didn't ask me."

"He *didn't?* I thought for sure he would." Andrea began to look anxious. "He's not dating anyone else, is he?"

"Not that I know of."

"Well . . . that's good. Maybe you should give him a little nudge in the right direction. You're not getting any younger, and if you want to have kids . . ." Andrea stopped in mid-sentence and sighed. "Sorry, Hannah. I'm beginning to sound like Mother."

"Yes, you are."

"But at least I stopped before I got to your biological clock ticking down."

"No, you didn't. You just said it."

Andrea looked nonplussed for a moment, but she recovered quickly. "I *said* I was sorry. Look, Hannah . . . I know it's a touchy subject with you. I apologize for bringing it up."

Hannah's mouth dropped open. Andrea didn't apologize often. She had to squelch the urge to rush down to Lake Eden Neighborhood Drugs to buy a box of gold stars like the ones Miss Gladke had used to mark special days on the classroom calendar. She was about to say she accepted Andrea's apology when Lisa came back to the table.

"It's good news and bad news," Lisa informed them. "Which one do you want to hear first?"

Hannah made an instant decision. "The bad news. We'll save the good for last."

"That was the caterer. Pamela's parents canceled the wedding. She had a big fight with Toby and she eloped with the boy she used to date in high school."

Hannah groaned. "I think you'd better tell us the good news now."

"I told the caterer we'd baked all the cookies and she

promised to pay us for them. She said she'd send a check and we could keep them."

"That's nice. But what are we going to do with them? We can't sell cookies with the bride and groom's initials on them, unless . . ." Hannah reached out for a paper napkin and flipped it over so she had a perfectly blank square. "Do you have a pen?"

"I always have a pen." Andrea reached in her briefcase and pulled out her gold Cross pen.

Hannah drew a large circle and wrote Pam's and Toby's initials inside. She stared at it for a moment and then she turned to Lisa. "Will you get one of the wedding cookies for me? I've got an idea."

A moment later, a sample cookie was resting on a napkin in the center of the table. Hannah studied it for a moment, then looked up at Lisa with a grin. "Is there room to squeeze an 'H' and an 'A' in front of Pam's initials?"

"There's plenty of space. I had to leave room for the purple heart."

Andrea looked surprised. "Was the groom a war hero?"

"No, but he deserves to be for putting up with Pamela." Hannah turned to Lisa again. "How about a 'Y' at the end of Pam's initials?"

"That's easy. What are we doing to Toby's initials?"

"Not much. All we have to do is put a big number four in front."

"I get it!" Andrea said, sounding excited. "Then they'll say, 'HAPPY 4TH.' The cookies are white. If you do all the letters in blue and the number in red, they'll be Independence Day cookies."

Lisa pushed back her chair. "It's perfect, Hannah. I'll get started on them right now. I need to match that blue frosting before it dries."

"Won't the cookies get old before the Fourth?" Andrea asked. "It's five days away."

"Not if we decorate them and pop them in the freezer.

We'll thaw them the night before and give them out at the parade."

"Tracey can do that for you," Andrea offered. "She's almost five and that's old enough to be in the parade. She could ride on The Cookie Jar float and pass out the cookies."

Hannah shook her head. "That's a nice idea, but we don't have a float."

"No float?" Andrea looked shocked.

"We wanted to build one, but we didn't have time, not to mention the money it would have cost us."

"But you've got to have a float! Everybody's having a float. I'll build it for you, Hannah. It'll be a fun project for me."

Hannah opened her mouth to say that "fun" was a noun, not an adjective, but she didn't have the heart to correct Andrea. Her sister was obviously serious about wanting to build the float. With Tracey in preschool and Bill at work, she must be at loose ends. "Have you ever built a float before?"

"Not exactly, but how hard can it be? Please let me do it, Hannah. Think of it as a favor. You'll be saving me from terminal boredom and it won't cost you a dime. Bill's dad has a hay wagon I can borrow and I've got tons of decorating supplies in the garage."

Hannah found it hard to resist the pleading look on her sister's face. Andrea hadn't looked this excited since she'd planned her own wedding. "But are you sure you want to tackle a rush project like this?"

"Of course. I've got loads of time. Just say the word and I'll get started right away."

Hannah knew she might live to regret it, but she nodded. "Okay."

"You're the best sister in the whole world!" Andrea jumped up and rushed around the table to hug her. "I'm going to run down to Kiddie Korner and tell Tracey. She'll be so excited."

"Don't forget about your meeting with Norman. You have to be back by nine-thirty with the house papers."

"I'll be here. Thanks again, Hannah. You've given me a whole new lease on life."

Hannah sighed as Andrea raced out the door, climbed into her Volvo, and drove away. She was glad her sister was happy, but giving her permission to build the float might have been a strategic mistake, especially since Bill was being so overprotective. How would he feel toward Hannah when his pregnant wife announced that she'd be working long hours designing and decorating a float for The Cookie Jar?

Lemon Meringue Pie

Preheat oven to 350 degrees F.,
with rack in middle position.

1 nine-inch baked pie shell

FILLING:

3 whole eggs
4 egg yolks *(save the whites in a mixing bowl and let them come up to room temperature—you'll need them for the meringue)*
1 cup white sugar *(granulated)*
½ cup water
¼ cup cornstarch
⅛ cup lime juice
⅓ cup lemon juice
1 to 2 teaspoons grated lemon zest
1 tablespoon butter

(Using a double boiler makes this recipe foolproof, but if you're very careful and stir constantly so it doesn't scorch, you can make the lemon filling in a heavy saucepan directly on the stove over medium heat.)

Put water in the bottom of a double boiler and heat it until it simmers. (*Make sure you don't use too much*

water—it shouldn't touch the bottom of the double boiler top.) Off the heat, beat the egg yolks with the whole eggs in the top of the double boiler. Add the ½ cup water and the combined lemon and lime juice. Combine sugar and cornstarch in a small bowl and stir until completely blended. Add this to the egg mixture in the top of the double boiler and blend thoroughly.

Place the top of the double boiler over the simmering water and cook, stirring frequently until the lemon pie filling thickens *(5 minutes or so)*. Lift the top of the double boiler and place it on a cold burner. Add the lemon zest and the butter, and stir thoroughly. Let the filling cool while you make the meringue.

MERINGUE: (This is a whole lot easier with an electric mixer!)

4 egg whites
½ teaspoon cream of tartar
⅛ teaspoon salt
¼ cup white sugar *(granulated)*

Add the cream of tartar and salt to the egg whites and mix them in. Beat the egg whites on high until they form soft peaks. Continue beating as you sprinkle in the sugar.

When the egg whites form firm peaks, stop mixing and tip the bowl to test the meringue. If the egg whites don't slide down the side, they're ready.

Put the filling into the baked pie shell, smoothing it with a rubber spatula. Clean and dry your spatula. Spread the meringue over the filling with the clean spatula, sealing it to the edges of the crust. When the pie is completely covered with meringue, "dot" the pie with the flat side of the spatula to make points in the meringue. *(The meringue will shrink back when it bakes if you don't seal it to the edges of the crust.)*

Bake the pie at 350 degrees F. for no more than 10 minutes.

Remove the pie from the oven, let it cool to room temperature on a wire rack, and then refrigerate it if you wish. This pie can be served at room temperature, or chilled.

(To keep your knife from sticking to the meringue when you cut the pie, dip it in cold water.)

(This is Lisa's favorite pie—she loves the zing of the lime juice.)

Chapter Three

Andrea pointed to a line marked with a blue checkmark. "You're next, Hannah. Sign here."

Hannah signed her name where Andrea indicated, right under the lines with the green, red, and purple checkmarks. Andrea had explained the color-coded system when they had first taken their seats at the tables in the rear of the cookie shop. Norman was green, Rhonda Scharf was red, Andrea was purple, and Hannah was blue. It seemed that Norman's first step into the world of home ownership began with a polychromatic autograph assembly line, but he didn't seem to mind. Hannah watched him smile as he signed his name on the next paper and when he looked up at her, she smiled back.

Howie Levine held his hand out for the paper she'd just signed and Hannah handed it over. Howie notarized the signatures and placed the paper on the stack of completed pages by his left elbow. The pile was growing with each passing minute. Hannah wondered how long it would take to top the one-inch mark.

Hannah glanced over at Rhonda Scharf and caught her checking her watch. It was clear Rhonda was pleased at selling her great-aunt's property, but they'd been signing papers for the past fifteen minutes and the novelty had worn off. Rhonda had dressed for the occasion in a pink knit pantsuit with a cloud of iridescent butterflies appliquéd on the front. The largest and most colorful butterfly was perched just below the vee of her low-cut neckline and called attention to her considerable cleavage. Rhonda, at fifty, still had a voluptuous figure and she liked to show it off. The only jarring note was her shoes, lime green tennis shoes that had been dyed to match the smock Rhonda wore behind the cosmetic counter at Lake Eden Neighborhood Drugs.

"Only ten left." Andrea signed and passed another document to Rhonda. Rhonda signed and handed it to Norman. When Norman had signed with the Rhodes Dental Clinic pen that Hannah had located, he handed the paper to her. From Hannah it went to Howie, who notarized it and placed it on the top of the stack.

It seemed to take forever, but at last they were almost finished. The only thing left was for Rhonda to sign the deed.

"Excuse me . . . Howie?" Rhonda hesitated, her pen poised over the deed. "Before I agreed to the sale, I asked Norman if I could go out there over the weekend to pick up a few family mementos. Do we need a separate agreement for that?"

Howie turned to Norman. "Is that all right with you?"

"Sure. I already told Rhonda that she could."

"Then it shouldn't be a problem. A verbal agreement is fine for something like that."

"Okay. I just wanted to make sure," Rhonda said and signed the deed.

Once the deed had joined the stack of completed papers and Rhonda was in possession of Norman's cashier's check, Howie pushed back his chair and stood up to shake hands with Rhonda and then with Norman. "I'll file these papers today, but since it's a Friday, you'll have to wait until Monday morning to take possession."

When Howie had left, Hannah turned to her sister. "Is that all?"

"That's it." Andrea looked relieved. "Congratulations on

the sale, Rhonda. And congratulations to you, Norman. You bought a great piece of property."

Hannah started to get up from the table, but Norman beat her to her feet. "The cookies are on me," he announced, grinning at all the patrons in the shop. "I just bought my first house."

"And I just sold my first house." Rhonda stood up next to Norman. "I'll pay for the cookies. Thanks to Norman, I'm the one with all his money."

There was a burst of laughter from her customers and Hannah headed off to the counter, leaving Norman and Rhonda to hammer out the details. The Cookie Jar was packed with dozens of people who'd already paid, but Hannah didn't know of a single one who would turn down the chance to have a free cookie. She called that phenomenon "buffet mentality." You could be full to bursting, but if the food was all-you-can-eat, you'd pig out way past the point of comfort. It was the same mind set that caused women to fill their purses with free perfume samples they'd never try, and that gave guests at fixed-price New Year's Eve parties champagne hangovers for the bowl games the next day.

Lisa was carrying coffee refills from table to table when Rhonda came up to the counter. "I won," she said, looking pleased. "I'm paying for the first free cookie and Norman's going to pay for the second."

Hannah added up Rhonda's bill. Once it had been settled, she expected Rhonda to leave, but Rhonda slid onto a stool at the counter.

"The house isn't much," she confided. "I don't blame Norman for wanting to tear it down. It'd cost more to remodel than it'd ever be worth. It's a nice piece of property though, and you'll love the view. I hope you and Norman will be very happy in your new home."

Warning bells rang in Hannah's head. She knew she had to tread carefully. Rhonda wasn't the biggest gossip in town,

but she was definitely a contender. "It won't be my home,
Rhonda. All I did was design it with Norman."

"But I thought . . ." Rhonda stopped speaking and began
to frown. "When Norman told me he was building the house
you designed for the contest, I just naturally assumed that . . .
You aren't going to marry him?"

"No."

"But you'll never find anybody nicer!"

"That's probably true."

"Then why won't you marry him?"

Hannah sighed. Rhonda had the persistence of a door-to-
door salesman. "Norman hasn't asked me."

"He *hasn't?*" Rhonda looked shocked, but she covered it
quickly and reached out to pat Hannah's hand. "Don't lose
heart, dear. I know you're nearly thirty and all of your
friends are married, but I'm sure Norman's just waiting until
the house is built. As a matter of fact, I'm *sure* that's what
he's doing."

Hannah decided that it was best to change the subject. She
was tired of being on the defensive about Norman's failure to
pop the question. "Congratulations on the sale, Rhonda. Are
you planning to do something special with the money?"

"Yes. I'm taking a real vacation for the first time in my life
and it's a dream come true. Thanks to Norman I can afford it
now and I booked the ticket last night. I leave Monday
morning for Rome!"

Rhonda's eyes lit up and Hannah caught some of her excitement. "That sounds wonderful. How long are you staying?"

"Two glorious weeks! That should give me enough time to
see everything I've always wanted to see." Rhonda reached
for her purse and slung it over her shoulder. "I've got to run
or I'll be late to work. If I don't see you before I leave, *bon
voyage.*"

Hannah bit back a grin as Rhonda slid off the stood and

walked toward the door. *Bon voyage* meant "good voyage" and she should have said it to Rhonda, not the other way around.

Once Norman and Andrea had left, Hannah manned the counter in the cookie shop while Lisa went back to the kitchen to work on their Independence Day cookies. When the predictable lull came at eleven-thirty, Hannah stepped back to the kitchen to see the results.

"What do you think?" Lisa asked, putting the finishing touches on the last tray of cookies.

"They're perfect. No one would ever know they're recycled."

"I gave a couple of my mistakes to Freddy and Jed." Lisa motioned toward the pantry where Freddy and his cousin were hanging the new shelves that Hannah had bought. "I'll deliver our cookie orders if you want to stay here."

"That's fine with me. Did you mention that ceiling fan?"

Lisa shook her head. "No, I forgot all about it."

"I'll tell them. This would be a good time to fix it."

A few minutes later, the ladder had been set up in the cookie shop and Freddy steadied it while Jed climbed up to look at the defective fan. He yanked the pull cord, but the blades didn't move. Then he loosened the screws on the hub and peered inside.

Freddy looked anxious as he watched Jed overhead and Hannah put her hand on his arm to reassure him. "Don't worry, Freddy. I'm sure Jed can fix it."

"But I'm the one that did that fan," Freddy sounded every bit as upset as he looked. "I must have done it wrong."

Jed looked down at his cousin. "No, you did it right. The wires came loose, that's all. It could have happened to anyone. I'll fix it and it'll work just fine."

"But I should fix it," Freddy insisted. "It's my fan and a man's got to stand behind his work."

Jed smiled and Hannah could tell that he approved of what Freddy had said. "You're right, buddy. I'll come down and you can fix it. Hold the ladder like I taught you, okay?"

"Okay. I'm holding it, Jed."

As Freddy gripped the ladder tightly, Hannah realized that he looked different. His hair was shorter and his clothes were clean, but there was another change. Freddy was dressing better now that Jed had moved in with him. Instead of donning the baggy green trousers and old work shirts that had belonged to his father, Freddy now had jeans that fit him and cotton knit shirts with a pocket in the front. He even had new work boots that had replaced his battered old tennis shoes.

"Good job, Freddy." Jed stepped off the ladder and patted Freddy on the back. "That ladder didn't move an inch."

"Nope. I held it real tight, just the way you taught me."

Jed walked over to his toolbox and removed a rubber-handled screwdriver and a roll of black electrical tape. "Where's your tool belt, Freddy?"

"Gotta think . . ." Freddy stared up at the ceiling for a moment. "It's in the pantry, Jed. You told me to take it off when it bumped you."

"Right. Go get it, then. You're going to need it to carry tools up the ladder."

Hannah waited until Freddy had gone back to the kitchen and then turned to Jed with concern. "Are you sure Freddy should be working with electricity? It's pretty dangerous."

"As long as I'm here, he'll be fine. Freddy knows better than to try it alone."

Hannah studied the young man standing in front of her. He was like a savvier, more animated version of Freddy and no one would doubt that they were cousins. They had the same athletic build, the same sandy hair, and the same blue-gray eyes. They were both just under six feet tall and they were dressed the same, whether it was planned or by accident. The only difference was that Freddy's face was fuller, more childish, and Jed's features were sharply defined.

"Look, Hannah . . ." Jed reached out to place his hand on her arm. "It's good for Freddy to learn new things. Everyone in Lake Eden protects him just like his mother did and that holds him back. I know you do it out of kindness, but that's not really helping Freddy in the long run."

Hannah sighed. Jed had a point. "Maybe you're right. We're just concerned, that's all."

"Well, you can relax now. I'm here and I'm going to take care of Freddy. He's my buddy. We played together when we were kids and I've always liked him. I want to see him lead a good life and do all that he can do."

"I got it, Jed." Freddy came through the door with a smile on his face. His tool belt was buckled around his waist and he looked determined to tackle the defective ceiling fan.

"Good." Jed handed him the screwdriver and the tape. "Find a place for this on your belt. Do you remember what to do when you get to the top of the ladder?"

"I remember. First you turn off the power."

"That's right. Hold on a second and I'll throw the circuit."

Once Jed had turned off the power, Hannah stood to the side and watched as Freddy climbed the ladder. He was a bit more hesitant than Jed had been, watching every step to make sure his feet were in place, but he climbed up steadily.

"Do you see those two wires hanging down from the hub on the fan?"

"I see 'em, Jed."

"Wind the black one around the base of the black screw and tighten it down. When you're through with that, put a strip of tape over it so it doesn't come loose. Do the same with the red wire and the red screw."

"Okay. I can do that."

Hannah watched as Freddy tackled the job. It took him a while, but he was wearing a big smile when he'd finished. "I did it, Jed."

"Yes, you did. Come on down, Freddy."

"Okay. I'll take it real slow, Jed. Getting down is a lot

harder than getting up. My head's up so high I can't see where my feet are going."

"Can you get down on your own? Or should I help you with your feet?"

Freddy looked confused and Hannah could understand why. Jed had asked two conflicting questions and now Freddy had to decide which one to answer first.

"Yes, I can get down," Freddy answered at last. "And no, I don't need you to help. Here I come, Jed."

Both Hannah and Jed watched as Freddy climbed down the ladder. There was a proud smile on his face, but he gave a big sigh of relief when his feet touched the ground. "Can I be the one to test it?"

"Sure," Jed said. "Let me turn on the juice and then you can try the wall switch."

Once Jed had given him the okay, Freddy flicked the switch and the blades started to revolve in perfect tandem with the other ceiling fans. "Look at that. I did it! Was that good, Jed?"

"That was real good." Jed patted Freddy on the back and then he turned to Hannah. "If it's okay, we'll take our lunch now. We'll be back here at one to work on those shelves."

"Sure, go ahead."

"What do you say, Freddy?" Jed clamped an arm around Freddy's shoulders and walked him toward the door. "You want to have lunch at the café?"

"I like the café. Can I have chili?"

"Sure, if that's what you want."

"And a chocolate shake?"

"Sure, Freddy. Knock yourself out."

"Why do I have to do that?"

"Do what?"

"Knock myself out."

Jed laughed and glanced back at Hannah. "It's just an expression, Freddy. I didn't really mean that you should hit yourself."

"What did you mean, then?"

"I meant that you should order whatever you want and I'll pay for it."

"Okay. I'll have chili, and onion rings with ketchup, and a chocolate shake, and pickles. And maybe I'll have coconut cake, too."

Hannah was grinning as the door closed behind them. Freddy didn't get the chance to eat at the café very often and it sounded like he was ready to take full advantage of the unexpected treat. If Jed didn't keep an eye out, Freddy would eat up their whole day's salary and then some.

Chapter
Four

Her weekend had been boring beyond belief and Hannah was not in the best of moods on Monday morning as she began to bake the cookies they'd need for the day. With Mike in Iowa and Norman busily calling contractors and getting estimates on the work to be done, Hannah had decided she'd finally do the spring housecleaning she'd put off for three months.

When The Cookie Jar had closed at five on Saturday, Hannah had driven straight home to feed Moishe and fix her evening meal. She'd done her utmost to pretend that her green dinner salad was a piece of buttery garlic bread, her boneless skinless chicken breast was a thick slab of country ham, and each floret of steamed broccoli was a crispy French fry, but her powers of self-deception had failed her before she'd even raised the fork to her mouth. She'd eaten most of it anyway and shared a few bites of her chicken with Moishe, who'd seemed delighted that she was dining on one of his favorite meats. Once her dishes were stashed in the dishwasher, she'd grabbed one of her ever-present steno pads to make a list of the tasks she needed to tackle and before she'd crawled under the covers at eleven, her kitchen floor had been spotless, all the burned-out lightbulbs in her condo had been replaced, every inch of her carpet had been sucked free of dirt and unidentified fibers, and all the clothes she'd sprinkled and stuck in the freezer to avoid mildew attacks before she got around to ironing them had been neatly pressed and were hanging in her closet.

Sunday had been more of the same. Hannah had risen early, eaten one piece of dry toast and a half grapefruit for breakfast, and salivated for a full two minutes when she'd smelled bacon frying in a neighbor's apartment. She'd read the Sunday paper and then she'd tackled the rest of her to-do list. She'd carried the contents of Moishe's litter box down to the Dumpster in the garage, scrubbed the fixtures in her bathroom until they were sparkling, and straightened the linen cabinet. After a big bowl of mixed vegetables for lunch, she'd rearranged her spice drawer, washed all the windows, dusted the bookshelves, and emptied the trash. She'd even cleaned out the kitchen cupboards, although it had taken every ounce of willpower she possessed to toss out the half-eaten canister of caramel corn that Bertie Straub had given her for Christmas.

Dinner had been a nice piece of fish with a small baked potato sans sour cream and butter, and another mixed salad with low-cal dressing. Since Hannah had never been fond of fish, Moishe had gotten the lion's share of that. She'd alleviated her urge to snack by munching celery sticks as she'd watched several insipid movies, and she'd crawled under the covers at ten, hoping that sleep would silence the rumbling of her stomach.

"Hi, Hannah," Lisa greeted her as she walked in at seven-thirty. "Something smells good."

"That would be cookies. I'm just glad my nose is stuffed up!"

"The diet's getting to you?" Lisa gave her a sympathetic look.

"Yes. 'Diet' has a lot in common with some other four-letter words."

"I understand. Why don't you go in the shop and put on the coffee? I'll finish up in here."

"Thanks, Lisa." Hannah turned and walked toward the swinging door that led to the coffee shop. "I had the most awful urge to spoon down all that cookie dough. Raw."

Once temptation was behind her, Hannah felt much better. As she measured out the coffee grounds, she reminded herself that the waistband on her jeans had been looser this morning and this was not the time to falter in her resolve. If she could keep it up, she'd be thin and beautiful. Well . . . maybe not beautiful, but certainly thinner. She'd feel better, she'd have more energy, and she might even have the nerve to buy a new bathing suit before the swimming season was over for the year.

Hannah had just plugged in the coffee when the phone rang. They weren't open for business yet, but it could be someone calling with an advance order. She lifted the receiver and answered in her most professional voice. "This is The Cookie Jar. Hannah speaking."

"I'm glad I caught you, dear."

"Hello, Mother." Hannah glanced up at the clock. It was ten to eight and that was much later than Delores usually called.

"I hate to disturb you at work, but I need to ask for your help."

This was a new wrinkle! Delores never asked, she demanded. "What is it, Mother?"

"Norman told Carrie that we can take any furnishings we want from the Voelker place. The only catch is, he found someone to start demolishing it on Saturday and we have to get the things out before then."

"And you want me to help you move them?" Hannah's muscles began to cramp at the thought. The last time she'd helped her mother move antiques, she'd been stiff and sore for almost a week.

"No, Luanne's taking care of all that. She's rented a truck and hired a couple of high school boys to do the heavy lifting. She's absolutely wonderful, Hannah. Her talents were simply wasted at the café."

"I'm glad it's working out so well," Hannah said, smiling to herself. As far as she was concerned, Luanne Hanks was a story of success in the face of adversity. The Hanks family lived at the end of Old Bailey Road, right next to the town dump and a mile past Freddy Sawyer's house. The youngest of six children, Luanne had dropped out of school in her senior year to have a baby, but she'd studied at home and passed her high school equivalency exam. Instead of taking the easier way out and giving her daughter up for adoption, Luanne had decided to raise Suzie as a single mom. For the first two years, she'd supported her widowed mother and her baby by working at Hal & Rose's Café as a waitress and selling Pretty Girl Cosmetics door to door.

Delores had come into contact with Luanne when she'd done the makeup for the old-fashioned portraits Norman had taken at the Lake Eden Winter Carnival. Impressed with Luanne's eagerness to learn about antiques, Delores and Carrie had hired her as their assistant when they'd opened Granny's Attic in May.

"I'm going out to the Voelker place this afternoon to tag the things we want to take. I thought it would be fun if we went out there together."

Hannah searched her mind for an ulterior motive. Her mother always had an ulterior motive. Hannah knew very little about antiques, and Delores was an expert. There was no way her mother needed her help with that. As far as she knew, her mother's car was running just fine and she was perfectly capable of driving out there by herself. Perhaps Delores just wanted to spend a few hours with her eldest daughter? No, that couldn't be it.

"Do you have time to go with me, Hannah? I'd really appreciate it."

"I guess," Hannah said, a bit reluctantly. There was something afoot, but she couldn't think of what it could be. "I'm catering coffee and dessert at the St. Jude Society prayer meeting, but I should be back here by one."

"That's perfect, dear. Norman's got an eleven-thirty appointment and he should be free by then."

"Norman's going?"

"Yes, dear. He wants to take another look at the place before they tear it down."

"But if Norman's driving out there anyway, why don't you ride with him?"

"We'd rather ride with you, dear." Delores sounded a bit uncomfortable and she cleared her throat. "You've got such a nice big truck and Norman says there's quite a bit of artwork on the walls. I thought we could pack that up and bring it back with us."

Hannah grinned in sudden understanding. Delores wanted her for the cargo space in her cookie truck. She thought about refusing. Her truck was not a moving van. But it was a small thing to ask and she did want to take a look at the property that Norman had bought.

"Okay. I'll call you when I get back here and we'll go pick up Norman. Tell him to expect us about one-fifteen."

"I'll do that, dear. I'm sure he'll want to show you all around and discuss the new house while I'm tagging the antiques. Who knows? If the timing is right, something might just happen."

Hannah was grinning as she hung up the phone. Not only had she identified her mother's primary motive, she'd found a second. Delores hoped that if she threw Hannah together with Norman, he might propose. Hannah didn't think that would happen, but it was a nice try on her mother's part.

It was ten o'clock and Hannah was manning the cash register when she spotted Mike's Jeep pulling up in front of her shop. Her heart began to hammer and her insides turned to mush as he got out and strode toward the front door. With a start, she realized that the mug of coffee she was holding was sloshing and she set it down quickly before any of her customers could notice. Mike always had this effect on her. It was as if she'd received a jolt of electricity that made her tingle all over.

The door to The Cookie Jar opened and Mike walked in. He looked determined, like a man on a mission, and Hannah watched his eyes rove over the customers that lined the tables in her small shop. When he spotted her behind the counter, he strode up to her quickly. "We need to talk."

"Okay. What is it?"

Mike shook his head. "Not here. Let's go in the back and send Lisa up here."

The switch was accomplished with a minimum of fuss and Hannah motioned to a stool at the workstation. "Sit down, Mike. Do you want a cup of coffee?"

"No. Am I too late, Hannah?"

Hannah glanced at the clock. "Actually, you're early. Andrea said you'd be in about noon."

"Not *that!* Am I too late?"

"Too late for what?" Hannah asked, genuinely puzzled.

"Don't play games with me, Hannah. Bill told me all about Norman's new house."

"Oh, *that!*" Hannah did her best not to smile as she met Mike's eyes. He was jealous, pure and simple. The green-eyed monster had sunk its claws into the most handsome man in Lake Eden. Of course Mike didn't have any reason to be jealous, but he didn't know that, and Hannah was enjoying his discomfort too much to tell him quite yet. "Is there some reason why Norman can't build on that property?"

"Not that I know of."

"But you seem upset."

"Of course I'm upset! I was only gone for three days and when I come back, I find out that Norman's building your dream house!"

"It's *our* dream house," Hannah corrected him. "Norman and I designed it together."

"Then you're going to marry him?" Mike asked, clenching his fists.

"No," Hannah said, knowing that she'd milked Mike's jealousy for all it was worth and any more would be cruel. "Norman's just building the house, that's all. It doesn't have anything to do with me."

Mike exhaled with an audible whoosh and Hannah could see that he was relieved. "But that house is too big for Norman, isn't it?"

"Four bedrooms, three baths."

"That's what I mean. What's he going to do with all that room?" Mike began to frown. "Do you think he's going to ask you to marry him when it's finished?"

Hannah laughed. "If I knew that, I'd set up a hotline and rake in the cash as a telephone psychic."

"What if he does? Will you say yes?"

"I don't know."

"Well, you can't!"

Hannah's heart jumped up into her throat. Was Mike about to propose? And how would she feel about it if he did? "Why can't I?"

"Because you'd never be happy with Norman. Promise me you'll tell me right away if he asks you."

"What good will *that* do?"

"I don't want to get blindsided. Promise me, Hannah."

"I promise," Hannah said. What else could she say? She didn't like to see Mike looking this miserable.

"Then everything's still status quo with us?"

"Status quo," Hannah repeated, beginning to smile as she wondered what that was, exactly.

Mike got up from his stool and pulled Hannah to her feet to give her a hug. "I don't want to change anything. Everything's great just the way it is."

And then Mike kissed her. It was a long, sweet kiss that was just beginning to kindle into a blaze when Hannah heard someone open the back door.

"Hannah? I just wanted to ask you about . . ." It was

Andrea and she stopped abruptly as she saw what she'd interrupted. "Sorry. I'll come back later."

Mike motioned Andrea in. "That's okay. I was just leaving. If you see Bill before I do, tell him I'm going home to take a quick shower and put on a fresh uniform. I'll catch up with him at the station after lunch."

"What was all that about?" Andrea asked after Mike had left.

"Nothing much." Hannah shrugged, leaving it at that. "What did you want to ask me?"

"It's about Tracey's costume." Andrea eyed the cookies that were cooling on the baker's rack. "Are those Almond Kisses?"

"They're for my catering job, but I baked extras."

"Then I can have a couple?"

"Of course." Hannah watched as Andrea grabbed three cookies. "What were you saying about Tracey's costume?"

"I need to know what kind of shoes the Statue of Liberty wears."

"Really big ones," Hannah quipped, but Andrea didn't look amused. "I think it's sandals, but I'm not positive."

"How would I find out?"

"Run down to the library and look it up in the encyclopedia. There's bound to be a picture."

"Good idea. I asked Janice Cox, but she wasn't sure either. I'm going to dress Tracey up as Lady Liberty. Won't that be cute?"

"Tracey would be cute in any costume."

"I know, but she really wants something with a crown. Is she right-handed?"

"Probably," Hannah said, assuming that Andrea was asking about Lady Liberty and not her daughter. "The torch goes in the right hand, if that's what you're asking. You're not going to put Tracey in green makeup, are you?"

"No. The green's just tarnish anyway. I wonder why they don't polish her up. She'd look a lot better."

"That's easier said than done. Remember when that citizens group got the idea to clean the dome on the county courthouse? They dropped it in a hurry when they found out it would take three years and cost a fortune."

"Time and money. They're always the deciding factors. I'd better run, Hannah. I'm short on time this morning, and I'll be short on money if I don't get out to CostMart in time for their white sale. I'm picking up new towels for the bathroom. Ours are practically in shreds. Is there anything you need while I'm there?"

"Thanks, but I can't think of anything I . . ." Hannah stopped speaking as her neck gave a twinge. She reached up to rub it and sighed. "There is one thing. Remember when we went shopping last year and I bought that new pillow?"

"The goose-down?"

"That's the one. I need a second pillow just like it."

Andrea's eyes narrowed. "But you already have one. Does that mean you're contemplating . . . uh . . . sleepover company?"

"No, it just means that Moishe keeps stealing it. And every time he does, I wake up with a stiff neck. I'm going to give him mine and get a new one for myself."

"You really ought to train him not to do that."

"That's impossible. Cats train their owners, not the other way around. It took Moishe a whole year, but he's trained me to buy a new pillow."

Andrea laughed. "Okay. I'll pick one up for you, but it might be expensive. The last time I priced them, they were over fifty dollars."

Hannah sighed. She'd forgotten that goose-down was that expensive. She didn't really want to shell out an extra fifty dollars, but it would be worth it for a pain-free neck. "Just get it, whatever it costs. I can spend fifty dollars for a pillow, or I can spend fifty dollars for a chiropractor. At least with a pillow, I won't have to go back for another adjustment."

Almond Kisses

Preheat oven to 350 degrees F.,
with rack in middle position.

1 ½ cups melted butter *(3 sticks)*
2 cups white sugar *(granulated)*
1 teaspoon vanilla
1 teaspoon almond extract
⅛ cup molasses *(2 tablespoons)*
1 ½ teaspoons baking soda
1 teaspoon baking powder
1 teaspoon salt *(if you use salted almonds, cut the
  salt to ½ teaspoon)*
1 ½ cups finely ground almonds *(grind them up in
  your food processor with the steel blade—they
  don't have to be blanched)*
2 beaten eggs *(just whip them up with a fork)*
4 cups flour *(no need to sift)*
13 oz. bag Hershey's Kisses *(or small squares of
  milk chocolate)*

Microwave the butter in your mixing bowl to melt it.
Add the sugar, the vanilla, the almond flavoring, and the
molasses. Stir until it's blended, then add the baking
soda, baking powder and salt. Mix well.

Grind up the almonds in your food processor. Measure *after* grinding. Add them to the bowl and mix.

Pour in the beaten eggs and stir. Then add the flour and mix until all the ingredients are thoroughly blended.

Let the dough firm up for a few minutes. Then form it into walnut-sized balls and arrange them on a greased cookie sheet, 12 to a standard sheet.

Cut the Hershey's Kisses in half *(from the top down, so that each half has a point and a base.)* Press the halves into the middle of your cookie balls, cut side down. They'll look pretty on top as a yummy decoration. If you want to splurge a little, press a *whole* Hershey's Kiss into the center of the dough ball, base down and point sticking up. *(If you do splurge, you'll need double the amount of Hershey's Kisses or squares of chocolate. If your kids help you unwrap the Kisses, you should probably triple the amount!)*

Bake at 350 degrees F. for 10 minutes, or until the edges are just beginning to turn golden. *(Don't worry—the Hershey's Kisses won't melt.)* Cool on the cookie sheet for 2 minutes and then remove to a wire rack to finish cooling.

Yield: 10 to 12 dozen cookies, depending on cookie size. *(If that's too many, just cut the whole recipe in half.*

And if you have any Kisses left over, the baker deserves a treat!)

(Norman says these cookies taste the way he always wished marzipan would taste.)

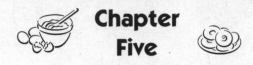

Chapter Five

"This is a nice location," Hannah commented, stopping her truck as close to the front door as she could get. "You can see the lake from here."

"You'll be able to see it even better when I prune the bottom branches on those pines." Norman hopped out of Hannah's truck and opened the door for Delores.

"It's a nice little house," Delores said, taking Norman's arm and heading for the front door. "It's almost a pity to tear it down, but I suppose it's much too small for you with only two bedrooms. Once you make the smallest one into an office, there's no room at all for . . ."

"Houseguests," Hannah interjected quickly, shooting her mother a warning glance. Now was not the time to fish around for a proposal.

"Yes, guests." Delores looked slightly embarrassed. "Well, I'll go straight to work. I don't want to keep you two out here all afternoon."

Norman opened the front door. "I'd better turn on the lights so you can see better. The windows are small and it's fairly dark inside."

"The electricity's still on?" Hannah was surprised. She'd assumed that Rhonda had turned it off to save the expense.

"I told Rhonda to switch it over to my name. I'll have it

turned off on Saturday morning before the demolition crew gets here."

When Hannah stepped inside the house, she was pleasantly surprised. She'd expected to be assailed by the clouds of must and dust that inevitably gathered when a house was unoccupied, but the only odor she could detect was lemon-scented furniture polish. "It's so clean in here!"

"I know. That's why I didn't bother to change clothes." Delores glanced down at the pale yellow dress she was wearing. "Andrea told me that Rhonda had a cleaning woman."

"What for? There hasn't been anyone living here since Mrs. Voelker died."

"I know, but the house wasn't selling and Andrea thought it might show better if it was cleaned. You know how some people are. They can't see past the dust and the cobwebs. Rhonda didn't feel like doing it herself, so she hired a cleaning lady. Come on, Hannah. We'll start in the living room and work our way through to the back."

The living room was cluttered with furniture and artwork, but with all three of them working, it didn't take long. Hannah put red tags on the furniture and artwork that Delores indicated, and Norman packed the smaller items in boxes.

The guest room didn't yield much for Granny's Attic, just a handmade patchwork quilt that Delores thought she could sell, but the master bedroom was a different story. Delores chose two Maxwell Parish prints and an old wooden rocking chair. Then she pointed to the quilt on the bed. "I'd like to take that."

"Why?" Hannah asked. She was almost sure that the quilt was machine-made, the type that anyone could buy from a mail-order catalogue. "It's not an antique, is it?"

"No, but Reverend Strandberg can use it for the homeless shelter."

Hannah agreed and pulled the quilt from the bed. But instead of a bare mattress similar to the one they'd found in the guest room, this bed was complete with sheets, pillowcases, and a blanket. "I wonder why Rhonda kept this bed made up? Do you suppose she stayed out here sometimes?"

"I doubt it, dear. Why would she want to stay way out here when she has an apartment of her own? The cleaning woman probably made it up by mistake."

"Do you want the rest of the bedding for Reverend Strandberg?" Norman asked, holding one end of the quilt while Hannah folded it.

"Yes. And if there's a linen closet, I'll take whatever's there. I think I'm through in here. Let's tackle the kitchen."

"Why don't you two go ahead," Norman suggested. "I'll load up the artwork and join you as soon as I'm through."

Hannah was the first to enter the large farm-style kitchen and what she saw made her stop cold. "That's one of my pie boxes on the table!"

"You're right. I wonder how long it's been here." Delores marched past her, lifted the lid on the distinctive box Hannah used for pies, and stepped back with a startled exclamation. "Yuck!"

"My pies are *yuck?*"

"They are when they're covered with ants."

Hannah walked closer, peered inside, and made a face. It was one of the lemon pies she'd baked on Friday. Only one piece had been eaten and the rest was crawling with an endless line of small black ants that were industriously carting away the sweet pastry. "You're right, Mother. This pie is ant fodder. I'll dump it in the garbage."

"Here, Hannah." Delores walked over with a plastic garbage bag she'd found in a box under the sink. She held it open near the edge of the table and motioned to Hannah. "I'll hold the bag. You slide the box off the table, dump it inside, and carry it out."

"Yes, Mother," Hannah said obediently, resisting the urge to giggle. Delores was treating her like a backwards child, but the plan was a good one and to object would be petty.

Once the box was safely transferred to the garbage bag, Hannah carried it to the back door and took it outside.

Two garbage cans sat on a cement slab next to the old garage. Hannah peeked in the garage window, hoping to see an antique car up on blocks, but the interior was completely filled with fireplace wood. She'd have to remember to tell Norman about that. There was enough wood in Mrs. Voelker's garage to carry him through several winters. All he had to do was move it to another location before they tore down the garage.

Hannah held her bag at the ready and lifted the lid on the garbage can. She expected it to be empty and she was surprised to see several items in the bottom of the plastic liner. There were two Styrofoam boxes with see-through plastic lids, the kind used for restaurant takeout dinners. One dinner was partially eaten and the other looked untouched. Both were osso buco, one of Hannah's favorite entrées. She recognized it by its distinctive marrowbone. Rhonda must have ordered takeout on the night she packed up the last of her great-aunt's effects and since there were two containers, it was obvious she'd expected someone to join her for dinner.

It was probably an invasion of privacy to go through someone else's garbage, but Hannah was curious about that uneaten dinner. She lifted the liner partway out of the can, and peered down at the other items in its depths. There was an empty Chianti bottle, and two plastic wineglasses. Rhonda had poured wine for someone, but that someone had left before dinner.

Hannah shrugged and added her garbage bag to the mix. She didn't understand why Rhonda hadn't taken the untouched entrée home. Even if she hadn't wanted it, she could have given it to one of her neighbors. For that matter, why had she left the pie? The same reasoning applied. One of Rhonda's neighbors would have loved it.

Just as she was about to close the lid, Hannah heard the rumble of a trash truck approaching on the road that ran past the house. Monday must be garbage day. Hannah lifted out the liner, tied it off, and rushed to the front to hand it to the driver.

"What took you so long?" Delores asked when Hannah came back into the kitchen.

"The garbage truck came so I carried out the bag." Hannah sniffed the air. "You must have found some ant spray."

"It was under the sink. Look at these dishes, Hannah. They're Carnival glass."

Hannah surveyed the rainbow of colored dishes Delores had stacked on the counter. "I thought Carnival glass was orange."

"That's the most common, but they made it in other colors, too. See this purple bowl? It's fairly rare and it'll bring a good price. Could you climb up and look in the top cupboards, dear? There may be more."

Hannah dragged a chair over to the counter and climbed up on the seat. She opened one of the cupboard doors and her eyes widened as she recognized a distinctive design. "Here's a big Desert Rose platter. You want that, don't you?"

"Yes. Hand it down to me."

Hannah handed the platter to her mother and reached for a stack of plates. "This looks like Blue Willowware, but it's green. I think there's a whole set of it."

"Let me see." Delores sounded excited as she reached up for a plate. She flipped it over and she gasped. "What a find! It's genuine Green Blue Willowware!"

Hannah coughed to cover a laugh. How could a plate be Green Blue Willowware? It sounded like a contradiction in terms. "Here's some pink. Do you want that, too?"

"Yes! Pink Blue Willowware is a collector's dream. Just hand me everything, Hannah. And be careful you don't drop any pieces. I'm just glad Rhonda didn't go through the cupboards. She missed some real treasures."

By the time Norman joined them in the kitchen, Delores

had every flat surface stacked with dishes and glassware. "It looks like you found some things you want."

"Oh my, yes!" Delores turned to smile at him. "Are you sure you don't want a percentage? Mrs. Voelker had some valuable dishes and glassware."

Norman shook his head. "It's all yours and Mother's. I've been living with her rent-free and it's the least I can do."

"Well . . . that's very generous. Just wait until I tell Carrie and Luanne. They're going to be *in alt* over these fabulous dishes."

Hannah chuckled as she climbed down from the chair. *In alt?* It was obvious that that her mother had attended a meeting of her Regency Romance group recently. Delores had explained that *alt* referred to altitude, and the heroines in Regency novels often spoke of being *in alt* when something took them to the heights of pleasure.

When they'd packed up the glassware and dishes and Norman had carried the boxes out to the truck, Delores gave one last glance around. "I think that's all. I've looked in every room."

"How about the basement?" Norman asked. "I haven't been down there, but Rhonda said her great-uncle used to do some woodworking."

"Antique tools!" Delores's eyes began to gleam. "They're going for a premium right now. Do you have time for me to take a quick peek?"

"I've got time. How about you, Hannah?"

"It's fine with me." Hannah handed Delores the apron she'd discovered hanging over the back of a kitchen chair. "You'd better put this on, Mother. It might be dusty down there."

Delores tied on the apron and headed for the basement stairs. "Aren't you coming, dear?"

"I can if you need me," Hannah said, giving her mother an exaggerated wink.

"Of course I . . ." Delores caught the wink and interpreted

it correctly. "Actually, I don't. I'm perfectly capable of exploring the basement by myself. Stay right here and keep Norman company. You're both so busy, you don't get much time to spend together and I know you'd like to discuss your plans for the house."

"Right," Hannah said, rolling her eyes at the ceiling. Her mother was about as subtle as a sledgehammer. "Holler if you need us and we'll come right down."

Norman waited until Delores had switched on the light and gone down the stairs, and then he turned to Hannah. "What do you think about a picture window in the kitchen? Since it faces the woods, it would be a nice view."

"Yes, it would." Hannah could picture herself sitting at the kitchen table in the morning, sipping a freshly brewed cup of coffee and watching the deer emerge from the trees. That thought was dangerous to her preferred single state, so she quickly asked another question. "How about the living room? That window will face the lake, won't it?"

"That's right, but the master bedroom will have the best view. That's where I'm building the balcony."

Hannah didn't want to think about the master bedroom with its wood-burning fireplace and incredible view. It was just too appealing. She changed the subject again, asking Norman about how he planned to furnish the house. That was interesting and it was only when she glanced up at the old kitchen clock on the wall that she realized almost fifteen minutes had passed and they hadn't heard a peep out of Delores.

"Maybe I'd better check on Mother. She's been down there a long time."

"I'll go with you." Norman led the way to the basement doorway. "Delores? Are you all right down there?"

Hannah stood behind Norman, waiting for her mother to respond. When there was no answer, she felt a jolt of fear. "Move over, Norman. I'm going down there."

"Not without me, you're not." Norman had gone down

three steps when he stopped abruptly. "Here she comes, now. Back up to give her room."

Hannah backed up, but she gazed over Norman's shoulder to watch her mother climb the stairs. Delores didn't appear to be hurt, but her mouth was set in a tight line. Something had happened in the basement. And judging by the way her mother was gripping the handrail, that something wasn't good.

"Water," Delores croaked as she reached the top of the stairs, and Norman rushed to get her a glass. She took one sip, handed the glass back to him, and shivered visibly.

"You look like you just saw a ghost," Hannah commented and immediately wished she hadn't when her mother's face turned even paler.

Delores gave a small smile, so small that it could only be classified as a grimace. "Not a ghost. I found . . . a body!"

Chapter
Six

Delores sighed and leaned back against the headrest in the passenger seat of Hannah's truck. "You were right, Hannah. The chocolate helped."

"Chocolate always helps." Hannah held out the bag of leftover Chocolate-Covered Cherry Cookies. When she'd started her business, she'd vowed never to sell day-old cookies. She always had some in her truck and she gave them away as samples, telling everyone that if they thought her leftover cookies were good, they should come in and taste them fresh out of the oven. People did, and they were hooked. Business at The Cookie Jar was thriving. "Have another cookie, Mother. I guarantee you'll feel even better."

Norman peered closely at Delores. "Your color's coming back and you're beginning to look like yourself again. When you feel up to it, tell me exactly what you saw. I need to go down to the basement to check it out."

"I'm not going with you!"

"Nobody expects you to," Hannah assured her. "I'll go with Norman if you'll tell us exactly where to look."

"In the furnace room, just like I said. It's way in the back. I was standing by a shelf filled with jars when I saw the pile of dirt."

"Okay," Hannah said, reaching in through the open window to pat her mother's arm. "Do you want to come inside with us and sit in the kitchen while we look?"

"No! I'm not setting foot inside that house again, not with that dead body in there. I'll stay right here, thank you very much."

"That's fine, Mother. Just honk the horn if you need us. And if it makes you feel better, roll up the windows and lock all the doors."

Norman led the way toward the house and Hannah followed. They went down the hallway to the kitchen and approached the basement door.

"You don't have to go, Hannah." Norman turned to look at her. "I can take care of it."

"And let you have all the fun?" Hannah gave him a grin. "I want to be there when we discover it's a pile of rags, or a bag of old clothes."

"You don't think your mother saw a body?"

"I doubt it. Andrea said looky-lous have been traipsing through this house for the past three months. If there was anything in the basement, one of them would have found it."

"Maybe they didn't go down there. Your mother was very descriptive, Hannah. She said the body was partially buried in a grave."

"A grave is nothing but a hole and someone could have dug up the floor to fix the plumbing. Mother said the furnace room light was burned out and she admitted that she couldn't see very well. I know her better than you do, Norman. I'm sure she saw something, but she's a drama queen. I'll never forget the time she swore she saw a black bear going through our trash can and it was only our neighbor's French poodle."

"That's good to know," Norman said, looking relieved. "But we still have to look. Did you bring those flashlights?"

"Of course I did." Hannah handed him a flashlight and kept one for herself.

Norman started down the steps first and Hannah let him.

It was clear he was exercising his manly prerogative, and that was fine with her. She really didn't think her mother had found a body, but it would be negligent of them not to check.

As they reached the bottom of the stairs and started to walk across the basement floor, Hannah looked around her curiously. The basement ran the full length of the house. It looked cavernous in the light from the single string of bulbs that hung from the rafters and the shadows were deep and slightly menacing.

"It's creepy down here," Hannah said, her voice much louder than she'd intended.

"It's also a mess," Norman added, stepping over a pile of old newspapers and detouring around a stack of decaying boxes. "Rhonda's cleaning woman didn't clean down here."

As they picked their way past piles of greasy rags, old paint cans, and stacks of old magazines tied up with twine, Hannah let her flashlight play over the walls. One wall was covered with floor-to-ceiling shelves that held an array of home-canned vegetables and fruit. The jars were laden with years of dust, but she could still see the brightly colored contents and she was impressed. "Look at all those preserves. Mrs. Voelker must have spent a lot of hours canning."

"Rhonda said she used to win blue ribbons for her jams and jellies at the county fairs."

"Really?" Hannah stepped closer and let the beam of her flashlight play over the jars. "I don't see any. These are pickles, and canned corn, and things like that. Maybe Rhonda took all the jam."

The door to the furnace room was open and hanging by one hinge. Hannah was surprised that her mother had ventured so far into the basement without a flashlight. The lure of antiques must have been stronger than her distaste of spiders and grime.

"Hold on, Hannah." Norman held up his hand. "I want to make sure this door doesn't fall. I'll hold it to let you through and then I'll find something to prop it up."

Norman held the door and Hannah stepped into the furnace room. It was much larger than most, a rectangular, dirt-floored space with the furnace near the center. There was a coal chute set into the outside wall, and Hannah surmised that this room had once been the entire basement. A homemade set of shelves was sitting against one of the walls. Hannah saw that it contained jam. A few jars were broken and she stepped over the shards of glass as she made her way past the furnace.

"Something's been digging back here," she called out to Norman, as she spotted a mound of dirt. "It was probably a big badger or mole."

"Do you think that's what your mother saw?"

"Maybe. I don't see anything resembling a body, though. Mother's imagination must have been working overtime."

"Where are you?" Norman asked, his voice floating eerily into the darkened silence.

"In back of the furnace. Go around it to the right. Be careful where you step. There's some broken glass on the floor near the shelves."

Hannah stepped closer, shining her light over the mound of dirt. Just beyond it, there was a large hole in the dirt floor and she could see why Delores had assumed it was a grave. She moved closer, letting the beam of her flashlight play over the partially filled-in hole, and she drew her breath in sharply as she saw something that couldn't be explained by any animal, no matter how large. It was a tennis shoe and it was attached to a human foot.

"Oh!" Hannah gasped, turning and almost bumping into Norman.

"What is it?"

"I'll tell you later," Hannah said, grabbing his hand and pulling him toward the doorway. "Let's go."

"Was it a body?" Norman asked, puffing a little as he hurried to catch up with Hannah.

"Yes!"

"In the hole?"

"Yes!" Hannah took a deep breath. "Mother was right. We have to get out to the sheriff's station and tell them about it."

Hannah left Norman getting coffee for Delores at the bank of machines that lined the lobby. The coffee was awful; she'd had it before, but even bad coffee was good in a pinch. She'd driven out to the sheriff's station on autopilot, trying not to think about the gruesome discovery they'd made. The tennis shoe she'd seen had been lime green and the only person in Lake Eden who wore shoes that color was Rhonda Scharf.

"Hannah," Mike smiled as he saw her coming toward his desk. "How's it going?"

"Not good. Is there somewhere private we can talk?"

Mike nodded, led her to one of the conference rooms, and closed the door. When he motioned her to a chair, Hannah noticed that he looked anxious. "Don't tell me that . . ."

"Norman didn't propose," Hannah said, guessing what was foremost in his mind. "This is something entirely unrelated."

"What?"

"There's a body in the basement at the Voelker place. I don't know for sure, but I think it's Rhonda Scharf."

Mike looked stunned for a moment and then he pulled out his notebook. "You found another body?"

"Not this time. Mother had that honor."

"Delores?" Mike looked even more stunned. "Is she all right?"

"Yes, if she survives the coffee in your vending machine. Norman's with her and I gave her a triple dose of chocolate."

"What happened?"

"We were out there looking for antiques and Mother went down to the basement to search for old tools. When she came back up, she told us she'd found a body. Norman and I checked it out, and she was right."

"Hold on a second," Mike interrupted her. "Let me get Bill in on this, and we'll take your statement right now. We'll catch your mother later, after she calms down a little."

"Good idea," Hannah said, settling down for a lengthy session. These things always took time and there was no rushing it. She knew that from prior experience.

By the time Hannah got back to The Cookie Jar, it was almost four in the afternoon. Jed and Freddy had finished work for the day, the customers had thinned out, and almost all of their cookies had been sold. Hannah joined Lisa behind the counter to tell her what had happened, but she didn't say anything about the identity of the body. That could wait for official confirmation.

"Well, at least your *mother* was first on the scene," Lisa said, speaking in an undertone so their customers couldn't hear her. "This time she can't accuse you of trying to embarrass her by finding dead bodies."

"Oh yes she can. I'm not sure how, but I know this'll wind up being all my fault."

"You could be right," Lisa conceded, grabbing a towel and wiping an already spotless counter. "You're going to look into it, aren't you?"

"No way. We've got a lot to do to get ready for the Fourth of July party, and Mike and Bill were pretty bent out of shape the last time I interfered in one of their cases. I am curious about one thing, though. When we got out to the Voelker place, there was one of our Lemon Meringue pies on the kitchen table. I was wondering how it got there."

Lisa looked thoroughly stumped. "I know Norman didn't buy a pie, and Rhonda didn't, either. Do you want me to check my customer list?"

"What list?"

"I keep a record of everyone who buys our pies. I call them up if you're going to bake their favorite."

Hannah was impressed. "That's smart marketing."

"It works," Lisa said, smiling broadly. "Most of them want me to save one for them and a couple have standing orders. Mrs. Jessup told me to put her down for two pies every time you bake apple."

"And you have a record from last Friday?"

"It's at home, but I'll call you tonight and read off the names. It'll probably be after ten. I'm going out to dinner with Herb."

"That's fine. I really want to know who bought a whole pie and only ate one piece. It's practically an insult."

"I know, especially when it's your Lemon Meringue." Lisa looked up to see a customer holding his coffee mug aloft. "Mayor Bascomb wants a refill. Do you want to get it while I mix up a batch of Walnuttoes for tomorrow? Donna Lempke called and ordered six dozen for her cousin's birthday party."

"I'll do the Walnuttoes. You do the coffee."

"But are you sure? They're chocolate and you're on a diet."

Hannah gave an ironic grin. "That's okay. Seeing that body took my appetite away."

"The Dead Body Diet?" Lisa started to grin as she picked up the carafe. "I'm surprised someone hasn't thought of it before. What do you want me to say if anyone asks me about what you saw in the basement?"

"Nobody will. Bill and Mike won't release any information until they confirm the identity, and Norman won't say anything because they asked him not to."

"But how about your mother?"

"Oh-oh," Hannah groaned. It was a sure bet that Delores had told someone by now. Actually, the odds were good that she'd told hundreds of someones. "Just say that Mike and Bill are handling it and I'm not involved."

Lisa snorted. "They'll never swallow that."

"Maybe not, but it's true. Wild horses couldn't drag me

into this one. As of right now, I'm officially retired from the murder business."

"Then you think it was murder?" Lisa's eyes grew round.

"All I know is someone's dead. It's up to Doc Knight to determine who, when, and how."

Hannah turned and headed back to the kitchen before Lisa could ask more questions. She was convinced that the body they'd found was Rhonda Scharf, and as she got out her recipe book, Hannah swallowed past the lump in her throat. Rhonda had never been one of her close friends, but she hadn't disliked her. And no one should have to die in a gloomy, moldy basement only hours before leaving on the best vacation of her life. Of course Rhonda had been murdered. The fact that someone had tried to bury her confirmed that. If Rhonda had died accidentally, the person who'd found her would have called the sheriff's department to report it.

It didn't take long to mix up the dough for the Walnuttoes. Hannah had baked them twice a week for the past two years, but she still took the precaution of checking off the ingredients on the laminated surface of her recipe. She was preoccupied with Rhonda's death and preoccupation led to mistakes.

Once she'd finished, Hannah covered the bowl with plastic wrap and carried it to a shelf in her walk-in cooler. She was just emerging from the chilly interior when the back door opened and Mike stepped in.

"Hi, Hannah. We took your mother's statement and I need to check a few facts with you."

"Sure." Hannah motioned to a stool at the stainless-steel workstation. "Coffee?"

"That'd be great." Mike waited until Hannah had brought him a mug of coffee before he opened his notebook. "Did your mother go down to the basement alone?"

"Yes. Norman and I didn't know anything was wrong until she told us what she'd seen."

"Where were you while she was in the basement?"

"We were sitting at the kitchen table. We told her to call out if she needed us and the basement door was wide open."

Mike began to frown as he referred to his notes. "You didn't run down there when you heard her screams?"

"Mother didn't scream. There wasn't a peep out of her. That's why we got worried and went to the stairwell to check on her. We called out to her and when she didn't answer, we started to go down the stairs. But then we saw Mother coming up."

Mike made a note in his book. "Was the house still creaking when you went down there?"

"Creaking? No."

"Then the wind had stopped?"

"There wasn't any wind."

"Interesting," Mike said, referring to his notes again. "How about the rats? Were they as large as your mother said?"

"What rats? We didn't see any rats."

Mike began to grin. "I think your mother must have embellished her story just a bit. How about the gruesome trail of glistening blood?"

"No blood," Hannah said, shaking her head.

"Okay. We'll just file your mother's statement under 'f' for 'fiction' and go with the ones that you and Norman gave us. At least they match what we found at the crime scene." Mike took another sip of his coffee and stood up. "Thanks, Hannah. I've got to run. The fingerprint team should be finished by now."

Hannah reached out to grab his arm. "Not so fast. Was I right?"

"About what?"

"About the shoe. Was it Rhonda's?"

Mike looked as if he didn't want to say, but then he nodded. "Yes. Doc Knight made a positive identification."

"Poor Rhonda." Hannah sighed deeply. "How did she die?"

"It's too early to tell."

"But was she murdered?"

"The autopsy report isn't in yet."

"I'm asking for your personal opinion." Hannah gave an exasperated sigh. "Do you think that Rhonda was murdered? Or did it look like an accident?"

Mike thought it over for a moment and then he relented. "This is unofficial. If you quote me I'll deny it, but it didn't look like an accident to me. Now don't ask me any more questions, Hannah. That's all I'm saying."

"Just one more thing. Why didn't Rhonda's killer finish burying her? She told everyone that she was going on vacation and no one would have missed her for two weeks. Her killer could have bought himself a lot more time if he'd finished burying her."

"I know that."

"Then you think he was scared off before he could finish filling in her grave?"

"That's possible."

"What I can't figure out is why anyone wanted to kill Rhonda. She could be exasperating at times, but everyone I know seemed to like her well enough. How about the crime scene? Did you find any clues?"

Mike's eyes narrowed. "You're not going to interfere with our investigation, are you? You don't have any reason to get involved this time around."

"You're right," Hannah said, meeting his eyes squarely. "I've got enough to do without solving murder cases. Of course I'll tell you if I hear anything important, but that's as far as it'll go."

"Good." Mike gave her one of his melt-your-heart smiles and pulled her into his arms for a hug. "Bill and I are perfectly capable of running a murder investigation without you."

"Of course you are," Hannah said, hiding her grin against the maroon lapel of his sheriff's uniform. She'd already helped them solve several murder cases, but Mike was clearly asserting his professional independence.

"I won't deny that you helped us a lot in the past, but I don't want people to think we can't do our job without you."

"I understand," Hannah breathed, snuggling a little closer. Mike's hugs were wonderful. He was tall and rugged, and being in his arms made her feel fragile and feminine.

Mike's cell phone rang, disrupting the moment, and he answered it. He listened for a moment. "Okay. I'll be out there in ten minutes."

"You have to go?" Hannah asked, already knowing the answer.

"Yes, but I'll call you later. The forensic guys are finished and Bill's waiting for me out at the crime scene."

"Take some cookies with you," Hannah said, heading for the counter to put some in a bag.

"Thanks. We probably won't get a break until late and they'll tide us over." Mike took the cookies and gave her a lopsided grin. "Remember what I said, Hannah. Bill and I can handle it."

Walnuttoes

Do not preheat oven—
dough must chill before baking.

2 cups chocolate chips *(a 12-ounce bag)*
1 ½ cups brown sugar
¾ cup butter *(1 ½ sticks)*
4 eggs
2 teaspoons vanilla
2 teaspoons baking powder
1 teaspoon salt
2 cups flour *(not sifted)*
2 cups finely chopped walnuts
approx. ½ cup additional white sugar in a small
    bowl

Melt chocolate chips with butter. *(Microwave on high for 2 minutes, then stir until smooth.)* Mix in sugar and let cool. Add eggs, one at a time, mixing well after each addition. Mix in vanilla, baking powder and salt. Add flour and mix well, then add nuts and mix in.

Chill dough for at least 4 hours, overnight is even better.

When you're ready to bake, preheat oven to 350 degrees F., rack in the middle position.

Roll walnut-sized dough balls with your hands. *(This is messy—wear thin plastic gloves if you wish. If dough becomes too warm between rollings, return it to the refrigerator.)*

Drop dough balls into a small bowl with white sugar and roll around to coat. Then place them on a greased cookie sheet, 12 to a standard sheet. Smush them down with a greased spatula.

Bake at 350 degrees F. for 12 to 14 minutes. Let cool on cookie sheet for 1 minute, then remove to wire rack. *(If you leave them on the cookie sheet too long, they'll stick.)*

Yield: 8 to 10 dozen, depending on cookie size.

(Delores says these cookies taste like the Walnetto caramels she loved as a child. She also told me that she likes the cookies better, because they don't pull out her fillings.)

Hannah was ready to return to the coffee shop when the back door opened and Delores poked her head in. "Are you busy, dear?"

"I've got a minute," Hannah greeted her. "Come in and have a cookie. I've got Peanut Butter Melts, Apricot Drops, or Chocolate Chip Crunches."

Delores sat down on the stool Mike had vacated at the stainless-steel workstation. "I'll take a Chocolate Chip Crunch. You're going to investigate, aren't you?"

"No," Hannah answered, pouring a mug of coffee and setting it down in front of her mother.

"But you've got to investigate!"

"Why?"

"Because Rhonda's dead and we need to find out who killed her."

Hannah gulped. She'd told no one except Mike about the lime green tennis shoe. "How do you know it was Rhonda?"

"Bill told Andrea, and Andrea told me. I just got off the phone with her."

"What else did you learn?" Despite her resolve, Hannah's curiosity was aroused.

"Rhonda was stabbed with a knife."

"Bill told Andrea that?"

"No, Bill and Mike don't know it yet. Minnie Holtzmeier told me."

"How does Minnie know?"

"Her son was driving the ambulance that took Rhonda to the morgue and he heard the two paramedics talking in the back. One of them said that it was a single stab wound and the blade of the knife went in between two ribs to puncture Rhonda's heart. The other one said Rhonda must have died instantly and that was a blessing."

"That's interesting, but I promised Mike I wouldn't interfere." Hannah placed two cookies on a napkin and carried them over to Delores. Her mother had only asked for one, but she always ate two and it would save her a return trip. "Don't pass that information around, Mother. It might hamper the investigation and it's really none of your business."

"Of course it's my business. I have a vested interest."

Hannah was puzzled. "What vested interest?"

"I'm the one who found Rhonda! I owe it to her to do everything in my power to see that her killer is caught. Haven't you heard that when you save someone's life, you bear a responsibility to them?"

Hannah had heard that line in a score of bad movies. "But you didn't save Rhonda's life. Rhonda was already dead when you found her."

"I know, but it still amounts to the same thing."

Hannah shook her head to clear it. Her mother's logic left a lot to be desired. She thought about pointing out the dissimilarities, but she wisely kept her silence. Arguing with Delores was an exercise in futility.

"You have a vested interest, too."

"What's my vested interest?" Hannah asked, regretting the question the moment it had left her lips.

"Rhonda's last meal was a piece of your Lemon Meringue Pie. If that's not a vested interest, I don't know what is! You have to help me investigate. It's your duty."

"But you told me you didn't want me to investigate any more murders."

"That's perfectly true. It's not the sort of thing I want my daughter involved in, but these are extenuating circumstances. I'll run the investigation and you can just help me." Delores took a bite of her cookie and chewed thoughtfully. "What do you think we should do first?"

Hide under the bed until this blows over? Lock ourselves in a cell to save Mike and Bill the trouble of doing it later? Hannah bit her tongue hard to keep from voicing any of her thoughts.

"I think we should make a list of the people who wanted Rhonda dead. That's the logical place to start. Get out your notebook, dear."

Hannah reached for one of the blank steno pads she kept handy. There was no way she was getting involved in Rhonda's murder investigation, but Delores didn't seem capable of taking no for an answer and it couldn't hurt to write down what her mother dictated. "Okay. I'm ready."

"Write down Norman."

"Norman?!" Hannah was so startled her pen dug a little hole in the page. "Why would Norman want Rhonda dead?"

"Because he bought her house. If he thought he paid too much for it, he would have been mad enough to kill her."

"That doesn't fly, Mother. Norman told me he made Rhonda a lowball offer and he got the house at a steal."

Delores frowned slightly and it was clear she wasn't happy about Hannah's revelation. "If you say so, dear. The house wasn't the motive then, but it doesn't mean that Norman didn't kill her. It's motive, means, and opportunity . . . isn't that right?"

"It's right enough for the cop shows."

"That's good enough for me. Norman had the opportunity. He knew that Rhonda was going out there over the weekend to pick up some mementos."

"That's true," Hannah said, but she set down her pen. "I agree that Norman had the opportunity, but how about the means? I'm not even sure Norman owns a knife."

"He could have bought one. They've got all sorts of knives at Lake Eden Hardware. And since Norman has medical training, he would have known exactly how to stab Rhonda."

Hannah laughed. She couldn't help it. The thought of Norman as a mad killer wielding a knife he'd just purchased was ridiculous. "Norman's a dentist. If he'd used his medical knowledge to kill Rhonda, he would have shot her full of Xylocaine or something like that."

"You've got a point." Delores sighed deeply. "That's all right. I didn't really think Norman did it anyway. We'd better move on to someone else."

"Who?"

"Rhonda's boyfriend. Couples always have a reason to kill each other, especially if it's a passionate relationship."

Hannah picked up her pen. She was still determined not to get involved, but the idea of a boyfriend had definite possibilities. "Okay, who is he?"

"I don't know."

That stopped Hannah cold for a moment. "But you think Rhonda had one?"

"All that flirting must have amounted to something. Rhonda tried to entice every man that walked into the drugstore."

Hannah nodded, glad that her mother hadn't gotten wind of Rhonda's flirtation with Bill. It had happened less than a year ago when Hannah and Bill had gone to Rhonda's cosmetic counter to ask her about a lipstick mark that had been part of the evidence in Bill's first murder case. All the while they'd asked questions, Rhonda had flirted with Bill outrageously. When Hannah had mentioned it later, Bill had brushed it off. He'd said that Rhonda always flirted with the guys and it didn't really mean anything.

"A flirt isn't necessarily any more than that," Hannah reminded her mother. "Rhonda might have run for the hills if a man had tried anything."

"Don't be silly, dear. I'm positive that Rhonda had a boyfriend."

"How do you know?"

"It's deductive reasoning. Bertie told me that Rhonda had a standing appointment to have her roots touched up. And a woman doesn't have her hair colored unless she's trying to look younger for a man."

"Really?" Hannah's eyes narrowed and she eyed her mother closely. At the time of her father's funeral, her mother's dark hair had been sprinkled with gray.

Delores noticed Hannah's expression and she colored slightly. "Of course there could be other reasons. Rhonda might have wanted to look good for her job. As a matter of fact, I have Bertie touch up my hair every month or so. It makes me look more professional."

"Right," Hannah said, accepting her mother's excuse at face value. There was no way she wanted to consider the possibility that her mother had a love life.

"I'm almost positive that Rhonda was involved with someone. There was just too much gossip and where there's smoke, there's fire. Everyone was talking about Rhonda and the UPS man a while back. Of course I didn't pay much attention to it. I don't approve of gossip."

Hannah did her best to keep a straight face. Delores had called her with the story about Rhonda and the UPS man the moment it had hit the telephone wires. "Do you want me to write down the UPS man?"

"Just put down a question mark. I'll know what it means."

Hannah made a big question mark and underlined it. "We only have one suspect and that's a question mark. Who else do you want to add?"

"I'm not sure. I'll call you later when I've had a chance to think about it." Delores slid off the stool and headed for the door. "You don't have to be anything except my sounding board, dear. Since you told Mike you wouldn't get involved, I'll solve Rhonda's murder all by myself."

"Do you really think you can do it?" Hannah couldn't resist asking.

"Of course. I'm an intelligent woman and I love solving puzzles. I'll find out who killed Rhonda. Trust me."

Hannah stared at the door as it closed behind Delores. In her experience, only people who didn't know what they were doing said 'trust me.' Perhaps she was grossly underestimating her mother's crime-solving abilities, but Hannah had doubts about trusting the woman whose VCR had been flashing twelve A.M. for the past four years.

"I still can't believe she's dead," Lisa said, reaching into her purse and pulling out her car keys. It was already five-thirty and she'd stayed an extra half hour to help Hannah finish mixing up dough for the next morning. "Did you know it was Rhonda when you told me about it?"

"I suspected it was, but I didn't want to say until they made a positive identification."

"And you're still not going to investigate?"

Hannah shook her head. "Mike and Bill don't need me and I have things of my own to do."

"Well . . . if you change your mind, I'll take over the work-load."

"Thanks, Lisa." Hannah flashed her a smile. "Now get out of here so you have time to change clothes before your date."

Once Lisa had left, Hannah rinsed off the things they'd used and stacked them in the industrial dishwasher. The brochure that had come with the dishwasher claimed that there was no need for pre-rinsing, but old habits died hard. She was about to pour in the detergent when there was a knock at the back door.

"Hannah?" Norman's voice carried through the door. "I need to talk to you for a minute."

Hannah set the detergent on the counter and hurried to the door to let him in. "Hi, Norman. I just ditched the last of the coffee, but I can offer you a cookie."

"No, thanks. I gained some weight and I'm trying to take it off. No more snacking between meals."

Hannah eyed Norman closely. He didn't look like he'd gained an ounce. "How many pounds are we talking about here?"

"Three."

Hannah came very close to losing it. Three pounds were hardly worth going on a diet. She had almost seven times more to lose.

"What?" Norman asked. "You look angry about something."

"That's because I have more weight to lose than you do. And I'm not really angry. This is my regular I'm-on-a-diet expression."

"Why are you dieting? You look great to me."

"You're not just saying that?"

"I never *just say* anything. And I think people should look real, not like fashion models."

"But you think the models are attractive, don't you?"

Norman shrugged. "Sure. But I wouldn't want to date one, if that's what you mean."

"Why? They're really glamorous."

"I know, but that's not a big selling point for me. I think women should look like . . . well . . . women. They shouldn't look like starving teenagers."

Hannah found herself feeling better by the minute. Perhaps she wasn't that overweight after all. Both Lisa and Norman had said that they didn't think she had to lose weight.

"I came to ask a favor, Hannah." Norman abruptly switched

gears. "Mother called earlier and I know the body in the basement was Rhonda. I want you to investigate her murder."

Hannah blinked. Norman really ought to beep when he reversed directions like that. "Why do you want *me* to investigate?"

"Because you're good at it. And because I have a vested interest."

Hannah sighed. Not the vested interest thing again! Norman was echoing her mother's reasoning. "Is it because you saw Rhonda's body and you feel a certain obligation?"

"Not really. It's just that the sheriff's department roped off the whole house as a crime scene and they won't let me tear it down until the case is solved. I've got the demolition crew coming on Saturday and I really hate to cancel. Maybe it's selfish of me, but I'm on a tight time schedule. If I don't start building before winter comes, I'll have to wait until the spring."

Hannah felt her stress level rise and she squelched the urge to grab a cookie. Her mother wanted her to investigate and now Norman was climbing on that bandwagon. What was a girl to do?

"Mike and Bill don't want me involved," Hannah said, not meeting Norman's eyes. Her excuse sounded weak, even to her.

"That's never stopped you before. Come on, Hannah. I'm asking you as a friend. After all, it's our dream house."

"I know," Hannah said. It *was* their dream house and a little digging around could do nothing but help Mike and Bill. She loved the blueprints they'd made together and she wanted to see their house built almost as much as Norman did.

"Then you'll do it?"

Hannah considered her options and discarded them one by one. She could bow out and risk alienating her mother and Norman, two of the most important people in her life. Lisa would be disappointed in her, too. She'd offered to take over the workload and that meant she wanted Hannah to investigate. Mike and Bill wouldn't be happy if she got involved, but they were the only ones. And wasn't there something about the greater good? Pleasing three people was more important than pleasing only two.

"At least think about it," Norman urged, reaching out to take her hand. "This is very important to me, Hannah."

"It's important to me, too. Give me some time, Norman. I'll think about it tonight and let you know what I decide in the morning."

"That's good enough for me." Norman stood up and smiled at her. "I know you'll do the right thing. You always do."

It was a good exit line and Norman took it, going out the door without another word. Hannah was left in a thoughtful mood as she started the dishwater, did her nightly check of the exits, and made sure everything was securely locked. Once that was done, she loaded up the leftover cookies and placed them in a box. She was just carrying it to the back door when the telephone rang.

Hannah groaned. She had a good notion to walk straight out the door and lock it behind her, but it was difficult to ignore a ringing phone. She set the box she was carrying on a stool and walked over to pick it up. "The Cookie Jar. This is Hannah speaking."

"What are you doing there so late?"

It was Andrea and Hannah sighed. "I was just about to leave, but the phone rang."

"I'm sorry. I didn't mean to hold you up."

"That's okay," Hannah said, starting to grin. "I had to come back to answer the phone anyway."

"No, you didn't . . . I mean . . . That doesn't make any . . . You're kidding me, right?"

"Right." Hannah laughed out loud. Andrea's sputtering reaction was even better than she'd hoped for. "What did you want to tell me?"

"Two things. I couldn't get your pillow at CostMart, because they were all out. They're getting more in, but not until later in the week. I made them give me a rain check so you'll still get the sale price."

"Thanks, Andrea." Hannah was grateful. She probably wouldn't have thought to ask for a rain check. "What's the second thing you had to tell me?"

"Mother called and she told me she was going to investigate Rhonda's murder."

"That's true. She told me the same thing."

"You've got to talk her out of it, Hannah. You're older and she'll listen to you."

"No, she won't. She's *never* listened to me."

"Just try it. Tell her she can't do it."

"Why not?"

"Because Mother doesn't know anything about investigating murders, and all she'll do is mess up the case for Bill and Mike. She might even get into trouble."

"That's possible," Hannah agreed.

"And that's why you have to talk her out of it. I don't want Mother to get into trouble. Just tell her that you're going to take over and she'll back right off. That's what she really wants anyway."

Hannah sighed deeply. "I know."

"Then it's all settled and you'll investigate?"

"Nothing's settled. I haven't made up my mind yet."

"But you have to do it. Say you will, Hannah. I have a vested interest."

"*Everybody* seems to have a vested interest. Mother wants me to investigate because she found Rhonda's body and she feels obligated. Lisa wants me to investigate because she likes to take over the workload. And Norman wants me to investigate because Mike and Bill won't let him tear the Voelker place down until the case is solved. What's *your* vested interest?"

Andrea was silent for a moment. "It's not as important as theirs."

"What is it?"

"I want you to investigate because I'm bored and I want to help."

"How can you be bored when you're building The Cookie Jar float?"

"I already took care of that."

"You mean it's all finished?"

"Not exactly. But when Janice Cox saw my plans, she volunteered to build it. Tracey's classmates and the people at the Senior Center are helping her."

Hannah chuckled. Andrea was a master a delegating authority. Janice would end up doing all the work and she'd never realize what had hit her. "What's the float like?"

"I'm keeping that a secret until the morning of the parade. By the way, I talked to Mayor Bascomb and he wants our float to lead off the parade, right behind his convertible."

"Really?" Hannah was surprised. Usually that honor went to the oldest business in town.

"It's all arranged. Now I need something else to do. This inactivity is driving me crazy. I just know I'll get horribly depressed if you don't let me help you investigate."

"But even if I do decide to investigate, I can't let you help me."

"Why not?"

"Because you're pregnant and murder investigations are dangerous."

"I know, but I'm not talking about going along with you, or anything like that. I can make calls and gather information. You'll let me do that, won't you?"

"Sure," Hannah said, responding once again to the pleading note in her sister's voice. It was the very same note that had convinced her to return her sister's library books, help her with her homework, and bake cookies for her friends. "You can help me if I decide to investigate."

"You will. You won't be able to resist. Besides, Bill wants you to."

"Really?" Hannah took that with a grain of salt. Andrea tended to hear only what she wanted to hear. "What makes you say that?"

"When he called me to tell me about Rhonda, he said this case would be different since you weren't involved."

"And that made you think he wanted me to investigate?"

"Absolutely. He sounded sad when he said it and I read between the lines. Bill wants your help. I'm sure of it."

"Okay, if you say so."

"What shall I do first?" Andrea asked, sounding eager.

"You're jumping the gun. I haven't decided to do it yet."

"But you will and we might as well get started. Give me some phone calls to make. I'm sitting on the couch with my feet up because that's what Bill wants me to do, but I'm right next to the phone."

Hannah was about to say she couldn't think of any calls for Andrea to make, when she remembered the two takeout dinners that had been in Rhonda's trash can. "Grab the Yellow Pages and make a list of the restaurants in a ten-mile radius of the Voelker place. Call them and ask if they served takeout dinners over the weekend. When you get a yes, ask if their menu included osso buco."

"Got it. Why do you need to know?"

"There were two containers of osso buco in Rhonda's trash can."

"*Two?*"

"That's right, but one wasn't touched. I figure Rhonda must have been expecting company. There were also two plastic wineglasses with dried red wine in the bottom. The person she invited showed up, but didn't eat."

"That doesn't matter. The fingerprint guys should be able to get a print off the wineglass."

"No, they can't."

"How do you know that?"

"Because they don't have it. The garbage truck came before Mother found Rhonda's body and I tossed out the bag."

Andrea groaned. "That's bad luck! What are the chances of the garbage truck showing up on the very day Mother finds Rhonda's body?"

"One in seven. They pick up every week. But that's why I need you to check out that takeout."

"Okay. Don't worry, Hannah. I won't mention it to Bill, since we're already on top of it. And just as soon as I find that restaurant, I'll call you at home and tell you."

After Hannah hung up the phone, she retrieved her box of day-old cookies. She was just opening the back door when her phone rang again.

"I don't care who you are, I'm not going to answer," Hannah snapped, turning on her heel and walking out. She was going home to Moishe and her boring vegetable salad. Her caller could just call back when she opened in the morning.

The air outside was hot and humid, nearly eighty degrees with a moisture content to match. As Hannah walked the short distance to her truck, she heard the grumble of thunder in the distance. The blacktop in the parking lot was spongy under the soles of her shoes, and she felt the perspiration break out on her skin.

The sun was still up and Hannah knew all about the greenhouse effect. She opened the driver's door of her truck, reached in to stick her key into the ignition, and pushed the buttons to lower all the windows. Her leftover Chocolate Chip Crunch Cookies would be mush if she didn't cool off the interior of her truck. Judging by the brief moment her arm had been inside the truck, it was almost as hot as her oven.

Thunder sounded again, low and rumbling like the growl of some predatory beast. Hannah stood there with the cookie box balanced in her arms and thought about the melting point of chocolate. Who would want to eat a mushy Chocolate Chip Crunch Cookie? Even if it was free? She stashed the box in the back of her truck, grabbed the bag that contained the Chocolate Chip Crunches and marched back inside The Cookie Jar to put it in her walk-in cooler. Driving home with chocolate in the back of her truck was too much of a temptation anyway. She'd give the bag to Jed and Freddy when they came in to finish the pantry shelves in the morning.

Hannah was just sliding into the driver's seat when her mother's car pulled into the lot. Delores parked behind her, so she couldn't back up, exited her car, and rushed up. "I'm glad I caught you! Sally's serving coq au vin tonight and I'll take you out to dinner."

Hannah's hand froze near the ignition. Delores knew her weak spot and she wasn't shy about hitting it. Coq au vin was one of Hannah's favorite entrées at the Lake Eden Inn.

"We need to discuss my murder investigation. I told Carrie all about it and she wants to help."

"Oh, joy," Hannah muttered. Carrie had been itching to get involved in her last three murder cases.

"Don't be like that. Carrie knows everybody in Lake Eden and she'll be a valuable resource. Besides, I'm picking up the tab for dinner. When do you want to go?"

The thunder was growing louder by the minute and Hannah recognized a handy excuse when she heard it. "I'd love to join you and Carrie, but Moishe always gets a little crazy when it thunders. He'll tear up the sofa if I don't get home in time to turn up the volume on the television set."

"That's not a problem. You go on home and I'll call Sally. I'll make reservations for eight and pick you up at seven-thirty."

Hannah bristled. Her mother always wanted to be in control of everything. "I don't need anybody to pick me up. I have my own transportation."

"That's fine," Delores smiled. "You can meet us there.

Make sure you wear something appropriate, dear. You never know who you'll run into and it's always smart to look your best."

Hannah thumped her fist on the steering wheel as her mother climbed back into her car and drove away. She'd had no intention of going out to dinner with her mother, but she'd been outmaneuvered. As she put her truck into gear, Hannah vowed not to use this as an excuse to break her diet. All she had to do was stay away from the delicious things like sauces, and Sally's homemade rolls, and her yummy twice-baked potatoes, and the confections on the dessert cart. With all those restrictions, she'd probably end up with meat and a salad, but at least she wouldn't have to fix it herself.

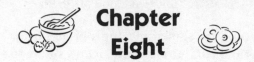

Chapter Eight

Driving from her condo to the Lake Eden Inn took twenty minutes and even though it was seven-thirty in the evening, there was no need for Hannah to turn on her headlights. Only a week had passed since the summer solstice and June twenty-second was the longest day of the year. Darkness wouldn't fall for another two hours and the summer sun was still slanting through the branches of the pines that lined the lakeshore, creating a venetian-blind effect on the dusty gravel of the road. Only the shadows were lengthening. When they reached a proportion longer than the height of the trees that teamed with the lowering sun to create them, they would take on a bluish hue. As night fell, their color would deepen to purple and then to velvety black.

Hannah switched off her air conditioner—it never cooled down her truck adequately anyway—and lowered all her windows to enjoy the breezes that blew across the lake. She'd have to brush her hair again when she got to the Lake Eden Inn, but driving with the windows down was pleasant. She'd dressed for dinner in a wraparound skirt, a sleeveless cotton blouse, and the leather thong sandals she'd purchased during her college years. They were made of water buffalo hide and no longer imported, but political correctness wasn't one of her top priorities. The water buffalo in question had died long ago and giving up her favorite pair of sandals wouldn't bring him back to life.

The pines along the shore grew in clusters and Hannah caught glimpses of fishing boats on the shining mirrored surface of Eden Lake as she drove past the gaps in the trees. Eden Lake was known for its record walleyes and most metropolitan families with a fisherman in residence were lured by the promise of trophy fish. They rented the cabins that the locals owned, and from dawn to dusk, Eden Lake was peppered with anglers.

As she drove, Hannah thought about Rhonda's murder and by the time she'd taken the turnoff for the Lake Eden Inn, she'd reached a decision. Mother, Andrea, Norman, and Lisa all wanted her to investigate. Since she also wanted to investigate, that made five. From what Andrea had said, she could assume that Bill was neutral. He wasn't firmly on the side of her involvement, but he wouldn't put up much of a fuss. Mike was the only one who was firmly against it.

Five for, one neutral, and one against. Hannah tallied it up as she brushed her hair, got out of her truck, and headed for the entrance of the inn. The numbers were definitely on her side, and who was she to argue with the statistics? She'd just have to think of some way to deal with Mike's resistance that wouldn't land her in jail.

As Hannah walked up the path, she noticed that Dick's topiary bear was filling out. It no longer looked skinny and it had grown to almost five feet. For a former stockbroker, Dick had turned out to be a decent gardener. He'd also done a great job of decorating the inn for summer. The porch had been hung with lights that looked like Japanese lanterns and their soft glow was festive. The Lake Eden Inn looked better every year. What had been a risky investment for Sally and Dick was paying off.

Hannah opened the double doors and stepped inside. The little alcove just to the right of the door had been decorated for summer with a small, self-contained fountain and a grouping of wicker furniture. In the winter it would contain the massive wooden boot rack and benches that were necessary in Minnesota.

"Hi, Hannah." The hostess looked up as Hannah approached the restaurant door. It was Carly Richardson, Michelle's friend from high school.

"I thought you were off at college, Carly."

"I am," Carly said. "I just came home for summer break and Sally hired me to fill in while her regular girl's on vacation."

"Do you know that Michelle's coming back to town tomorrow night?"

"I know. She called Tricia and we're all getting together for lunch on Wednesday. You're out here for dinner, right?"

"Right. Mother's supposed to join me."

"Oh, Sally just seated your mother's party. Just follow me and I'll take you to their table."

Her mother's *party?* Hannah sighed as she followed Carly through the crowded dining room and into the bar. Her mother had told her to wear something appropriate and that should have rung alarm bells in Hannah's mind. She hoped this wasn't another attempt to fix her up with an eligible male.

As Carly walked toward the rear of the bar, Hannah found herself lagging behind. Sally had designated that section for private dining. There were four tables on a raised platform, separated from each other by carved wooden partitions that contained frosted glass. The space that faced the rest of the bar was hung with gauzy curtains that the occupants could draw, or leave open. The fact that her mother had requested one of the private tables and closed the curtains could mean only one thing. Delores had set her up again. The only question in Hannah's mind was the identity of the man her mother was attempting to trap for her.

"Here's Hannah, Mrs. Swensen," Carly announced, pulling

aside the corner of the curtain. "Since your party's all here, shall I send the waitress to take your orders?"

"Not quite yet, dear," Delores responded. "Give us five minutes and then we'll be ready."

Hannah wished she could turn on her heel and go back home, but her mother would never forgive her. She took a deep breath, plastered a smile on her face, and stepped inside the curtain. When she saw Norman, her smile turned genuine. "Hi, Norman. Hi, Carrie."

"Come in and sit down, dear." Delores motioned toward the spot they'd saved for her.

Hannah sat down and turned to Norman. "This is a nice surprise. Mother didn't tell me you'd be here."

"Just a minute, dear," Delores hushed her, reaching out to arrange the curtains to hide them from general view. "I really don't think we need everyone in town to see us discussing Rhonda's murder."

"Seeing us doesn't matter, as long as they don't hear us. And they'll be less inclined to eavesdrop if they can see us."

"You've got a point," Delores conceded, opening the curtains again. "I'd never invade someone's privacy like that, but I'm sure some people would."

Hannah just barely managed to squelch a chuckle. She'd seen Delores take the long way around to the ladies room several times in the past, and once she'd even dropped her purse by the row of private booths so she'd have more time to listen.

"I have a question for you, Hannah." Delores stared hard at her. "Norman says he asked you to investigate and you promised to think about it and let him know in the morning. Is that right?"

Hannah hesitated. She'd never been any good at walking on eggshells and this situation had the earmarks of a giant omelet in the making. What if Delores really wanted the job as chief investigator and she'd resent it if Hannah took over? Was there any explanation Hannah could give for her change of heart that wouldn't lead to infanticide? Or was infanticide called something else when a mother killed her grown daughter?

"Well?" Delores glared at her. "I'm waiting for an explanation, Hannah Louise."

Her mother only called her Hannah Louise when she was in big trouble and Hannah thought fast. "Norman told me that Mike and Bill roped off the entire Voelker house as a crime scene and he can't tear it down before they solve Rhonda's murder. That means he might have to delay building our dream house until spring, and . . ."

"That's enough, dear," Delores interrupted her. "I understand perfectly and I think you made the right decision. It was a matter of priorities."

Hannah felt a bit guilty as she basked in her mother's approval. Delores thought their dream house had made all the difference. If Hannah weren't careful, her mother would be sending out invitations to a bridal shower that would never happen.

Norman looked eager as he turned to Hannah. "Does that mean that you're going to do it?"

"Of course it does," Delores answered for her. "And I'm glad we got all this settled. We'll all do everything we can to help you, Hannah. I made some calls this afternoon and I'm almost positive that Rhonda led a double life."

"Really?" Norman looked interested. "What kind of a double life?"

Delores leaned across the table and lowered her voice. "I think she had a boyfriend, perhaps even more than one. But let's not go into all that now. Why don't we order? Once we've eaten, we can discuss Rhonda's murder in detail over dessert."

Hannah's dietary resolve wavered dangerously when their waitress wheeled up the dessert cart. Sally's delicious flourless chocolate cake was sitting in the center of the display. Hannah started to salivate the moment she spotted it.

"I'll have the chocolate cake," Delores declared. "I ordered it the last time I was here and it was simply scrumptious."

"The same for me," Carrie echoed.

"Nothing for me." Norman glanced at Hannah. "How about you?"

"Just coffee." Hannah forced the words past her lips. She'd followed her diet to the letter so far, eating only her salad and her serving of coq au vin. She'd even ordered steamed broccoli in place of potatoes.

Once their coffee had been replenished and the cake had been served, Delores turned to Hannah. "Well? What do you want us to do first, dear?"

Eat your cake fast, before I cave, Hannah thought, her eyes glued to the rich confection on her mother's dessert plate, but of course she didn't say that. If Delores found out that she was on a diet, she'd have to listen to hours of unsolicited and unhelpful advice. "Just keep your ears open for any facts about Rhonda's private life that might have led to a motive for her murder."

"I think I can find out who her boyfriend was," Carrie volunteered. "When I get home tonight, I'll make some calls."

"How about the UPS man?" Delores asked.

"Sam?" Carrie sounded shocked. "Oh, he was Rhonda's cousin on her father's side. That's why he used to drop by to have lunch with her."

"Is Sam still in the area?" Hannah asked, wondering about Rhonda's family history. If Rhonda's cousin was jealous over the fact Rhonda had inherited the Voelker place, he might have had a motive for murder.

"No, he went back to Utah a few months ago. Rhonda said his uncle was wealthy and they owned some high-tech corporation. Sam took over as president when the uncle retired."

Hannah sighed, mentally scratching Sam from her list of suspects. Not only was he several hundred miles away, he was now running a successful business. Sam wasn't likely to care that his cousin had inherited an old wreck of a house in Lake Eden, Minnesota.

"Would it help to talk to Rhonda's cleaning woman?" Norman asked.

"Absolutely." Hannah beamed at him. Cleaning women often knew a lot more than they let on. "Do you know who she was?"

"Luanne's mother, Marjorie Hanks. She called and left a message on my answering machine at the clinic to see if I wanted her to keep on cleaning the house. I told her I didn't, but I hired her to clean the dental clinic."

Hannah took out her notebook and jotted down the information. Marjorie Hanks was no fool. She might have noticed something at the Voelker house that could provide them with a clue.

Delores pushed her partially eaten cake across the table toward Hannah. "Would you like to finish it, dear? My eyes were bigger than my stomach and I know it's one of your favorites."

Despite her best intentions, Hannah glanced down at the cake. It looked moist and delicious, and the scent of chocolate wafted dark and heady in the air. Hannah had the insane notion to utter the words, *Vade retro, Satana,* undoubtedly prompted by the fact that she'd watched a rerun of *The Exorcist* over the weekend. She reminded herself that it hadn't helped Max Von Sydow and it probably wouldn't help her, either. Her only solution was to move herself out of harm's way.

"Thanks, but I'll pass," Hannah said, rising to her feet before she could grab the remaining cake and stuff it into her mouth. "Excuse me. I need to find Sally to tell her how much I enjoyed the dinner."

After a fruitless search of the dining room, Hannah found

Sally in the kitchen. She was sitting at the small desk in the corner, writing out the lunch specials for the next day.

"Hi, Hannah," Sally greeted her. "Did you enjoy your dinner?"

"It was delicious. Do you have any idea how many calories there are in . . . never mind. I don't want to know. I was just wondering if you'd served osso buco lately, like over the weekend?"

Sally shook her head. "I haven't been able to get a good cut of veal in a month. Why? Did you want some?"

"I always want some, but that's not why I'm asking."

Sally looked slightly confused for a moment, and then she recovered. "I guess it must have something to do with Rhonda's murder. You're investigating, aren't you?"

"Yes, but keep it under your toque."

"It won't do any good. He's bound to find out."

"He who?" Hannah asked, feeling a bit like a Swiss yodeler.

"Mike. He *always* finds out. He's mad at you for a day or so, and then he gets over it. Why don't you just tell him now and get it over with? That way he can't say you weren't upfront with him."

Hannah stared at Sally for a long moment. It was a good suggestion. "You're a wise woman, Sally."

"The jury's still out on that one. Just let me know if there's anything I can do to help you."

"Thanks." Hannah turned and started for the door, but she reversed direction as she thought of something. "Do you know if Rhonda ever came in for dinner with a man?"

"Not offhand. I'm only in the dining room part of the time. The rest of the dinner hour, I'm here. Do you want me to ask my waitresses?"

"Yes, and call me if anything turns up."

"I will. Are you working on the jealous boyfriend angle?"

"It might be a bit premature. I don't even know if Rhonda *had* a boyfriend."

"You'll find out. You're good at this. If I wasn't so crazy about your cookies, I'd urge you to switch jobs."

As Hannah returned to the crowded dining room, she thought about Rhonda and she had to work to keep the smile on her face. She hadn't been very curious about Rhonda in the past, but now that she was dead, her life had taken on a new importance. It seemed that people could walk through life without causing a ripple, leading ordinary and uneventful lives. It was only after they'd been murdered that people took notice of them. And that thought was depressing.

Hannah sighed as she approached the private booth where her mother, Carrie, and Norman waited. There was only one cure for depression and that was chocolate. If her mother's cake wasn't gone by now, it would be shortly.

Chapter Nine

When Hannah reached her turnoff, she pressed the buttons to close the windows in her truck, leaving only the driver's window open. She'd lowered them all to enjoy the night air while she drove home, but she had to stop to use her gate card to get into her condo complex, and a stationary vehicle was a prime target for the voracious blood-sucking insects that outnumbered the human population of the state of Minnesota by millions. Some people claimed that the mosquito was the state bird, but Hannah always denied it to the tourists who came into her cookie shop. She conceded that the mosquito might be the state insect, but that would be a close call with the competition from the moths that fluttered around every yard and porch light, the June bugs that flung themselves at the screens, and the deerflies that dive-bombed careless hikers who were foolish enough to wear shorts in the woods. Insects loved Minnesota with its ten thousand lakes. The climate was moist, the air was muggy, and they multiplied with wild abandon.

Once Hannah had driven through the complex and parked in her spot in the underground garage, she climbed up to street level and headed for the covered staircase that led to her upstairs unit. When she reached her door, she slipped her key in the lock, set down her purse, stood firmly on both feet, and opened the door. Just as she'd anticipated, a flying ball of orange and white fur hurtled itself through the air.

"Hi, Moishe." Hannah caught her cat expertly, using both arms. After almost a year of this enthusiastic method of greeting, she was used to his antics. "You're glad to see me, right?"

Moishe started to purr as Hannah retrieved her purse with one arm and carried him inside with the other. She chucked him once under his chin, set him down on the back of the couch, and went straight to the kitchen to get him his nightly treat.

Hannah smiled as she dished vanilla yogurt into one of the expensive cut-glass dessert dishes that had been a Christmas present from her mother. According to Delores, the dishes had appreciated in value, and although her mother would certainly disagree, Hannah figured that Moishe deserved to eat from expensive crystal.

As she put the yogurt back into the refrigerator, Hannah eyed the green glass jug of white wine on the bottom shelf. She had been good tonight, forgoing the rolls and dessert, and eating only her salad, chicken, and vegetables. A glass of chateau screwtop was only eighty calories and she deserved a treat. Besides, she still had to call Mike to tell him she'd changed her mind about getting involved in Rhonda's murder investigation, and the argument they'd have was bound to burn a lot of calories.

Hannah knew she was rationalizing, a no-no for a person on a diet, but her mind was spinning with possible suspects and motives, and she was sure she'd never be able to get to sleep without a small glass of wine. It was obviously the correct thing to do for her health and well-being, and who was she to argue with that? She carried the dessert dish into the living room for Moishe and went back to pour a glass of wine for herself. One sip and then she'd call Mike and face the music.

Once she'd taken up her favorite position on the couch and tasted the forbidden fruit of the vine, Hannah reached for the phone and called the sheriff's station. A moment later, she was smiling. Mike wasn't in. If her luck held, he wouldn't be home either, and she could put off their argument until morning.

Hannah crossed the fingers on both hands and punched in Mike's home number, no easy feat. Then she held her breath as the phone rang once, twice . . .

"Hello?"

"Hi, Mike." Hannah sighed deeply. Her luck had turned rotten and perhaps it was a good thing she hadn't bought more than one ticket for the quilt the Lake Eden Altar Guild was raffling off. "I need to talk to you about Rhonda's murder case."

"Now? I'm in a rush, Hannah. I just stopped off to grab a clean shirt. Bill's waiting for me in the cruiser."

"It won't take long. I just wanted to tell you that I changed my mind about investigating. I'm going to do it."

"I sort of figured you would," Mike said, and then he shocked Hannah by chuckling.

"You're laughing?" Hannah heard her voice squeak in surprise.

"Of course I'm laughing. I was wondering how long it would take you to change your mind. It's only ten-thirty and that means I won."

Hannah's mouth dropped open. "You won *what?*"

"The office pool. I took the lowest number. Bill thought you'd cave in by midnight, but I figured it wouldn't take you that long. Rick Murphy said eight tomorrow morning and Sheriff Grant thought you'd hold out until noon. The others were all somewhere between that, except for Lonnie, Rick Murphy's younger brother. He had you down for two full days."

"How many people were in on this?" Hannah asked, not really sure if she wanted to know.

"A dozen. We each put in ten bucks, so I just won a hundred and twenty."

"A hundred and ten," Hannah corrected him. She was still fuming about the fact that she'd been the subject of an office pool and her words hissed out like droplets of water skittering across the surface of a hot griddle. "It's only a hundred and twenty if you forget to subtract your own ten dollars."

"You're prickly tonight." Mike sounded amused.

"Of course I am. You're betting on me like a football game and I don't like it. Besides, office pools are illegal."

"I guess you could turn us all in, but then you'd have to explain what the pool was about. I don't think you'd like to do that."

"You're right. I wouldn't," Hannah said, giving it up as a bad job.

"Thanks for winning me a bundle, Hannah. I'll take you out to dinner with it. If there's nothing else, I've got to run. I'll drop in to see you tomorrow and we'll compare notes, okay?"

"Uh . . . okay." Hannah hung up the phone with a sigh. She wasn't sure what she should be feeling. Of course she was relieved that Mike hadn't been upset at what he'd always referred to as her *interference,* but it seemed that no one at the sheriff's station had expected her to keep her word about not getting involved.

Hannah thought back to the scene of Rhonda's death. Something was bothering her, niggling at the back of her mind, and she couldn't help feeling that she'd missed an obvious clue. She went over the scene of the crime in her mind, trying to remember everything she'd noticed. The Voelker house had two entrances. They'd gone in through the front and she'd used the back door when she'd carried out the garbage. She'd gone through every one of the rooms, helping Delores tag the items she wanted. The only things that might have been clues were her pie on the kitchen table and the takeout containers and disposable wineglasses in the garbage. There had been nothing else unusual or out of place, no signs of a struggle, and nothing that would lead anyone to suspect that Rhonda's body was in the basement.

The stairs to the basement had seemed perfectly ordinary, in good repair and clear of debris. Once she'd followed Norman down into the basement, she hadn't noticed anything alarming. There had been the usual clutter and moldy smell, but it was a rare basement that wasn't cluttered and moldy. The door to the furnace room had been hanging from one hinge, but since Hannah hadn't examined it closely, she had no idea whether it had pulled loose recently, or had been that way for years.

Hannah took herself through the door to the furnace room in her mind. Other than the broken jam jars on the dirt floor, there hadn't been any visible clues. Who had broken those jars? Delores, in her shock at seeing Rhonda's grave? Or Rhonda's killer, as he'd struggled with her?

"Sorry, Moishe." Hannah reached out to run her fingers through his glossy fur. "This may upset you, but I need to call your least favorite person."

Hannah picked up the phone, punched in her mother's number, and a few seconds later she had her mother on the line. "Thanks again for dinner, Mother."

"You're welcome. It was fun seeing you and Norman together. Carrie and I talked about it on the way home and we both think you make such a nice couple."

"Thanks," Hannah said, leaving it at that. Delores sounded perky and chipper, and Hannah admired her mother's energy. Most women approaching their sixtieth birthday would be exhausted after working all day and going out to dinner, not to mention finding a murder victim. "I need some information, Mother."

"About Rhonda? I just got home and I haven't had a chance to make any calls yet."

"Not about Rhonda, at least not directly. I need to know about those broken jam jars in the furnace room. Are you absolutely sure you didn't drop them on the floor?"

"I'm positive. I didn't even touch them. I remember stepping around them and thinking that someone ought to clean them up."

"Okay. Thanks, Mother. You've been a big help. I'll let you go now and I'll see you . . ."

"Just a minute, Hannah," Delores interrupted before Hannah could hang up the phone. "I just want you to know that I'm very heartened about this thing with Norman."

"What thing?"

"The fact that you sided with him, instead of Mike. That means a lot to a man and you made the right decision. I like Mike well enough, but he's not good husband material."

Hannah drew a deep breath and let it out again slowly. Then she said, very carefully, "Don't get your hopes up, Mother. Neither one of them has proposed yet. And I'm not sure what I'd say if they did."

"Good girl, Hannah!" Delores exclaimed, giving a light-hearted laugh. "I always told you it wasn't smart to wear your heart on your sleeve."

Hannah knew she should leave well enough alone, but she couldn't resist. "Andrea did and it worked for her. Everyone knew she was crazy about Bill."

"That's different. They were young and he gave her his class ring when she was a senior. That made them pre-engaged. And after that, they were recognized as a couple, and everyone expected them to get married. It's really not fair to compare your current situation with your sister's. Andrea never dated two men at the same time."

Hannah clamped her mouth shut and didn't say a word. She happened to know that her sister had dated two boys in high school who'd never known about each other. It was obvious that Delores hadn't known about them either, and Hannah wasn't going to be the one to tell her.

"I've got to run, dear. I'm starting to crack."

"Crack?"

"My face. I'm giving myself a facial and my fifteen minutes

are up. If I don't wash it off now, I'll have to peel it. Good-night, dear."

When she'd hung up the phone, Hannah glanced at Moishe, who'd been listening to her conversation. His tail was swish-ing back and forth, his ears were back, and he'd puffed up into attack mode. Hannah grinned and reached out to smooth his fur. "It's okay. I hung up and I don't have to talk to her again tonight."

But Moishe wasn't that easily soothed. His tail continued to flick and he regarded her with baleful eyes.

"Come on, Moishe." Hannah reached out for him again. "If you come closer, I'll scratch your ears."

Moishe regarded her solemnly for several seconds and then he moved to the far side of the couch, putting as much space between them as possible.

"I'm not the enemy here, Moishe. As a matter of fact, I saved you from seeing Mother tonight. She offered to pick me up here and take me to dinner. If I'd agreed to that, she might have come in when she brought me home. Think about it. You would have hated that!"

Hannah wasn't sure what went on in a cat's mind, but Moishe seemed to take it all in. He stared at her for several seconds and then he turned around, inching forward until his head was resting in her lap.

"That's better," Hannah said, scratching his ears and earn-ing a rumble for her efforts. "I knew you'd see it my way. Aren't you glad I have my own wheels and I can drive my-self? I don't have to rely on . . ."

When Hannah stopped speaking and scratching his ears, Moishe lifted his head to stare up at her. His expression was as quizzical as a cat's expression could get.

"I just thought of something," Hannah told him. "I don't remember seeing Rhonda's car at the Voelker place. I know it wasn't in the driveway when I pulled up, and it couldn't have been in the garage. I looked through the window and it was filled with firewood."

Hannah interpreted the expression on Moishe's face to mean, *Yes? So what?* and she went on. "If Rhonda drove out there, her car would be there. But if she rode with someone else, her car should be parked in the garage at her apartment building."

Moishe made a sound, a cross between a yowl and a purr, and Hannah nodded, just as if he'd suggested another possibility. He was a social being and he liked to be included in the conversation. "You're right, Moishe. The only other possibility is that Rhonda's car was at the Voelker place and her killer stole it to make his getaway."

Hannah flipped to a blank page in her notebook and jotted a reminder to check Rhonda's apartment building for her car. If she found it parked in its assigned spot, her next step would be to canvas the neighbors to see if anyone had seen Rhonda leave.

The phone rang again, just as Hannah finished making her notes. She reached out to answer it and smiled when she recognized Lisa's voice. "Hi, Lisa. Did you find that list of pie buyers?"

"I've got it right here. I'm sorry it's so late, but I just got home."

"That's okay. Did you have a good time?"

"Yes. We went out to the Corner Tavern for a steak and then we dropped in at the bowling alley. They were short a couple of people on one of the teams, so Herb and I filled in."

"How did you do?"

"Not bad. I averaged two hundred a game and that's good for me. When we finished, it was time for Herb's night rounds and I rode along."

Hannah knew all about Herb's night rounds. Unlike Bill and Mike, who were with the county sheriff's department, Herb Beeseman was on the Lake Eden city payroll. During the day he enforced parking regulations and ticketed drivers who committed driving infractions within the city limits.

Two months ago the city council had asked Herb to patrol the business district every evening. Local business owners had given Herb keys to use in case of emergency, and the extra precaution had worked out well. In the two months that Herb had been patrolling at night, he'd spotted a broken faucet in the café that had saved Hal and Rose a massive cleanup, and he'd turned off a smoldering halogen lamp in Stan Kramer's office.

"It's usually boring, but tonight we had some excitement," Lisa went on. "The alarm went off just as we were driving past Granny's Attic."

"Mother had a break-in?"

"No. Herb used his key to check out the inside and everything was fine."

Hannah was puzzled. "Why did the alarm go off if no one broke in?"

"It was the electricity. Remember that pole the owner put up between The Cookie Jar and Granny's Attic?"

"Of course," Hannah said. The pole was an eyesore, but the owner had assured them he'd take it down just as soon as Granny's Attic was rewired.

"The problem is with the circuits. The same circuit that runs your mother's alarm is the one that runs our freezer and our walk-in cooler. If our cooler and freezer happen to kick in together, there's a sudden drop in power that triggers the alarm at Granny's Attic."

"That doesn't sound good. Does Herb think it could happen again?"

"It could, but your mother's taking care of it. Herb just spoke to her and she's going to call the alarm company in the morning. They'll send a man out to move her alarm system to a circuit that's not so heavily loaded."

"Good. How about our freezer and walk-in cooler? Are they okay?"

"They are now, thanks to Herb. It didn't affect our freezer

at all, but our cooler's got some kind of internal circuit breaker that shuts it off during a brownout. Herb hit the reset button and it started right up."

"Tell Herb he's a doll."

Lisa laughed. "I'll tell him. Do you want those names of pie buyers now?"

"Sure." Hannah reached for her steno pad and a pen. "Okay, I'm ready."

Lisa read off the names and Hannah wrote them down. No one on the list seemed likely to have given Rhonda a pie, but she thanked Lisa, told her she'd see her in the morning, and hung up the phone. It was past bedtime and morning would come much too soon.

Hannah performed her nightly ritual, making sure the doors were locked and preparing the coffeemaker for its automatic timed brew in the morning. She washed her face, brushed her teeth, and got into the oversized shirt that she wore for a nightgown. She was just about to crawl into bed when the phone rang again.

"Hello?" Hannah answered at bedside, using the shocking-pink Princess phone she'd picked up at the thrift shop. The little light no longer worked, but the phone was still operational.

"Hi, Hannah. It's me." Andrea's voice floated out of the tiny holes in the receiver. "I'm sorry it's so late, but I didn't get a chance to call earlier."

"That's okay. I wasn't in bed yet."

"Good. I made some calls right after I talked to you, but the finer restaurants weren't open yet. I hit pay dirt about an hour ago, but Bill came home and I didn't want to call you until he went to bed."

"What did you find out?"

"It's Alfredo's Ristorante. That's the new place out at the lake. They served osso buco for takeout on Friday night."

"Good job!" Hannah said, jotting down the name. "Thanks, Andrea."

"No problem. It was easy. What do you want me to do next?"

Hannah thought about the leads she had to follow. "Do you know where Rhonda's apartment building is?"

"Sure. I've got her address in my client file. She lives at the apartment building that Beatrice and Ted Koester bought last year."

"Could you run over there in the morning and check to see if her car is still in the garage? It would save me a trip."

"I can do that. What do you want me to do if it's there?"

"Nothing. Just drop by The Cookie Jar and tell me. We'll decide what to do about it then."

"Okay. I'd better get to bed before Bill starts wondering what I'm doing out here. I'll see you in the morning, Hannah."

Hannah hung up and opened the bedroom window to catch any night breezes that might blow her way. Then she doused the light to stop the moths from trying to commit suicide against her screen and crawled under the sheet she used as a quilt in the summer. There was a thump, resembling a mini-earthquake, and a furry shape crept up in the near darkness. Hannah grabbed her pillow protectively and glared in his direction. "This pillow is mine. I won't let you have it until my new one comes."

There was a rustle and then another thump as Moishe settled down on the other pillow, the foam one she'd designated for his use. Silence filled her bedroom for several moments and then Hannah heard a rumbling purr. She reached out and stroked Moishe's soft fur three times and pulled her hand back. Experience had taught her that four strokes would cause him to move to the bottom of her bed. Hannah checked to make sure her alarm clock was set correctly and then she seized her pillow in a death grip and closed her eyes, hoping that her arms wouldn't loosen as she slept so that Moishe could steal it again.

Chapter Ten

Hannah awoke to an inky black bedroom and the infernal electronic beeping of her alarm clock. It took her a minute to sit up and shut it off, but when she did, she realized that her head had been lying on the mattress. She flicked on the light and turned to eye her goose-down pillow. Moishe had commandeered it once again.

Even though she wanted to settle back down for another few minutes of rest, Hannah tossed back the sheet, placed her feet firmly on the floor, and got out of bed. It was a psychological trick she'd learned in college and it worked for those mornings when she was tired and wanted nothing more than to go back to sleep. Once she'd thrown back the covers and was standing by the side of the bed, the task of straightening the bedding to climb back in seemed like more work than starting the day.

Hannah stuffed her feet into her slippers and walked down the hallway to the kitchen. Once she got there, she switched on the light and headed straight for the coffeepot. There was coffee in the carafe and the little red light was glowing. She sent up a short, thankful prayer for modern conveniences and poured her first cup of the day.

The coffee was hot, practically scalding, but Hannah sipped gratefully. Even the kink in her neck seemed to straighten out somewhat with the invigorating infusion of Swedish Plasma.

She drank one cup standing, leaning one hip against the counter, and then she poured a second. Her eyes were no longer at half-mast and her brain was beginning to function again.

There was a plaintive yowl from the direction of Moishe's food bowl and Hannah turned to frown at him. The new pillow couldn't come soon enough to suit her! Even though her neck was still stiff as a result of Moishe's nighttime theft, her heart wasn't hard enough to resist the appeal in his round yellow eyes.

Once Hannah had given Moishe fresh water and filled his bowl with kitty crunchies, she carried her second cup of coffee to the table and opened her steno pad. It was time to organize her day, now while she was still only three-quarters awake. If she waited until she was fully alert, the task would seem daunting.

Hannah glanced at the calendar that hung on the kitchen wall, an exact duplicate of the one in the kitchen at her cookie shop. She had a two o'clock cookie-catering job for the Lake Eden Quilt Society at Trudi's Fabrics, and a three o'clock at the community center for the Lake Eden Friends of the Library. She jotted those down, then turned to other matters. She had to mail off the rent check for The Cookie Jar, change the batteries on the flashlights she carried in her truck, and buy a bag of lettuce and some sliced low-fat turkey breast for her dinner salad. These were small things, easily accomplished, but they all took time. And somewhere between her trip to the grocery store, her baking, and her catering, she had to find time to investigate Rhonda's murder.

"Shower time," Hannah said, glancing at Moishe, who was more concerned with crunching down his breakfast than anything she might have to say. His bowl was still half full, but Moishe was a pessimist. A half-full bowl was half empty to him, and he'd panic if any part of Garfield's picture on the bottom came into view. Hannah added another scoop for insurance before she headed off to the shower.

In exactly fifteen minutes, Hannah emerged from her bedroom, dressed and ready for her day. She owned three short-sleeved cotton pantsuits that she wore for summer catering jobs and she'd chosen the green one this morning. As she'd pulled on the pants, she'd noticed that they'd felt a bit looser. It was difficult to judge with elastic waists and perhaps it was only wishful thinking on her part, but she really thought her diet was working.

Since she still had a few minutes before she had to leave, Hannah retrieved the steno pad she was using for Rhonda's case notes and sat back down at the kitchen table. She'd written down what Norman had told her, that Marjorie Hanks had been the one to clean the Voelker place. She'd even thought about calling Luanne's mother when she'd gotten home last night, but she'd decided that it was too late. Now it was too early. Even if Marjorie rose before sunrise, she wouldn't appreciate getting a phone call first thing in the morning.

Hannah flipped to the next page. She'd copied the list of pie buyers that Lisa had given her and it was time to go over them again. Perhaps she'd see a connection now that it was morning and she was more alert.

There were ten names. Hannah checked them off one by one. Most were repeat customers, mothers who always came in for pie on Friday to serve it to their families that night. There was no way any of them had given their dinner pie to Rhonda. The two men on the list were easy to eliminate. One lived out at the retirement home and shared Hannah's pie with his friends. The other was a Jordan High student who took Hannah's pies to his girlfriend's mother when he went to her house for Friday night dinners.

Hannah shook her head. There was one name left, Claire Rodgers. And Claire had bought three pies. Hannah stopped to think about that for a moment. Claire was single and she lived alone. If she'd bought three pies, she must have planned to take them somewhere. Was it possible she'd given one of her pies to Rhonda?

Several more sips of idea-generating caffeine and Hannah had come up with a possible scenario. What if Rhonda had gone into Claire's shop on Friday afternoon to purchase a new wardrobe for her trip? If Claire had already picked up her pies, Rhonda might have seen them and mentioned that she liked lemon meringue. Claire might have given one pie to Rhonda as a thank-you, especially if Rhonda had just spent a lot of money on clothes.

Hannah knew her scenario was reasonable. It could have happened that way. She'd drop by Beau Monde the first chance she got and ask Claire if she was right.

The sky was beginning to lighten by the time Hannah turned into the alley behind The Cookie Jar, but she didn't turn off her headlights. They were still necessary to distinguish the dark blobs of the Dumpsters from the darker blobs of the buildings.

Hannah parked in her spot and shut the windows, but she left an inch gap on the driver's side to defeat the greenhouse effect. She grabbed the old beach towel she kept on the passenger's seat, folded it twice because it was so threadbare, and draped it over the steering wheel. The seats in her truck didn't get that hot. They were upholstered in fabric. But her steering wheel was covered in black vinyl and it soaked up the sun. All would be well if she'd wear oven mitts to drive, but she didn't.

As Hannah stepped out of her truck, the air hit her like a tangible force. She'd never really thought about air having weight before, but this air was like walking through invisible pudding. It was so heavy with moisture, the humidity had to be close to the hundred-percent mark.

The first thing Hannah did when she stepped inside her kitchen was switch on the air conditioning. The next thing she did was to check to see if the cooler was running. It was, and she heaved a big sigh of relief as she carried out the bowls of cookie dough and set them on the surface of the workstation. She had the urge to drag a stool into the cooler and sit there for a while, but there was work to do and she didn't have time. She fired up her ovens, clamped one of the little paper caps mandated by the health board over her unruly red curls, and washed her hands thoroughly. Then she tied on an apron and got right to work. There were multiple batches of cookies to bake and she wanted to finish before Lisa came in. Her partner had enough work to do waiting on their customers, taking phone orders, and boxing up cookies for special orders.

Just as she'd planned, Hannah had finished the baking when Lisa arrived. Racks of cooling Black and Whites, Oatmeal Raisin Crisps, and Twin Chocolate Delights filled the kitchen, and other varieties of cookies were already in the glass jars they used for display behind the coffee shop counter.

"You've been busy!" Lisa exclaimed, glancing around her. "How many did you snitch?"

"None. I didn't even taste the Cinnamon Crisps and that's my newest recipe."

"Where did you get it?" Lisa asked, reaching for one and taking a bite.

"I made it up. My dad used to make us cinnamon toast for breakfast when Mother was out antiquing. I thought that cookies with the same taste would be good."

"They *are* good," Lisa said, taking another bite. "They're crunchy and simple and absolutely delicious."

"You really like them?"

"Well . . . I'm not exactly sure, now that I think about it." Lisa gave an impish grin. "I might have to eat a few more before I can make up my mind."

Hannah laughed. "Go ahead. This batch is a test run. I won't sell them until I get them perfect."

"They're perfect." Lisa grabbed two more cookies and headed for the swinging door to the coffee shop. "I'll start the coffee and fill the rest of the serving jars."

The chores didn't take long with both of them working together. When they'd finished, they had twenty minutes before it was time for them to open, and they carried mugs of coffee to their favorite table in the back of the coffee shop.

"Did you decide?" Lisa asked, taking the chair across from Hannah.

"About the Cinnamon Crisps?"

"No, about Rhonda. You're going to catch her killer, aren't you?"

"I'm going to try."

"Good." Lisa shivered slightly and cupped her hands around her mug of coffee. "I just can't get over it. She was here one day and dead the next. How about that pie you found? Do you think it has anything to do with her murder?"

"Maybe, but even if it doesn't, it'll help me establish a timeline for the day of her death. I need to know where she went, who she talked to, and what she did."

"That seems like a good place to start. What can I do to help?"

"Just keep your ears open. People talk and someone may know something about Rhonda's last hours. If you pick up anything, tell me right away and . . ." Hannah stopped speaking and winced.

"What's the matter?" Lisa asked, looking concerned.

"I'm getting a terrible headache. I swear I can actually hear my head pounding."

"That's not your head. It's some kind of noise coming from outside. Hold on a second and I'll go look."

Lisa unlocked the front door and peered out. When she came back, she was grinning. "You were right. It's a headache, all right."

"What is?"

"The Jordan High marching band. What you heard was

their bass drum. I'll get the aspirin bottle. They're headed this way."

After she'd washed down two aspirin, Hannah watched as the band came into view. Even though the doors and windows were closed, she could hear the mutilated strains of "The Stars and Stripes Forever."

"They're awful," Lisa said, reaching up to cover her ears.

Hannah did the same. The trumpet section could certainly use a review lesson in sharps and flats, and she shuddered to think of what would happen when they got to the piccolo obbligato, since there wasn't a piccolo in sight.

Hannah held her breath as the band reached the critical measures and then she groaned aloud. Two girls on clarinets were attempting the part, and it was obvious they weren't at all skilled on the upper registers.

"Maybe they'll get better in time for the parade," Lisa mused, but after a glance at Hannah's pained expression, she shook her head. "You're right. That's probably asking too much."

When the hands of their wall clock reached nine, Lisa unlocked the door and customers began to come in for morning coffee and cookies. Business was brisk for the first hour and it took the efforts of both Hannah and Lisa to serve their customers. Things didn't slow down until after ten and that was when Andrea walked in. By the smile on her sister's face, Hannah knew she had information about Rhonda.

"What is it?" Hannah asked, pouring Andrea a glass of orange juice.

Andrea glanced around her. The only other people at the counter were Amalia Greerson and Babs Dubinski, engrossed in a conversation of their own. "The subject's car is still there."

"You mean Rhonda's?"

"Shh!" Andrea put a finger to her lips.

"It's okay." Hannah leaned forward across the counter. "Babs is trying to play matchmaker."

"You mean for her son?"

"Right. And Amalia's not buying it. She thinks he's too old for her granddaughter."

"He is. She just graduated from high school and there's got to be at least a fifteen-year difference. And the fact that he's a tax accountant tacks on another ten years."

"You're right," Hannah said, remembering the ill-fated evening when Delores had set her up with Babs's son. To say that it had been boring would be kind. "What else did you find out? When you came in, you were grinning like the Cheshire cat."

"Let's go in the back," Andrea suggested, picking up her glass of orange juice and leading the way. She was mum until she'd taken a stool at the workstation and then she grinned proudly. "I got the autopsy report from Doc Knight this morning."

"You mean you saw Bill's copy?"

"No, he doesn't have it yet. I had to drop off a sample for Doc Knight and I asked him about it."

"A sample?"

"You know, a *sample*. I couldn't give him one yesterday and it's all Mother's fault. Remember how she always said to go before we left the house?"

Hannah caught on immediately. "So you did, and then you couldn't give him a sample?"

"That's right. It was a good thing, though. I asked him about Rhonda, just making conversation, and he said he thinks she was killed between eight and nine on Friday night. And then he talked about stomach contents. Your lemon pie was there and so was the osso buco."

Hannah was surprised. "Doc Knight actually identified it as osso buco?"

"No, but the ingredients were right."

"How do you know?" Hannah was puzzled. "You've never made it, have you?"

Andrea shook her head. "I looked it up in a cookbook."

"You have a *cookbook?*"

"Of course I do. My friends got together and gave me a whole set for a wedding present. The only ingredient that didn't fit was ripe olives."

Hannah made a mental note of that. "Did Doc Knight think Rhonda had anything else to eat?"

"No, but she drank some red wine. That was when he started talking about some other tests he'd run and I stopped listening because I was getting a little queasy."

Hannah shoved a rack of cooled Chocolate Chip Crunch Cookies closer to her sister. "Have a couple of cookies. The chocolate will settle your stomach. And while you're at it, bag up a half-dozen for Claire Rodgers."

"You're going to Beau Monde?"

"Yes. Lisa offered to take over for me until my two-o'clock catering gig."

"Your diet's working and you're buying smaller clothes?" Andrea guessed.

"Not exactly. Claire bought three lemon pies on Friday and I need to find out if she gave one to Rhonda."

"I'm coming along," Andrea announced, taking a cookie for herself and bagging another half-dozen for Claire. "Claire left a message on my machine that my maternity clothes came in. You can talk to her while I try them on."

Hannah groaned. Andrea wasn't exactly speedy when it came to trying on clothes. On the other hand, Claire would be delighted at the prospect of a big sale, so she might be more forthcoming about answering questions.

"How long are you free for?"

"Until one-thirty," Hannah answered, trying not to wince at her sister's sentence structure. When they were still in high school, she'd tried to break Andrea's habit of tacking on a final preposition, but her grammar lessons hadn't had any appreciable effect.

"Then you've got a couple of hours. When we're through at Claire's, let's run out to Rhonda's apartment building and interview her neighbors. I checked the mailboxes and almost everyone's retired. They should be home in the middle of the day."

"Okay," Hannah agreed. Interviewing Rhonda's neighbors wouldn't be at all dangerous and Andrea was good with people.

"When we get through, I'll help you with your catering. I can pour coffee while you do the rest."

Hannah smiled. Catering was always easier with two people. "All right, but it's only fair to warn you."

"Warn me about what?"

"My first job is at Trudi's Fabrics."

"What's wrong with that? I like Trudi Schuman."

"So do I, but she's hosting a Lake Eden Quilting Society meeting and your mother-in-law will be there."

"Oh." Andrea rolled her eyes toward the ceiling. She didn't get along well with Regina Todd. Bill's mother was constantly complaining that Andrea should quit her job and be a stay-at-home mother and wife. "It should be all right, Hannah. I'll wear one of my new maternity outfits and that'll win her over. She's crazy about Tracey, but she really wants a grandson."

"All right, if you can handle it." Hannah pushed away a mental picture of Regina haranguing Andrea about quitting her job and Andrea spilling scalding coffee on Regina's hand. "It shouldn't take more than a half hour. When we're through, I'll drop you back here and load up for my three o'clock."

"Where's that one?"

Hannah was so pleased by Andrea's question, she almost forgot to answer. Were her years of correcting her sister's grammar finally paying off? Or had Andrea merely forgotten to add the final, unnecessary *at?* "It's in the library at the community center. Marge Beeseman is holding her monthly Friends of the Library meeting."

"I'll help you with that. Tracey needs a new book and I have to stop by the library anyway. She didn't like the last one Bill read to her out of."

Cinnamon Crisps

Preheat oven to 325 degrees F.,
with rack in middle position.

2 cups melted butter *(4 sticks)*
2 cups brown sugar *(loosely packed)*
1 cup white sugar *(granulated)*
2 beaten eggs *(just whip them up with a fork)*
2 teaspoons vanilla
1 teaspoon cinnamon
1 teaspoon baking soda
1 teaspoon cream of tartar *(critical!)*
1 teaspoon salt
4 ¼ cups white flour *(not sifted)*

Dough-ball rolling mixture:

½ cup white sugar
1 teaspoon cinnamon

Melt the butter. Add the sugars and mix. Let the mixture cool to room temperature while you beat the eggs, and then stir them in. Add the vanilla, cinnamon, baking soda, cream of tartar, and salt. Mix well. Add flour in increments, mixing after each addition.

Use your hands to roll the dough into walnut-sized balls. *(If dough is too sticky, chill for an hour before rolling.)*

Combine the sugar and cinnamon in a small bowl to make the dough-ball rolling mixture. *(Mixing it with a fork works nicely.)* Roll the dough balls in the mixture, then place them on a greased cookie sheet, 12 to a standard sheet. Flatten the dough balls with a greased or floured spatula.

Bake at 325 degrees F. for 10–15 minutes. *(They should have a touch of gold around the edges.)* Cool on the cookie sheet for 2 minutes, then remove the cookies to a rack to finish cooling.

Yield: Approximately 8 dozen, depending on cookie size.

(Lisa loves these cookies—it's the only time I've seen her eat a half-dozen of anything at one sitting.)

"I didn't expect you this soon, Andrea." Claire looked surprised as she opened the door of her dress shop and let them into the back room. The space wasn't very deep, only about six feet, but it ran the entire width of the building and was crowded with racks of clothing, unassembled Beau Monde dress boxes, Claire's small desk, and her ever-present ironing board and sewing machine. "I just left a message for you at home and it couldn't have been more than ten minutes ago. How did you get here so fast?"

"I was already next door. I retrieved your message from my cell phone, and since Hannah wanted to come over here anyway, I tagged along. I know you're not open yet. If I'm too early, I can always come back later."

"You're not too early. I'm just glad I pressed your maternity outfits first." Claire ran a hand over her sleek hair and looked slightly embarrassed. "I've been unpacking my new shipment and I planned to change my clothes before I opened."

Hannah let her sister say all the right things to ease Claire's embarrassment. She didn't think it was possible for Claire to look rumpled, even in the slacks and casual cotton blouse she was wearing. Andrea and Claire were two of a kind, the type of women who could wear gunnysacks with house slippers and still generate admiring glances.

"I love this color," Andrea said, reaching out to touch a lavender silk suit hanging on the rack of clothing that Claire had indicated. "Do you think it's too Easter-ish?"

Hannah set her bag of cookies by the coffeepot and tuned out as Claire and Andrea began to discuss colors and their association with various holidays and seasons. Fashion wasn't one of her interests. Instead, she mentally reviewed the questions she wanted to ask. Of course she'd find out about the pies, but Claire might have some other useful information. As Andrea was fond of saying, everybody who was anybody in Lake Eden bought designer clothes at Beau Monde. While the stores at the Tri-County Mall might be less expensive, Claire provided the personal touch that pampered women everywhere craved. Her customers often arrived in pairs and while they were trying on clothes, they gossiped. It was possible that Claire might have overheard something about Rhonda's private life.

"How about this, Hannah?" Andrea asked, holding up a maternity top.

"You're asking *me* a fashion question?" Hannah laughed.

"Second thought, I'll just try it on." Andrea exchanged a grin with her sister and then she turned to Claire. "If you don't mind, I'll try all of them on."

"I don't mind at all."

Claire gathered the hangers and led Andrea toward the dressing rooms, leaving Hannah to fend for herself. It wasn't for long. Claire was back before Hannah even had time to walk over to the racks to look at the new shipment.

"Your sister's all set," Claire said, heading toward the small coffee machine she kept next to the sink. "I just put on a fresh pot of coffee. Would you like a cup?"

"Sure," Hannah said, even though Claire's coffee was nothing to write home about. Conversation over coffee tended to be candid and invited confidences. "I brought you a half-dozen cookies."

"Thanks, Hannah. What kind are they?"

"Chocolate Chip Crunch."

"Oh, good. I could use a pick-me-up. I've been pressing out wrinkles since eight. Take my desk chair and I'll get the coffee. How about one of your own cookies?"

"No, thanks."

Claire poured two cups of coffee while Hannah sat down. She carried one to the desk, set it neatly on a coaster, and then perched on a stool with her coffee in one hand and a cookie in the other. "You've lost weight."

"Do you think so?" Hannah felt a swell of pride. Claire studied everyone's appearance. If she thought Hannah had lost weight, it was probably true.

"I make it my business to notice things like that. If one of my ladies comes in and she's gained weight, I need to substitute a larger size without commenting on it."

"And you can tell that by just looking at her?"

"Of course. I have a very discerning eye."

Hannah was thoughtful. Claire's discerning eye might provide a way for her to avoid the dreaded scale. "Can you tell me how much weight I've lost?"

"I'd say about three pounds. Your face is thinner and I think you dropped a bit from your upper arms."

"Wonderful," Hannah said, disappointment setting in. She wasn't trying to lose weight on her face or her upper arms. It was her waist and her hips that concerned her.

"Andrea said you wanted to ask me something?"

"I do." Hannah relegated weight-loss thoughts to the back corner of her mind. "Lisa said you bought three lemon pies last Friday. I was wondering if Rhonda ended up with one of them."

Claire's eyes widened in surprise. "That's right! How did *you* know that?"

"Just a lucky guess."

"Are you working on Rhonda's murder investigation?"

"Yes. And I already told Mike, so it's no secret this time. Do you know anything personal about Rhonda that might have given someone a motive to kill her?"

Claire sipped her coffee and thought for a moment. "I don't think so, but I did hear some rumors last year. Someone said that Rhonda had a boyfriend, but no one seemed to know anything about him."

"I've heard that. Any guesses?"

Claire shook her head. "No name was ever mentioned."

"Anything else about Rhonda's personal life?"

Claire thought for a moment and then she shrugged. "Not much. Most of my customers seemed to think that Rhonda was a little silly, wearing all that makeup, and dressing young, and flirting with every man who walked up to her cosmetic counter to buy perfume for his wife. But no one took it seriously and I don't think anyone ever harbored her any ill will."

"Okay. Let's get back to the pie. Did Rhonda give you the money and ask you to pick it up for her? Or did she just free-load one of yours?"

"She freeloaded one of mine," Claire said with a chuckle. "She came in here on Friday afternoon and bought some out-fits for her trip. The pie boxes were stacked on my counter. She noticed them when I rang up her purchases."

"And she mentioned that lemon was her favorite so you almost had to give her one?"

"That's exactly how it happened. She spent over six hundred dollars and I figured the least I could do was give her a pie."

Hannah preened a bit. Her scenario had been correct. "I'm curious, Claire. What were you going to do with *three* pies anyway?"

The color began to rise in Claire's cheeks. She looked as guilty as a kid caught going through the lunch line twice. "If I tell you, will you keep it to yourself?"

"Yes, if it doesn't have anything to do with Rhonda's murder."

"It doesn't. You heard that our church is trying to raise the money for new hymnals, didn't you?"

Hannah had heard about the hymnal fund the last time she'd catered a Redeemer Lutheran board meeting.

"We had a meeting two Sundays ago to discuss fund-raising ideas. I suggested holding a weekly bake sale on Saturday mornings."

"I bet they roped you into organizing it," Hannah guessed, knowing how local church politics worked.

"You're right. They nominated me and I couldn't say no, since it was my idea in the first place. And of course I had to contribute something, but I don't bake."

"So you bought three of my pies to take to the bake sale?"

"Exactly. I repackaged the two I had left and I didn't exactly say I'd baked them, but I didn't say I hadn't, either. Do you think that's cheating?"

"Maybe technically, but it was for a good cause and I don't mind. How much did they sell for?"

"Ten dollars apiece. The bake sale was a huge success, Hannah. Bob was very impressed."

"Bob who?" Hannah asked. It was a fairly common name in Lake Eden, and she knew at least a dozen local Bobs.

"Reverend Knudson. He asked me to call him Bob."

Hannah watched the color come up on Claire's cheeks again and one possible explanation occurred to her. Claire had broken off her long-standing affair with Mayor Bascomb last winter. As far as Hannah knew, Claire hadn't dipped her toe into the dating pool again, but the pink rising in her cheeks was a dead giveaway. Unless Hannah missed her guess, something new was going on in Claire's love life. "Hold on a second, Claire. Are you dating Reverend Knudson?"

"Not exactly. But we're really good friends and I just adore his grandmother."

A tactless question popped into Hannah's mind and she asked it before she could stop herself. "But don't you find him boring after all that time with the mayor?"

"No, not at all. You wouldn't think Bob was boring if you knew him as well as I do. He has a wonderful sense of humor."

Hannah hoped she didn't look as dubious as she felt. Reverend Knudson's sermons about the wages of sin hadn't seemed the least bit humorous to her. Of course, the subject matter didn't leave a whole lot of room for jokes.

"Before you ask, Bob knows all about my affair with the mayor," Claire interrupted Hannah's thoughts. "I told him myself."

"What did he say?" Hannah held her breath. Reverend Knudson had never struck her as the liberal type.

"He said it wasn't important and I shouldn't worry about it."

Hannah blinked. "Reverend Knudson said an affair wasn't important?"

"That's right. He's not as strict and proper as you think he is, Hannah. Bob's really a lot of fun once you get him out of his clerical garb." Hannah's eyebrows shot up at that turn of phrase and Claire started to giggle. She sounded giddy, like a teenage girl, and her eyes sparkled with pure laughter. "I didn't mean it *that* way!"

Hannah and Claire were still laughing when Andrea appeared in the doorway, wearing one of the outfits. It was a dark green cotton dress with large gold sunflowers scattered over it. "I'm taking them all, Claire. And I'm wearing this."

"I'm so glad you like them." Claire looked pleased. "That dress is wonderful with your coloring."

"I think so, too. I'm helping Hannah with her catering this afternoon and I need to look my best." Andrea turned to Hannah. "Why don't you pick out something else to wear, Hannah? I'll even pay for it. Our greens clash."

Hannah felt herself climb firmly on the defensive. It was the old Queen-of-the-Hill battle they'd played countless times before. "*You* pick out something else. I was wearing my green first."

"But yours is at least two years old and mine is new. New takes precedence over old."

Hannah shook her head. "My green stays. The caterer takes precedence over the assistant."

The two sisters locked eyes, four orbs burning with equal intensity. But after a moment, what would have led to a pitched battle in the past suddenly dissolved into laughter.

"I'm sorry, Hannah," Andrea said through a volley of chuckles. "You're the caterer. You win."

"No, you're the one who's pregnant and facing your dragon of a mother-in-law. You win."

"Really?" Andrea's smile was as radiant as the sun after a sudden downpour. "Are you sure?"

"Yes, and you don't even have to buy me a new outfit. I'll just put it on my almost-maxed-out credit card."

Ten minutes later and eighty dollars poorer despite the huge discount Claire had given her, Hannah walked out of Claire's shop. She was wearing her new outfit and it was in her very favorite color, one she'd always despaired of being able to wear. It was a summer-weight skirt and jacket in an odd shade of red that miraculously failed to clash with her hair. Claire had chosen the outfit from her new shipment and it had been worth every penny Hannah had spent. She felt svelte and gorgeous.

"I'll drive to Rhonda's apartment building," Andrea said, hurrying to keep up with Hannah's longer stride as they walked across the parking lot toward the back door of The Cookie Jar. "You don't have a hook in the back of your truck and I want to hang my new outfits so they won't wrinkle."

"Okay." Hannah opened the door, walked through the kitchen, and stashed her old pantsuit in the small cubicle that the owner called a bathroom. "Let's go. I have to be back here by one-thirty."

"No problem." Andrea led the way through the coffee shop and out to her car. She opened her car doors with a click and slid under the wheel while Hannah got into the passenger's seat. "I thought you were going to give me a hard time about wanting to drive."

"Why would I do that?"

"Because I drive too fast and I don't keep my eyes on the road."

"That's true," Hannah said, reaching for her seat belt and buckling it. "It's a source of wonder to me that you haven't had an accident."

Andrea started her engine and pulled out into the street. "If I'm that bad, why are you letting me drive?"

"I'm an eternal optimist. I keep hoping you'll get better."

Andrea considered that a moment, then shook her head. "I don't believe it. There's some other reason you want me to drive. Come on, Hannah. Tell me what it is."

"You're my sister and you deserve another chance?"

"No way."

Hannah sighed. Andrea was persistent. She'd get it out of her sooner or later. "I love your air conditioning. Mine isn't working right."

"I knew there was something!"

Hannah glanced out the windshield and pushed her foot against a nonexistent brake pedal. "Slow down, Andrea. That light's turning."

"I've got plenty of time," Andrea argued, whizzing through the intersection. "See? I told you. It was yellow almost all the way through."

"Tell me when we get there." Hannah leaned back against the leather seats, reminded herself again that Andrea had never been involved in an accident, and shut her eyes. It was the coward's way out, but she knew she'd feel a lot safer if she didn't watch.

Chapter Twelve

It was noon by the time they finished canvassing Rhonda's neighbors and Hannah was depressed. They hadn't learned anything of value, but that wasn't the cause of her depression. Not every lead in a murder investigation panned out and she knew it.

"Are you upset that nobody saw Rhonda leave?" Andrea asked, noticing Hannah's dejected expression as they walked down the sidewalk and headed toward her car.

"No."

"Then what's the matter?"

"Nothing."

Andrea stopped and put her hands on her hips. "There's something wrong when your sister looks like she just lost her best friend. Now tell me what it is."

"I thought I looked good in my new outfit."

"You do."

"Then why did all Rhonda's neighbors tell you that you looked adorable, and then say, *And you look very nice too, Hannah.*"

"That's because I'm wearing maternity clothes. You know how people treat you when you're pregnant."

"No, I don't."

"Well I do. I've been through it before." Andrea unlocked the doors to her car and climbed in. She waited until Hannah had buckled her seat belt before explaining, "Pregnant women look like blimps. It's a fact of life. Rhonda's neighbors were just saying I looked nice to make me feel better."

Hannah knew that Andrea was trying to spare her feelings. She appreciated the effort, but it wasn't working. Usually Hannah didn't mind when people complimented Andrea lavishly and then threw her a bone to be polite. Today it had gotten to her. It was a rerun of high school and the comments their teachers and friends had made when they saw tall, gangly Hannah with beautiful and dainty Andrea.

"You're taking things too personally," Andrea chided her gently. "I think it's because you're on a diet. That'll get anyone's spirits down."

Hannah realized that Andrea was right. "I hate it when you're more mature than I am."

"So do I. Being mature isn't what it's cracked up to be." Andrea started the car and pulled out from the curb. "Is there anywhere else you want to go? We've got almost two hours before we cater."

"Let's go out to the Quick Stop."

"Why?" Andrea asked.

"I want to pick up a toy for Suzie Hanks, and then I thought we could drive out to see Luanne's mother. Norman found out that she cleaned the Voelker place for Rhonda."

"She could know something," Andrea mused. "Cleaning ladies notice all sorts of things. But we don't have to go out to the Quick Stop first. My place is closer and I've got a whole bag full of toys I picked out for Suzie."

"Tracey's things?" Hannah asked, knowing that Andrea had given Suzie cartons of clothing and toys that Tracey had outgrown in the past.

"No, they're new. The toy store at the mall had a huge sale last month."

"If they're new toys, you'd better have some sort of excuse for giving them to Suzie. You know how Luanne and her mother are about accepting anything they think is charity."

"You're right. I'll say they were Tracey's. After all, they *could* have been hers. She had so many toddler toys she didn't even get a chance to play with them all."

"You're devious, Andrea." Hannah turned to smile at her sister. "And you're generous, too. I'm really proud to be your sister."

"Thanks, but I'm not that devious, at least not more than any other real estate professional. And I'm proud of you, too."

"All this for Suzie?" Marjorie Hanks gasped as she looked inside the shopping bag Andrea and Hannah had toted into her small cabin. She was a short but compact woman in her fifties with dark brown hair and hazel eyes. "Are you sure Tracey can't use any of these?"

"She cleaned out her closet herself," Andrea said, pulling out a pink velvet teddy bear dressed in fake fur with a string of fake pearls around its neck. "Tracey especially wanted Suzie to have this. You know how girls are when they reach a certain age. She thinks pink is too young for her."

Marjorie picked up the bear and stroked its soft fur. "Suzie will love it. I'll give it to her the minute she wakes up from her nap. But isn't this one of those new bears like they have in the toy store out at the mall?"

"It can't be," Andrea stated with what sounded like complete sincerity, "unless they reissued them, or something like that. One of my friends gave it to Tracey for a christening gift."

Hannah figured it was time to step in before Andrea dug an even deeper hole. "I need to ask you about Rhonda, Mrs. Hanks. I'm investigating her murder and Norman told me that you cleaned the Voelker place for her."

"That's right. I did. I'm sorry the job's over. It was one of the best I ever had."

"But wasn't it a lot of work?" Andrea asked, jumping in to help with the questioning.

"The only hard part was the first day. Rhonda warned me that her great-aunt had been in a wheelchair since nineteen-eighty, and she said the place was a real mess. It sure was! That companion Mrs. Voelker had living with her didn't do much in the way of cleaning."

"It must have taken you a long time to whip it into shape," Hannah commented.

"Not that long. All I had to clean was the ground floor. Rhonda said the attic was bare and the basement could stay the way it was. And I had Freddy and Jed to help me. They were out there doing some other work for Rhonda and they hauled out all the heavy trash bags."

"What sort of work were they doing?" Hannah was curious.

"Handyman things. They did a real good job replacing some of the glass in the windows."

Andrea nodded and returned to her first line of inquiry. "But the place wasn't hard to keep up once you'd cleaned it the first time?"

"Heavens no! All I had to do was dust and vacuum and that was it . . . except for the bedroom."

"The bedroom?" Hannah's interest rose. "What did you have to do in there?"

"Dust and vacuum, clean the bathroom, and change the sheets on the bed. I know Rhonda had her own place in town, but she stayed out there some nights. Now I don't want you to repeat this to a soul, but I think Rhonda had overnight company, if you know what I mean. There were always at least four dirty towels on the floor and once I found a razor in the wastebasket. It was right on top of one of those little travel bottles of aftershave."

"What kind of razor was it?" Hannah asked, hoping for something distinctive that she could track down.

"Just one of those blue disposable kind you can buy a dozen to a bag at CostMart."

"How about the aftershave? Do you remember the brand?"

"Sure do. It was Old Spice and I almost kept the bottle because it was kind of cute. Suzie loves to pick dandelions and I was thinking I could use it for a little vase on her table." Marjorie paused for a moment and then she frowned. "Is it important?"

"It could be," Hannah told her. "If we had it, the crime lab could dust for fingerprints. The man who spent the night with Rhonda might be able to tell us something about her murder."

Marjorie shivered slightly. "Or he could've killed her. Now I wish I'd saved the bottle and the razor, too. They'd be evidence. But I just tossed them into a garbage bag and carried it out to the trash can."

Hannah frowned slightly. She'd unwittingly sent evidence off to the dump and so had Marjorie Hanks.

"Don't worry about it," Andrea jumped in. "Hannah can catch Rhonda's killer without those things."

Hannah turned to give her sister a startled glance. Either Andrea was just attempting to make Mrs. Hanks feel better, or she really had confidence in Hannah's abilities. Unfortunately, Hannah didn't feel all that confident. With the exception of the fact that they now knew Rhonda's boyfriend was real and not just gossip, they were still back at square one.

"Thanks, Mrs. Hanks. You've helped a lot." Hannah put on her brightest smile. "Norman told me he hired you to clean his office. I'm really glad you got a new job."

"So am I. Doctor Rhodes said he'd pay top dollar, and he promised us a discount anytime we need our teeth fixed. He even said he'd hire me to clean that new house he's building for you."

"It's not for me," Hannah corrected her. "It'll be Norman's house, not mine."

Marjorie shrugged. "Whatever. I'm willing to bet you'll

change your tune by the time it's ready. You can't find a nicer man than Doctor Rhodes."

There was nothing Hannah could say to argue with that, so she kept mum. She did, however, shoot her sister an entreating look and Andrea took over the conversation. After they'd discussed how bright Suzie was and how she was already learning her numbers, Hannah and Andrea headed back the way they'd come on Old Bailey Road.

"That was good, wasn't it?" Andrea asked, zipping out to the highway and driving toward town. "I mean, we learned something."

"Yes. We already suspected that Rhonda had a boyfriend, but now we know it for sure."

"Because of the aftershave?" Andrea asked, pulling out to pass a truck loaded with lumber.

Hannah reached down to make sure her seat belt was fastened securely. "Unless Rhonda preferred the scent of Old Spice to all the expensive perfumes she sold down at the drugstore, there's a man in the picture."

After Hannah loaded up the last box of cookies, Andrea glanced down at her watch. "We've still got twenty minutes and I really don't want to get there early. Could we run next door to Granny's Attic? Mother said Luanne found an antique rosewood cradle at an estate sale last weekend. She thinks it would be perfect for the new baby."

"Good idea. I want to check with Mother and Carrie anyway. They were going to ask around and try to find out who Rhonda's boyfriend was."

Hannah locked up her truck and the sisters walked across the parking lot to their mother's shop. The back door was unlocked for the convenience of customers who parked in the rear, and they made their way past boxed acquisitions and some pieces of old furniture.

"Norman's right. They need more storage space," Hannah

muttered as she came perilously close to tripping over a three-legged table.

"I know. They've got things stacked up to the ceiling back here. I told Mother I'd look around for a garage they could rent."

"Hello, dears!" Delores called out when she spotted them. "Go take a look at that cradle, Andrea. It's right next to the curved highboy with the leaded-glass doors on the east wall."

"Any news about Rhonda's boyfriend?" Hannah asked, joining her mother and Carrie at the counter.

"I'm afraid not." Delores frowned slightly. "We called everyone we could think of, but we still don't have a name."

"We did find out one thing," Carrie said, smiling slightly.

"What's that?"

"Rhonda got a little tipsy at the Goetz's New Year's Eve party. She told Geraldine that she was seeing someone, but she couldn't marry him."

Hannah added this to her small store of personal facts about Rhonda. "Did Rhonda say why?"

"Geraldine asked her, but she just said that there'd have to be a funeral first."

"A funeral?"

"Your mother and I think he was married and that was Rhonda's way of saying that he wouldn't divorce his wife."

Hannah thought about that for a moment. "You could be right."

"We did find out another interesting thing," Delores said, lowering her voice even though there were no other customers in Granny's Attic. "Bridget Murphy threatened Cyril last night."

Hannah had to work to keep her mouth from dropping open. Bridget Murphy was one of the sweetest, gentlest women in Lake Eden and there'd never been a hint of trouble in her marriage to Cyril. "You mean . . . with a weapon?"

"Of course not. Remember that car he gave her for her

birthday? Well, it's broken down three times. Bridget told Cyril that if he didn't fix it right this time, she'd paint a giant lemon on it and tow it down Main Street at the tag end of the parade."

It was four o'clock when Hannah let herself in through the back door of The Cookie Jar. Her two catering jobs had gone well, and Andrea's new maternity outfit had totally tamed her mother-in-law. Their only private conversation had been about which color quilt Andrea would prefer for the nursery.

"Hi, Lisa." Hannah stepped into the coffee shop, joining Lisa behind the counter. "Do you need a break?"

"No, I'm fine. We had a big rush around three, but it's slowing down now. Mike was in earlier, looking for you."

Hannah sighed. "I was afraid I'd miss him."

"He said not to worry, that he was pretty tied up, but he'd call you before you left for the day. Did you see Jed when you came through the kitchen?"

Hannah shook her head. "No. I just set down my purse and came straight in here."

"Well, he wants to talk to you. He sent Freddy in about twenty minutes ago to say they were almost through in the pantry. I think he was looking to get paid for the day."

"Okay. I'll pay them and then I'll start mixing up the dough for tomorrow."

Hannah greeted a few regular customers before going back to the kitchen. The new pantry shelves were all up. Jed was just tightening the last screw. "Hi, guys. That looks nice."

"Thanks. Come in for a second, Hannah. I want to show you an improvement we made." Jed waited until Hannah had stepped inside the pantry, then pointed to the small, rectangular space between the inside of the door and the wall. "This spot isn't big enough for shelves, so we made you a pocket rack as a thank-you for giving us the work."

Hannah eyed the structure Jed had called a pocket rack

with interest. It consisted of a long narrow board painted the same color as the wall with see-through pockets made out of wire mesh.

"It's for small things that might get pushed behind bigger things on the shelves. They won't drop out because of the mesh, but you can see at a glance what's in there."

Hannah was pleased. She was always looking for the left-over nuts she'd chopped, or almost-empty bags of chocolate chips and marshmallows. "That's very clever. Where did you get the idea?"

"From the last industrial kitchen I worked in. If there was a space that was too small for a shelf, it had a pocket rack."

"It'll come in really handy. Thanks for thinking of it, Jed." Hannah led the way out of the pantry and retrieved her purse to pay them. She was just counting out the money when she realized what Jed had said. "You said you worked in a kitchen. Were you a cook?"

"No, I was on the maintenance crew and I learned all about kitchen appliances. If something in your kitchen breaks down, I can probably fix it."

"I'll keep that in mind." Hannah slipped their pay into en-velopes and handed one to Freddy and the other to Jed. "Thank you for my new pocket rack. Both of you did a won-derful job."

Freddy took his envelope and gave Hannah a big smile. "Thanks, Hannah. Betcha didn't know that Jed used to work in the joint."

"The joint?" Hannah frowned slightly as she turned to Jed. "Was that the name of the restaurant?"

"No, it really *was* the joint. That's what Freddy calls prison."

Freddy looked embarrassed. "I'm sorry, Jed. I forgot I wasn't supposed to tell."

"It's okay to tell Hannah, but some people might get the wrong idea." Jed turned back to Hannah to explain. "I was a civilian worker, not a prisoner."

Hannah nodded, but she wondered if Jed was telling the truth. Most people who'd been in prison would go to any length to hide it. "Did you work there long?"

"Just for a couple of months until I saved enough money to move on. There was one good thing about the job, though. They gave the maintenance crew some kind of retroactive raise and I got a big check in the mail today. Right after we're through here, we're going down to Cyril Murphy's car lot with that old car that belonged to Freddy's mother to trade it in on a pickup truck."

"But doesn't that car belong to Freddy now?"

"Sure, but he can't drive anyway, and it was a wreck before I got it running again. It's still no great shakes. I have to park it on top of a hill."

"A hill?"

"I replaced the starter, but it still doesn't work right. Half the time, we have to roll it down the hill in first gear to start it. Besides, Freddy wants to ride in a truck."

"You betcha!" Freddy gave Hannah a big smile. "I'd really like for us to have a truck. Jed says the girls really like guys who have trucks."

Hannah was thoughtful as Freddy and Jed gathered up their things and left. She didn't really believe Jed's story about being a civilian worker at the prison and she intended to check on it. She also didn't like the new attitude she saw in Freddy. As far as she knew, he'd never been interested in girls before. Jed might have good intentions, but he was teaching Freddy some things that could lead to trouble down the road.

Hannah glanced at the clock as she hung her apron on a hook. "That's it, Lisa. Take the rest of those Oatmeal Raisin Crisps for your dad and go home. It's past six-thirty."

"Okay. You won't get any argument from me." Lisa finished stashing the last bowl of dough in their walk-in cooler, and hung up her apron next to Hannah's. "Are you going to stick around for Mike's call?"

"For a while. Then I'll go home. He knows the number."

"See you tomorrow then," Lisa said, picking up the half-dozen leftover cookies and heading for the door.

After Lisa left, Hannah did a check of their stock in the pantry, made out the order that had to be placed the next day, and got ready to leave. It was almost seven-thirty. It was unlikely that Mike would call this late. She had just picked up her purse and was heading out the door when the phone rang. Hannah stopped in her tracks and stared at the phone, wishing that it could tell her who was on the other end of its line.

Should she? Or shouldn't she? Rather than debate that question any further, Hannah rushed across the kitchen to answer. If it was Delores, she could always think of an excuse to cut the call short. "Hello?"

"Hi, Hannah." There was an apologetic tone in Mike's voice. "I'm sorry I didn't get back to you, but I've been tied up. Do you have plans for dinner?"

"Tonight?"

"Yes. I thought we could go out to a nice dinner and talk about Rhonda. I'll even let you pick the place."

"It's a deal," Hannah said, realizing that she could kill three birds with one stone. "Could we go to Alfredo's Ristorante? And could you take me to the Quick Stop after dinner so that I can meet Michelle's bus? And then could you drive her out to Mother's lake cottage?"

"No problem. I'll make the reservations if you tell me what time."

Hannah glanced up at the clock and figured out the logistics. It was seventy-thirty on the nose, so traffic would be light. It would take her fifteen minutes to get home and two minutes to pour some kitty crunchies into Moishe's bowl. That was a total of seventeen minutes. She didn't need time to dress because the outfit she was wearing was perfect for dinner out. She'd need another three minutes to wash her face, brush her teeth, and comb her hair, and she'd tack on an extra ten minutes just to be on the safe side. "Make our reservations for eight-thirty and pick me up at my condo at eight."

"You can drive home and get ready to go out in half an hour?"

Hannah started to grin. Mike had sounded shocked. "Of course I can."

"But most women take longer than that to get ready for a date."

"I'm not *most* women. I'll be ready when you get there. Just buzz me and I'll walk out to the road to meet you."

Hannah glanced at the clock as she refilled Moishe's food bowl. It was ten minutes to eight. Her face was washed, her teeth were brushed, and her hair was secured in the clasp that Michelle had sent her last year from the Macalester College Arts Fair. She'd even taken time to spritz on a little perfume from the bottle her college roommate had given her. She was ready and she had ten minutes to kill before Mike buzzed her from the gate.

There was a yowl from the direction of the food bowl and Hannah turned toward her resident feline. "Don't worry. Mike's just taking me out to dinner, and then we're going to pick up Michelle at the bus stop."

That seemed to satisfy Moishe because he lowered his head to his food bowl again and didn't look up as Hannah sat down at the kitchen table with her steno pad.

Five minutes passed in relative silence, if one didn't count Hannah's sighs as she went over her notes on Rhonda's murder and the sound of Moishe's dinnertime crunching. She really hadn't learned much so far. She knew that Claire had given Rhonda the lemon pie. At least that mystery was solved. And she'd find out tonight if the takeout osso buco had come from Alfredo's Ristorante. If luck was with her, Rhonda's boyfriend had picked up the takeout and someone would remember him. If not, she'd just have to dig deeper to uncover his identity.

Learning that Rhonda really had a boyfriend had given Hannah several new motives to explore. If the man was married, as Carrie and Delores suspected, his wife could have murdered Rhonda in a fit of jealousy. She'd have to be a strong woman. Digging a grave for the "other woman" in the earthen floor of the basement furnace room would have taken some muscle.

One by one, other motives and possibilities occurred to Hannah and she jotted them down. If Rhonda's affair had led to the breakup of a marriage, anyone involved, even a teenager, could have retaliated by killing the woman who'd led his or her dad astray. It was a little far-fetched, but not impossible that several siblings had banded together to get rid of their mother's rival.

There was also Rhonda's big mouth to consider, especially if her gossiping had really hurt someone. Carrie and Delores could check out that possibility for her.

Then there was Rhonda's job at the drugstore. If Rhonda had been instrumental in getting a coworker fired, that person could have taken revenge. She'd run down to Lake Eden Neighborhood Drugs tomorrow to check with Jon Walker, the pharmacist and owner.

The buzzer by the phone sounded and Hannah pressed the switch that opened the wooden arm at the gate. She said good-bye to Moishe, topped off his food bowl for the final time, grabbed her notebook, and went out the door. It was a beautiful evening if you ignored the muggy air and the mosquitoes that descended like miniature Draculas on any carelessly exposed patch of skin.

Mike's car was just rounding the bend and Hannah took the shortcut through the planter. Even though the condo association had forbidden the practice, almost all of the residents took the shortcut instead walking down the much longer winding sidewalk to the street. Use of the shortcut had become so widespread that the association had been forced to cave in and instruct the gardeners to place stepping stones over the path the residents' shoes had worn.

Mike gave a little toot on his horn as Hannah approached and Hannah raised her hand to wave. That was when she realized that she still held her steno pad in her hand. She shoved it down into the bottom of her shoulder bag. Mike had seemed much more tolerant of her investigation this time around, but flaunting the tangible proof of her detective work would still be a little like waving a red flag.

Hannah smiled happily as she looked around her. Alfredo's Ristorante was impressive and so was their cuisine. Mike had reserved a table by the window overlooking Eden Lake and while she'd ordered pollo picotta, a boneless chicken breast sautéed with lemon and capers, she'd talked Mike into the osso buco. Just as she'd expected, it had come with a garnish of sliced ripe olives.

"Don't you want your pasta?" Mike asked, eying the side dish the waitress had placed by Hannah's entrée.

"Of course I want it, but I can't have pasta on my diet."

"Do you mind if I eat it then?"

Hannah shook her head, even though she minded a lot. According to the menu, the pasta was homemade fresh rigatoni tossed with first-press, extra-virgin olive oil and butter, and liberally sprinkled with parmigiano reggiano, the best Parmesan cheese money could buy. She couldn't have it, but she really didn't want Mike to eat it. It was the spurned lover's reaction, *If I can't have you, nobody can.* And that was a possibility she hadn't thought of before. If Rhonda had been involved with two men and she'd made noises about leaving one for the other, the loser could have killed Rhonda rather than let her go. It was one of the reasons why so many love triangles ended in tragedy.

"What are you thinking about?" Mike asked, swallowing the last of her pasta. "You look really intense."

"Dessert, and how I can't have any."

"That's not it." Mike shook his head. "You'd look sad if you were thinking about missing dessert. What was it?"

Hannah thought about dissembling, but she couldn't come up with a likely subject. Perhaps the truth was her best bet. "Actually, I was thinking about Rhonda and how jealousy could make someone mad enough to kill. I figured that Rhonda might have been part of a love triangle."

"Rhonda was involved with a married man and his wife killed her?"

"Maybe, but I was thinking of another way. If Rhonda was involved with two men, one of them could have killed her rather than let the other one have her."

Mike thought about that for a moment. "That makes more sense. Doc Knight said a woman could have stabbed Rhonda. It doesn't take that much force to kill someone with a knife if the blade hits a vital spot. But we've got to assume that the person who killed her is the one who dug that grave and that dirt is as hard as concrete. Bill and I tried to dig a hole in the corner and it was tough going."

"Then how did the killer manage to do it?"

"He used a pickax and then he shoveled it out. We found the tools in the corner of the basement."

"Were there any prints?"

Mike shook his head. "Not even a partial. The fingerprint guys are sure he wore gloves."

"How about the murder weapon? Did you recover it?"

"No. We think it was a hunting knife with a long blade, the kind you can buy almost anywhere for field-dressing big game. The killer probably took it with him and ditched it later. Unless we get lucky, we probably won't find it."

There was a note of frustration in Mike's voice and Hannah could understand that. Every hunter in Minnesota had a hunting knife. "How about Rhonda's apartment? Did you search it?"

"Of course we did, but we didn't find anything that related to her murder."

"Was there anything unusual about the autopsy?"

"Not really. Rhonda ate dinner that night and her stomach contents helped Doc narrow down the time of death. Her blood alcohol level showed that she drank almost a whole bottle of red wine with her dinner."

"Then she was pretty tipsy when she went down the basement stairs?"

"She must have been. Good thing she wasn't driving. Since her car is still parked at her apartment building, we figure someone must have dropped her off at the Voelker place."

"Do you know who?"

Mike shook his head. "We spent hours trying to track that down, but we got nowhere. How about you?"

"I got the same place you did." Hannah felt cheered. Mike wasn't asking her to back off and he hadn't even mentioned locking her up to keep her from interfering. "So you're okay with me doing my own investigation?"

"I'm not happy, but I'm okay with it. Maybe *reconciled* would be a better word. Just keep out of trouble and tell me if you discover anything you think I should know."

"Haven't I always?" Hannah sidestepped any promises. "How about the crime scene? I didn't really look around that closely. Did you find any clues?"

"Just one. We thought we had a suspect, but it turned out to be nothing."

Hannah leaned forward. This was the first she'd heard about a suspect. "Who was it?"

"Jed Sawyer. We found an old Minnesota Twins baseball cap in the basement and Bill remembered that he'd seen Jed wearing one just like it. We questioned him, but it turns out Rhonda hired Jed and Freddy to do some handyman work when she was getting ready to sell the Voelker place."

"That's true. I heard they fixed some of the windows."

"That fits with what Jed told us. He says he remembers taking off his cap while he was replacing one of the basement windows and he must have forgotten it down there."

"And you believe that?"

"It checks out. We took another look at the crime scene photos and the window that Jed said he replaced still had the sticker on the glass."

"Too bad," Hannah said with a sigh.

"What's the matter? Don't you like Jed?"

"It's not that I don't like him. It's just that . . . I'm not sure he's a good influence on Freddy."

"What do you mean?"

"It's probably nothing."

Mike gave her a stern look. "Spit it out, Hannah. It's not like you to beat around the bush."

"I think Jed's pushing Freddy too hard and giving him ideas he can't handle."

"Like what?"

"Like trading in his mother's car for a truck and going out to attract girls. Freddy idolizes Jed and he wants his approval. He'll do anything Jed says and that worries me." Hannah thought back to her conversation with Jed and that gave her an idea. "Would you check out something for me?"

"Maybe. Does it have anything to do with the murder investigation?"

"No, I'm just curious. Jed said that he worked on the maintenance crew at the prison and he made a point of telling me that he was a civilian worker. I don't have any reason to think he's lying, but there's something about Jed I don't quite trust."

"That was my impression. I'll find out if he was an inmate. Which prison?"

"I don't know. I didn't ask. But since he said *the* prison, instead of *a* prison, I'm assuming it's in Minnesota."

"Okay. I'll get on it first thing in the morning."

"Thanks, Mike." Hannah smiled at him. "Would you excuse me for a minute?"

"Sure. Shall I order you an after-dinner drink?"

"No, thanks. More coffee would be nice, though. I need to keep up my energy level and I'm running about a gallon short."

Hannah left Mike sitting at the table and headed toward the entrance of the dining room. It was time to check out the restaurant's takeout menu and see if anyone remembered who'd picked up the containers of osso buco that had landed in Rhonda's garbage.

The hostess was at her post by the entrance. Hannah put on a friendly smile as she approached. "I notice that you have osso buco on the menu and that's my mother's favorite. Does Alfredo's do takeout?"

"Yes, and we alternate our entrées." The hostess returned Hannah's smile. "Osso buco is available every Friday evening from six to eight. You have to call in advance with your order."

"That's reasonable. I'll bet Friday nights are popular for takeout."

"No, it's actually our slowest night. Hold on a minute and I'll show you what I mean."

Hannah held her smile as the hostess flipped through pages on a clipboard. She was close to getting the information she wanted, but she wasn't quite there yet.

"Here you go." The hostess tapped a perfectly manicured nail on the page she'd chosen. "Six orders of osso buco. That's all we sold last Friday, but I know we ran out in the kitchen. That means most people came out here and ordered it from the menu."

Hannah was impressed. "Your system is very efficient. You actually keep the names of the people who ordered takeout?"

"We have to. It's my job to make sure the takeout goes to

the proper person at the time they specified. See? Three people ordered takeout, two orders apiece."

Hannah blessed the fact that she could read upside down. She'd first learned that skill when Andrea was a child and used to sit facing her with a schoolbook. When Andrea had faltered over a word, Hannah had taught herself to read it upside down, so she wouldn't have to move. And that just went to prove that laziness sometimes paid off.

"Would you like one of our takeout menus?"

"I'd like several." Hannah accepted the printed menus the hostess gave her. "I'll call in on Friday and order osso buco for my mother and her friends."

"Not this Friday. We're closed for the Fourth."

"Right," Hannah said. She'd been so intent on tracking down the takeout dinners, she'd forgotten all about the holiday. "I'll call in next Friday. Thanks for the information."

Hannah gave the hostess a parting smile and headed off to the ladies room. Once there, she pulled her steno pad out of her purse and jotted down the names from the takeout list. The first was Ken Purvis, Jordan High's principal. Hannah really had to stretch her imagination to imagine Ken as Rhonda's boyfriend. The second was Gil Surma, the high school counselor, and that also seemed impossible. The third name was even more unlikely because it was Reverend Knudson. He wasn't married, but he lived with his grandmother. Hannah supposed that Rhonda could have been referring to Priscilla Knudson when she'd made her comment about not being able to marry unless there was a funeral. Mrs. Knudson had suffered a stroke only weeks before the Goetz's New Year's Eve party and Rhonda'd had no way of knowing she'd completely recover. Finding out which of the three men was involved with Rhonda would take time, but there was a pay phone in the ladies room and there was no time like the present to start narrowing the field.

Bonnie Surma, Gil's wife, answered on the first ring. Hannah fixed a smile on her face—she'd heard that telemarketers used this technique to sound friendly—and took a deep breath. "Hi, Bonnie. It's Hannah Swensen. I'm out here at Alfredo's Ristorante and . . ."

"Take my advice and order their osso buco," Bonnie interrupted her. "Gil picked it up for us on Friday night and it was marvelous."

Hannah's phony smile turned into a real grin. If Gil had taken osso buco home to Bonnie, he wasn't Rhonda's boyfriend.

"Friday was our anniversary and Gil wanted to do something special. I didn't feel like getting dressed up and going out, so he ordered dinner and brought it home."

"That was sweet of him," Hannah said, scrounging for a pen in the bottom of her purse and crossing Gil's name off her suspect list.

"It would have been sweeter if he hadn't left for a meeting right after dinner, but even a good marriage can't be perfection. Gil and I rub along very well together."

Perfection. Rub along very well. Hannah came close to chuckling. Bonnie must have been at the same Lake Eden Regency Romance Club meeting as Delores.

"Did you need something, Hannah? Gil's at a city council meeting. He said he'd call before he left for home, so I need to keep the line free."

"Uh . . . yes. Yes, I did." Hannah thought fast. She should have had an excuse for her call all prepared. "Tracey was talking about joining the Brownies the other day. She wanted to know how old she had to be."

"I'm glad Tracey's so interested. She's still too young, but I'll mail a packet to Andrea tomorrow with the guidelines."

"Thanks, Bonnie. That's all I needed. I'll let you go." Hannah hung up the phone and let out a relieved sigh. She liked Bonnie and Gil and she was glad that Rhonda hadn't been a threat to their marriage.

The next name on Hannah's list was Kenneth Purvis. Hannah had trouble visualizing Jordan High's principal, a man whose most notable habit was polishing his glasses, in a steamy embrace with Rhonda, but she couldn't discount the possibility. Ken *had* picked up two orders of osso buco on Friday night.

Hannah had learned her lesson from Bonnie. She needed a good excuse for her call. When Ken or his wife, Kathy, answered, she'd ask about the community outreach night classes Jordan High was planning to hold in the fall. There had been an article about it last week in the *Lake Eden Journal.* She could pretend to be interested in signing up for basket weaving, or fly casting, or something like that.

Hannah looked up the number and dialed. The phone rang several times and then their answering machine clicked on. Rather than leave a message, Hannah hung up and turned to the third name on the list, Reverend Knudson.

"Redeemer Lutheran," Reverend Knudson's grandmother answered on the second ring.

"Hi, Mrs. Knudson. It's Hannah Swensen."

"Hello, Hannah." Mrs. Knudson sounded pleased to hear from her. "The reverend isn't home right now, but I can take a message and have him call you in the morning."

"That's okay. Maybe you can help. I meant to call earlier, but I forgot. I'm out here at Alfredo's Ristorante. Have you ever had their osso buco?"

"No, but it's one of my favorite dishes."

"Maybe your grandson could pick it up as takeout for you," Hannah said, hoping to solicit more information. It was obvious that Reverend Knudson hadn't taken osso buco to his grandmother, but he'd left Alfredo's last Friday night with two takeout orders. "They have it on their menu every Friday night."

"You might know it would be Fridays!" Priscilla Knudson gave an exasperated sigh. "The reverend is always gone on Friday nights. Church-related meetings, you know."

"Of course," Hannah said, drawing a circle around Reverend Knudson's name. If he'd gone to a church-related

meeting on Friday night, she was willing to bet he hadn't arrived with two orders of takeout osso buco from Alfredo's
Ristorante.

"You said earlier that you thought I might be able to help
you. With what, Hannah?"

Mrs. Knudson's question brought Hannah back from her
speculations and she launched into the excuse she'd prepared. "I heard about the bake sale Redeemer Lutheran is
holding on Saturdays and I wanted to contribute something.
How about a box of cookies?"

"Why, that would be lovely, Hannah. I'm sure the reverend will be delighted. Can we count on you for this Saturday?"

"Absolutely."

Hannah smiled as she hung up the phone. A box of free
cookies was a small price to pay for the information Priscilla
Knudson had given her. She'd eliminated Gil Surma and she
had yet to reach Principal Purvis, but Reverend Knudson had
just jumped to the top of her suspect list.

Chapter Fourteen

Hannah glanced at her watch in the light from Mike's dashboard as they came over the crest of a long steep hill and neared the Quick Stop. They still had almost fifteen minutes before Michelle's bus was due to arrive. "Let's park on the side and go in. I want to see how my cookies are doing for Sean and Ron."

Mike pulled into a spot at the side of the building and shut off his engine. "We can go in, but I already know your cookies are selling really well."

"How do you know that? Did you ask Sean and Ron?"

"I didn't have to ask. The guys at the station used to stop for doughnuts and coffee on their way to work, but now they bring in coffee and your cookies. Nobody buys doughnuts anymore."

"Thanks for telling me." Hannah was pleased. She'd started to supply the Quick Stop with cookies several months ago and the volume of their orders had been steadily increasing. That was a good sign, but she hadn't been sure if Sean and Ron were selling more cookies, or just eating more of them.

"You can go in if you want to." Mike turned to smile at her. "I'll stay here and meet Michelle if her bus comes in early."

Hannah laughed. "Thanks, but that won't work."

"Why not?"

"You've never met Michelle. You don't even know what she looks like."

"Yes, I do. There's a picture of the three of you on the mantel over your fireplace. I recognized Andrea and you, so I figured Michelle had to be the one in the middle with the brown hair."

Hannah was impressed, even though she knew Mike had been trained to notice things. "You're right, but that's an old picture. You might not recognize her now."

"She can't be that different. Her hair could be another color and she could have gained or lost weight, but her basic bone structure is the same. I'll spot her. You don't have to worry about that."

Hannah began to grin. "I guess any cop who can recognize a suspect from his DMV picture wouldn't have much trouble with an old family photo."

"That's right." Mike lowered his window, looked out for a moment, and then he turned to grin at her. "It's a good thing you didn't go inside. Here comes the bus now."

Hannah glanced out his window, but all she saw was an empty road. "Where? I don't see anything."

"You'll see it when it comes over the hill."

"Who do you think you are?" Hannah asked, eyeing him with some amusement. "Supercop with x-ray vision?"

"No, but I might try out for Supercop with subsonic hearing."

"You *heard* the bus?"

"That's right. A diesel engine's got a certain high-pitched whine to it. On a still night it'll carry for a long way."

Hannah stared at him, but he didn't seem to be putting her on. "Okay, I believe you even though I've met the bus lots of times and I never heard a whine."

"You probably wouldn't notice."

"Because it's a cop thing?"

"No, it's a trucker thing. My father was an owner-operator

and I drove most of his short runs every summer. It gets boring, driving the same route day after day. I looked for ways to amuse myself and I started concentrating on the sounds trucks make. I got so good, I could tell a Peterbilt from a Kenworth a quarter-mile away."

Hannah had been aware of a low rumbling noise while Mike spoke and it had increased in volume. Her eyes widened as a Greyhound bus crested the hill and began its descent. "You were right. There's the bus. I hope Michelle's trip wasn't too boring."

"I'm sure she found someone to talk to. She's a very pretty woman."

"Girl," Hannah corrected him. "She's still a teenager."

"Just barely. I've known a few nineteen-year-olds. They'd much rather be thought of as young women."

"I suppose you're right." Hannah gave him a sharp glance as she climbed out of the car. She wanted to know more about the nineteen-year-olds he'd known, but it wasn't a good idea to ask. Mike didn't talk about his past very much and he'd already told her about driving his father's truck. That was enough for one night.

As they walked, Hannah glanced up at the halogen lights by the bus loading and unloading area. Moths were fluttering around the bulbs in uneven halos, attracted to the hot light despite its danger. As she watched, several fell back down to the pavement and were crushed under the feet of the people who had gathered to meet the bus.

Mike found a spot near the front of the crowd and Hannah stood close to his side. He reached out to take her arm and smiled down at her. "Are you excited about seeing her again?"

"Yes," Hannah said, smiling back. There were times when she indulged in a bit of nostalgia, remembering how she'd helped Delores soothe Michelle through bouts of colic when she was a baby, carrying her on mile-long treks around the living room until she'd finally gone to sleep.

The bus pulled up with a loud snort and a squeal of brakes, spewing out a black plume of what Hannah now knew was diesel exhaust. There was a moment of expectation while the driver flicked on the interior lights and checked something on his clipboard. Then the door opened with a mechanical hiss and a plump woman in a nurse's uniform climbed down the steps. She was followed by a man carrying a raincoat, a mother with a baby in her arms, and an older gentleman wearing a straw hat.

There was a long pause as a young man struggled to navigate the steps with a package large enough to contain a tuba. Once he'd successfully disembarked, two teenage girls in jeans and sweaters stepped off the bus.

Hannah began to frown. There was only one more passenger waiting to get off the bus and it wasn't Michelle. "Oh-oh. I think she missed the bus."

"No, she didn't. She's right there at the top of the stairs."

Hannah gave the woman a second glance. She had bright green streaks in her hair and a tattoo on her left shoulder, an in-your-face rendition of a coiled snake. She was wearing a shiny gold top that was so tight Hannah could see every breath she took, and her red pants were hip-height at the waist, exposing her navel. As far as Hannah could see there was no one standing behind her waiting to get off. "I don't see her. Where is she?"

"Right there. With the green hair."

Hannah took another look. The apparition was still at the top of the stairs and she appeared to be having trouble with one of her gold, high-heeled tennis shoes. The heel was stuck in the metal grating of the step.

"That's not Michelle," Hannah said, shaking her head.

"Yes, it is. Watch this."

Mike stepped closer to wave at the green-haired woman. "Hi, Michelle. Over here!"

The woman's face lit up in a smile and she waved back. "Hi, Hannah! Just a sec. My shoe's stuck."

It *was* Michelle. Hannah groaned. She knew that college students often followed the newest clothing fads and she'd expected that Michelle might have a slightly different look, but nothing could have prepared her for seeing her baby sister in an outfit that looked like . . .

"I'll go help her," Mike said, interrupting the thoughts that Hannah didn't want to think anyway. "Don't worry. It's probably just some stage she's going through."

"Some stage," Hannah muttered, managing somehow to put a welcoming smile on her face. She averted her eyes as Mike bounded forward, wondering if her mother had grounds to sue the college. She'd check with Howie Levine in the morning. Better yet, she'd call him the moment she got home to her condo.

"Here she is," Mike announced, arriving at Hannah's side with Michelle in his arms and her left shoe dangling from his fingers. "I'm going to carry her to the car so she can change shoes. Her luggage is being unloaded right now and there's only one piece, a pink duffle bag. Can you get it?"

"Sure," Hannah said brightly, heading off to collect the pink bag. Perhaps the college wouldn't admit full responsibility. Michelle had lived off campus for a semester. But at the least, they ought to refund the tuition money.

"So. How was your trip?" Hannah asked, after she'd retrieved Michelle's bag, stashed it in the trunk, and taken her place in the passenger's seat.

"Exciting. I almost missed the bus." Michelle grinned at her big sister. "I just wish I'd brought my camera. I'd give anything to have a picture of your face when I got off that bus."

"You do look . . . uh . . . pretty spectacular," Hannah said, reminding herself that they had an audience and it would be better to wait until they were alone to read Michelle the riot act.

"I wish Mother could see me like this, but I don't think that's a good idea."

"Probably not," Hannah said, knowing that she'd just made the understatement of the year. "As far as I know, she doesn't have heart problems . . . yet."

Michelle cracked up and Hannah immediately felt better. At least her sister's new look hadn't leeched her sense of humor.

"Could we go to your place so I can wash this green stuff out of my hair?"

"It washes out?"

"It's supposed to. It's a spray I got from the makeup department. You don't think I look like this all the time, do you?"

"You don't?"

"Of course not. I don't dress like this, either. It's just that I was in a student play tonight. If I'd taken the time to change out of my costume, I would have missed my bus."

"You're wearing a *costume!*" Hannah exclaimed, beginning to smile. "Mike and I thought it was a new kind of fad. How about the tattoo? Is that real?"

Michelle shook her head. "It's just one of those press-on things that washes right off with soap and water. If I can use your shower, I'll be as good as new in less than twenty minutes, I promise."

"Hannah's place it is," Mike said, reaching out to pat Hannah's hand as he started the car and pulled out of the parking lot. "The tattoo's impressive. I know a woman who has one just like it."

"Here in Lake Eden?" Hannah asked, turning to him in absolute shock.

"No, in Minneapolis. I busted her three times when I was a rookie."

Chapter Fifteen

Hannah took another sip of coffee. Her nerves were jangling with the infusion of even more caffeine than usual, but she had to do something to wake up. They'd stayed out at the cottage with Mother and Michelle until almost one in the morning, and then she'd spent long minutes with Mike at her door, debating about whether or not she should invite him in. One glance at her watch had settled that question. One-thirty was too late, especially for a small-business owner who had to get up at five the next morning to bake. She'd gone inside alone, fed Moishe, and crawled into bed. And this morning, when she'd come into work, she'd found two frantic messages on her answer machine. Both were rush orders that had come in the previous evening. Loretta Richardson had called in a panic. She'd been deluged with unexpected guests for the Fourth and she needed five-dozen Praline Charlottes. The second order had come from Doc Knight, who wanted three pans of Lovely Lemon Bar Cookies for his nurses.

"Hannah?" Lisa pushed the swinging door to the kitchen open and stuck her head in. "Norman's on the phone and he wants you to meet him down at the clinic at twelve. He says it's important. Then he wants to take you to the café for lunch."

Hannah was about to say yes when she remembered that

Lisa needed her lunch break. "How about you? Can you wait until one for lunch?"

"No problem. Just bring me back one of Rose's hamburgers."

"It's a deal." Hannah started to smile. It would be good to see Norman.

"And Mike just came in. He wants to see you."

"Okay. Will you coffee him and send him back here?"

"Sure. Did you finish the Praline Charlottes for Loretta?"

"Yes, and I'll deliver them on my way to see Norman." Hannah gestured toward several boxes she'd stacked on the counter. "I have extras if you want to give them out for samples."

Lisa shook her head. "They're too good for samples. I know you're just using them for catering and advance orders right now, but I think we should add them to the cookie menu."

"We'll have to charge a little more. The frosting takes time."

"People will pay it. They're delicious, Hannah. I just wish Cousin Charlotte could taste them."

"I agree, especially since we named them after her. I'll package up a few and we'll send them to her by overnight mail."

Lisa looked happy as she went back out to the coffee shop. Her mother's cousin, who ran a cleaning service in New Orleans, had sent Lisa a box of pralines for Christmas. Hannah had tasted one and been so impressed, she'd decided to try to make a praline cookie.

Hannah had just finished packaging the cookies when Mike came in with a coffee mug in his hand. "Hi, Hannah. I checked on that little problem we discussed last night."

"What little problem?"

"Just a second." Mike walked over to the pantry and glanced through the open door.

For a moment Hannah thought he'd lost his marbles, but

then she realized that he wanted to give her his report on Jed's job at the prison. "Jed and Freddy finished their work for me yesterday. There's no one here except you and me, and the weevils in the flour."

"You have *bugs* in your flour?"

Mike started to frown and Hannah wondered if he was thinking of turning her in to the Health Department. She didn't think he would, but she knew she'd better correct his misconception in a hurry. "Relax, Mike. I was just kidding. I always store my flour in canisters and tape a bay leaf to the inside of the lid to keep out the weevils."

"And that works?"

"It's never failed me. The only other way is to freeze the flour in airtight containers, but I don't have the freezer space for that."

"I learn something new every day in this job." Mike gave her a grin. "Do you want me to tell you about Jed?"

"Please do. Pull up a stool and sit down."

Mike took the stool across from Hannah and took out his notebook. "I checked when I got to the station this morning. Jed was a civilian worker on the maintenance crew at Stillwater. He didn't lie to you, but I doubt he told you the whole truth."

"What's the whole truth?"

"He was fired. I talked to his supervisor and he said that Jed was unreliable. He came in late most mornings and there were several times when his supervisor suspected that he'd been drinking on the job. He finally caught Jed with a bottle and fired him on the spot."

"Jed didn't mention anything about that."

"Of course he didn't. My big concern is for Freddy. You said you think Jed's a real influence on him?"

"I know he is. Freddy thinks the world of Jed."

"Then we'd better hope that Jed's drinking hasn't developed into a pattern. Do you think he was drinking when he was working for you?"

Hannah thought about it for a moment and then she shook her head. "I don't think he was. I'm pretty sure I would have noticed. Maybe he learned his lesson?"

"Either that, or he's just being more careful not to get caught. Who are they working for now?"

"I don't know."

"I'll find out and keep an eye on Jed." Mike finished his coffee and stood up. "Break time's over and I've got to run. I'll give you a call later."

The moment Mike left, Hannah pulled out her steno pad and added the new information he'd given her. It didn't have anything to do with Rhonda's murder, but she liked to keep all her information in one place. Then she checked her list of things to do and saw her notation about Reverend Knudson. Priscilla thought her grandson had attended a church-related meeting on Friday night, but Hannah had her doubts. If Lisa could spare her, she'd run next door and ask Claire if she knew where the reverend had gone with his two orders of takeout osso buco.

"Is there something wrong with the outfit you bought yesterday?" Claire asked when she answered Hannah's knock on her back door.

"Are you kidding? I wore it when I went out to dinner with Mike and he said I looked like a goddess."

Claire smiled. "It's the simple truth. That outfit does wonders for you."

"Thanks." Hannah appreciated the compliment, but it was time to get to the point. "Something's come up and I need to talk to you about Reverend Knudson. Do you have a minute?"

Claire glanced at her watch. "I have exactly five. Becky Summers just went into the dressing room and she always struggles with her zipper for at least five minutes before she calls me in to help."

"Then I'd better hurry." Hannah took a deep breath as she

stepped inside Claire's back room. "I know that this is a delicate subject, but do you know where Reverend Knudson was on Friday night?"

"Is this about Rhonda's murder?"

"Yes. Rhonda had a guest at the Voelker place on Friday night and he brought two takeout dinners with him. I know Reverend Knudson got takeout that night. I'm hoping he wasn't Rhonda's visitor."

"He wasn't."

"Are you sure about that?"

"As sure as I can be. Bob was *my* visitor."

"What time did Reverend Knudson get to your place, and when did he leave? And what did he bring you for dinner?"

"Do you really need to know all that?" Claire's green eyes narrowed. "Or is it just prurient curiosity on your part?"

"I'm never prurient . . . or at least not often. I really need to know, Claire. I realize you want to keep your relationship with the reverend private and that's one of the reasons I'm asking. If I can eliminate him from the suspect list, I won't have to mention him to Mike."

Claire thought about that for a moment. "All right. Bob got to my apartment at seven and he didn't leave until after midnight. And he brought me osso buco."

"Good. I can cross him off the list." Hannah gave a relieved sigh. "If you don't mind my asking, why did his grandmother think he was at a church meeting?"

Claire gave a little smile. "Because that's where he was *supposed* to be. It was Ecumenical Council night, but they canceled. Bob found out late that afternoon and we . . . well . . . we just took advantage of the moment. By the way, he's an incredible dancer."

"Reverend Knudson?"

"Yes. He put himself through college by working part time as a dance instructor. Bob can tango better than anybody I know. He's just wild."

Hannah blinked. She really had trouble imagining the solemn man who stood behind the pulpit at Redeemer Lutheran dancing a wild tango. "You went out dancing?"

"Not out. We shoved back the furniture and danced in my living room. Bob's just wonderful, Hannah. I've never been so happy in my life. He's almost got me persuaded to let him announce our engagement to the congregation and let the chips fall where they may."

Hannah sighed. She wished Claire well, but those would be some pretty big chips.

"I know what you're thinking, but even when I was involved with Richard, I stayed active in the church. I can always be the reformed sinner that Bob redeemed."

Another thought occurred to Hannah that she knew she shouldn't ask, but that had never stopped her before. "Do you really think you could be a small-town minister's wife?"

"I think so. I know I'd like to be Bob's wife. There's only one thing stopping me."

"Your past?"

"No, Bob doesn't care about that. But I don't read music and every other minister's wife in town plays the organ."

Hannah glanced at her watch as she pulled into a space in front of the Rhodes Dental Clinic. She was twenty minutes early for her lunch date with Norman despite the fact that she'd stopped off to deliver Loretta's Praline Charlottes. She got out of her truck, locked it up, and walked into the waiting room. She could hear voices in the back, coming from one of the examining rooms. Norman was still with a patient. Rather than sit and page through magazines she didn't want to read anyway, Hannah decided to dash up the block to Lake Eden Neighborhood Drugs and talk to Jon Walker about Rhonda's work at the drugstore.

The heat was shimmering up in little waves from the sidewalk as Hannah walked to the drugstore. Main Street was practically deserted and she could understand why. Anyone with half a brain was inside with curtains drawn and fan blades whirling as fast as they could to move the sluggish air. The heat today was powerful enough to make Hannah wish that the Lake Eden City Council would legislate required siestas.

As Hannah walked, she caught herself stepping over the cracks in the sidewalk. Grandma Ingrid had once told her that if she stepped on a crack, she'd break her mother's back. The old rhyme had evidently sunk deeply into her subconscious. Of course she didn't believe it. She doubted she'd believed it then. But twenty-five years had passed since she'd first heard that childish warning and she was still altering her pace to avoid the cracks.

There was a large revolving fan on a stand in the open doorway of the drugstore and Hannah moved around it to step inside. The lighting was dim compared to the brightness of the summer sun. She stopped several feet from the door to let her pupils adjust. When her eyes had done their retinal magic and enabled her to make out obstacles again, she realized that she was standing next to the candy counter and quickly moved over to a display of stuffed toys.

"Hello, Hannah."

A voice greeted her from the dusky interior. Hannah gave a little wave as she spotted Linda Nelson. "Hi, Linda. I didn't know you were working here."

"I'm Beth Halverson's summer replacement. She got a scholarship to science camp."

Hannah nodded. Beth was the piccolo player who would be sorely missed by everyone who heard the Jordan High marching band. "I need to talk to Jon. Is he around?"

"He's in the pharmacy. Come with me and I'll call him."

Hannah was surprised. The last time she'd come in to talk to Jon, one of the clerks had just slipped behind the counter, opened the door to the pharmacy, and told Jon that Hannah wanted to see him. "Why do you have to call him?"

"New regulations. We're not allowed behind the pharmacy counter and the door is kept locked. If someone wants Mr. Walker, we have to call him on the phone."

"You had a break-in?" Hannah guessed.

"I don't know. Mr. Walker just told us the new rules when we came in to work Friday morning. He didn't explain why."

Hannah followed Linda to the front of the pharmacy counter and watched as she punched a series of numbers into the phone. It rang in the pharmacy, the door behind the counter opened, and Jon Walker came out. He was a full-blooded Chippewa Indian, born at Red Lake Reservation. When it had been time for Jon to start high school, his family had moved to Lake Eden and Jon had graduated from Jordan High. He'd gone on to college and come back to Lake Eden to buy the drugstore and take over the pharmacy.

"What can I do for you, Hannah?" Jon asked, locking the door behind him.

"I need some information. Can we step inside the pharmacy so we can talk privately?"

Jon shook his head. "Sorry. The pharmacy's off limits to everyone except me. We can go to my office, though."

Hannah followed Jon through the storage area at the back of the store and into the small cubicle he called his office. It was closet-sized, barely large enough to hold his desk and two chairs, but it was private and that suited Hannah's purpose.

"Coffee?" Jon asked, gesturing toward a small coffee-maker. It was clear the carafe hadn't been cleaned in recent memory and it was half-filled with dregs of a brown liquid that looked lethal to Hannah.

"Thanks, but no. What's with all these new rules you have? Did somebody break into the pharmacy?"

"No, nothing like that. I just decided we were getting too lax and it was time to beef up our security."

Hannah gave him a challenging look. "Come on, Jon. Nobody fixes something that isn't broken. Level with me and tell me what gives."

Jon dropped his eyes and refused to meet hers. "Let's just say we had an unfortunate incident and I had to make certain it couldn't happen again."

"Unfortunate incident? You sound like a politician, Jon."

"Maybe I do, but I can't tell you any more than that."

Hannah studied Jon carefully. His mouth was set in a straight line and he looked determined not to say more. "Okay. If Rhonda wasn't involved in this incident of yours, I don't have to know what it was."

There was complete silence from Jon, although he looked very nervous, and Hannah put two and two together. "Rhonda *was* involved."

"Yes. I see where you're going, Hannah. You think this might have something to do with Rhonda's murder. Are you working with the sheriff's department again?"

"I've never worked with the sheriff's department. They've always taken great pains to let me know that they don't want me."

"I guess that's true." Jon gave a small, humorless laugh. "But you *are* investigating Rhonda's murder, aren't you?"

"Unofficially, yes. And that's why I need to know."

"What I say has to stay with you. You can't tell anyone else."

"You've got it," Hannah said and sat back to wait. Jon had caved and this might be good.

"Rhonda was working late last month, making out her order for the cosmetic department. I'd already left for home and she was the only one here. Around eight o'clock Reggie York pulled up and he hammered on the door. He told Rhonda he'd called in a prescription from work, but traffic was heavy and he'd just gotten back to town."

Hannah knew Reggie was Gus and Irma York's oldest son and they were very proud that he'd landed a job as a pilot for Worldways Airline. The last time Hannah had seen Irma, she'd complained that Reggie's commute to and from the airport in the Twin Cities took longer than most of his flights.

"Rhonda did exactly what I would have done. She let him in. Since she was my manager, she had a master key. She unlocked the door to the pharmacy and found his prescription on the shelf."

"Rhonda filled his prescription?"

"No, it was filed alphabetically and all ready to go. She rang it up and then she asked Reggie if he was still flying."

"What's wrong with that?"

"Nothing. Not then. When Reggie said he was, Rhonda said she thought pilots who had glaucoma were grounded."

"How did she know Reggie had glaucoma?"

"Her great-aunt, Mrs. Voelker, had glaucoma. Rhonda used to pick up her medicine and deliver it to her. That's how she recognized the name of the eyedrops Reggie used."

"Let me guess," Hannah said with a sigh. "Rhonda blabbed, somebody reported it to Worldways, and Reggie was grounded?"

"That's exactly what happened. Reggie's glaucoma was mild and it was completely under control, but Worldways has very strict rules about their pilots. Reggie applied for a desk job right after he was diagnosed, but it hadn't come through yet and he could have been fired for concealing his condition."

"So Reggie was angry with Rhonda for blabbing?"

"Angry wasn't the word. Reggie was fit to be tied. He called me at home on Thursday night and threatened to sue me for breach of confidentiality."

Hannah's mouth dropped open. "Reggie's suing you?"

"No, I managed to calm him down. He wasn't really angry with me, but he was furious with Rhonda for gossiping about his disease. He demanded that I change the lock on the pharmacy door and guarantee that no one except a registered pharmacist could get inside. And he also demanded that I fire Rhonda."

"Oh boy," Hannah groaned. "Did you fire her?"

"I had to. I told her on Friday morning when she came in to work. I felt bad about it, especially since it was her last day before her vacation, but I knew that people would take their prescriptions to another pharmacy if they found out about it."

"How did Rhonda take it?"

"That was the surprising thing. I expected her to beg me to reconsider, or tell me off, but she didn't seem upset at all. She just said she could understand why I had to let her go and she went out the back way smiling."

"That's strange. How about your other employees? Do any of them know about this?" Hannah asked the question even though she thought she already knew the answer.

"I didn't see any point in telling them. I just tightened security the way I promised Reggie I would."

"I've got a tough question for you," Hannah warned him. "Do you think Reggie was mad enough at Rhonda to kill her?"

Jon thought about it for a moment and then he sighed. "I don't like to think so, but I suppose it's possible. Reggie really loved to fly."

"Thanks for being honest with me, Jon. I only have one more question and I don't want you to take it personally. Where were you on Friday night?"

"You think *I* killed Rhonda?" Jon looked utterly shocked.

"Of course not, but you did have a motive."

"*What* motive?"

"If things had gone differently, Rhonda could have cost you your business. I've got to put you on my suspect list, but I can cross you off if I know where you were."

"I guess it can't hurt to tell you. I picked Judy up right after I locked up at five, and we drove to Mille Lacs Lake for my mother-in-law's birthday. You can check with Judy. We stayed over that night and drove back early Saturday morning so that I could open at nine."

"Thanks, Jon." Hannah slipped her steno pad back into her purse and stood up to leave. She glanced at his coffeemaker as she passed it and sighed. "The next time you come in The Cookie Jar, the coffee's on me. You could probably bottle that stuff of yours and sell it for rat poison."

Praline Charlottes

Preheat oven to 350 degrees F.,
with rack in middle position.

1½ cups melted butter *(3 sticks)*
1½ cups brown sugar
2 teaspoons vanilla
1½ teaspoons baking soda
1 teaspoon baking powder
1 teaspoon salt *(decrease to ½ teaspoon if you use salted pecans)*
1½ cups finely ground pecans *(grind them up in your food processor with the steel blade and measure AFTER grinding)*
2 beaten eggs *(just whip them up with a fork)*
3 cups flour *(no need to sift)*

Microwave the butter in your mixing bowl to melt it. Add the sugar and vanilla. Stir until blended, and then add the baking soda, baking powder, and salt. Mix well.

Grind the pecans in your food processor. *(Remember to measure AFTER grinding.)* Add them to the bowl and mix. Pour in the beaten eggs and stir. Then add the flour and mix until all the ingredients are thoroughly blended.

Let the dough sit for a few minutes to firm up. Then form dough into walnut-sized balls and arrange them on a greased cookie sheet, 12 to a standard sheet. *(If the dough is too sticky to form into balls, chill it for a few minutes and try again.)*

Flatten the balls with a fork in a crisscross pattern. *(If the fork sticks, either spray it with Pam or dip it in flour.)*

Bake at 350 degrees F. for 8 to 10 minutes or until they're golden brown around the edges. Cool on the cookie sheet for 2 minutes, then remove to a wire rack to finish cooling. When they're cool, prepare the frosting.

Praline Frosting

¾ cup butter *(1½ sticks)*
3½ cups powdered sugar *(not sifted)*
2 teaspoons vanilla *(or 1½ teaspoons vanilla and
    ½ teaspoon almond flavoring)*
⅓ cup cream
½ cup finely chopped pecans
Approx. 6 dozen pecan halves for decoration *(optional)*

Before you start, arrange the cooled cookies on racks or on sheets of waxed paper. Then heat the butter in a saucepan over medium heat, stirring occasionally, until it turns a medium shade of brown *(the color of peanut butter)*. Remove the pan from the heat, and add the vanilla *(and the maple flavoring if you use it)*. Blend in the powdered sugar, the cream, and the finely chopped pecans. Stir the frosting with a spoon until it's well mixed, but don't let it cool completely.

Frost the cookies and place a pecan half *(optional)* on top of each cookie for decoration. *(It's like spreading butter; you don't have to spread it all the way out to the edges.)* If your frosting hardens before you're through, scrape it into a microwave-safe bowl and heat it for 30 seconds to 1 minute on high in the microwave to soften it so that you can spread it again.

Let the finished cookies rest on racks or on waxed paper until the frosting has hardened *(at least an hour)*. Then store the cookies in a cookie jar or other closed container.

Yield: Approximately 8 dozen, depending on cookie size.

Note: These cookies, unfrosted, make a delicious "tea" cookie with a light, delicate flavor. The only changes you have to make are to roll the dough balls smaller and press them down with the heel of your impeccably clean hand. Bake them for about 8 minutes or until the edges begin to turn golden. Andrea says they're EXCELLENT with hot chocolate.

Chapter Sixteen

When Hannah got back to Norman's clinic, she still had four minutes to wait. She took out her steno pad and jotted a note to speak to Reggie York at the first opportunity. Rhonda's gossip had almost cost him his job and that was certainly a motive for murder. Then she placed Reggie second on her list of suspects, right after Ken Purvis. Since she'd eliminated both Reverend Knudson and Gil Surma as Rhonda's possible dinner companion, Ken was left holding the bag, or rather, the boxes of osso buco.

The sliding glass door that separated the receptionist desk from the waiting room opened and Norman's smiling face appeared. "Oh, good. You're here. We'll be right out."

Hannah heard Norman giving his patient last-minute instructions, something about a soft toothbrush and a special brand of toothpaste, and then the interior door to the waiting room opened. Norman stood aside to let his patient precede him and Hannah smiled as she saw her baby sister. "Hi, Michelle. I didn't know you were here."

"Hi, Hannah. Dr. Rhodes is wonderful. Just look at what he did for me!"

Michelle smiled and Hannah gasped in shock as she saw two gemstones embedded in her sister's front teeth.

"Isn't it wonderful?" Michelle reached up to tap her front

teeth. "This one's red and this one's blue. Now I'm unique and I'm patriotic, too. It's just perfect for the Fourth of July."

Hannah struggled to make a sound, but she was so flustered, she couldn't say a word. Michelle's front teeth were ruined! She took a deep breath, called upon her vocal cords to do their thing and managed to croak out a response. "How *could* you, Norman?!"

Norman exchanged a glance with Michelle and they both started to laugh. Hannah got up, preparing to storm out of the clinic and banish Norman from her life forever, but Norman grabbed her arm.

"I didn't really do anything, Hannah. They're just temporary."

"What do you mean?"

"The teeth with the gemstones are attached to a retainer that fits in Michelle's mouth. Her regular teeth aren't affected at all."

"Oh," Hannah said, sinking back down in the chair. "Then they're fakes?"

"I prefer to call them a miracle of modern dentistry, but you can call them fakes. Show her, Michelle."

Hannah watched as Michelle loosened the caps and took them out of her mouth. She smiled and Hannah breathed a big sigh of relief as she saw that her sister's teeth were intact. "Thank goodness for that! I really didn't think you'd do anything permanent, Norman."

"Yes, you did. I saw that fire in your eyes. You were all ready to kick me from here to the next county, maybe even out of the state."

"Well . . . maybe," Hannah conceded.

"Don't worry, Hannah." Michelle slipped the retainer into a little plastic box and placed it inside her purse. "I'll tell Mother they're fake before I even take them out of the box."

"Good girl. Mother can't stand another shock. Finding Rhonda's body really took the wind out of her sails."

"I know. She told me." Michelle turned back to Norman. "Are you sure I can't pay you? I've got some money saved."

"Keep your money. We already worked out a payment plan."

"Were they expensive?" Hannah asked. She hadn't bought Michelle's birthday present yet, and she was sure that Andrea would split the cost of the retainer with her.

"They were *very* expensive, but we worked out a deal." Norman winked at her. "Your sister's on my special time-payment plan. For every 'A' she gets, I deduct fifty dollars from her bill. And every 'B' is worth twenty-five. She tells me she's a good student, so I figure that by the end of her junior year she'll own her retainer free and clear."

Michelle shook her head. "It won't take me that long. I plan to get perfect grades next semester and I'll send you a copy."

"Make sure that you do. And stop by the next time you come home so I can see how they're holding up."

"I will."

"How about lunch? Hannah and I are going over to the café."

"Thanks, but I can't. I promised to meet some friends for lunch. 'Bye, Hannah. And thanks again, Dr. Rhodes. These teeth are going to just blow the girls away!"

"More coffee, Hannah?" Rose approached the booth with the pot in her hand.

"No, thanks."

"How about that salad? Do you want me to take it away?"

"Might as well. I already ate all the good stuff."

Rose glanced down at the remains of Hannah's Chicken Caesar and nodded. "I can see that. The only thing left is lettuce. Don't you like romaine?"

"I like it just fine, but I've had enough lettuce to last me for a month. Maybe more than a month."

"You must be on a diet," Rose guessed, sliding into the other side of the booth. "I noticed it when you came in with Norman. I even said to Hal, *Hannah looks thinner.*"

"You did?" Hannah felt her spirits perk up. They'd hit rock bottom about ten minutes ago, when Norman's pager had gone off and he'd told her that he had to go back to the clinic to handle a dental emergency.

"I'm not even going to say what I have for dessert. No sense in tempting you."

"I'm already tempted. The minute I set foot in here, I started dreaming about your coconut cake."

"Then you're in luck." Rose leaned forward and grinned at her.

"No, I'm not. I can't have it."

"I know that. I was just about to say that Mayor Bascomb took the last piece back to his office. Does that make you feel better?"

"Only if I can get over to his office and mug him before he eats it."

Rose laughed and Hannah knew she was pleased. Her coconut cake was legendary, but she never got tired of hearing people rave about it.

"Mind if I sit for a minute?" Rose asked.

"Not at all," Hannah said. Rose was already sitting, so the question was moot.

"Everybody loves that coconut cake. When Irma York was in this morning, she ordered two for Reggie's bachelor party."

Hannah's ears perked up at the mention of Reggie's name. "I didn't know Reggie was getting married."

"Neither did Irma until Friday night. He's been dating this girl in Hawaii. She's a reservations agent for Worldways. When Reggie found out he got promoted on Friday morning, he flew straight to Honolulu to ask her to marry him."

"That's wonderful news," Hannah said and she silently added, *in more ways than one.* If Reggie had flown to Hawaii on Friday, he couldn't have murdered Rhonda.

"Irma's all excited about going to Hawaii for the wedding. They're getting free tickets from Worldways since the kids are both employees." Rose glanced at her watch and slid out of the booth. "Lisa's burger should be ready by now. I told Hal to put on extra pickles and mustard, and he's throwing in an order of fries for you to share. People on diets should have more vegetables. I read that in a magazine."

"Here you go, Lisa." Hannah handed her partner the bag from the café and gestured toward the kitchen. "Go eat. And then find something to do for an hour. And I don't mean baking, either. You need a break."

"Are you sure?"

"I'm sure. You haven't had any time off in a week."

"Okay." Lisa gave her a big grin. "When I'm through with lunch, I'll run down to Kiddie Korner. All the seniors are there and they're helping Tracey's class decorate the float."

"That's nice. Have you seen it yet?"

"I saw it last night. It's going to be spectacular, Hannah. Andrea really had a great idea."

"She did?" Hannah felt her curiosity rise. "What colors are they using?"

Lisa shook her head. "I can't tell you. I've been sworn to secrecy about everything. Andrea and Janice don't want you to know anything about it until the day of the parade."

Hannah gave up. Lisa could keep a secret better than anyone she knew and it was a lost cause.

"Hi, Hannah." Andrea popped through the front door of The Cookie Jar just as Hannah had finished refilling the coffee mugs. "I've got great news. Danielle Watson is back in town. She looks absolutely wonderful, much better than she did when she was married to the coach."

"I'm really glad to hear that." Hannah knew she'd never forget how terrified Danielle had been when everyone in town thought she'd killed her husband. "Is she back for a visit?"

"No, for good."

"Really? I thought you sold her house for her when she went to stay with her mother in Florida."

"I did. Danielle said there were too many unhappy memories and she didn't want to keep it. Now that she's back, she's looking for a condo. Are there any units for sale in your complex? There's nothing listed, but sometimes people try to sell on their own."

Hannah tried to think of any likely candidates. "You could try Mrs. Wozniac. Her sister's husband died and she was talking about moving in with her."

"Thanks. That's a good lead." Andrea pulled out her leather-bound appointment book and jotted down the name. "Anybody else?"

"Not that I know of, but check with Sue Plotnik. Phil's president of the homeowners' association and nobody can put up a For Sale sign without his approval."

"That's another good lead. Have you ever thought of going into real estate, Hannah?"

"Never." Hannah knew she'd better change the subject before Andrea tried to recruit her. "Is Danielle going to look for a job in town?"

"Not exactly. She's opening a dance studio and I found the perfect spot for her. I showed her the loft above Red Owl Grocery and she rented it on the spot. She absolutely fell in love with the high windows and the hardwood floor. And that reminds me, did you know that Red Owl used to be a big grocery chain? The chain went under, but our store petitioned the board of directors and got permission to keep the name."

"That's interesting. When is Danielle going to open for business?"

"In September, right after school starts. She said it wouldn't take much work to convert the loft. All she needs to do is resurface the floor, install floor-to-ceiling mirrors, and decorate it."

"Good for her." Hannah was pleased.

"I'm just glad I thought to show it to her. It's been on the books for over three months and I thought I'd never get it rented. I really hope Danielle can make a good living teaching dance in Lake Eden and it won't end up on the books again."

Hannah clamped her lips shut. She knew that Danielle could afford to run her studio at a loss, but Danielle's finances were her own personal business.

"I just popped in for a minute. I've got a million things to do before Tracey gets out of preschool. You're going to the dinner tonight, aren't you?"

"What dinner?"

"At the lake cottage. We're all invited. I wonder why Mother hasn't called you yet."

Hannah experienced a fleeting moment of relief. Perhaps Delores had forgotten. Then she wouldn't have to put her diet to the test again tonight. But Delores never forgot things like that.

"She'll call," Hannah said, as certain of that as she was of the sun rising in the morning. "She's probably nursing a sore ear from all those phone calls she's been making about Rhonda."

"I'm back." Lisa came in from the kitchen with a smile on her face. "They're having a ball down at Kiddie Korner. Janice really had a great idea involving the seniors. The kids don't seem to notice that some of them have failing memories."

"Kids that age are very accepting. If we could just get them to keep that attitude, it might be a kinder world."

"You said it!" Lisa said with a sigh, but she immediately brightened. "Janice is talking about making this a regular thing. She said that if the seniors could spend one afternoon a week with them, it would be good for both groups."

"I think she's right. Some of Tracey's classmates don't have grandparents in the area. And the seniors have the same problem in reverse."

Lisa moved behind the counter and began to make a fresh urn of coffee. "Did any new orders come in while I was gone?"

"Just one. Donna Lempke's throwing a sweet-sixteen party for her daughter and she wanted to know if we could make ice cream sandwiches."

"Can we?"

"I told her we could. Remember how soft the Pecan Chews got the last time we baked them?"

"I remember. They tasted great, though."

"I think it was the humidity. It's still just as humid, so I thought we'd bake another batch. We'll sandwich vanilla ice cream between them, wrap them individually, and freeze them."

"Let's do half vanilla and half chocolate," Lisa suggested. "Then people can choose."

"That's a good idea. If they turn out really well, we'll add them to the summer cookie menu. In weather like this people might like something frozen."

"Do you want me to start on them now?"

"Not quite yet. I have someone I need to see. Could you man the counter for an hour?"

"Sure. Does it have anything to do with—" Lisa stopped and glanced around her, but the customers at the tables were busy with their own conversations "—with Rhonda's murder?"

"Yes. I'll be back as soon as I can."

"Take as long as you need. I told you I'd run the shop while you investigated. Is there anything I can do while I'm waiting on our customers?"

Hannah thought about that for a moment. "Nothing specific, but keep your eyes open and be the invisible coffee mug filler."

"That actually works," Lisa said with a laugh. "They just go right on talking like I'm not even there."

"I know. That's one great advantage we have. Just listen for anything that has to do with Rhonda and tell me about it when I get back."

"Can you tell me who you're going to see?"

It took Hannah no more than a split second before she decided. Lisa never blabbed what she shouldn't. "Kenneth Purvis."

"Mr. Purvis?" Lisa's eyes widened. "Do you think *he* killed Rhonda?"

The concerned look on Lisa's face made Hannah decide to hedge a bit. "I just think he might have some information that could help me. I'll give him a call and see if he's at home."

"He's probably at the school."

"How do you know that?"

"Mrs. Purvis was in last Wednesday and I heard her tell Gail Hanson that she was driving to Rochester for a family reunion and she wasn't coming back until the third. She said Mr. Purvis had a lot of work to do on the fall schedule and he'd practically be living at the school until she got back."

Hannah smiled. "The invisible coffee mug filler trick worked."

"Actually, it was the invisible cookie boxer trick. She came in to get three dozen Old-Fashioned Sugar Cookies to take to her mother."

Chapter Seventeen

After promising to stop and pick up some vanilla and chocolate ice cream, Hannah went out through the kitchen. Once she reached her cookie truck, she unlocked the doors and lowered the windows to let out the stifling air. On a day like today, when the mercury was flirting with the ninety-degree mark, she'd give her kingdom for air-conditioning that worked.

It didn't take long to drive to the school. Hannah pulled into the Jordan High faculty lot and parked next to Ken Purvis's car. The only other car in the lot belonged to the music teacher and she could hear the marching band practicing on the football field. Hannah walked across the steaming concrete, grimacing at the strains of music she heard. It was good they were practicing. They needed it.

The interior of the school was slightly cooler than the blazing heat outside. Hannah walked down the deserted hallway, smelling the same unique combination of sweeping compound and chalk dust that had welcomed her as a child. She still felt a pang on the first day of school, when freshly washed school busses carried spiffed-up students to the Lake Eden school complex. The first day of the school year had always been her favorite. Dressed in her new school clothes with summer freckles still dancing a line across her nose, she had carried her new book bag into a classroom that had sported completely clean blackboards, long pieces of perfectly formed chalk, and bigger desks.

Hannah stopped at the end of the hall and peeked around the corner at Ken Purvis's office. The door was open and the secretary's desk was unoccupied. She breathed a sigh of relief as she stepped into the outer office, glad that she didn't have to make up an excuse to see Ken privately.

There was the sound of rustling papers from the inner office, Ken's domain. Hannah approached the open door and stopped in her tracks as she smelled a familiar scent. Old Spice. There could be no mistake about it. Her father had used Old Spice aftershave and the scent was as familiar to her as chocolate. Ken Purvis had been Rhonda's boyfriend. Hannah was certain.

Ken glanced up as Hannah knocked on the open door. He looked startled at the interruption, but the moment he saw that it was Hannah, he smiled. "Come in."

Hannah entered the inner sanctum that caused most high school students to tremble in their sneakers and took a chair in front of Ken's desk. She was trying to think of something polite to say to warm Ken up for the ensuing conversation when he beat her to it.

"It's always good to see you, Hannah. You're not planning to enroll for the fall semester, are you?"

Hannah laughed at the standard principal's joke. "No, I've got something else on my mind."

"What can I do for you?" Ken removed his reading glasses and placed them upside down, bows crossed, on the pile of papers he'd been reading.

Hannah hesitated. She wanted to handle this tactfully, but she couldn't think of a way to do it. "Why did you bring two takeout dinners to Rhonda Scharf at the Voelker place on Friday night?"

All the color in Ken's face fled and so did his smile. "How do you know *that?*"

"I know."

"Does anybody else know?"

"Not yet. Maybe they won't have to if you're honest with me."

Ken sighed and it was like letting all the air out of a basket-ball. Hannah could almost see him deflate before her eyes. "What you're thinking is right, Hannah. I'm not proud of it, but I was involved with Rhonda."

"Does that *involved* mean what I think it means?"

"Yes. It's entirely my fault that it went this far and I take full responsibility. I just hope that Kathy won't have to find out about it."

Hannah could understand his concern. Ken's wife had a fiery temper and she wouldn't take the news of her husband's infidelity lightly. "This is just between you and me right now. Tell me how it started."

"I was having troubles at home with Kathy." Ken sighed deeply. "You don't need to know about that, do you?"

"No."

"Well . . . I wanted to ease the situation a bit and I went to the drugstore to buy a bottle of perfume as a peace offering."

Hannah decided to cut to the chase. She knew about Rhonda's bag of tricks. "And Rhonda came on to you?"

"That's exactly what happened. It was right after she in-herited her great-aunt's place. She said she really wanted to go out and look at it, but she needed the help of a big strong man. And . . ."

"Never mind, I get the picture," Hannah cut him off. "And you went out there for another . . . uh . . . rendezvous with Rhonda on Friday night?"

Ken shook his head. "Not exactly. Kathy and I worked out our problems. When she left on Wednesday to go to her fam-ily reunion, I decided the time was right to break it off with Rhonda."

"Because Rhonda would have two weeks to get over being mad at you before she came back from her vacation?"

"That was a factor," Ken admitted. "I was trying to make it easier on everybody involved."

"Including you?"

"Including me."

Hannah gave Ken a long hard look, but he appeared completely sincere. "And you decided to bring Rhonda dinner before you broke the bad news to her?"

"It sounds a little strange now, but that's exactly right. I called and asked to see her, but she said she had to go out to her great-aunt's place to pick up some things. I told her that was fine, that I'd take her out there and then I'd go get us some dinner. She thought that was fine and she offered to bring dessert."

Hannah was sure that Ken was telling the truth, but that didn't mean that he hadn't killed Rhonda. She felt slightly uncomfortable for a moment, wondering if she should have brought some kind of weapon, but she quickly dismissed that concern. Ken wasn't a large man and Mike had taught her some good self-defense moves. "Tell me exactly what happened that night and don't leave anything out."

"All right," Ken agreed, but he looked very uncomfortable. "Just let me take a pill first."

Hannah watched as he pulled out his center desk drawer and took out a prescription pill bottle. "What are you taking?"

"Something Doc Knight prescribed for my bursitis. He said it would work, but it hasn't had much effect so far." Ken shook out a pill and downed it with a sip of water from the glass that was sitting on his desk. "You want to hear everything?"

"Yes."

"I had an appointment with Doc Knight at five on Friday afternoon. After that, I went straight over to Rhonda's apartment and drove her out to her great-aunt's place."

"What time was that?"

"About six."

Hannah jotted down the time in her notebook. "What happened when you got there?"

"I dropped her off and then I went to pick up our dinners. I figured I'd tell her after we ate."

"The takeout was from Alfredo's Ristorante?"

"Yes. I ordered in advance. They have osso buco on Friday nights and Rhonda said she liked it."

"Where was Rhonda when you got back?"

"In the kitchen. She was taking a break, waiting for me to get back. We sat down at the table and I opened the wine. I brought a really good bottle of Chianti, because I thought it might ease the situation."

"Right." Hannah tried not to sound too sarcastic. Ken was a fool if he thought a bad situation would improve with alcohol.

"I sat down to dinner but I was so nervous, I couldn't eat much. I just had the garnish off the osso buco and that was it. Rhonda noticed that I wasn't eating and she asked me if something was wrong. That's when I told her."

"And was her reaction as bad as you thought it would be?"

"It was worse. She got angry and accused me of treating her like a . . ." Ken stopped speaking and cleared his throat. "Do you really need to know what she said?"

"No. What happened next?"

Ken reached for his glass of water and took a sip. "She started screaming at me and calling me names. They were really ugly names, if you get my drift."

"I do. Go on."

"By this time I'd taken just about all I could take. I knew there was nothing I could say to calm Rhonda down, so . . . I left."

Hannah pulled out her notebook. "What time was that?"

"Around seven-thirty."

"Where did you go?"

"I drove home and called Kathy at her mother's house."

Hannah groaned. "Did you tell Kathy what had happened with Rhonda?"

"Of course not. I realize I was irresponsible and stupid when I started this whole thing with Rhonda, but I've never harbored a death wish."

Hannah had to grin at that. "What *did* you tell Kathy?"

"Just that I'd had a rough day and I needed to hear her voice. We talked for quite a while about the reunion and the cousins she hadn't seen since she was little. When I finally hung up, I felt a lot better. I also felt hungry, because I skipped lunch and all I'd eaten were the sliced olives on top of my dinner. There wasn't much to eat in the house, so I decided to go out and get a hamburger or something. I went back out to my car and that's when I realized that I'd left Rhonda at the Voelker place with no way back to town."

"I was wondering when you'd get to that. So you drove back out?"

"Yes. I didn't want to, but I couldn't just leave her there. It was too far to walk back to town."

"What time did you get back there?" Hannah held her pen at the ready. The time frame would be crucial.

"At nine-thirty or so. The lights were on so I figured that Rhonda was still there. I sat there in the car for a minute or two. I really didn't want to go in and start fighting with her again. But I'd driven out there to give her a ride and I figured I might as well do it."

Hannah flipped back to the page where she'd listed Rhonda's time of death. If Doc Knight was right, and he usually was, Rhonda had been dead and cooling off in the basement when Ken had knocked on the door. "Were there any other cars in the driveway when you drove up?"

"No. I wouldn't have stopped if there'd been another car. Whoever it was could have given Rhonda a ride."

"What happened when you went in?"

"I didn't go in, not right away. I knocked on the door and waited for her to answer. And when she didn't, I knocked again. Then I opened the door and went inside."

"What's the first thing you did when you stepped inside?"

"I called out for Rhonda. It's not a big place and I knew she could hear me. When she still didn't answer, I got nervous. I thought maybe she'd had an accident, or something like that. I went from room to room, looking for her, but she wasn't anywhere in the house. I even went out in the backyard to search for her."

"What made you think that Rhonda might have been out there?"

"The takeout boxes were gone and the back door was standing open. I figured she'd gone out with the garbage and . . ." Ken stopped talking and swallowed hard. "Do you think Rhonda's killer went out that way?"

"It's possible."

Ken shivered. "I guess I could have scared him away. I never thought about that. If he was still in the basement when I drove up, he could have run out the back way."

Hannah nodded as another piece of the puzzle clicked into place. She'd discussed the grave with Mike. Both of them thought that the killer had intended to fully bury Rhonda, but someone or something had frightened him away before he could finish his grisly task. Ken Purvis could be that someone. If Rhonda's killer had been in the basement when Ken's car drove up, he would have had plenty of time to flee out the back door.

"Maybe the killer was still there when I went to the backyard," Ken speculated, his voice shaking slightly. "I didn't hear anything, but it was dark and he could have been hiding anywhere."

Hannah figured she'd better reassure Ken. His face had turned a sickly shade of gray and drops of nervous perspiration were beading on his forehead. "My guess is that he was long gone. Let's get back to what happened. After you checked the backyard, you . . . ?"

"I came back in and shut the back door. I figured she could come back in after I left."

"Think back to how the kitchen looked. Was the basement door open?"

Ken frowned in an attempt to remember. "It must have been closed. If it had been open, I would have gone down there."

"So you never considered that Rhonda might be in the basement?"

"It never even occurred to me," Ken said, sighing deeply. "I really wish I'd thought to check. If I'd found her, I could have gone for help, or taken her to the hospital myself."

"Forget it, Ken. Doc Knight said Rhonda died instantly. Even if you'd found her, you couldn't have saved her life."

"Thanks for telling me, Hannah." Ken reached for his glass and took another sip of water. "That makes me feel a little better. It's still awful, but at least I know there was nothing I could have done to help her."

"What did you think when you searched the house and you couldn't find Rhonda?" Hannah asked.

"I figured one of her friends had seen the lights, dropped by to see her, and given her a lift home. Or maybe she'd walked out to the road and flagged someone down. Those were the only explanations I could think of."

"So you didn't think there was anything wrong when Rhonda wasn't there at the house?"

"Not really. I did think it was a little odd that she'd left on the lights, but Rhonda tended to storm off when she was mad and I thought she'd just forgotten to turn them off. It was wasting electricity since there was no one there, and—" Ken's voice trailed off and he took another sip of water "—I turned them off and left. I didn't know about Rhonda then."

"I understand. Where did you go after you left the Voelker place?"

"I drove to the Quick Stop to get some gas, and then I went to the Corner Tavern for a burger and fries."

Hannah closed her steno pad, shoved it back into her purse, and got to her feet. "That's all I need for now. Thanks for being honest with me, Ken."

"Wait a second." A look of panic crossed Ken's face. "You don't think that *I* killed Rhonda, do you?"

"Of course I don't. And there's a way you can prove it right now if you want me to clear you completely."

"I do! What do you need? Telephone records so you can prove I went home to call Kathy? My gas receipt from the Quick Stop?"

"Those wouldn't do it, but your bursitis will."

"It will? How?"

"Just call Doc Knight and have him verify that your bursitis was acting up on Friday."

"I can do that. I'll call him right now." Ken reached for the phone and punched in a series of numbers.

While Ken explained what he needed to Doc Knight, Hannah glanced around his inner sanctum. There was an array of Jordan High graduation class photos that ran the length of three walls, one for every year since the school had been built. She found hers and grimaced slightly as she saw her younger face. No doubt the photographer had told them to say "cheese" because she was smiling so widely, she had chipmunk cheeks.

"Here, Hannah," Ken said, handing her the phone. "I told Doc Knight to give you any information you needed."

Hannah took the phone and leaned across the desk, so the cord wouldn't stretch out too much. "Hi, Doc."

"Hello, Hannah. Ken says you need to know about his bursitis. When I saw him last Friday, it was in an acute stage and his range of motion was severely limited."

"How limited?"

"He couldn't raise his right arm any higher than his waist and his left arm was even worse. You're working on Rhonda's murder?"

"That's right."

"You should have asked me before you put Ken through the wringer. Even if he'd been mad as blazes, there's no way he could have stabbed Rhonda. She was standing with her back turned to her assailant at the time and they're approximately the same height."

"Would it work if she was standing in the hole?"

"No. The angle would be wrong. Take him off your list, Hannah. Ken's not your man."

"I'm glad to hear it. Thanks, Doc. You've been a big help."

Hannah hung up and turned to smile at Ken. "Okay. Doc Knight says you couldn't have done it. You're in the clear."

"Then nobody has to hear about my . . . uh . . . relationship with Rhonda?"

"I don't know what you're talking about," Hannah said as she headed for the door. "I was just here to check some old school records that you were kind enough to find for me."

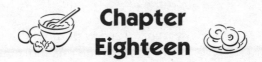

Chapter
Eighteen

Business was brisk when Hannah got back to The Cookie
Jar. After she had stashed her vanilla and chocolate ice
cream in the freezer, she managed a brief private word with
Lisa. She said nothing to tarnish the image of Lisa's former
principal and she certainly didn't mention his liaison with
Rhonda. She just said that she'd needed to check some old
school records and that Ken had been very helpful.

It didn't take long to mix up a batch of Pecan Chews and
in less than an hour they were baked and cooling on the
racks. Hannah was about to soften the ice cream to make the
sandwiches when Freddy Sawyer knocked on the back door.

"Come in, Freddy," Hannah invited. "Have a cookie or
two."

"Thanks, Hannah. I love your cookies. They're almost as
good as the ones my mom used to bake."

Hannah took that as a compliment. As she remembered,
Mrs. Sawyer had made very good cookies. She poured a glass
of milk for Freddy, set two cookies on a napkin for him, and
waited until he had finished munching.

"I wish I knew how to bake," Freddy said, wiping his
mouth with the napkin. "Miss Cox promised to teach me,
but I'm too busy helping Jed right now. We're making real
good money. Did you know that?"

"I know."

"Did you see my new watch?" Freddy pointed down at the watch on his wrist. "Jed bought it for me this morning and it cost almost ten dollars. It was in the window and the girl climbed in to get it for me. She said it was a sports watch. I don't play sports, but that's okay, isn't it?"

"That's fine. Lots of people who don't play sports wear sports watches."

"Why is that?"

Hannah shrugged. She'd never really thought about that before. "I'm not sure, but I think it's because they're more rugged."

"I like that answer." Freddy smiled widely. "Jed's always after me to be more rugged. He thinks I should stand up for myself if somebody teases me, and he's even teaching me to fight."

Hannah wasn't sure she liked that idea. She was sure that Freddy could defend himself in a pinch quite well enough already. But it was a chance to ask a few questions about Freddy's cousin. "Does Jed know how to fight?"

"You betcha! Jed told me he once licked a guy twice his size. Put him right in the hospital. I don't understand how being licked could put you in the hospital, though. Mrs. Cox's dogs lick me all the time and it doesn't hurt me any."

"That's true, but what I think Jed means is . . ." Hannah paused, trying to think of a way to explain slang usage to Freddy.

"Oh, gosh! I forgot the time!" Freddy glanced down at his new watch and sighed. "I'd like to stay and talk to you more, but I have to meet Jed at the café in fifteen minutes."

Hannah remembered what Lisa had told her about Janice Cox teaching Freddy to tell time. It seemed he had the concept down pat. "That watch is going to come in really handy for you, Freddy."

"I know. I was careful to pick out the one with hands instead of just numbers. That's the one I learned how to do."

Freddy stood up and headed for the door, but Hannah

stopped him. "Was there something you needed, Freddy? Or did you just come in to say hello?"

"Oh, boy! I guess Jed is right and I really *am* a dunce!" Freddy thunked his forehead with the heel of his head. "It just went clean out of my head, Hannah. I wanted you to save something for me. Will you?"

"Sure," Hannah said, guessing that it was a rock or some little object Freddy had come across in his handyman work.

"I've got it right here. Be real careful of it. It's precious." Freddy pulled a battered shoebox out of his backpack and handed it to Hannah.

Hannah accepted the box gingerly. It was tied up with twine and it didn't look too clean. "It's not alive, is it?"

"No." Freddy gave a little laugh. "And it's not a sandwich, either. It won't spoil."

"Good. Can you tell me what it is?"

"It's something Jed lost. I found it in the trash right before the garbage truck came. I'm going to shine it all up and give it to him for a present. Boy, will he be surprised!"

"That's nice," Hannah said, wondering if Jed would appreciate getting something he'd thrown away as a present. "Where do you want me to keep it?"

Freddy glanced around and then he pointed to the walk-in cooler. "How about in there? Nobody will find it there."

"Okay. Come with me." Hannah carried the box to the cooler and opened the door. She stepped in and Freddy followed her inside. "I'll put it right here, on the shelf behind the milk cartons."

Freddy nodded, watching while Hannah removed the cartons and slipped the shoebox in the back. "That's real good, Hannah. Nobody'll see it there."

"Just tell me when you want it back and I'll get it for you," Hannah said, leading Freddy to the door.

"Okay. Thanks, Hannah. Good friends are like sunshine. A day is gloomy without them." Hannah turned to give Freddy a quizzical look and he grinned. "Mom used to say that. She had a lot of friends and she said they were my friends, too."

Hannah had just finished mixing up the next day's cookies and stashing them in the cooler when Lisa came into the kitchen waving a ten-dollar bill.

"Look at this, Hannah. There's something funny about it."

"Funny ha-ha, or funny peculiar?" Hannah asked, repeating the words of Mrs. Carlson, her third-grade teacher.

"Funny peculiar. You must have had Mrs. Carlson, too." Lisa gave a little laugh. "Just look at it, Hannah. I've never seen an old one that's this new before."

Hannah walked over to take a look and she didn't point out the inconsistency in Lisa's statement. The issue date was nineteen seventy-four, but the old-style bill was crisp and clean, and it looked as if it had just been minted. "That *is* strange."

"Do you think it's counterfeit?"

"It could be. We'd better ask at the bank." Hannah glanced up at the clock on the kitchen wall. It was past three and the bank would be closed, but Doug Greerson, the president of First National Mercantile, stayed in his office until five. "I'll run over and check with Doug. Do you have any idea who gave it to you?"

Lisa looked a little worried. "I think it was your sister."

"Andrea?"

"No, Michelle. She stopped by while you were having lunch with Norman and bought a half-dozen Short Stack Cookies to take to her friend's house. The only reason I remember was that we were running short on fives and I had to give her all one-dollar bills in change."

Hannah frowned as she looked down at the bill. "If Michelle had it, it could have come from the Twin Cities area. I'm going out to the cottage tonight to have dinner with the family. If Doug says it's counterfeit, I'll ask Michelle if she remembers where she got it."

Doug Greerson looked surprised to see Hannah standing outside the front door of the bank and holding up a ten-dollar bill. He motioned for her to wait a moment, then walked back to a keypad that was partially hidden from her view. After he'd entered some numbers, he came back to the door and unlocked it, a lengthy procedure that involved several complicated locks.

"Thanks, Doug." Hannah stepped in, waving the bill. "This came into the shop this afternoon. Lisa and I both think it looks funny peculiar."

Doug chuckled. "Mrs. Carlson, third grade. I'll never forget her for that. Go on back to my office and make yourself comfortable. I'll be there as soon as I reset the alarm. There's some coffee in the pot. It's a combination of Columbian, Guatemalan, Brazilian, and Sumatran."

"Sounds good."

"It is. It's darkly roasted, heavy-bodied, and it has a smooth finish."

"I'll have to taste that," Hannah said with a grin as she walked back to Doug's office. He'd discovered gourmet coffees at Christmas when his wife, Diana, had given him a sample pack of beans and an electric coffee grinder.

Doug's coffeepot was spotless, a sharp contrast to the one in Jon Walker's office. Hannah had just poured herself a cup and taken one of the chairs in front of the desk when Doug came in.

"So what do you think of the coffee?" he asked.

Hannah took a sip and smiled. "It's really good."

"Just wait until next week. I ordered a shipment of Blue Mountain from Zabar's in New York. It's supposed to be the finest coffee in the world."

"It'd have to go some to beat this," Hannah declared and took another sip. "Take a look at this bill, Doug."

Doug took the bill Hannah handed him, switched on his halogen desk lamp, and took what looked like a jeweler's loupe from his desk drawer. He examined the bill for several moments and then he shook his head. "It's not counterfeit."

"But look at the date. It says nineteen seventy-four. Don't you think it's odd that it looks so new?"

"Not really. Somebody could have kept it in a safe deposit box or under a mattress all these years. And sometimes people just like to save money in mint condition."

"You mean collectors?"

"There's nothing collectible about this bill, but it could have been some sort of a keepsake, framed and put under glass. When people give money as a gift, they usually come in to get new bills."

Hannah nodded and reached out to take back her bill.

"What's the matter?" Doug asked her. "You look a little disappointed."

"Lisa and I thought maybe we'd stumbled onto a counterfeiting ring. It would have been interesting."

Doug gave a small, humorless laugh. "I don't think you want to get involved with something like that. If that bill were counterfeit, you'd have federal agents breathing down your neck in two seconds flat."

"New customers," Hannah said with a grin, slipping the bill inside her purse and getting up from her chair. "Thanks, Doug. I guess we'll never know the story behind that new-old bill. I thought it might be contraband and someone had sat on it for years, afraid to spend it before now."

"Wait a second, Hannah. You might have something there. Let me check the serial number."

"What will that tell you?"

"When a bank gets new bills, they come in packaged by denomination and serial number. If this one was stolen in a bank robbery and they took packaged bills from the safe, the bank would have reported the serial numbers to the authorities."

"And you can check that?"

"Of course. The computer's in the middle of an automatic backup right now, but I've got hard copy of the loot list."

"Loot list?"

"That's what we call it. The official title is about twenty words long. It's a cross-reference index by year and serial number."

"And it lists money from bank robberies?"

"It lists some of it. If a robber comes in and empties the cash drawer, there's no record of the serial numbers. But if he takes money from the safe, there is. And it's not just from bank robberies. It's also a list of marked money."

"Like the cops give out when they're trying to track down a ring of scam artists?"

"That's right. Hold on a second and I'll get the printout."

Hannah poured herself more coffee while Doug was gone. It was so good, she even considered installing a gourmet coffee bar in The Cookie Jar, but she didn't think that would go over well in Lake Eden. New fads took years to catch on and the residents in Lake Eden would balk at paying three or four dollars of their hard-earned cash for a cup of designer coffee.

"I've got it," Doug said, coming in the door with a large three-ring notebook. "Read off that serial number and I'll see if it's in here."

Hannah gave him the serial number and Doug flipped the pages to the proper section. He ran his fingers down a long line of numbers and then he looked up with an excited expression. "I knew it was a long shot, but it's in here. Your ten-dollar bill was part of the cash that was stolen from the Redwing City Bank in June of nineteen seventy-four."

"Stolen money?"

"That's right. Keep your eye out for more and tell Lisa to do the same. I'll copy this page and give it to Sheriff Grant. He can have his deputies distribute it to every merchant in town, and we might be able to catch ourselves a bank robber.

Think back, Hannah. Do you have any idea who gave you this bill?"

Hannah assumed the most innocent expression she could muster as she shook her head. She remembered what Doug had said about federal agents breathing down her neck, and she wasn't about to involve her baby sister in a bank robbery investigation until she'd had the chance to talk to her first.

Chapter Nineteen

Of course Delores had called to invite her to the family party. Once Hannah had fed Moishe, she changed into a pair of old jeans that had become threadbare through frequent washings and were perfect for summer. The waist felt a bit loose and that made her wonder just how many pounds she'd lost.

Hannah glanced in the mirror as she slipped into a cotton pullover sweater with short sleeves. It was in one of her favorite colors, a muted teal that looked good with her red hair. She'd worn it for good until she'd dripped mustard on the front at the volunteer fire department's picnic last year. The mustard had come out, but the stain remover she'd used had lightened the material. Rather than relegate the sweater to the ragbag, she'd dabbed the stain remover on in a random pattern all over the material, washed it again, and now she had several dozen dime-sized circles of light teal dancing down the front and back of her new "designer" sweater.

It didn't look half bad, Hannah thought, glancing in the mirror. She skinned her hair back into a ponytail, a style she knew was probably too young for her, but she planned to drive with her windows open and she could ditch the elastic band once she got to the lake. Then she went back to the kitchen to refill Moishe's bowl for the final time, slung her purse over her shoulder, and hurried down to her truck to drive to Eden Lake.

Twenty minutes later, Hannah found a parking place at the side of the dirt road that ran past the lake cottage that had been in the Swensen family for the past thirty years. It had belonged to her grandparents, who had rented it out every summer for the extra income. When her father had inherited it, he'd done the same. As a child, Hannah had spent two weekends at the cottage every year. One had been at the beginning of May when it was still too cold to set foot in the lake. They'd spent that weekend getting the cabin spruced up and ready for the summer rental season. Hannah's second summer weekend had been at the tail end of August right after dog days, when the surface of Eden Lake had been covered with algae so thick, Hannah hadn't been allowed to swim. That time had been spent winterizing the cottage, shutting off the water and bleeding the pipes, covering the screens with heavy plastic to protect them from the icy winter winds, and packing up the dishes and silverware to store for the next summer.

Hannah sighed as she thought back to her childhood. She'd always dreamed of staying at the cottage during the height of the tourist season, when the tiny grocery store was stocked with a dozen flavors of Popsicles, and there would be other kids from fascinating places like Iowa and Wisconsin to swim with. Now she was here, at the height of the season, and she didn't even own a swimsuit. And she couldn't have any Popsicles because she was on a diet. Sometimes life just wasn't fair.

Hannah got out of her truck and walked past Andrea's Volvo. Her sister and niece were here early. There was Norman's car, too. And Carrie's. Delores must have invited the whole extended family. That was good. With more people here, it would be easier for her to pull Michelle off in a corner and ask her about the ten-dollar bill.

As she approached the screen door of the cottage, Hannah sniffed the air. She expected to catch a whiff of Hawaiian Pot Roast, or E-Z Lasagna, her mother's favorite company dishes. Hannah wasn't particularly fond of either one, but the fact that she couldn't eat them made them sound delicious. All she could have was salad and Delores had promised she'd have plenty of that.

Norman walked over to greet her the moment she walked in the door. At first Hannah was puzzled by the relieved expression on his face until she realized that he'd been talking to Delores. No doubt her mother had been asking him all sorts of personal questions about why he was building such a big house and if he had any plans for the future. "Mother's been giving you the third degree?" she asked.

"You could say that."

"Then it looks like I got here just in time."

"In more ways than one," Norman told her with a smile. "Bill and Mike went to pick up the pizza and they should be back any minute."

"Did you say they were bringing *pizza?*"

"Yes, and your mother ordered a low-cal one for you."

Hannah started to frown. "That's got be a contradiction in terms. How could a pizza be low-cal?"

"Maybe they put on low-fat cheese?"

"That wouldn't do it. There's still all that wonderful crust, and the spicy sauce, and pepperoni, and sausage, and olives, and anchovies, and . . . ."

"Hold it," Norman said, handing her his handkerchief. "You're drooling."

Hannah took it and made a show of wiping her face even though she knew he was teasing. "Pizza is one of my very favorite things and just one bite would blow my diet."

"Don't you think you've lost enough weight? You're looking positively skinny."

"I am?" Hannah stared up at him with a look that was at least a first cousin to adoration.

"I really didn't think you needed to lose any weight in the first place."

"You didn't?" If they'd been alone, Hannah would have grabbed him and given him a big kiss. As it was, she felt grateful tears well up in her eyes and she covered her embarrassment at being so emotional with an attempt at humor. "How's your eyesight?"

"Twenty-twenty . . . as long as I wear my glasses."

"Glasses? But you're not wearing any . . ." Hannah stopped and gave him a stern look. "You're kidding, right?"

"Not entirely. I do need to wear glasses, but I switched to contacts a couple of years ago."

"Here comes dinner!" Delores called out from her post at the window. "Bill and Mike just drove up. Who wants to run out and help them carry the pizzas in?"

"I do." Hannah turned on her heel and headed for the door. If she couldn't eat the pizza, at least she could get in a couple of good sniffs while she carried it in to the table.

After dinner, Hannah carried in the box of assorted cookies she'd brought and Delores got out the rest of the dessert. Her mother's contribution was a huge tub of ice cream with a whole array of jarred toppings from the Red Owl. Hannah took one look at the fudge sauce and wished she had a full complement of talismans to ward off evil. Since she had nothing, not even a necklace of garlic to protect her, she grabbed Michelle while everyone else was munching cookies and building sundaes.

"Will you walk out on the dock with me?" Hannah asked her. "We need to talk."

"Sure. I ate so much of that low-cal pizza, I don't have any room left for dessert."

"What was on it anyway?" Hannah was curious. Since there had been a big tub of salad, she'd filled up on that.

"Skim-milk mozzarella with sun-dried tomatoes, shredded chicken breast, and asparagus tips. The crust was low-cal too because it was thinner than their regular crust."

"So you had to eat twice as much to fill up?"

Michelle started to grin. "You're right. I usually eat two pieces and tonight I ate four."

Just as Hannah and Michelle were about to go out the door, Andrea saw them and rushed up. "Do you want some company? I'm passing on dessert, too."

"Come on then," Hannah told her. "We're going out to sit on the dock."

"Oh, good. I'm going to dangle my feet in the water. I ran all over town today and my ankles are swelling."

"You two go ahead," Hannah said. "I'll get the mosquito repellent and meet you down there. They're really bad this time of night and they'll eat us alive."

Hannah sprayed on her repellent as she walked down the steps to the dock. Once she got there, she tossed the spray bottle to Michelle and handed the lotion to Andrea. "I remembered what you said about aerosols, so I brought you some lotion."

"Thanks, Hannah." Andrea slapped at a mosquito that had already discovered her arm. "Doc Knight's got a real thing about it while I'm pregnant. I can't use hair spray, or perfume, or even cooking spray."

Hannah laughed. "I don't think there's much danger with the cooking spray."

"That's true," Andrea conceded good-naturedly. "Bill uses it for his eggs in the morning, but he always waits until I leave the kitchen."

"I thought you cooked breakfast for him." Michelle looked surprised.

"I used to, the first year we were married. I made scrambled eggs every morning, but Bill decided I burned too many frying pans. Now he makes his eggs and I do the toast."

Hannah felt like asking how much toast Andrea had managed to burn, but she curbed the question and turned to Michelle. "You gave Lisa a ten-dollar bill today, didn't you?"

"Yes. I stopped by to pick up some cookies for Carly while you were out to lunch."

"Do you have any idea where you got that bill?"

"I'm not sure." Michelle thought for a moment and then she shook her head. "I really don't remember. Why do you need to know?"

"It turns out it was stolen from a bank. Doug Greerson looked it up on a list the banks get."

Andrea looked surprised. "Bill didn't say anything about it. Does Sheriff Grant know?"

"Doug said he'd alert him." Hannah turned back to Michelle. "That's why it's so important to know when and where you got it. They want to track it back to the source."

"I'm pretty sure I didn't bring it with me. When I got to the bus station in Minneapolis, I had four twenties I got from the bank machine, and a couple of ones."

"How about your bus ticket?" Andrea asked. "Did you pay for that in cash?"

"Yes. I wish I could remember how much it was. I think it was almost twenty dollars, so I wouldn't have gotten a ten back in change."

Andrea took out her cell phone and punched in a number. "Did you buy a round-trip, or a one-way?"

"Round-trip."

Hannah and Michelle listened to the one-sided conversation as Andrea asked about the ticket. She thanked the person on the other end of the line, hung up, and turned back to them. "It didn't come from the bus station. A round-trip ticket to Lake Eden is eighteen dollars and change."

"Then I got it right here in town. But I didn't buy anything. I'm sure I didn't. The only store I went into was . . ."

"Where?" Hannah zeroed in when her sister hesitated.

"The drugstore. I needed two gemstones so I ran to the drugstore and bought a little package of colored rhinestones."

"Rhinestones?" Andrea made a face. "They're so tacky. You should have called me if you wanted gemstones. They have some very nice synthetic stones that aren't expensive. We could have gone out to the mall and . . ."

"Relax, Andrea," Hannah interrupted. "Michelle didn't need good stones. They were just for her teeth."

"Her *teeth?*"

"Her fake teeth. She'll explain later." Hannah turned back to Michelle. "How much were the rhinestones?"

"Less than ten dollars. And I must have paid with a twenty. That means I would have gotten a ten and some coins back in change."

"Makes sense," Hannah said, considering the possibilities. She wasn't sure how it all tied in, but Rhonda had worked at the drugstore. Maybe the fact that some of the stolen money had ended up there didn't have anything to do with Rhonda's murder, but it was certainly interesting.

"Are you thinking what I'm thinking?" Andrea turned to her.

"Yes," Hannah said quickly. "We need to find out more about that old bank robbery."

"Hello down there!"

All three sisters turned to see Norman standing at the top of the steps that led to the dock.

"Is it okay if I come down? Or is this a sisterly bonding moment?"

"We're already bonded," Hannah said with a laugh.

"That happened the first time Mother tried to make us eat canned peas. Come on."

Once Norman had joined them on the dock, Hannah tossed him the mosquito repellent. "You'd better use this. The mosquitoes are thick tonight."

"Thanks, but I don't need it."

"What do you mean, you don't need it? They're bloodthirsty. I thought I was going to need a transfusion before I could get the cap off the bottle."

"Mosquitoes don't bite me."

"What?!"

"It's true," Norman said and he looked perfectly sincere. "I don't know why, but mosquitoes just leave me alone."

"Do you take some kind of vitamin supplement?" Michelle asked.

"No."

"How about soap?" Andrea suggested. "Do you use a special kind?"

"Just whatever's on sale at CostMart."

Hannah began to frown. As far as she knew, mosquitoes bit everyone. They certainly regarded her as a five-course dinner, complete with dessert and beverage. Norman must be putting them on and she'd call his bluff. "I don't believe you, Norman. Roll up your sleeve and stick out your arm. I want to see this for myself."

"Okay," Norman said agreeably, rolling up his sleeve.

All three sisters watched as a small cloud of mosquitoes descended, each of them emitting a high-pitched, irritating whine. One of them almost landed on Norman's bare arm, but it veered away at the last minute.

"See?" Norman grinned. "They just don't like me."

Hannah gave up in defeat. It was true. Mosquitoes didn't like Norman. But could she love someone the mosquitoes didn't like? She'd have to think about that later. Right now, they still had the problem of Michelle's ten-dollar bill to solve.

"I guess I'd better bring you up to date," Hannah told him. "Michelle got a ten-dollar bill today and we found out it was part of the loot from a bank robbery."

Norman listened while Hannah explained. "And you need to find out more about that old bank robbery?" he asked.

"That's right."

"And it happened in Redwing in nineteen seventy-four?"

"That's what Doug Greerson told me."

"Then it's easy. It must have been a lead story in the local newspapers at the time. I'll check to see if any of them have archives on-line."

"You can do that?" Hannah was impressed. Her computer skills were limited.

"No problem. I've got my laptop in the car. Do you want me to get on-line right now?"

"Not now." Hannah shook her head. "I want to keep this private."

"Private, as in not telling Bill or Mike?"

"That's right. I'm already involved in investigating Rhonda's murder and they're okay with that. But if they find out that Michelle is the one who had that ten-dollar bill, they'll have to tell the Feds. Michelle doesn't need that. They'll ask her a million useless questions and ruin her vacation."

"You've got a point. How about if I come over to your condo with my laptop when the party breaks up?"

"That'd be great." Hannah looked up as she heard footsteps. Mike and Bill were coming down the stairs.

Bill was the first on the dock and he walked over to Andrea. "We've got to take off, honey. We just got word that the autopsy report's in and we need to go over some things with Doc. Tracey wants to know if it's okay if she stays out here overnight. Delores and Carrie promised to play a board game with her."

"Tell her it's fine. She loves to stay overnight with Grandma."

"That'll work out perfectly," Michelle said. "Tracey can have my bed and then Mother won't be alone."

Hannah turned to her youngest sister in surprise. "Alone? Where are *you* going?"

"I've got a date."

"Don't let him take you to any isolated spots," Mike jumped into the conversation. "We still haven't caught Rhonda's killer."

Michelle laughed. "You don't have to worry about me. I'll be perfectly safe."

"Are you sure?" Mike still looked concerned.

"I'm positive. I'm going out with Lonnie Murphy."

Hannah stifled a laugh. That ought to take the wind out of Mike's sails. Lonnie was the newest hire at the Winnetka County Sheriff's Department and Mike liked him. Lonnie's older brother, Rick, had been with the department for three years, and Mike had told Hannah that eventually the two Murphy brothers might make a good detective team.

"You said Tracey could have your bed," Mike reminded Michelle. "Are you planning to stay out all night?"

"Of course not, but Lonnie and I went to high school together and we've got a lot of catching up to do. It could be a late night. I don't want to wake Mother when I come in, so I was going to ask Hannah if I could stay with her."

"Of course," Hannah agreed quickly, before Mike could think about giving any other dating advice.

"I don't like leaving you alone, honey." Bill sat down and slipped his arm around Andrea's shoulders.

"I won't be alone. I'll drive over to Hannah's. When you're through working, you can get Mike to drop you off there and we'll go home in my car."

"It could be three or four hours. We're meeting with Doc and then we have to catch up on the paperwork."

Andrea reached up to pat Bill's chest. "Don't worry about me, honey. If I get tired, I can sack out on Hannah's couch."

Hannah wasn't sure how she felt as she listened to this tender exchange. On the one hand, it was nice to have someone who was concerned about you. But on the other hand, you couldn't ever feel truly independent. Marriage was a trade-off. You gave up some things and you gained others. Since Hannah knew she'd balk at the trade-off aspect, it must mean that she wasn't ready for that walk down the aisle, at least not quite yet.

Hannah reached out for Moishe, who seemed fascinated with Norman's computer and was sitting on the coffee table, pawing at the keyboard. "Guard your computer, Norman. I'll carry him in the kitchen and fill his food bowl. Then he might leave you alone."

"He's okay. He's just curious." Norman scooped Moishe up and settled him down on his lap.

"He shouldn't be that close to your computer," Andrea advised, waving away some orange and white cat hairs that were floating around in the air. "He's shedding."

"That's what cats do. It's not his fault." Norman scratched Moishe behind the ears with one hand and typed with the other. "I'll blow out the keyboard with compressed air when I get home."

"Are there any more leftover cookies, Hannah?" Andrea picked up an empty bag and crumpled it.

"No, but I'm baking fresh. Let me go see how they're coming."

Hannah stepped into the kitchen and sniffed the air. The new cookies smelled wonderful, a blend of cinnamon, cardamom, and a secret ingredient that Norman and Andrea would never be able to identify. It was so unusual, no one would ever think of it and it would remain a mystery to anyone who tasted the cookies. And that's what she'd call them, Mystery Cookies.

As if on cue, the oven timer beeped and Hannah opened the door to take out the sheet of cookies. She'd gone into the kitchen to mix up this batch right after she'd noticed that Norman and Andrea were going through her bags of leftover cookies like starving wolves at a sheep convention. At first she'd planned to make Chocolate Chip Crunches, but she'd been out of chips and cornflakes. Peanut Butter Melts had been out, since the jar of peanut butter was nearly empty. Her Old-Fashioned Sugar Cookies would have worked, but they required chilling time and the wolves in the living room might attack if their stomachs weren't placated. She'd stared at her pantry shelf for a moment to assess her stock of ingredients, and then she'd flipped through her cookbook for the recipe Grandma Ingrid had called Red Spice Cake and adapted it for cookies on the fly.

Once Hannah had transferred the hot cookies to a rack and slipped another pan in the oven, she put the dozen cool cookies she'd made on a plate and carried them into the living room. "Here. These are ready and I've got more on the way."

"Thanks, Hannah." Andrea took a cookie with her left hand and munched while she continued to take notes from Norman's computer screen. "These are really good. They're moist and cinnamony and . . . is that a word?"

"Is what a word?"

"Cinnamony."

Hannah laughed. "If it's not, it ought to be."

"Mmm . . ." Andrea reached out for another cookie. "What are these?"

"Spice cookies. I'm going to call them Mystery Cookies."

"That's a good name." Norman grabbed a cookie before Andrea could take her third. "What's the mystery?"

"There's a secret ingredient and I don't think anyone can guess what it is. Except maybe Andrea."

"Me?" Andrea looked surprised. "How would I guess? You know I don't bake."

You don't cook, either, Hannah thought, but she didn't say it. Andrea had taken enough heat over the years about her lack of culinary skills. "Just think about Grandma Ingrid's Red Spice Cake and you'll know."

"But that was made with . . ." Andrea stopped abruptly and began to grin. "I think I get it. Does this mystery ingredient come in a red and white can?"

"Yes, and don't tell anybody. I'll have to tell Lisa because she'll be helping me mix the dough, but I'll swear her to secrecy."

"I'll never tell. I promise." Andrea raised her hand to her chest and gestured. "Cross my heart and hope to die. I wonder where that comes from."

"It's a reference to the crucifixion. It's like *knock on wood*. That's a reference to the wooden cross."

"Really?" Norman turned to stare at her. "How do you know that?"

Hannah shrugged. "I read it somewhere a long time ago. Little things like that stick in my head."

"If you had a computer you could find out all sorts of things like that on-line," Norman told her.

Hannah sighed. They'd had this discussion before. Norman was trying to pull her kicking and screaming into cyberspace. "Why would I need to find it out if I already know it?"

"You don't know it all. It's fun doing research on the Web and it's way past time for you to get a computer. As a matter of fact, I think you should have two."

"One for each hand?" Hannah quipped.

"No, one for here and one for The Cookie Jar."

"But why? I'm doing just fine without a computer."

"You could have a master file of your recipes," Andrea jumped into the fray. "Then you wouldn't have to make copies and keep them in both places. If you made a change in a recipe at work, you could send it to your computer at home. When you got home, you could print it out and then you'd always have the updated version."

"That's what I do now. I just run down to the drugstore and make a copy and bring it home."

"But that's the whole point." Andrea was insistent. "You wouldn't have to run down to the drugstore. You'd be saving money, too. That copier down there is expensive."

Hannah laughed. "And two computers aren't?"

"Not as expensive as you think," Norman took over the argument. "They're practically giving away last year's models. Since you don't need it for anything fancy, you wouldn't need to be state-of-the-art."

"You're ganging up on me," Hannah accused them. "And here I am, feeding you cookies. That's not nice."

Andrea reached out for her fourth cookie. "You're right. I wish you had a printer at home, though. Then I wouldn't have to copy all this stuff off Norman's screen. It's like copying off the blackboard at school and I hated doing that. I always got a terrible headache."

That's because you refused to wear your glasses, Hannah thought, but she wasn't mean-spirited enough to say it.

"Of course, that's because I wouldn't wear my glasses. I thought they made me look ugly," Andrea went on. "That's one of the things I like about using computers. If I get close enough, I don't have to wear them. I think I hear your timer, Hannah."

Andrea was right. Hannah got up to take another sheet of cookies from the oven. She stuck in another sheet, set the timer again, and when she came back, she found Andrea and Norman smiling broadly. "You found something?"

"Bingo!" Andrea said, and held up Hannah's notebook. "I copied it all down for you. There were two men and they stole over two hundred thousand dollars. One was apprehended that night, but the other one got away with the money. He was caught a week later, trying to cross the

Canadian border, but he only had five thousand dollars with him and he refused to say where he'd hidden the rest. Since one of the bank guards was killed in the robbery, both men were charged with murder and sentenced to life in prison."

"Which prison?"

"That's the one thing the article doesn't say. I can find out, though. First thing tomorrow morning, I'll call the prisons and ask if the robbers are there."

"I hate to put a damper on your spirits, but I don't think that'll work." Norman shook his head. "Prison officials don't give out that kind of information on the phone."

Hannah laughed. "They don't, not usually, but you've never seen Andrea in action."

"That's right." Andrea preened a bit. "I'm a real estate agent. We're trained to get confidential information out of people."

The doorbell rang and Hannah glanced at her watch. It was only eleven and Michelle had said she'd be late.

"Look through the peephole before you open the door," Andrea advised.

"I can't use it at night. The outside light's in the wrong place and all I can see is a silhouette."

"Then leave the chain on," Norman suggested.

Hannah thought it was silly, but she did leave the chain on. After all, there was a killer on the loose.

"It's me, Hannah," Michelle said, waving at Hannah through the crack in the door.

"You're early. Did something go wrong on your date?"

"No. Or maybe that's a yes. Lonnie got called back to the station."

"Did they catch Rhonda's killer?"

"No, nothing like that. Lonnie's the youngest deputy and they call him in to do all the grunt work."

"That's too bad," Hannah said, knowing exactly what Lonnie was going through. The most recent hire in any business had to do all the things the veteran employees didn't want to do. "Wait just a second. I have to shut the door to take off the chain."

When the chain was off and the door was fully open, Michelle stepped inside. She made a maneuver that would have made any running back proud, and neatly blocked Moishe's headlong rush to the door. "Hi, Moishe. You remember me from last night, don't you?"

"He remembers the smoked salmon you brought him for Christmas. Listen to that. He's purring already."

"I don't have any salmon this trip, but I do have this." Michelle reached into her purse and brought out a cellophane wrapper with a long string tied around it.

"He really doesn't play, Michelle," Hannah said, as Michelle dropped the wrapper on the rug.

"He'll play with this. Just watch."

Hannah watched as Michelle began to walk forward, tugging the wrapper behind her. And then the cat Hannah had thought was non-playful began to chase the wrapper. Moishe pounced, Michelle jerked the wrapper away, and then they did it all over again, all the way to the sofa where Andrea and Norman were sitting.

"I'll be!" Hannah said, heading for the kitchen to take the last pan of cookies out of the oven. She'd spent a fortune on high-priced kitty toys when Moishe had first moved in with her, and he hadn't played with any of them. Now it seemed that all she'd needed was a crumpled cellophane wrapper and a piece of ordinary string.

When Hannah came back with a fresh plate of cookies, Michelle dug right in. She ate two in rapid succession and then she gave Hannah a thumbs-up. "These are great. I waited for you to get back so I could tell you all together. The reason Lonnie had to go back to the station is that Freddy Sawyer got in trouble tonight."

"Is Freddy okay?" Hannah asked, imagining the worst. Freddy had told her that Jed was teaching him to fight.

"He's fine now, but he got hauled in for drunk and disorderly. Jed promised that it would never happen again and they let him off with a warning."

"I didn't think Freddy drank." Andrea looked puzzled.

"He didn't before his cousin got here," Hannah said with a sigh. "But now that Jed's in the picture, he's teaching Freddy all sorts of things that aren't good for him."

"I got the same impression," Michelle said. "Lonnie and I sobered Freddy up and then we drove him home to sleep it off. Lonnie had to go back to the station to file the paperwork, so he dropped me off here."

"I'm sorry your date didn't work out," Norman said. "Lonnie seems like a really nice guy."

"You know him?" Michelle looked surprised.

"He's been coming in every Saturday morning since he got his dental insurance. It's part of the county heath package. His teeth were in good shape to start with, but we did a few things to correct his bite."

"Right. You never know when you have to bite someone in the line of duty," Hannah joked, and then she turned to Michelle. "Tell us what happened with Freddy. Was he in a bar fight?"

"No, nothing like that. He was riding in the back of that pickup truck Jed just bought and mooning people as his cousin passed them on the road."

Hannah was shocked. It wasn't really a serious offense since no one had been hurt, but it would offend a lot of people. "As far as I know, Freddy's never been in trouble with the law before. And that doesn't sound like something he'd think of to do, all by himself."

"You're right. According to Lonnie, the girl Freddy was drinking with in the bar admitted that she'd egged him on. She said she thought it was funny."

Hannah felt sick. "Freddy's drinking, getting involved with girls in bars, and mooning people on the road? If this is Jed's way of teaching him to be a man, I don't like it one bit!"

"Neither do I," Norman said. "Freddy did some work for me when I was remodeling the clinic. He was always a good, responsible worker and he seemed a little shy to me. This just doesn't sound like it's in character for him."

"You're right," Andrea agreed. "Jed's the one who's giving Freddy ideas. And now that Freddy's mother is dead, there's no one to really look out for him. I don't think Mrs. Sawyer approved of Jed. He never came around when she was alive."

"I'll try to talk to Freddy tomorrow," Norman promised, setting his laptop in its carrying case and zipping it up. "Jed has a lot of influence with him, but that's because we let him. We're all too busy with our own lives and we don't take enough time to really get involved."

After Norman had said his good-byes to Andrea and Michelle, Hannah walked him to the door. She followed him out on the landing, closed the door behind them, and gave him a big hug. "You're a good man, Norman."

"Thanks, but I didn't do that much. Looking up things on-line is simple."

"Not that. I was talking about Freddy. It's really good of you to offer to get involved."

"But you're involved. You always take time to talk to Freddy, even when you're busy. There's no reason why I can't find the time to help him, too."

"That's what I mean. You're a good man." Hannah hugged him again.

Norman's arms tightened around her and he started to grin. "Is this your idea of a reward for good behavior?"

"Maybe. What's wrong with that?"

"Absolutely nothing. I just think I need a little bigger reward." Norman tipped her face up and kissed her.

It was a sweet kiss and Hannah didn't want it to end. It felt good to be this close to Norman. It was comforting, and warm, and nice, and exciting, too. And while her bones didn't melt and her legs didn't tremble in the same way they did when Mike kissed her, she didn't have that little doubt in the back of her mind about how many other women he'd kissed in exactly this way.

"Good night, Norman," Hannah said, when their kiss had ended. "Thank you."

"For the kiss?"

"Yes. And for being you."

Norman smiled and started down the stairs, but he stopped halfway and turned to look back at her. "I'm glad I'm me, especially tonight. I'd really don't like the idea of you kissing somebody that's not me."

Mystery Cookies

Preheat oven to 350 degrees F.,
with rack in middle position.

½ cup melted butter *(1 stick)*
3½ cups white sugar
2 beaten eggs *(just whip them up with a fork)*
1 can condensed tomato soup *(the regular plain
    kind, not "Cream Of Tomato" or "Tomato
    with Basil" or anything else fancy—I use
    Campbell's)*
2 teaspoons cinnamon
2 teaspoons nutmeg *(if you grind your own, use 1
    teaspoon instead of 2)*
2 teaspoons baking soda
2 teaspoons salt
2 cups raisins *(either golden or regular)*
2 cups chopped walnuts *(measure after you chop
    them)*
4½ cups flour *(no need to sift)*

Microwave the butter in your mixing bowl to melt it.
Add the sugar, let it cool a bit, and mix in the beaten
eggs. Open a can of condensed tomato soup, add that to
your mixing bowl, and then mix it all up. Stir in the cinnamon, nutmeg, baking soda, and salt. Then add the
raisins and the walnuts, and stir. Measure the flour and

add it in one-cup increments, mixing after each addition.

Let the dough sit for ten minutes or so. Drop the dough by teaspoons onto a greased or Pammed cookie sheet, 12 to a standard sheet. *(If the dough is too sticky to scoop, you can chill it for a few minutes, or dip your teaspoon into a glass of cold water.)*

Bake at 350 degrees F. for 10 to 12 minutes or until the cookies are golden brown on top. Let them sit on the cookie sheet for a minute or two *(no longer or they'll stick)*, and then transfer them to a wire rack for complete cooling.

A batch of Mystery Cookies yields about 10 dozen. *(I know that's a lot, but they'll be gone before you know it.)* They're soft and chewy and a real favorite. *(And if you don't tell the kids that they're getting a helping of tomatoes with their cookies, I guarantee they'll never guess.)*

Chapter
Twenty-One

"It's eleven-thirty. Aren't you tired?" Hannah asked her sisters when she came back into her living room.

"Not me." Michelle shook her head.

"How about you, Andrea?" Hannah turned to her. "You're the one who's sleeping for two."

Andrea laughed. "That's *eating* for two. There's no such thing as sleeping for two. The baby sleeps whenever he wants to. It doesn't matter whether I'm awake or not."

"Are you *sure* you're not tired?"

"You sound like Bill. Really, Hannah. I'm not a bit tired."

Michelle looked confused. "But I thought pregnancy was so tiring."

"It is, in the last couple of months. But that's when you're carrying around all that extra weight. I've only gained five pounds so far. My feet get tired if I stand all day, but that's the only part of me that does. I actually have more energy now than I did before I got pregnant."

"I'm a real lightweight when it comes to pulling all-nighters, like when I have to study for a test. Maybe I should get pregnant and then I'd have more energy." Michelle noticed the shocked expression on her sisters' faces and she giggled. "Just kidding. I want to wait to get pregnant until I'm as old as Hannah."

Hannah groaned. She wasn't sure if that was an insult, but it sure felt like it.

"That's a bad idea. Don't wait *that* long," Andrea advised.

Hannah groaned again. This time she was sure it was an insult. "Forget about my biological clock. Mother's already got that covered. If we're going to stay up and talk, I'll make us some hot chocolate. Andrea? You can bring Michelle up to speed on everything we learned about the robbery case."

It took a while to make the hot chocolate, because Hannah made it the old-fashioned way with cocoa, milk, and sugar. Once she'd poured it into two mugs and refilled her own mug with no-calorie coffee, she carried them back out to the living room. She caught the tail end of the conversation when she entered the room.

". . . like him a lot, but there's someone at school I'm dating." Michelle turned to smile as Hannah set down her mug of hot chocolate and went on. "It's not exclusive, but we're really good friends, if you know what I mean."

"*How* good?" Andrea asked, taking her mug from Hannah.

Hannah winced as she took her place on the sofa. She'd apparently missed a conversation about Michelle's boyfriends and it sounded as if Andrea was grilling their baby sister.

"Not *that* good." Michelle looked a bit exasperated. "I'm not sleeping with him, if that's what you're asking."

"Tell me about him. Is he a student?"

"Yes. He's twenty-four, he's going for his M.B.A., and his name is Raj."

It was time for her to step in and Hannah did it with a rush. She wasn't sure how Andrea felt about inter-cultural dating. "Will you ask Raj if his mother has a good recipe for curry? I know most families from India have their own blend of spices and I don't really like the bottled curry powder you can buy in the stores."

Michelle laughed. "Raj's family isn't from India. His full

name is Roger Allen Jensen. 'Raj' is just a nickname they got from his initials."

"Oh," Hannah said, feeling slightly foolish. Since she didn't enjoy that feeling, it was time to change the subject and fast. "I still can't believe that Freddy mooned people on the road, and I'm really disturbed about Jed. I wouldn't be a bit surprised to find out that he knows something about the stolen money and he somehow got his hands on it."

"Do you think so?" Michelle asked, looking relieved that the boyfriend discussion was over.

"It makes some kind of sense, especially if you got that ten-dollar bill at the drugstore. Freddy showed me his new sports watch today and I know the drugstore carries watches like that. Freddy told me it cost less than ten dollars and Jed gave him the money to buy it."

"But a lot of people shop at the drugstore," Andrea pointed out.

"Wait. There's more. Jed told me he used to work on a maintenance crew at Stillwater Prison. He said he got some back pay, some sort of retroactive raise, but I don't believe it."

"Do you think Jed was a prisoner?" Andrea asked.

"No. Mike checked it out and he wasn't. But he could have met the bank robbers while he was working there and they could have told him where they stashed the money."

Andrea shrugged. "I guess it's not impossible."

"I hope Hannah's right," Michelle said. "Is it illegal to spend stolen money when you're not the one who stole it?"

"I think so, if you know it's stolen." Hannah looked at Andrea. "Do you know?"

"It's got to be. But even if Jed claims he didn't know the money was stolen, it still might be enough to separate him from Freddy, at least for a while."

"That would be good," Michelle said with a sigh. "Lonnie and I tried to explain things to Freddy when we took him home, but I don't think we did any good. Freddy still doesn't realize that Jed was the one who got him into trouble in the first place."

Hannah sighed. "That figures. Freddy's always been very loyal and trusting. It'll take a lot to convince him that Jed isn't a good guy. He's honest, though. If he finds out that Jed's been spending stolen money, that might be enough to change his opinion."

"That's a good place to start." Andrea motioned to Hannah. "Hand me my purse, Hannah. My cell phone has free long distance. I'll call Stillwater and see if the two bank robbers are there."

"Now?" Hannah stopped in the act of reaching for Andrea's purse. "But the prison offices will be closed."

"I know and that's just perfect. Whoever answers the phone might not know the rules and they'll give me the information I need."

"But won't they just tell you to call back when the office opens up in the morning?"

Andrea shook her head. "They might tell somebody else that, but not me. I've got a perfect reason for calling right now and they're going to fall over backwards getting me what I need. Now will you please hand me my purse?"

Hannah gave Andrea her purse, watched as her sister took out her cell phone, listened as she got the right number from directory assistance, and came very close to crossing her fingers as Andrea began to speak to someone at the prison. If Andrea could verify that the bank robbers were in Stillwater Prison, they'd be one step closer to proving that Jed was trafficking in stolen money.

"I'm really sorry to call so late, but I'm trying to balance my mother's checkbook and I noticed she sent a check to a man by the name of Loren Urlanski." Andrea paused and winked at them. "That's right. Urlanski. He's supposedly an inmate at Stillwater and my mother made a contribution to his appeal fund. Since it's a fairly large check, I wanted to make sure that Mr. Urlanski is really an inmate." Andrea paused again and then she smiled. "Of course. I'll be happy to hold while you check."

"You did it!" Michelle whispered, gazing at Andrea in awe.

Andrea shook her head. "Not quite yet. But he said he'd check the computer."

Hannah just shook her head. Andrea could lie like a trooper when the occasion warranted.

"Yes, I'm here," Andrea said, speaking into the phone again. "He's not? Are you sure?" She paused to make a note in her book and then she continued. "How about David Aspen? My mother also contributed to his appeal fund. Could you check that name for me?"

Hannah grabbed Andrea's pen as she waited and scribbled a note to her sister. It said, *Transferred? Dead? Paroled?* Andrea glanced at it and turned back to the phone. "He's not, either? That's exactly what I was afraid of. How about if they were transferred? Or if they died? Or if they're out on parole? Is there any way your computer can tell that?"

Hannah held her breath as she waited for the answer. If neither bank robber had been an inmate at Stillwater, their theory was a washout.

"I see. Well, thank you so much for checking. I really appreciate it. I'll turn these canceled checks over to the proper authorities in the morning. Obviously somebody is running one of those scams that targets the elderly."

Hannah waited until Andrea hung up and then she started to laugh. "The *elderly?* If Mother had heard that, you wouldn't have a chance to *get* elderly."

"You're right. She'd kill me." Andrea grinned from ear to ear. "But she's never going to find out about it . . . right?"

"Right," Michelle said.

"Absolutely," Hannah agreed. "Thanks for checking on it, Andrea. You were incredible."

"Anytime. What do you want me to do next?"

"I don't know." Hannah sighed deeply. "My theory about

Jed is blown. If the two bank robbers were never at Stillwater, Jed couldn't have met them there. It's a shame. I really wanted him to be the one who was passing that stolen money."

"Me, too," Michelle said. "He's a jerk."

"I know, but I guess not every jerk is a criminal." Hannah picked up her notebook and paged through it. "We're spinning our wheels with this bank robbery thing, especially when we can't prove it has anything to do with Jed or with Rhonda's murder. Maybe we'd better tell Bill and Mike what we know and drop it."

When her alarm went off the next morning, Hannah had to squelch the urge to throw it across the room. The only thing that stopped her was that she didn't have the energy to lift her hand. It had been almost one in the morning by the time Bill had come to collect Andrea and close to one-thirty by the time she'd gotten Michelle settled in the guest room. It would be a two-pots-of-coffee morning before she was alert enough to drive to work.

"That new pillow had better come in soon," Hannah grumbled, rubbing her neck as she crawled out of bed. She'd ended up with the foam pillow again because she'd been too tired to dislodge Moishe from hers.

After a quick shower that eased some of the pain in her neck, Hannah dressed in cotton pants and a short-sleeved top. She slipped her feet into a pair of moccasins and padded to the kitchen with Moishe, who was following on the trail of his breakfast. Once she'd filled his food bowl and given him fresh water, Hannah poured her first cup of coffee, grabbed her master file of recipes, and sat down at the table to page through it while she woke up. Today was the day before the Fourth, and she still hadn't decided what type of dessert to bring to the potluck picnic and barbecue.

Long minutes passed while Hannah paged and sipped. When the hands of her apple-shaped kitchen clock approached five o'clock, the time she'd decided to leave for work, she was no closer to deciding which dessert to bring than she'd been before she'd started. She might have actually welcomed the diversion of a morning call from her mother, but it was too early, even for Delores. Hannah finished the first cup of coffee from the second pot and poured the rest in her insulated car coffee caddy. She wrote a quick note for Michelle, telling her to come down to the shop when she woke up, and propped it up against the saltshaker where she'd be sure to see it. Then she refilled Moishe's food bowl for the final time, slung her purse over her shoulder, and stepped out into the muggy early morning air.

The air outside was like a sauna and Hannah imagined that she could hear steam hissing up as the water hit the rocks. It would be another scorcher today. If this heat wave didn't let up before tomorrow, the students in Jordan High's marching band would be dropping like flies in their uniforms at the parade.

Hannah drove through the still morning with her windows down, attempting to catch every breath of wind. Crickets chirped in the fields, somewhere a cow was lowing, and several frogs hopped dangerously close to her wheels as they crossed the road to a pond on the opposite side of the road.

The sun was just beginning to peep over the horizon when Hannah parked in back of The Cookie Jar. The first thing she did after she unlocked the door was to beat a path straight to the air conditioner and turn it on full blast. Then she got down to the business of baking the cookie dough that she'd mixed up with Lisa before they'd left the shop the previous night.

In less than an hour, Hannah was very grateful for the cool air that circulated in her kitchen. With the ovens baking and cookies cooling on the racks, it was warm, but not hot. It made her wonder how she'd ever managed without her window unit.

When Lisa came in, at seventy-thirty, she was smiling. Hannah took one glance at her partner's happy face and was instantly curious. "What's up? Did Herb propose?"

"No, it's Dad. He's Uncle Sam!"

"What?"

"The Seniors Center rented him a costume and Dad's leading his whole group in the parade. He's going to be the best Uncle Sam they ever had!" Lisa stopped and frowned slightly. "That's strange, Hannah."

"What's strange?"

"I just remembered something. Dad got all excited when I got to be the Easter Bunny in my second-grade play. He told all his friends that I was going to be the best Easter Bunny they ever had. And now I'm doing the same thing for him, just like I'm *his* proud parent. I guess it's true that roles get reversed when you get older."

"I guess so." Hannah tried to think of something to say to cheer Lisa up. She'd been smiling, but now she looked sad. "You should take some pictures of your dad and his group in the parade. They might like to put them up on the bulletin board at the center."

Lisa started to smile again. "That's a great idea. I already bought a disposable camera to take pictures of our float."

"How's it coming?" Hannah asked. She wasn't about to miss a golden opportunity to see if she could find out more about The Cookie Jar float.

"It's almost finished. Tracey's class is putting on the final touches today. It's absolutely precious, but that's all I'm allowed to say."

"But can't you just tell me . . ."

"No," Lisa interrupted, grinning widely. "You'll see it tomorrow at the parade."

Hannah recognized the stubborn set of Lisa's chin. She could beg and plead, but she wouldn't get any more information. "Delores and Carrie are coming to watch the parade with us, and they can help us take pictures of your dad and the seniors. Andrea can help, too. Take some money out of the till and run down to the drugstore as soon as they open to get more disposable cameras."

"Thanks, Hannah. We should get lots of good pictures that way."

"Even if we don't, we've always got Norman as a backup. He'll be here with his own camera."

Lisa smiled happily. "I'm really looking forward to tomorrow. I love the parade and the whole celebration out at Eden Lake. Have you decided what dessert we're going to bring?"

"Not yet. I tried to think of something special this morning, but I'm fresh out of ideas."

"I'll take care of it," Lisa offered. "You've got enough on your mind with Rhonda's murder. What did you find out about that ten-dollar bill I gave you yesterday? Did Mr. Greerson think it was counterfeit?"

"Sit down for a second and I'll tell you." Hannah gestured toward a stool at the workstation. And then she told Lisa all about the robbery and the stolen money that had surfaced in Lake Eden.

Lisa's eyes were round with surprise by the time Hannah finished. "I guess a lot happened after I went home last night!"

"There's more," Hannah said, and told her about Freddy Sawyer's drunk and disorderly charge.

"This just gets stranger and stranger." Lisa shook her head. "We've had a mooning, a murder, and money turning up from an old bank robbery, all in one week."

"People who think small-town life is boring ought to move to Lake Eden!"

"I guess," Lisa said, and then she began to frown. "Do you think all those things could be related somehow?"

"I can't find a connection. And believe me, I tried. I'm giving up on the stolen money and concentrating on Rhonda's murder. I really don't have a clue, so far."

"Maybe you should tell me everything you know," Lisa

suggested. "It'll put your thoughts in order and I might be able to catch something you missed."

"You think so?"

"It's possible. It could be a little like walking into a room where someone's doing a jigsaw puzzle. Sometimes you spot the piece they're looking for right off the bat."

"Fresh eyes?"

"That's it. Except this time it's fresh ears."

"It's certainly worth a try." Hannah gave Lisa a smile. "Go put on the coffee and when you come back, we'll finish the baking. And while we work, we'll talk bloody murder."

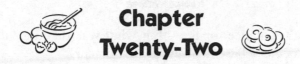

Chapter
Twenty-Two

By the time Hannah was through telling Lisa everything except the identity of Rhonda's boyfriend, the cookies were baked and the display jars behind the counter were filled. The big urn of coffee had perked, and Hannah and Lisa sat down at their favorite table in the back of the coffee shop to take a break.

"Well?" Hannah turned to her partner. "Do you think I missed anything?"

"No, but I can't help thinking about Ron LaSalle. Remember what you said when he was murdered?"

"I said a lot of things." Hannah sighed. Thinking about her favorite Cozy Cow deliveryman still made her sad.

"But you pointed out that Ron's only mistake was being in the wrong place at the wrong time. Or is it the wrong place at the right time? Or the right place at the wrong time? Or . . ."

"It doesn't matter," Hannah interrupted her. "I know what you mean. Do you think that's what happened to Rhonda?"

"Maybe. What if the killer was in the basement and Rhonda went down there and caught him doing something he didn't want anyone else to know he was doing? If that happened, he might have . . ."

"Killed Rhonda to keep her from talking," Hannah finished Lisa's sentence for her. "But what was the killer doing in Mrs. Voelker's basement in the first place?"

"I don't know, unless he was looking for antiques to steal, or something like that. You were in the basement. What was down there, anyway?"

"The only things I saw were cobwebs, dust, moldy junk, and shelves of old preserves."

Lisa shrugged. "That sounds like a perfectly ordinary basement to me. How about the furnace room?"

"Not counting the grave and Rhonda's body, there wasn't much there. There was the furnace, of course, and one wall had some homemade shelves for jams and jellies. A couple jars of jam were broken and there was glass on the floor."

"Are you sure that's all there was?"

"Pretty sure. But once I spotted Rhonda's body, I didn't look around at much else." Hannah thought about it for a moment. "You've got a point, Lisa. I should take a second look."

"How are you going to do that? Isn't the whole house taped off as a crime scene?"

"Yes, but that shouldn't be a problem since I don't have to go inside. There's a window in the furnace room and I can take a peek through the glass."

"Why don't you take pictures?" Lisa suggested. "Then both of us could look at the crime scene."

"Good idea. I'll run home and get my camera."

"I've got the disposable I bought last night. It's still in a bag in my car. You can use that."

It didn't take Lisa long to return with the camera. Hannah examined it and began to frown. It had a built-in flash that went off with every picture. That could present a problem, especially since she'd be taking pictures through the glass.

"What's wrong?" Lisa asked, noticing Hannah's frown.

"I have to figure out some way to block the flash so it won't glare off the windowpane."

Lisa jumped up again. "You can mask it with electrical tape. We've got some in the kitchen drawer."

Once the camera was modified, Hannah set off for the Voelker place. She'd heard that a deputy had been stationed there to keep out the ghoul-seekers who wanted a peek at the crime scene, and she'd armed herself with a half-dozen cookies and a cup of takeout coffee. She planned to present the deputy with an early morning snack and then give him her excuse for driving out. Since the Voelker place was a good ten minutes away, she'd have plenty of time to dream up something convincing before she got there.

Hannah gave a relieved sigh as she parked at the side of the driveway and spotted Lonnie's older brother, Rick Murphy, sitting in a wicker chair on the front porch. Rick loved her Short Stack Cookies. He'd be so pleased to get some, he'd be sure to buy her story. She slipped off her watch, pushed it out of sight under the passenger seat, and got out of her truck. "Hi, Rick. I brought you a little something for breakfast."

"Hey, Hannah. That's really nice of you." Rick smiled as he accepted the cookies and coffee. "What are you doing way out here?"

"I'm looking for my watch. I think I dropped it inside the day we found Rhonda's body. Mother and I were packing up things for her store and it must have fallen off my wrist."

"I wish I could let you look, but I can't let anyone inside."

"That's okay, Rick. I figured that. But you can go inside and look for it, can't you?"

"I'm not allowed inside, either. The only authorized personnel are the detectives working the case. Sorry, Hannah."

Hannah gave a deep sigh and then she brightened visibly. "How about just peeking in through the windows? If we spot it, I can ask Bill or Mike to get it the next time they come out here."

"Well . . . I guess that'd be okay. They didn't say anything about looking in through the windows."

"Great." Hannah gave him a warm smile. "I'll start on one side of the house and you can start on the other. That way you'll be back at your post twice as fast."

"Sounds good. What does this watch of yours look like?"

Hannah froze for a millisecond. She should have anticipated that question. To cover her momentary lapse, she described her present watch. "It's a waterproof watch with a round face and it's got a black band."

"Like the ones in the window at the drugstore?"

"Exactly. As a matter of fact, that's where it came from. I know I didn't take it off, so the band must have broken. It's probably on the floor in one of the rooms."

The moment Rick disappeared around his side of the house, Hannah made a beeline for the basement windows on the other side. She pulled Lisa's camera out of her purse and clicked off a dozen fast shots, alternating between the four basement windows. By the time she was finished, Rick was rounding the back of the house and Hannah quickly stuffed the camera back into her purse. "Hi, Rick. Any luck?"

"No. You didn't spot it, either?"

Hannah shook her head, doing her best to appear disappointed. "I'm not even sure I lost it out here, but I thought it was worth a look."

Once she'd chatted with Rick for a few more moments, Hannah walked back to her truck. She didn't think he'd been suspicious about her request, but she didn't put her watch back on until she pulled up in front of the Rhodes Dental Clinic, ten minutes later.

"Hi, Norman," Hannah called out when she came through the door. "I've got a photographic emergency."

"A what?" Norman slid aside the little glass doors at the reception desk and peered out.

"A photographic emergency. I just took some pictures and I need to have them developed as fast as I can."

"Let me check my schedule." Norman flipped the page in his appointment book. "Okay. I've got Mrs. Walters coming in at nine, but Mayor Bascomb canceled his ten o'clock. If I don't have an emergency, I'm free from ten to twelve-thirty."

"Then you'll develop my film?"

"That depends," Norman said. "I assume it has something to do with Rhonda's murder?"

"Photos of the crime scene. I ran out there this morning and took them through the basement window. Don't mention that to anybody. I had to pull a fast one to do it."

"Okay. Did you use a flash?"

"No. I taped over it so it wouldn't glare against the glass."

Norman looked pleased. "I should have known you'd think of that. How about the light? Was it dark in the basement?"

"Yes, but there was some light coming in through the windows. The disposable camera I used didn't have any way of changing the settings."

Norman took the camera Hannah passed through the window and glanced at it. "It'll be okay. I can push the negatives."

"What's that?"

"It's like baking your cookies at a higher temperature to make them crisper."

"If I did that, I'd burn them!"

Norman laughed. "I never claimed to be a baker. Don't worry about it, Hannah. I'll play some tricks in the darkroom and get all I can for you."

"Thanks, Norman. Do you think you can have them ready by noon and drop them off at The Cookie Jar?"

"Yes, but I didn't say I'd do them yet."

"You didn't?"

"No. When you asked me, I said, *It depends.*"

"On what?"

"On your Orange Snaps. Would you bake a couple dozen for me to give to my mother? She's almost forgiven me for not consulting her about the house and your Orange Snaps are her favorites. I figure they ought to get me back in her good graces."

"I'll mix them up the minute I get back to the shop."

The street door opened and Mrs. Walters walked in. Hannah greeted her and then she headed back out to her truck. She'd bake the Orange Snaps because Norman had asked her to, but his plan wouldn't work. Carrie was every bit as stubborn as Delores and there wasn't a cookie in the world that could pull either mother out of a snit.

"Mike's here, Hannah," Lisa said, poking her head into the kitchen. "He says he has to talk to you about something important."

"Okay. Will you give him a cup of coffee and send him back here?"

Hannah sighed as she finished packaging the Orange Snaps for Norman. Mike had probably found out about her early morning trip to the Voelker place and he'd come to find out what she'd really been doing.

"Hannah," Mike greeted her when he came into the kitchen. "What's all this about a watch you lost at the crime scene? Didn't you have it on last night when we got together at your mother's cottage?"

Hannah sighed and decided to tell the truth. "The watch was just an excuse. I needed to take another look at the basement and I didn't have time to call you or Bill for permission."

"So you made up that story and Rick bought it?" Mike looked absolutely incredulous.

"Yes, but I didn't go inside. I just looked in through the windows to see if the basement was the way I remembered it."

Mike shook his head. "Rick's going to have to develop a basic mistrust of people or he'll never be a good detective."

"Is that what you have? A basic mistrust of people?"

"I guess so."

"Isn't life a lot harder that way?"

Mike opened his mouth and Hannah could tell he was ready to deny it, but then he shrugged. "I guess it is. That's a big difference between us. You trust almost everybody and I don't trust much of anybody."

"But you do trust me, don't you?"

"Yes, and I shouldn't. You've lied to me enough times."

"I never lied!" Hannah's eyes flashed a warning. "I just . . . omitted a few things and misled you."

"Water under the bridge," Mike said, looking amused as he took a stool at the work island. "So you needed another look at the crime scene?"

"That's right. I realized that after I spotted Rhonda's body, I really didn't look around at anything else."

"Okay. I'll buy that. But why didn't you just ask me if you could see the crime-scene photos?"

"If I'd asked, would it have done me any good?"

"Probably not." Mike laughed and suddenly he was much friendlier. "I'm sorry, Hannah. I'm just not used to sharing the details of an investigation with anyone. I work best alone."

"How about Bill?"

"He's got access to the case file. I don't cut him out of it deliberately, but I tend to keep things to myself, especially those crazy theories that come to me in the middle of the night. I've always been that way. I guess I'm just a loner by nature. We're really a lot different, you know? Maybe that's why I value you so much."

"I'm the yin to your yang?"

"Yeah." Mike chuckled. "So . . . what did you find out?"

"Not a darned thing."

"Nothing?"

"Not really. Everything in that basement was just as I remembered it. It was probably a wasted trip."

Mike stood up and walked over to put his arm around her shoulders. "It's usually a wasted trip, but we have to keep on trying. That's one thing I'm sure of. Rhonda didn't deserve to die violently. We have to find her killer and punish him."

"I know." Hannah felt real warmth for this man who haunted her dreams. He had ideals, he was compassionate, and he'd said, WE *have to find her killer and punish him.* Mike had included her, and that meant he'd accepted her. "So are you going to tell me what you've found out so far?"

"No."

"No?"

"Maybe later, but not now. I've got something I've been working on and I'm not ready to tell anybody about it."

Hannah's mouth dropped open. "But you expect me to tell you all about *my* investigation?"

"Of course I do. You're the amateur and I'm the professional. That's not meant to put you down, Hannah. That's just the way it is."

"But . . ."

"I've got to run." Mike set down his coffee cup and pulled her into his arms for a quick hug. "See you later, okay?"

After Mike left, Hannah stared at the swinging door until it stopped wiggling. Then she turned back to her work with a scowl on her face. Either Mike hadn't noticed her lack of response when he'd hugged her, or he'd ignored her anger, intending to deal with it later. Neither possibility pleased her. There was still fire in her eyes ten minutes later when Lisa stuck her head into the kitchen again.

"Norman's here," Lisa announced before she noticed the expression on Hannah's face. "Oh-oh. Did you have a fight with Mike?"

"I did. He didn't. I don't think he even knew I was mad at him."

Lisa opened her mouth to respond, but she must have

thought better of it because she just shrugged. "Do you want me to send Norman back here?"

"Yes. Thanks, Lisa. And if Mike comes back in, cut off his free coffee and cookies. He can pay just like everybody else."

"How about Norman?" Lisa asked.

Hannah's anger evaporated and she started to grin. "You can give him whatever he wants . . . at least for now."

Orange Snaps

Don't preheat the oven yet—
this cookie dough has to chill

1½ cups melted butter (*3 sticks*)
2 cups white sugar
½ cup frozen orange juice concentrate (*I use
     Minute Maid*)
2 beaten eggs *(just beat them up with a fork)*
4 teaspoons baking soda
1 teaspoon salt
½ to 1 teaspoon orange zest*
4 cups flour *(you don't have to sift it)*
⅓ cup white sugar for later

*The orange zest adds a burst of flavor. Zest is finely grated orange peel, just the orange part, not the white. You can use a grater to scrape peel from an orange, or a zester which removes thin layers of peel in strips. If you use a zester, you'll have to finely chop the strips of peel with a knife.

Melt the butter in a large microwave-safe bowl. Add the sugar and orange juice concentrate, and stir. Let the mixture cool slightly. Add the eggs, baking soda, salt, and orange zest, stirring after each addition. Add the flour in increments and mix thoroughly. Cover the bowl and refrigerate the dough at least 2 hours *(overnight's even better)*.

When you're ready to bake, preheat your oven to 350 degrees F., with rack in the middle position.

Roll the chilled dough into walnut-sized balls with your hands. Put ⅓ cup white sugar in a small bowl and roll the balls in it. Place them on a greased cookie sheet, 12 to a sheet. Press the dough balls down just a little so they won't roll off on the floor when you put them in the oven.

Bake for 10 to 12 minutes at 350 degrees F. The dough balls will flatten out all by themselves. Let the cookies cool for 2 minutes on the cookie sheet and then move them to a wire rack to finish cooling.

These cookies freeze well. Roll them up in foil, put them in a freezer bag, and they'll be fine for 3 months or so, *if* they last that long.

Yield: approximately 10 dozen thin cookies, depending on cookie size.

(Tracey loves these cookies and she's almost managed to convince Andrea that she can have them in place of orange juice for breakfast.)

Chapter
Twenty-Three

"See anything new?" Norman asked after Hannah had rifled through the stacks of prints.

"Not a thing. How about you?"

"I don't know if this is important, but the canning jars in the furnace room are a lot smaller than the canning jars in the rest of the basement."

"That's right. The ones in the furnace room are small-size mayonnaise jars and Mrs. Voelker used them to put up her jams and jellies."

"Why not use regular canning jars?"

"Some people do, but canning jars are more expensive and you can put jam in any kind of glass container if you seal it with wax on the top."

"I didn't know that."

"It's true. When my college roommate got married, I was a bridesmaid and by the time I'd paid for my dress, I didn't have much money left for a gift. I bought a dozen wineglasses on sale, filled them with homemade grape jelly, and gave them as my wedding present."

"That's very you, Hannah."

"What do you mean?"

"It's sweet, and practical, and . . ." Norman shrugged. "It's just something you'd do, that's all. You'd make a great wife for a man with no money."

"Thanks . . . I think." Hannah chuckled. It was a strange thing to say, but she was sure it was meant as a compliment.

"I'd better get going. I've got a case of gum disease in ten minutes."

Hannah's chuckle turned into a laugh and she was still laughing as Norman picked up his package of Orange Snaps and headed out the door.

Lisa looked at the last print and shook her head. "I'm sorry, Hannah. I don't see anything even approaching a clue."

"Neither did we." Hannah gathered up the prints and stuck them back into the envelope Norman had brought. "I still have the feeling I'm missing something, but I don't know what it is."

"You could always borrow Dad's technique. He says if he thinks of something else, the thing he was trying to think of usually pops right into his head."

"At this point, I'm willing to try anything. I'll make the cookie deliveries. I always think best when I'm working."

"Okay." Lisa reached into her apron pocket and pulled out a list. "On your way back could you stop at the Red Owl? I thought of a dessert to make for tomorrow, but I need a few things."

"No problem. What are you making?"

"Cupcakes decorated especially for the Fourth. They're going to be really exciting, Hannah."

"I'm sure they will be." Hannah was smiling as she went back to the kitchen to pack up the cookies for delivery. She'd never thought of cupcakes as being particularly exciting before, but perhaps Lisa was on to something.

"Thanks for driving me, Andrea," Hannah said, collapsing into the passenger's seat and leaning her head back against the headrest. Andrea had arrived just as she was about to load her cookie deliveries and offered to drive

Hannah in her car. "That's the last of them. Just drop me at my truck and I'll run to the Red Owl."

"I can stop at the Red Owl. I have to pick up some things for tomorrow anyway."

"You're sure?"

"Positive," Andrea said and turned to smile at Hannah. "Besides, I want to collect my share of thanks for renting the second floor to Danielle. If she hadn't come along, it'd still be vacant."

By the time Andrea pulled up outside the Red Owl in her Volvo, the shower that had been threatening all afternoon with dark skies and occasional flashes of lightning had turned into a full-scale downpour. Andrea took one look at the fat raindrops pelting down on the windshield and suggested they wait until the worst of the rain had subsided.

"Good idea," Hannah said, wondering what they'd find to talk about. The Cookie Jar float was a taboo subject, but the murder case wasn't. "I'd like to show you some crime-scene photos."

"No way," Andrea said, shivering slightly.

"Why not?"

"Because I don't like gore in any way, shape, or form. I don't even let Bill show me crime-scene photos."

"These aren't gory. It's just Mrs. Voelker's basement and the furnace room, that's all."

"Then there's no body?"

Hannah shook her head. "No body."

"That might be okay. But if there's nothing there, why do you want me to see them?"

"Just look and tell me if you see anything that looks out of place."

"What's wrong with this picture?" Andrea asked, smiling at her sister. They'd both had Miss Gladke in second grade and that had been one of her favorite techniques to get the class involved in a discussion.

"Right." Hannah reached in her purse and drew out the envelope of prints that Norman had developed.

Andrea took her time paging through the prints. By the time she'd finished examining each one, the inside of her windshield was steaming up. "What happened to the rain gutters?"

"Where?" Hannah asked, glancing down at the top photo on Andrea's stack.

"On cars. Heaven knows my Volvo was expensive enough and it's got everything else. Remember the little ledge Dad used to have above the windows in the Chrysler? He could roll down the windows and the rain wouldn't come in."

Hannah knew Andrea was off on a tangent, but she understood her sister's reasoning. It was getting pretty steamy in her closed car. "So did you notice anything in the pictures?"

"Nothing really jumped out at me except those mayo jars." Andrea flipped to the picture of the shelves behind the furnace.

"But they're not unusual. Lots of people save mayo jars for jams and jellies. Don't you remember how Grandma Ingrid used to bring us mayo jars full of rhubarb jam?"

"Of course I remember. I loved Grandma Ingrid's rhubarb jam, but that's not what I'm talking about." Andrea pointed to the photo. "I just thought it was odd that these three jars in the middle of the top shelf are red."

Hannah took a quick look. "They're just a different kind of jam, that's all."

"I know that, but Mrs. Voelker was so organized. Each section holds a different type of jam. The top shelf looks like peach, the middle shelf looks like blueberry, and the bottom shelf looks like strawberry."

"So?"

"So why did she move three jars of strawberry jam up to

the peach shelf? You can tell she did. There are three empty places on the strawberry shelf, way over here at the end."

Hannah looked again. Andrea was right. Somebody had moved three jars of strawberry jam up to the top shelf. "You're a genius, Andrea! That's what I've been missing and you spotted it."

"I'm glad, but I don't know what you're so excited about. Mrs. Voelker probably ate the peach jam and her companion moved the strawberry up where it would be easier to reach."

"I don't think so. Look at that strawberry shelf again. It's all dusty between the jars, but there are three perfectly clean spots where the strawberry jam used to sit."

Andrea studied the photo again. "You're right, Hannah. Mrs. Voelker died over six months ago. If her companion had moved that jam, those spots would be covered over with dust by now. Do you think Rhonda's killer moved them?"

"That's my guess."

Andrea shivered slightly. "Maybe we should tell Bill and Mike. They might be able to lift some fingerprints."

"I don't think so. Mike told me that the killer wore gloves."

"That's right. Bill mentioned it. But why would the killer bother to move them in the first place?"

"I don't know, but there's got to be an answer. All I have to do is find out what it is." Hannah wiped a spot clean on the steamed-up window and glanced out. "Come on, Andrea. The rain's let up and it's a sauna in here. And I still have to do Lisa's shopping."

Once they entered the store, the two sisters went their separate ways. Hannah headed straight for the produce to get some things for her nightly salad, and Andrea veered off toward the frozen dinners. It didn't take long for Hannah to pick up the items on Lisa's list and when she arrived at the checkout counter, she found Andrea waiting for her.

"What's all that?" Andrea stared at the contents of Hannah's cart.

"I'll be darned if I know." Hannah was just as puzzled as her sister. She'd picked up some fresh vegetables for her dinner salad and a bag of kitty treats for Moishe, but the large bottles of red and blue food coloring and the boxes of flat-bottomed ice cream cones were for Lisa. "Lisa's making special cupcakes for the picnic."

"With cucumbers, cat treats, and ice cream cones?"

"No, the cucumbers and cat treats are mine."

"Well, that's a relief!" Andrea said, looking greatly relieved. "They don't make blue Jell-O."

"I never thought that they did." Hannah pushed her cart into the shortest line and Andrea followed her. "Why did you want blue Jell-O?"

"For the town picnic. I thought I'd make a Jell-O mold in layers for Independence Day. Blue Jell-O in the bottom, red on top of that, and then white whipped cream. It would have been perfect."

Hannah did her best to look sympathetic, but it was a struggle. Her sister's idea of gourmet cooking was to dump a can of fruit cocktail into some Jell-O and squirt it with a can of whipped cream. "So what are you going to bring?"

"Chips and dip. I got a package of blue corn chips, and a package of white. I'm going to mix them in a bowl and put out some salsa. That's red."

"That should do it," Hannah said, sending a silent thank-you to Kraft Foods for not making blue Jell-O.

When Hannah got back to The Cookie Jar, she manned the counter while Lisa went back to the kitchen to bake. Thirty minutes from the time Lisa had gone through the swinging door to the kitchen, a delicious aroma began to drift out to titillate Hannah's nostrils. She resisted for as long as she could, but finally she excused herself to the customers sitting at the counter and stuck her head into the kitchen to see how Lisa was coming along. "It really smells good in here. Chocolate?"

"Chocolate fudge cupcakes. They're my mom's recipe. The kids just love them and so do the grown-ups."

"Great," Hannah said, just as the timer Lisa wore around her neck started to clang. "That's my cue to leave. I'll take care of our customers and you take care of the cupcakes."

The next half-hour was busy. It was always busy in the summer when the tourists came to town. Hannah often wondered why they came to the lake when they spent most of their time shopping in the Lake Eden stores, cooking in the kitchens of their rented cottages, watching the television sets they'd brought with them, and doing almost exactly what they'd be doing at home in the big cities. She figured they must come for the genuine small-town atmosphere, the friendly, open feeling they got in Lake Eden. In the big Minnesota cities, people locked and bolted their doors and they didn't speak to strangers on the streets. Here things were different. A stranger was a friend unless he or she proved otherwise.

By and large, the tourists who rented the lake cabins were nice folks. They were certainly getting behind the town's Fourth of July celebration. Tickets for the potluck picnic and barbeque at Eden Lake were selling like hotcakes. Mayor Bascomb had predicted that there would be more than five hundred out-of-town guests watching the parade, taking part in the activities on the shores of Eden Lake, eating the food the residents provided, and enjoying the fireworks in the evening.

Business was brisk and Hannah's old-fashioned cash register dinged almost continually. The locals dropped in, as they always did, and mingled with the lake cottage tourists. Friendships were formed, romances with some of the local girls and boys appeared to be blooming, and no one was thinking about Labor Day, when the tourist season would end. Hannah had explained why the town was called Lake Eden and the lake that was within the city limits was called

Eden Lake at least a dozen times by the time most of the customers had cleared out. She was just transferring some of the money from the till to the bank deposit bag when the bell over the door tinkled and Jed Sawyer walked in.

Jed gave her a friendly smile. "Hi, Hannah."

"Don't *Hi, Hannah* me!" Hannah said right back, glaring at him. "I heard what you did last night."

"What did you hear?"

"You got Freddy drunk and let him pick up a girl in a bar. I thought you honestly cared about Freddy, but it looks like I was wrong!"

"Hold on." Jed held up his hands in a gesture of surrender. "I don't know where you got all that from, but it's not what happened."

"Oh, no?"

"Look, Hannah . . . I'm sorry Freddy got drunk, but it didn't start out that way. I let him have one bottle of beer and it hit him like a ton of bricks."

"You should have known better."

"I know. I found out later that he'd never even tasted alcohol before, but I didn't know that at the time."

Hannah put her hands on her hips. There was no way she was letting Jed off the hook this easily. "You should have guessed it. Mrs. Sawyer was a complete teetotaler. She didn't allow alcohol in her house."

"She used to when Freddy's dad was alive. We drove to see them every summer and my dad and Uncle Jim always sat out on the dock in the afternoon, fishing and polishing off a six-pack."

Hannah sighed. It was up to her to point out the obvious. "But you didn't see Freddy drinking, did you?"

"No. We were both too young back then. But really, Hannah . . . Freddy's almost thirty and I had no idea he couldn't handle one beer. It'll never happen again. I can promise you that."

Hannah thawed slightly, but she still had a ways to go. "It's not just the beer, Jed. You shouldn't have let Freddy pick up that bar girl."

"She wasn't a bar girl. And Freddy didn't pick her up. It was like this, Hannah. We were going to the movies and my date knew I was bringing Freddy along. When we got to her house, she had a friend there to make it a foursome."

"How about the bar? You were there, weren't you?"

"Yeah, but we just stopped off for a quick one before we headed off for the movies. You gotta remember, I was driving and I had my eyes on the road. I didn't know what Freddy was doing back there until the deputy pulled us over."

"And you would have stopped Freddy if you'd seen him?"

"You bet! I would have pulled over and told him to knock it off. But I didn't know, Hannah. I never thought Freddy would do anything like that."

Hannah didn't say anything. So far Jed's story had the ring of truth, but she still wasn't completely satisfied.

"I had a long talk with Freddy this morning," Jed went on, "and he knows what he did was wrong. I'm not going to date that girl again, either. If her friend thinks it's funny to egg on a nice, simple guy like Freddy, I don't want to have anything to do with either one of them."

Hannah was appeased. It sounded as if Jed had taken the proper steps to make sure that Freddy wouldn't get into trouble again. "I heard that Freddy was pretty drunk. How's his head this morning?"

"He's got a hangover the size of Minneapolis and he's feeling pretty ashamed of himself. That's the reason I stopped in. I wanted to bring him some cookies to prove that I'm not mad at him."

"That's a good idea." Hannah pulled out a bag, filled it with a dozen cookies, and handed it to Jed. "Take these to Freddy and tell him they're from both of us."

"Thanks, Hannah. You're really a great person, you know?"

Once the door had closed behind Jed, Hannah gave another long sigh. She hoped that Freddy had learned his lesson and that Jed would keep a better eye on him.

The next few minutes were slow, so Hannah took advantage of her downtime by refilling the sugar dispensers and stocking the tables with packets of artificial sweetener. She'd never figured out why people who'd scarf down cookies would put artificial sweetener in their coffee, but they did. She'd just finished when Michelle walked in through the swinging door from the kitchen.

"Hi, Hannah." Michelle hugged herself and shivered slightly. "Lisa's cupcakes look fantastic, but I'm not supposed to say any more than that. It's really cold in your kitchen with that air conditioner running full blast."

Hannah stared at her sister's outfit. Michelle was wearing a pair of white shorts that were so tight she probably had to stretch out on the bed to zip them up. Her pink spandex top barely covered what it had to legally cover and while the outfit looked good on her, it wasn't the sort of thing the Lake Eden girls wore to town. Hannah knew she shouldn't say anything, Michelle was old enough to choose her own clothing, but she couldn't resist. "Maybe if you had more clothes on, you wouldn't think my kitchen was so cold."

"Not you *too!*" Michelle gave an exasperated sigh. "You're getting more like Mother every day!"

"That's not necessarily a bad thing," Hannah countered. "Mother has her good points."

"Name one!"

"Well . . . she's always . . . um . . ." Hannah paused and then she began to laugh. "All right. I can't think of any right off the top of my head, but I'm sure there are plenty. How did your lunch with the girls go?"

"Fantastic. I made your spinach quiche and the girls really raved about it. They all wanted the recipe, but I said I'd have to ask you first. It's not a secret or anything, is it?"

Hannah laughed. "No, you can give it to them."

"Good. I just came from Granny's Attic and we're all getting together out at the cottage tonight. You'll drive out, won't you?"

"Well . . ."

"Come on, Hannah. I don't come home that often and it's fun if we all get together. We're having Chinese. Since you're on a diet, Mother called in a whole order of vegetables for you. Lonnie's picking up the food on his way out to the lake."

"You're seeing Lonnie two nights in a row?"

"Yes," Michelle said, and her cheeks turned pink. "Our date got cut short last night with Freddy and all, and we've still got a lot of catching up to do."

Hannah decided not to say anything. As Delores might describe it when she was in her Regency-speak mode, Michelle had a *telling blush*.

"It's not serious, so don't start worrying. It's just that Raj and I are so different."

"Oh?"

"He grew up in New York City and he doesn't know anything about small-town life. When I called him last night, I told him about the potluck picnic and barbecue, and how everyone brings their best dish."

"And?" Hannah waited for the punch line.

"He said he'd never been to a potluck picnic, but it sounded like a lot of work to him. And then he asked me why they didn't just call someone in to cater the whole thing."

"Different cultures?"

"And different incomes," Michelle said with a sigh. "He told me his mother's never set foot in their kitchen. They have a full-time cook."

"Imagine that," Hannah commented, biding her time.

"Raj thinks everything I tell him about Lake Eden is amusing. It's almost like he thinks we're all country bumpkins."

Hannah had the feeling that Raj wouldn't be in the picture

for much longer. "I guess we might seem that way to someone who was raised in a cosmopolitan city."

"I know, but his attitude burns me sometimes. He thinks
he knows everything and I don't know anything." Michelle
glanced down at her watch. "I'd better hit the road. I'm running out to CostMart. Do you need anything?"

Hannah was about to say no when she remembered the
down pillow. "Will you see if their goose-down pillows came
in? Andrea tried to buy one for me, but they were sold out.
She brought me a rain check for the sale price."

"Sure." Michelle waited until Hannah had produced her
rain check and handed it over. "I'm going to buy a new
bathing suit. And before you ask, I'm getting a one-piece."

"A one-piece that doesn't have strategic holes? And isn't
cut up to here?" Hannah pointed to a spot on the outside of
her thigh that was almost as high as her waist.

"Don't worry. It'll be modest enough to please even
Mother. What time do you think you'll be out at the cabin?"

Hannah thought about her time schedule. There was no
cookie dough to mix for tomorrow. They were closed for the
Fourth and she was taking Saturday off to give them a three-
day weekend. "Right after we close, I'll run home to feed
Moishe and then I'll drive out. I should be there by six-thirty
or seven."

"Okay. I'll bring your pillow if they have them."

"Do you want me to give you some money?"

"Mother gave me her credit card. I'll use it and you can
settle up with her later."

Michelle went out the front door and Hannah watched as
a passing car slowed down so the driver could stare. The outfit her baby sister was wearing was what the older generation
of women in Lake Eden would refer to as a husband-catcher.
Hannah knew that Michelle wasn't thinking of marriage at
this point in her life, but the weatherman on KCOW radio
was predicting cooler temperatures and rain for this evening.

If Michelle wore her husband-catcher outfit tonight, what she'd catch would be a nasty summer cold.

It was five-thirty, The Cookie Jar was closed, and Hannah was adding up the day's receipts when Lisa came into the coffee shop. "I'm done, Hannah."

"Already?" Hannah was surprised. Lisa had made fast work of baking the cupcakes.

"The only thing left is to store them in the cooler. Go take a look and tell me what you think."

Hannah headed for the kitchen feeling slightly guilty. Their dessert for the town picnic and barbecue was all finished and all she'd done was dash to the Red Owl for a few items.

"Oh, my!" Hannah gasped, as she stepped through the swinging door and caught sight of the trays of cupcakes that Lisa had made. Some were frosted with bright blue icing, others with bright red, and the rest with white. The cupcakes were standing on six of Hannah's largest rectangular serving trays and each tray was arranged to resemble the American flag with alternating rows of red and white. The upper left-hand corner of each tray was a field of blue cupcakes and Lisa had even piped little white stars on the blue icing.

As she approached the trays, Hannah realized that the cupcakes were in edible containers. Lisa had used ice cream cones instead of cupcake papers.

"Well? What do you think?"

Hannah turned to see Lisa grinning at her from the doorway. "They're really wonderful!"

"I didn't know for sure if the cones would work, but I couldn't see any reason why they wouldn't."

"And you were right," Hannah said, walking over to give her partner a hug. "They're perfect for the Fourth, and every mother in town is going to thank you."

"Why?"

"Because they won't have to peel off the cupcake papers and wipe sticky fingers after dessert."

Lisa looked absolutely astounded for a moment and then she started to giggle. "You're right. These cupcakes are perfect for the kids, but I didn't even think of that when I made them."

"That isn't why you baked them in the cones?"

Lisa shook her head. "I did it because I looked in all the cupboards and I couldn't find enough cupcake pans."

Chapter
Twenty-Four

"Are you sure you don't want me to follow you home?" Norman looked concerned as he opened the screen door of the cottage for her. "It looks really nasty."

"I'll be fine," Hannah said, glancing up at the lightning that was zigzagging across the sky. The storm had rolled in across the lake during dinner and by the time Delores had opened the bag with the fortune cookies, Hannah had announced that she had to leave.

"Hold on a second. I'm coming along." Mike got up from his place at the table and joined them. "You're not going to be able to outrun that storm, Hannah. It'll hit before you get home."

Hannah stepped out the door with both men following her. The air was so humid, it was like someone had put on a giant teakettle and it was steaming away to humidify the whole county. "Maybe, but I've driven through hundreds of storms before."

"This looks like a bad one," Mike commented as they walked toward Hannah's truck. "How are your windshield wipers?"

"They're fine. I just replaced the blades."

"And your tires?"

"They're practically new. Stop being such a worrywart,

Mike." Hannah gave him a smile to show that she appreciated his concern even though she thought he was being ridic-
ulously overcautious. "If it starts coming down in buckets,
I'll pull off to the side of the road until I can drive safely
again."

"Will you call the cottage when you get home?" Norman
asked, opening the door of the truck for Hannah. "Then
we'll know you got there all right."

Hannah climbed behind the wheel and lowered the window. "I'll call the minute I walk in the door. Give me at least
an hour, though. It might take me that long to get home."

"I still think I should follow you," Mike said, beginning to
frown.

"Thanks, but that's not necessary." Hannah started her
car and gave a little wave as she drove off. She glanced in her
rearview mirror and chuckled slightly. Norman had one
hand half-lifted in a wave, but Mike was glowering like there
was no tomorrow. He really didn't like it when he didn't get
his way and he'd wanted to follow her home. The fact that he
was worried about her was flattering, but she didn't like
being cast in the role of a helpless female.

The tall pines around the shoreline of Eden Lake kept the
sky mostly hidden from view. Hannah didn't realize how
dark it had become until she turned onto the main road. The
first thing she noticed was the ominous blend of colors above
her. The sky was a deep charcoal gray, streaked with dirty
yellow. Purplish black storm clouds roiled up from the horizon and they reminded Hannah of a witch's caldron churning
and bubbling with an evil potion. It was the same ugly color
combination the artist had used in an oil painting hanging on
the wall of Granny's Attic. It was entitled "Disaster," and
Hannah was heartily sorry she'd remembered that.

The wind began to pick up as Hannah passed the Quick
Stop. She noticed that Ron and Sean had battened down the
hatches by taping huge cardboard sheets to the inside of their

front windows. They'd never done that before and Hannah turned on the radio to see if there might be a tornado warning in effect.

At first there was only static and then a faint announcer's voice that cut in and out. Hannah had only managed to catch the words, "storm" and "century" before a sharp gust of wind caught the side of her truck and caused her to swerve dangerously. Just as she'd righted her heading and maneuvered back into her own lane of traffic, another gust of wind from the opposite direction sent her perilously close to the ditch. Hannah was seriously considering the wisdom of stopping and waiting until the winds had subsided when the decision was taken out of her hands. The wind gusted a third fierce time, snapping off a branch from a giant oak tree by the side of the road and hurtling it through the air, straight toward the front of her truck.

Hannah cranked the wheel as hard as she could, but there was no avoiding the wooden missile. It crashed into her windshield with a mighty thunk that rattled her truck and then it bounced back off again, taking the radio antenna with it. Hannah hit the brakes and muscled the truck over to the side of the road, pulling to a stop in a churning spume of gravel. By the time she'd stopped shaking and gotten out to assess the situation, the rain was beginning to fall. The branch didn't seem to have done too much damage, at least none that a bottle of touch-up paint wouldn't cure, but her radio antenna had snapped off at the base, leaving dangling wires and a hole in her hood where it had been attached.

"At least I won't have to listen to the storm warnings," Hannah muttered, picking up the wires and poking them back through the hole. The antenna was nowhere to be found, but she was sure that Ted Koester would be able to replace it with a new one from his salvage yard. Her windshield was intact and her truck was still running, and those were the important things. She should be able to get the rest of the way home.

It was only after she'd slid back into the driver's seat that Hannah realized her blouse and jeans were soaked. There was nothing like driving home in a storm, sopping wet. This was the sort of thing colds were made of and Hannah hated summer colds. She reached into the back of her truck, shoved aside the down pillow that Michelle had picked up for her, and grabbed a towel from the stack she carried for catering. After her hair, face, and hands were dry, she felt much more in charge. This wasn't so bad. The log hadn't crashed through the windshield and she wouldn't melt like sugar just because she was wet. Hannah was preparing to pull back out on the road again when she realized that her passenger's-side windshield wiper had stopped working altogether and the one on the driver's side was limping along like a lame duck.

There was nothing to do but go for it. Sitting here at the side of the road wouldn't get her anywhere and there was no way she wanted Norman and Mike to find her in this helpless position. Hannah pulled out on the road again, thankful that the rain was light. Her wiper was operating in fits and starts. Every time the wind gusted, it stopped. Hannah inched along in the gathering darkness, hoping that no one would come up behind her at a speedy clip.

She'd gone only about a quarter of a mile when the rain began to fall harder. The small drops turned into larger drops and then into sheets of pouring rain. Her wiper stuttered with each new gust of wind, locked into a life-or-death battle with the elements. When it seemed certain that the elements would win, Hannah pulled over to the side of the road again and thumped her hand against the steering wheel in frustration.

"Oh, great!" Hannah groaned, accepting the inevitable. If she wanted to get home, there was only one thing to do. She lowered her window, poked her head out, and drove slowly down the shoulder of the road, listening for upcoming traffic and peering into the driving rain to look for her turnoff.

It was slow going. Every minute or so, Hannah had to stop

to wipe off her face and her hair. She could think of pleasant ways to spend an evening and this wasn't one of them. If she'd known this was going to happen, she would have encouraged *both* Norman and Mike to follow her home!

By the time Hannah reached the turnoff, she felt like a drowned rat. Her hair was hanging in limp strands and her cheeks were raw from the stinging rain. She glanced at her watch and groaned loudly. It was almost an hour since she'd left the lake cottage. Visions of Mike and Norman waiting for her at her condo when she arrived were daunting, and she knew she'd better call to let them know that she was all right.

The first place Hannah passed was the apartment where Rhonda had lived. She pulled into the garage, parked her truck in a spot designated for visitors, and headed straight for Beatrice and Ted Koester's apartment. They owned and managed the building and they'd let her use their phone.

"Hannah!" Beatrice looked shocked when she opened her door in response to Hannah's knock. "Did your truck break down?"

"Yes, and no. It's still running, but the windshield wipers conked out on me. I had to stick my head out the window and that's why I'm so wet."

"Well, don't just stand there. Come in and dry off." Beatrice held the door open wider. "I'll get you a bath towel."

Hannah smiled her thanks as she slipped out of her soggy sandals in the hall and padded into Beatrice's dry apartment. "Could I use your phone? Mother's waiting for my call and I want to let her know that I'm all right. I promise I'll try not to drip on anything."

"That doesn't matter." Beatrice gestured toward the wall phone in the kitchen. "I was planning on washing the floor tonight anyway. Ted likes a clean home. It's a nice contrast to all that dirt and grease out at the scrap yard. He makes a good living, though. Especially since he added the auto salvage. Go ahead, Hannah. I'll get you that towel and a cup of coffee. You look chilled to the bone."

Hannah accepted the towel Beatrice brought her and did her best to mop herself off. Then she called the lake cottage and Michelle answered the phone.

"Hi, Hannah. I'm so glad you're home. Mike and Norman were beginning to get worried. Hold on a second and I'll tell them."

Hannah opened her mouth to say she wasn't home, but Michelle had already set the phone down. She could hear her youngest sister talking in the background, conveying the message that Hannah was home and everything was fine.

"I told them," Michelle came back on the line. "The storm was pretty fierce out here. Did you run into much rain?"

"Oh yes," Hannah said, knowing that she was uttering a gross understatement. The rain was still drumming against Beatrice's windows with considerable force.

"Mike and Norman said they'll call you back. Mother's car got hit by lightning and the guys are going out to look at it."

Hannah thought fast. If Mike or Norman called her back at her apartment, they'd get her answer machine. "Tell them to give me at least forty-five minutes. I'm chilled and I'm going to take a hot shower."

"Okay, Hannah. I'll tell them. I'm really glad you got home okay. We were all worried."

"Here, Hannah." Beatrice presented Hannah with a cup of coffee the moment she'd hung up the phone.

"Thanks, Beatrice." Hannah took a sip of the hot brew and sighed gratefully. "This is just what I needed."

"The other thing you need is dry clothes. I'd give you some of mine, but I don't think they'd fit."

"Not on a bet." Hannah laughed. Beatrice was petite, about Michelle's size.

"I don't know . . ." Beatrice cocked her head to the side and sized Hannah up. "You've lost a ton of weight. One of my skirts might be okay, but you're so much taller."

"Don't worry about it, Beatrice. Now that I'm toweled off, I'll dry in no time."

Beatrice looked doubtful. "You can't drive the rest of the way home in those wet clothes. You'll catch your death. How about something of Rhonda's? Her clothes are still in her closet and she was about your size."

"You haven't rented her apartment?" Hannah was surprised. Beatrice and Ted ran a nice apartment complex and there was always a waiting list of people who wanted to rent from them.

"I can't rent it out yet. Rhonda paid me for July. I can take a deposit now, but no one can move in until the beginning of August."

"That seems like a waste when you have a waiting list."

"I know, but that's the law. At least I won't have to work to get it in shape. We put in new carpet and repainted it in June, and Rhonda just finished redecorating. Her place looks wonderful, Hannah. It's just a shame her relatives don't want her things."

"They don't?" Hannah was surprised. "What are you going to do with them?"

"They said to sell her car and send the money to them in Colorado, but we can do whatever we want with the rest. I'm going to rent the place furnished and I'll let my tenants have first pick on everything else. That's why I said you should go up there and get something to wear . . . if you don't mind wearing her clothes, that is."

"Why would I mind wearing something of Rhonda's?"

"Because she's dead. You know, a lot of people are sensitive about things like that."

"It doesn't bother me," Hannah assured her. She'd hoped to get a peek inside Rhonda's apartment and this seemed like a gift from the gods.

"The only thing is, I can't go up there with you. Ted's at a meeting and he said he'd call right before he left for home to see if I needed anything. And I do. I want him to stop and pick up some laundry detergent."

Even better. Hannah tried not to look too excited. "That's okay, Beatrice. I can run up to Rhonda's apartment alone."

"Are you sure you don't mind? I mean, with her being dead and all?"

"I don't mind," Hannah said, taking the key that Beatrice held out. "After all, she didn't die there. I'll grab something, put it on, and come right back down with the key."

"No hurry. Poke around a little and see if there's anything you can use. Everything she owned is up for grabs."

Hannah took a deep breath as she unlocked the door and stepped inside. She'd never been invited to Rhonda's apartment and it was little strange to be coming here now. It felt like intruding, but Hannah reminded herself that she had a perfect reason to search through Rhonda's things for clues since she was trying to solve her murder.

There was a switch by the inside of the door and Hannah flicked on the lights. Rhonda's apartment was pretty, like something out of a magazine, with color-coordinated cushions on the couch and a bowl of matching silk flowers on the coffee table. The kitchen was immaculate, but that was no surprise since Rhonda had been intending to leave on vacation.

First things first, Hannah reminded herself, and she went straight to Rhonda's walk-in closet. She grabbed the first items of clothing that came to hand, a pair of black slacks with an elastic waistband and a light blue pullover sweater. She wasn't here to scavenge through Rhonda's clothing unless it had some bearing on the murder, and anything that was dry would do.

Hannah dropped her own clothes in a heap on the floor and changed to Rhonda's. Although the pants were too short, they weren't as tight as she'd expected them to be and

Rhonda's sweater was positively bulky. Perhaps Beatrice was right and she really had lost a ton of weight. She checked the closet, but it contained nothing unusual and she wasn't interested in the number of outfits in Rhonda's wardrobe. Then she tackled the dresser drawers, going from top to bottom as fast as she could. She found a pair of socks to wear, but there was nothing else that could possibly relate to Rhonda's murder.

The plastic bags were in a holder under the sink and Hannah stuffed her wet clothing into one of them. Then she went through the cupboards and kitchen drawers, learning nothing except the fact that Rhonda owned a set of sterling silver fish knives and she must have been very fond of packaged macaroni and cheese.

The living room was next. Hannah headed straight for a small desk that Rhonda had placed under the windows. The center drawer was filled with loose receipts, and she sat down in the desk chair to glance through them.

Nothing caught Hannah's interest until she found a receipt from Browerville Travel. Not only had Rhonda driven all the way to Browerville to book her flight, she'd lied to Hannah about where and when she had done it. When they'd signed the house papers at The Cookie Jar, Rhonda had said she'd called the airlines and reserved her ticket the previous evening. She'd also said that thanks to Norman, she had enough money to fly to Rome on vacation. But this receipt from Browerville Travel was dated two weeks *before* Norman had made his offer on the house!

Rhonda's lie didn't seem to make much sense, but Hannah didn't have time to think about that now. She grabbed the receipt, stuck it into her purse, and went through the rest of the desk drawers. She was down to the last drawer when she discovered another strange item. It was a letter addressed to Rhonda's great-aunt.

"Strange," Hannah mused, staring down at the letter. This was the only item belonging to Mrs. Voelker that she'd found in Rhonda's apartment. It must be important if Rhonda had kept it and nothing else. Hannah stuffed it into her purse and stood up. One room left to search and she was through.

Four minutes later Hannah emerged from Rhonda's bathroom with a frown on her face. Searching Rhonda's medicine cabinet and bathroom drawers had been a waste of her time. She'd found nothing except a small fortune in cosmetics and time was growing short. Hannah grabbed her things, flicked off the lights, and raced down the stairs to return Beatrice's key. If she didn't hurry, she'd have the whole Winnetka Sheriff's Department and every member of her extended family waiting on her doorstep when she got home.

Chapter
Twenty-Five

Hannah got up with a smile the next morning. Since Moishe now had his own down pillow, her neck felt great for the first time in months. It didn't take long to dress for the Fourth and within the hour, Hannah was in her truck on her way to The Cookie Jar. The weather was gorgeous. Puffy white clouds floated lazily in a bright blue sky and it couldn't have looked less like rain. After the deluge they'd gotten the previous night, the grass was emerald green and there was a wonderful fresh scent in the air, the same scent candles and room fresheners attempted in vain to duplicate.

As Hannah drove through town, she noticed that everyone had gone all out for Independence Day with flags, banners, ribbons, and other patriotic items. Even the tall pine that served as the town Christmas tree in Lake Eden Park was decked out with red, white, and blue streamers.

By seven forty-five, Hannah arrived at her parking spot. She unlocked the back door and stepped inside, sniffing appreciatively as a welcome aroma wafted out to greet her. Lisa had put on the coffee. But where was her car?

"Happy Fourth, Hannah!" Lisa came in from the coffee shop before Hannah had time to look for her.

"The same to you. Where's your car?"

"I left it down at the Senior Center. Herb gave me a ride

here. Pour yourself a cup of coffee and go sit down in the shop. I'm going to make you a low-cal breakfast."

The aroma of freshly brewed coffee was enticing and Hannah was only too happy to do as she'd been told. She filled a mug, carried it to her favorite table, and took a seat facing the plate-glass window. The street outside fairly sparkled in the sunlight. Mayor Bascomb had ordered every inch of the parade route swept clean last night. Since the street was roped off, there was no traffic and nothing to watch. It was too early for spectators to gather and the only thing moving was a family of birds in the tall pine across the street.

Hannah sipped her coffee for a few moments, but she'd never been any good at sitting still for long. This was the perfect time to check out the receipt and the letter she'd found in Rhonda's desk.

One glance at the clock and Hannah decided to tackle the receipt first. The toll-free number for the airlines shouldn't be terribly busy this early. She retrieved both items from her purse and carried the receipt behind the counter where she could use the phone. This would take some fancy talking, but she'd taken several lessons on that subject from Andrea. She'd say she was calling for Rhonda, who'd missed her flight because of a sudden death in the family. That part was the truth. And then she'd fudge a little by saying that Rhonda wanted to rebook her ticket with exactly the same accommodations. If she got lucky, the airline employee would tell her all the facts about Rhonda's ticket when he or she rebooked the flight.

It took ten minutes, but at last Hannah hung up the phone and walked back to the table to take a huge swig of coffee. The information she'd been given was startling, to say the least. Nothing Rhonda had told her was true. She'd booked a one-way ticket, not a round-trip. And she'd been flying to Zurich, not Rome.

Hannah stared out the window at the silent street. No

wonder Rhonda had gone to Browerville Travel! She hadn't wanted anyone in town to know that she was leaving for good or where she'd gone.

Hannah thought about that to the faint sounds of pans clattering from the kitchen. A few moments later, she caught the hint of a delectable aroma and her mouth began to water. She didn't know what Lisa was cooking, but it certainly smelled delicious.

"Our float looks gorgeous," Lisa said, pushing the door open and sticking her head in the coffee shop. "Unless the judges are blind, we'll win first prize."

"I didn't know they were awarding prizes."

"Neither did I. Janice Cox said they decided to do it at the council meeting last night. The first-place float gets a hundred dollars, second place gets fifty, and third place gets twenty-five. Hold on a second. I have to flip something."

The door swung closed and Hannah was left with a gaping mouth. If they won, what would they do with the money? By the time the door opened and Lisa appeared again, she'd decided. "If we win, I think we should split the money between Kiddie Korner and the Senior Center. They did all the work."

"Perfect," Lisa said, smiling her approval. "That's exactly what I thought we should do. There's one more thing I have to tell you. Andrea said that more robbery money surfaced last night. It's only a little over four hundred dollars, but someone is definitely spending it in Winnetka County. Excuse me for a minute. I think these are ready."

Lisa disappeared again and Hannah leaned back in her chair. She still didn't know whether the robbery money had anything to do with Rhonda's murder case, but the possibility couldn't be dismissed out of hand.

"Breakfast is served," Lisa called out, coming through the swinging door with two plates in her hands. She served Hannah first, then sat down across from her.

Hannah glanced at her breakfast. "These look like pancakes with sliced peaches."

"That's right." Lisa handed her the container with packets of non-calorie sweetener. "Sprinkle a little sweetener over the top. They're really good that way."

Hannah tore open a packet and sprinkled it on top of the stack. Then she cut off a piece of pancake and tasted it. "They're wonderful, Lisa. When you said low-cal, I thought I'd be getting cottage cheese for breakfast."

"You are."

Hannah blinked. "These have cottage cheese in them?"

"That's right. My Aunt Kitty used to make them every time somebody in the family was on a diet."

"They're delicious." Hannah took another forkful and smiled as she chewed and swallowed. "Thanks, Lisa. This is a real change from all those cold salads and bowls of plain cottage cheese. Are you sure they're diet food?"

"I'm sure, but you can make them into regular food, too. Aunt Kitty used to serve them with sour cream and jam on the top. When she did that, she called them Poor Man's Blintzes. I'll give you the recipe if you want it."

"I'd love to have it," Hannah said, taking another bite.

They ate in silence for several minutes, polishing off the last of the pancakes. When they were through, Lisa pointed at the letter on the table. "What's this?"

"It's a letter to Mrs. Voelker that I found in Rhonda's apartment."

Lisa looked surprised. "Mike and Bill let you search Rhonda's apartment?"

"No, Beatrice Koester did. She told me to go through Rhonda's things to see if there was anything I needed. The relatives in Colorado didn't want anything."

"That was a lucky break for you," Lisa said with a grin. "Did you find anything else interesting?"

Hannah told Lisa about the receipt from Browerville Travel and Rhonda's one-way ticket to Zurich. "And that explains why Rhonda wasn't upset when Jon fired her. She wasn't planning to come back anyway."

"What does the letter say?"

"I haven't read it yet."

"You'd better read it. It could be something important."

"I know. I just feel funny about reading someone else's private mail, that's all."

"Then throw it away."

"I can't throw it away without knowing what it says!"

"Then read it." Lisa looked amused. "You're making a mountain out of a molehill, Hannah, and that's not like you at all. If the contents are private, don't tell anyone about them. But if it's important, you can turn it over to the right person."

"You're right, of course." Hannah drew the letter out of the envelope before she could dither about it any longer. She unfolded the single sheet of tablet paper and began to read. As she skimmed the words, she let out a little cry of distress.

"What is it?" Lisa leaned forward in concern.

"It's a tragedy," Hannah said, swallowing past the lump in her throat.

Aunt Kitty's Cottage Cheese Pancakes
(Poor Man's Blintzes)

2 cups cottage cheese
4 eggs
½ teaspoon salt
½ cup flour

Mix cottage cheese, eggs, salt, and flour together in a small bowl. Let the mixture "rest" in the refrigerator for an hour *(overnight is fine, too.)*

Heat a nonstick griddle to 350 degrees F., or use a frying pan that's been sprayed with nonstick cooking spray. *(The frying pan is ready when a drop of water sizzles and "dances" across the surface.)*

Spoon pancake batter in pan or on griddle and fry until the bubbles on the surface of the pancake remain open. *(You can check to see if the bottom side is done by lifting the edge with a spatula.)* When the bottom side is a nice golden color, flip the pancake over and cook until the bottom color matches the top.

Place the finished pancakes on a plate, sprinkle artificial sweetener over the tops and add sliced fruit of your choice.

Poor Man's Blintzes

Mix up the pancakes as directed and fry them. When they're done, spread each pancake with butter and sprinkle with sugar. Top with spoonfuls of jam, add a generous dollop of sour cream, and enjoy.

Yield: 8 medium-sized pancakes.

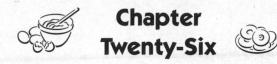

Hannah cleared her throat and began to read the letter aloud. *"I wish I was back in Lake Eden with you right now. They say I'm not going to make it and the guy next to me is going to find someone to take this letter out and mail it to you."*

"He's dying?" Lisa whispered as Hannah looked up.

"That's right. What makes you think this letter is from a man?"

"It sounds like he's in a hospital and they don't usually put a man and a woman together in one room."

"Good point," Hannah said and turned back to the letter again. *"Thank you for being nice to me when I was a kid. You were the only one who played games with me. Remember the one where you hid those notes and sent me all over the house to find them? You always started with the cookie jar and that sent me to the grandfather clock, or the Bible. You taught me to read with those clues. I never would have learned in school. And you always made sure I found the prize at the end."*

"I know that game," Lisa said. "Go on, Hannah."

"I just wanted to tell you that I love you. If you get this letter, I didn't make it. Keep putting up that peach jam of yours. It was always my favorite. And please say a prayer for me when you do it."

"That's so sad," Lisa commented, blinking away the tears that had gathered in her eyes. "Who sent it?"

"Someone named 'Speedy.' That's got to be a nickname. I don't know who Speedy is and anyone who might have known is dead."

"Where did the letter come from?"

Hannah shrugged. "I don't know. I can make out part of the date, it's nineteen eighty-something, but the rest of the cancellation is blurred."

"Well, at least Speedy had happy memories of his time in Lake Eden. He talked a lot about the Treasure Hunt game."

"That's what it's called?"

"That's what we called it. Mom used to play it with me every year on my birthday. She hid clues all over the house and she told me where to find the first one. When I found it, I read it and it told me where to find the second clue. There were always at least ten clues written out and when I came to the end, it told me where I'd find my birthday present."

Hannah felt jealous for one brief second. Delores had never played the Treasure Hunt game with her. But that was in the past. "Thanks for telling me about it, Lisa. It sounds like fun."

"It was. Do you want me to set out the rest of the day-old cookies? People might be hungry when they come in."

"Good idea." Hannah stuffed the letter back in her purse and shivered slightly. She'd just read the last words of a dying man, written to a woman who'd been dead and buried for months. To make things even more depressing, she'd found the letter in a murder victim's apartment. There was only one thing to do to turn her mood around. Normally, she would have eaten some chocolate. That was the best antidote for depression. But since chocolate wasn't one of the food groups allowed on her diet, Hannah did the next best thing. "Hold on and I'll help you," she said, levering herself up from the table and heading off to the kitchen to work.

* * *

By the time her extended family had arrived, Hannah was in much better spirits. They sat eating cookies, drinking coffee, and chatting until almost everyone who'd said they were coming had arrived.

"The only two missing are Mike and Bill," Hannah commented, turning to Andrea. "Where are they?"

"Oh, they're not coming. They're helping with The Cookie Jar float. Mike's towing it with his Jeep and Bill's taking care of the mechanics."

"The mechanics?"

Andrea looked contrite. "I shouldn't have said anything. I don't want you to know anything about the float ahead of time."

"I don't. And you didn't actually *say* anything."

"You'll understand what I meant once you see it. I got the idea from the animated floats they build for the Rose Parade. It's really a terrific concept."

"I'm sure it is," Hannah said, but she had to work to keep the smile on her face. If The Cookie Jar float was anything like the floats in the Rose Parade, Andrea had taken on a project that was much too difficult for a group of preschoolers and seniors to handle. It was bound to be a disaster, but it was too late to back out now and she was going to say she loved it, no matter what happened. She owed it to her sister.

Andrea reached out to squeeze her arm. "Don't look so worried, Hannah. It'll be great, you'll see. It was almost working when I left to come here."

"Great. I'm sure it'll be perfect." Hannah pushed back her chair. "The crowd's lining up out there. We'd better claim a piece of sidewalk before all the good spots are taken."

"No problem," Norman said, rising to take her arm. "Come on, everyone. Just follow me and I'll show you to your seats."

Hannah was surprised as Norman led her through the crowd. They usually stood up to watch the parade. Then she saw the row of folding chairs that had been set up near the

276 Joanne Fluke

curb. Their names were printed on signs hanging from the backs, and Hannah felt like an honored guest as she took the chair with her name.

"This is a great idea, Norman." Hannah smiled over at him.

"Thanks," Norman said, glancing down at his watch. "Only five minutes to go. I'd better get my camera ready."

There was flurry of activity as Lisa dispensed her disposable cameras and told everyone how to use them. She'd just finished when the vintage convertible carrying Mayor Bascomb and his wife rounded the corner. He was wearing a white straw boater with red, white, and blue ribbons around its brim, and she was dressed in a white dress with red and blue stripes. The parade had begun. The Cookie Jar float would be next.

Hannah applauded as the boys and girls from Tracey's class marched around the corner. They were wearing sandwich boards shaped and colored like cookies, and each one was carrying a white wicker basket lined with red and blue paper napkins. As Hannah watched, they scattered into the crowd, offering the patriotic cookies that Hannah had baked and Lisa had decorated.

"They're darling," Hannah said, snapping a picture of Bertie Straub as she accepted a cookie from one of Tracey's classmates. "Whatever you do, Norman, don't miss getting a shot of Tracey."

"I won't. Andrea already cued me in. I'm supposed to catch her at the apex."

"What apex?"

"You'll see."

The applause grew in volume and Hannah turned to look as two Jordan High students rounded the corner carrying a sign that read FIRST-PLACE WINNER.

"I told you we'd win!" Lisa shouted, running over to hug Hannah. Then she rushed over to hug Andrea, and all three of them laughed in excitement.

The applause grew even louder as Mike's Jeep began to round the corner. The kids and seniors had draped red, white, and blue bunting on the sides. Mike looked incredibly handsome in a shirt that was printed in an American flag pattern. Hannah's breath caught in her throat for a moment and her heart raced in her chest. To think that the most handsome man ever to set foot in Lake Eden chose to date her was very close to getting everything on your Christmas list. Reluctantly, she tore her eyes away from Mike and took her first look at The Cookie Jar float.

Hannah was aware that her mouth had dropped open, but she couldn't help it. The float was a masterpiece, a giant cookie jar done in red, white, and blue. As Hannah watched, the cover flipped back and Tracey rose from the depths, her smile as wide as Eden Lake.

"Oh!" Hannah gasped, staring at her niece in awe. Tracey was wearing a Lady Liberty costume, complete with torch and crown, and she was as cute as a button. She started to wave regally at the crowd, but her enthusiasm got the best of her when she spotted Hannah.

"Hi, Aunt Hannah!" Tracey yelled out. "Do you like it?"

"I love it!" Hannah shouted back, and then Tracey began to sink slowly out of sight inside the giant cookie jar, reaching up at the last minute to close the lid behind her.

"Do you really love it?" Andrea asked, looking a bit anxious.

"It's completely stupendous, marvelous, and fantastic," Hannah assured her. "And Tracey looks just adorable. I saw Mike driving, but where's Bill?"

"Can't you tell? Bill's down in the cookie jar, lifting Tracey up and down against counterweights."

"Of course. The mechanics." Hannah grinned at her sister. "Now I understand."

"I knew he'd get the kinks worked out. Tracey's standing in a box that Bill attached to counterweights. We were going to use hydraulics, but it made too much noise."

One by one the floats passed by. Hannah didn't think any of them could compare to The Cookie Jar float. She applauded with everyone else as the wheelchairs from the convalescent home came into view, the spokes of their wheels decked out with red, white, and blue crepe paper. Even the walkers were decorated with streamers and stars, and Jack Herman led the seniors in his Uncle Sam costume.

"Didn't Dad look wonderful?" Lisa asked, racing back from the street where she'd taken her pictures.

"He looked positively dashing," Hannah assured her. "Here's my camera. I used up the whole roll. The last one's a picture of Mrs. Robbins making eyes at your dad when he picked up the handkerchief she dropped."

"Do they still drop handkerchiefs?" Lisa wanted to know.

"I don't know, but Mrs. Robbins does. She's eighty-five if she's a day, so she might be a little behind the times."

The Boy Scouts came next and then Bonnie Surma's Brownies, followed by the Jordan High marching band. Hannah resisted the urge to cover her ears, especially when they stopped in the middle of her block to play. Their music was slightly less dreadful than before, and they were so enthusiastic, it made up for a multitude of missed notes and individual struggles with the tempo. Thankfully, blessedly, the bandleader had cut the piccolo obbligato and Hannah breathed a sigh of relief.

Delores, who didn't know a sharp from a natural, tapped Hannah on the shoulder after they'd finished playing and marched on. "Weren't they just wonderful?"

Hannah sputtered for a moment, trying to think of something honest to say. "They improved a lot from last year."

Several more floats rolled by, but they couldn't hold a candle to Andrea's creation. Hannah applauded for the veterans, resplendent in uniforms that had been retrieved from trunks in dusty attics, and she did her share of clapping for The Lake Eden Players, who were dressed in the costumes they'd wear later for their reenactment of the signing of the Declaration of Independence. When the parade was over and she still hadn't seen Bridget Murphy's lemon car, Hannah figured that Cyril had fixed it to save himself the embarrassment.

"That's it," Norman said, folding up his chair. "I'm going to take these back to the funeral home and then I'll develop the film."

"These chairs are from the funeral home?" Hannah asked, not sure exactly how she felt about that.

"I borrowed them last night. Digger said to take as many as I needed. Professional courtesy, you know."

"Professional courtesy?"

"He keeps hoping I'll send him some business."

"You mean like one of your patients dying?"

Norman shrugged, but there was a twinkle in his eye. "You know what people say about root canals. They're killers."

Hannah laughed as she helped Norman load the folding chairs in his trunk and she was still grinning when he drove away. Being with Norman always made her feel good. Then she said good-bye to the little group assembled on the sidewalk, went inside The Cookie Jar to help Lisa load up the cupcakes, and headed off to attend the municipal band concert before she drove out to the lake for an afternoon of games and other entertainment.

Hannah arrived at the area of lakeshore that had been designated for public parking with a smile on her face. The band concert in the park had been wonderful. The Lake Eden Municipal Band was a mixed conglomeration of musicians who had settled in the area. Anyone who wanted to put horn or woodwind in hand and practice every week at the community center was welcome. They'd played their full repertoire of Sousa marches and ended with the ever popular strains of "God Bless America."

The town had turned out in full force at Eden Lake and

Hannah trolled the parking area in vain for a spot. She finally settled for putting her truck in four-wheel drive and parking at the very edge of the lot, on top of the shoulder of the road.

Several hours later, after listening to two boring political speeches, attending one of the Lake Eden Players' performances, and watching some of the games and contests, she wandered over to the picnic area to see if there was anything she could do to help Edna Ferguson, who was in charge of the potluck dinner.

"Hi, Edna," Hannah said, trying not to stare at the older woman's hair. Edna's frizzy gray curls had undergone a transformation since the last time Hannah had seen her. Instead of Edna's natural steel gray, her curls were now blue.

"I know. Looks like you-know-what," Edna said, reaching up to swat at her curls. "Bertie talked me into a rinse the last time I was in and she didn't tell me it would take weeks to wash out."

"It looks very . . . colorful."

"That's tactful, Hannah, especially for you." Edna chuckled. "All I need is a couple of red and white bows and I'll be all decked out for the Fourth."

"I came over to see if there was anything I could . . ."

"Of course there is," Edna interrupted her. "You know no one else ever shows up when there's work to be done. What's the matter? Those two boyfriends of yours desert you?"

Hannah laughed. It was a waste of time to take offense at anything Edna said. She was outspoken and everyone knew it. "Not exactly. Mike had to go back to the station and Norman's home, developing the film he took of the parade. I'm all yours, Edna."

"Well good! You're a lot more help than some people I could name. I suppose your sister's bringing her Jell-O mold again. None of these young girls know how to cook. They're not like you and me."

Hannah bit back a choice retort. Edna was sixty if she was a day, and that made her at least thirty years older than

Hannah. She'd lived in Lake Eden all her life and that gave Hannah an idea, especially since Edna had grown up on the family farm right next to the Voelker place. "You knew Mrs. Voelker, didn't you, Edna?"

"Sure, I did. She put up the best peach jam in the county. Everybody around was real sorry when she got in that accident and ended up in the wheelchair. No more peach jam for the neighbors."

Hannah nodded, wondering if people would speak of her that way when she was dead, mourning not her, but the loss of her cookies. "Do you remember a boy named Speedy that visited Mrs. Voelker?"

"Speedy?" Edna started to shake her head. "No, I don't think . . . Yes, I do! He was some kind of shirttail relation and he spent a whole summer with her. That boy was a regular fishing fool. He used to race through his chores so he could get down to the lake to fish. That's why she called him Speedy. Half the time she ended up stripping the cows herself after the morning milking, but she told us he had a hard time at home and she was going to see he had fun for a change."

"Do you remember Speedy's real name?"

Edna sighed. "Can't say as I do. I suppose I knew it back then, but that was a long time ago."

"Will you tell me if you think of it?"

"Sure will. So, is she?"

Hannah blinked. Edna had obviously switched to another topic of conversation. "Is she what?"

"Bringing her Jell-O mold. Andrea, that is."

"Oh!" Hannah switched gears. "Not this time. She's bringing chips and dip for the appetizer table."

"Well, heaven be praised! One less Jell-O bowl to contend with. Why don't you dump some ice in the bottom of some of those coolers we borrowed so we can refrigerate the things that we have to keep chilled. You didn't bring a dessert with whipped cream, did you?"

"Would I do something like that?" Hannah asked, grinning at Edna.

"No, I don't guess you would. Marge Beeseman will though. You mark my words. And she'll put the whipped cream on at home, not leave it in the can the way it said to do in the flyer. And then she'll complain because it drooped!"

Chapter
Twenty-Seven

"**M**mm!" Hannah voiced her approval as she tasted the beef Norman had barbecued. "Delicious."

"Thanks, Hannah." Norman, who was sitting on her right side at one of the picnic tables, looked pleased by the compliment.

"It sure is," Mike commented from his spot at Hannah's left side. "I used to do a little barbecuing, but my beef was never this good."

"It's all in the sauce. A cut like this has to be marinated overnight. That way the flavor gets all the way through. It's not too much garlic for you?"

"Just right," Mike said, cutting off another bite. "Any less would be lost and any more would be overdoing it. I'd sure like that sauce recipe if you're giving it out."

"I'll give it to you. It works on chicken, too. All you have to do is double the mustard and cut back on the grated onion by half."

Hannah glanced from one man to the other, trying to keep herself from chuckling. They sounded like a couple of housewives comparing notes and even though they'd both wanted to sit with her, they seemed content to talk to each other and ignore her. She let them talk on, comparing the merits of charcoal over gas and which wood chips were preferable, while she glanced around at the crowds of people who were content-edly stuffing their collective faces.

The sun was lowering in the sky and Hannah knew she'd have to run back to her truck to get her mosquito repellent. That reminded her that they never bit Norman, and she turned to Mike. "Do mosquitoes bite you?"

"Mosquitoes?" Mike looked startled, as if she'd pulled him out of the most intriguing conversation of his life. "Sure. They bite everybody."

"Not Norman."

"Is that right?" Mike leaned in front of Hannah to stare at Norman. "What's your secret, Norman?"

Oh-oh. She'd started an all-male conversation again. Hannah sighed and turned back to people-gazing. Freddy Sawyer, dressed in jeans and a blue pullover with a picture of an American Eagle on the front, was leaning against a tree at the edge of the picnic area. Hannah was glad to see him here. Freddy had once told Hannah that the Fourth of July was his favorite holiday and he loved to watch the fireworks. Jed was only a few feet away, talking to a group of people Hannah didn't recognize. He looked handsome tonight in a white cot-ton shirt with the sleeves rolled up and a denim vest that was embroidered with stars and stripes. It looked expensive and Hannah wondered if he'd spent his whole paycheck on it.

A young woman in the group was flirting with Jed and he smiled at her as she reached out to put her hand on his arm. Although he was clearly flirting back, Hannah was glad to see him turn slightly, so that he could keep Freddy in sight. Jed was taking his responsibility toward his cousin seriously, keeping tabs on him in the crowd.

Several children in the crowd began to cheer and Hannah turned toward the source of the excitement. The Lake Eden volunteer fire department had arrived in their fire truck. The hook and ladder was followed by one of Cyril Murphy's dark green rental vans with light green shamrocks painted on the sides. Any child in the crowd old enough to remember the fireworks from the previous year knew that the van contained all the pyrotechnics for tonight's display.

Hannah glanced over at the food tables. There were only a few stragglers going back for thirds. It was time to start putting the food away. She stood up, and both men stopped talking and turned to her. "I'm going to help Edna with the cleanup."

"Sure," Mike said.

"Okay," Norman echoed the sentiment. "Do you need any help?"

"No, that's okay." Hannah headed off at a speedy clip, but not fast enough to miss hearing another all-male conversation begin. This one was about cars and the various advantages of the latest models.

By the time Hannah had helped with the cleanup and made a run to her truck to mosquito-proof herself and retrieve her quilt, she saw a fleet of rowboats heading out from the dock. The boats were riding low in the water and Hannah knew that the fireworks had been unloaded from the van and stacked in the bottom of the rowboats for transport to the rafts that would become launching pads. Most people in the tri-county area thought that the Lake Eden fireworks display was the best one around. The town council spent a small fortune every year on fireworks and the display seemed twice as large as it really was when the streamers of bursting colors were reflected off the surface of the lake. She found Mike and Norman on the lakeshore, sitting on the sand and claiming their patch of spectator space. They helped her spread out her quilt and before long the whole extended family had found spaces around them.

Darkness began to fall. Hannah could see dim lights, one on each of the rafts and more in the rowboats. She was sure that Joe Dietz was out there again this year. A retired warrant officer in Army Ordnance, Joe was in his seventies and he'd been directing the fireworks for as long as Hannah could remember. She spotted Jed moving through the crowd with a blanket roll under his arm. He'd put on a leather jacket over his shirt and vest, and Hannah wished she'd thought to bring hers. It wouldn't be needed in town, but there was always a breeze near the lake and it could turn chilly when the last rays of sun had faded. For a moment, Hannah was concerned that Freddy was nowhere in sight, but then she remembered the group that Jed had been talking to earlier and how friendly they'd seemed. Freddy and the group were probably sitting on the sand, saving a place for the blanket that Jed had gone to fetch.

Once the sun had disappeared below the horizon, night fell rapidly. Hannah crossed her legs and sat "Indian style," a phrase her first-grade teacher had used that was probably now politically incorrect.

Before Hannah really expected it, the fireworks began with a bang. It was a single bang and it was a loud one, causing her hands to fly up to cover her ears. She jumped, then laughed in delight. The Lake Eden fireworks always started this way, but it never failed to startle her.

The first loud bang was followed by a rapid series of bangs. Next there was a whoosh as a rocket shot up and burst overhead, raining down streamers of pink that were reflected on the surface of the lake. Hannah cheered with the rest of the crowd and at that exact moment, Norman reached out for her hand. A moment later, as a green blossom of fireworks burst in the sky, Mike reached out for her other hand.

Hannah sat there, hardly daring to breathe. What was the etiquette in a situation like this? Should she tell Mike she couldn't hold hands with him because she was already holding hands with Norman? Or should she refuse to hold hands with both of them? Hannah thought about it through another series of rockets and multicolored streamers and came to a decision. Miss Manners was bound to disagree, but since neither Mike nor Norman seemed to be aware that his rival was holding her hand, the best thing to do was relax and enjoy it.

The crowd gave a collective gasp and then a prolonged "Oooooh" as two more pyrotechnic stars burst overhead, one red and one blue. Joe Dietz was doing a good job of mixing large displays with the smaller displays to make the fireworks last as long as possible. It was a perfect evening for the show. There was a light breeze that cleared away the smoke, so each flash looked as brilliant against the night sky as the one that had come before it.

They were only five minutes into the fireworks show when Mike's police radio crackled and he held it up against his ear. He listened for a moment, responded with an "On my way," and turned to Hannah. "They called me in. There's a six-car pileup out on the highway with a bus involved."

Mike stood up and no more than a second later, so did Lonnie. Another moment and Bill also got to his feet.

"They called everyone in?" Hannah asked.

"Everyone. It's a bad one." Mike turned to Norman. "Have you seen Doc Knight? The dispatcher said she couldn't reach him on his pager."

"He was talking to Edna a couple of minutes ago," Norman said.

"Can you find him and tell him to go straight to the hospital? County's setting up triage out there and they'll be sending him some casualties."

"I'll find him and then I'll drive out. If you have any facial injuries, I can help. Where's the accident?"

"Two miles south of the Lake Eden turnoff. Thanks, Norman." Mike motioned to Bill and Lonnie. "I brought the squad car. You can ride with me."

In less time than it took to swat a mosquito, Hannah's two Lotharios had deserted her and she was left sitting in the center of her quilt alone. Michelle was also alone, now that Lonnie had left, and so was Andrea.

"If you marry a cop, you go through a lot of nights alone," Andrea commented with a sharp glance at Michelle. "You don't have to like it, but you do have to cope with it."

Hannah didn't like the way this conversation was starting. As far as she was concerned, Lonnie was a better choice for Michelle's boyfriend than the guy from New York who didn't know beans about small-town life and thought Michelle's descriptions of her hometown were humorous. She was about to horn in and change the subject when Delores reached back to tap her on the arm.

"Do you have an extra sweater in your truck, Hannah? It's getting a little chilly."

Hannah hesitated. If she offered her mother the ratty old hooded sweatshirt she carried in the back of her truck, it would lead to a long lecture about revising her wardrobe and weeding out the clothing that wasn't fit to be worn. "No, but I'll run to the cottage and get you a sweater."

"But you'll miss the fireworks."

"Not if I walk along the shoreline. I can see it just fine from there. And the cottage is only about a block away."

"Well, if you're sure you don't mind. . . . No! I've changed my mind! I don't want you to go, Hannah!"

"Why not?" Her mother had sounded panicked.

"Because . . . well . . ." Delores leaned back and turned her head to whisper, "The killer could be out there."

"Don't worry, Mother. The shore is crowded with people. He wouldn't attack me in front of all those witnesses."

"But they wouldn't be witnesses, not if they were looking up at the sky. And fireworks is perfect cover for a gunshot with all the banging and booming."

"Things like that only happen in the movies." Hannah was amused. Her mother was well intentioned, but totally irrational. "Besides, there wouldn't be a gunshot because the killer doesn't use a gun. Rhonda was stabbed, not shot."

"You're right. I forgot about that." Delores sighed deeply. "Do you think I'm overreacting?"

"Yes, Mother."

"Well . . . you're probably right, but you'd better stay here. I'd just worry the entire time you were gone."

"I'll go along with Hannah," Michelle offered. "There's no way anyone would take on both of us. That would make you feel better, wouldn't it, Mother?"

"Much better," Delores said, and she sounded very relieved. "And while you're there, you can put on the coffee. It would be nice to have a cup when the fireworks are over. And thaw that coffee cake I stuck in the freezer. Ten minutes in the microwave on defrost should do it. And would you carry out the garbage on your way back? I forgot to do it when I left."

"Sure, Mother," Hannah said, grabbing Michelle's hand and making a quick getaway before their mother could think of more tasks for them to do.

Chapter
Twenty-Eight

"We're done," Hannah said, gathering up the sweater they'd initially been sent to fetch and switching on the coffeepot. "Are you ready?"

"I'm ready." Michelle came out of her room wearing a sweatshirt and a pair of jeans.

Hannah opened the front door and they both stepped out. "I'm locking it. Do you have the key?"

"I've got it." Michelle whistled as a multicolored shower of streamers shot across the sky. "That was pretty spectacular. Is it the finale?"

Hannah glanced at her watch as another fiery flower blossomed in the sky. "Not yet. The show is supposed to run forty minutes this year. We've still got over twenty minutes left."

The two sisters climbed down the steps to the shore by the light of the fireworks that were bursting in the sky. As they reached the bottom, a huge white shower rained down and Michelle gasped. "What's *that*, Hannah?"

"What's what?"

"That big thing sticking out under the dock. It wasn't there this afternoon."

"I don't know, but I'll find out." Hannah walked closer and waited until another shower of lights illuminated the area. Her voice was sharp as she spoke again. "Is there a flashlight in the cottage?"

"Yes, Mother keeps one in the kitchen."

"Go get it and bring it down here."

Michelle turned and walked toward the steps. "Okay, but what is it?"

"Just get the flashlight, okay?"

The fates were kind and another volley of fireworks burst in the sky after Michelle had left. Hannah reached out toward the object and shuddered as she realized that the "thing" Michelle had seen was someone's leg. Delores hadn't been so crazy after all when she'd warned Hannah not to come here alone. Hannah stared at the leg for a moment and then she gave a deep sigh. There was only one thing to do and she was the only one here right now to do it.

It took all the strength that Hannah possessed, but she managed to free the ominously still form from its watery prison under the dock and pull it up onto the shore. By the time Michelle got back with the flashlight, Hannah had flipped it over. "Shine the flashlight, Michelle."

Michelle turned on the flashlight and both sisters stared at the inert figure for a moment, the beam of light illuminating the bloody wound on Freddy Sawyer's head.

"Is he dead?" Michelle asked, her voice shaking.

"Only one way to find out." Hannah dropped to her knees and felt for a pulse. "Not yet, but it doesn't look good. Run back to the cabin and call for an ambulance fast."

"But there aren't any. Lonnie said they were all called out to that accident out on the highway."

"Right." Hannah shook her head to clear it. The sight of Freddy's still face and the awful wound on his head had rattled her. "Okay. I'll take him to the hospital myself. I hate to ask, but can you stay here with him while I get my truck?"

"I'll stay," Michelle said.

Her baby sister sounded calm and that reassured Hannah.

"Okay, I'll be back just as fast as I can. Don't try to move him. If he starts to thrash around, talk to him and do your best to hold him still. We don't want that cut on his head to open up and start bleeding again."

Hannah raced for her truck and made short work of driving it down to the shoreline. She backed up as close as she could, opened the rear doors, and got out to find Michelle still sitting right where she'd left her, holding Freddy's hand. "Pulse?"

"It's still there." Michelle stood up and Hannah noticed that there were traces of tears on her cheeks. "How are we going to load him in?"

"Sideways. I'll take his head and shoulders and you take his legs. If he's too heavy for you, holler out and we'll put him back down."

"I can do it," Michelle said, and she knelt by Freddy's feet.

Hannah was about to lift Freddy's shoulders when she caught a whiff of a telltale odor. "Do you smell anything, Michelle?"

"Yes, booze. Do you think Freddy got drunk and hit his head when he passed out under our dock?"

"I don't know, but it's a possibility. I'm ready to lift if you are."

It wasn't easy, but between the two of them they managed to load Freddy into the back of Hannah's cookie truck. Hannah cushioned his head with the ratty old hooded sweatshirt her mother would have advised her to throw out, and shut the rear doors. "I'll drive him straight to the hospital. Call and tell them I'm coming. Say it's Freddy Sawyer and he's got a bad head wound. They should meet me at the emergency entrance with a stretcher."

"Okay, but don't you want me to ride along to help?"

"You don't have any medical training that I don't know about, do you?"

"No."

"Then you're better off here. Make that call to the hospital and then go and tell Andrea and Mother what happened. I want all of you to look for Jed Sawyer and tell him that I'm driving Freddy to the hospital. I'll call the cottage as soon as I have any news on his condition."

"Got it," Michelle said. "Good luck, Hannah."

Hannah got in behind the wheel and lowered the window. "You're really great in a crisis, Michelle."

"Thanks." Michelle gave a little smile. "I think I must have inherited that from you."

By the time Hannah took the turnoff for the Lake Eden Memorial emergency entrance, her nerves were shot. She'd driven a distance of only ten miles, but it had been gruesome. Freddy had cried out and mumbled from the back of her truck and what she'd been able to understand had been heartbreaking. Freddy was upset because Jed was mad at him. Jed hated him and thought that Freddy was stupid. If Freddy could only get that present back for Jed, then Jed might forgive him and not go away. Then they could be friends again and everything would be all right.

Hannah had attempted to talk back to Freddy to reassure him, but she didn't think he'd heard her. He'd just gone back to the mumbling again about how he had to give Jed the present.

About five miles from the hospital, Freddy had stopped mumbling. He'd groaned once or twice, and then he'd been disturbingly quiet. While Hannah had been hoping that Freddy would calm down and stop mumbling, his total silence had been worse. Hannah had tromped on the accelerator and prayed that he'd only lost consciousness and not died.

By the time she pulled up at the doors of the emergency room, Hannah was shaking like a leaf. She flicked her lights and honked her horn to let the E.R. staff know that she'd arrived, and then she cut her engine and leaned back in her seat, watching as the emergency room crew loaded Freddy on a stretcher.

Hannah sat for a few minutes, just working to get her breathing back to normal. When her legs had stopped shaking and she felt able to walk, she got out of her truck and went inside to the nurses' desk. "I just brought in Freddy Sawyer," she told the stern-looking older nurse who was behind the desk. "Is he . . . alive?"

"Yes. Doctor Knight's with him right now."

"Did he say anything about Freddy's condition?"

"It's borderline critical and they're working to stabilize the patient. Doctor said to tell you that you did your part and you should go home and get some rest."

"No way," Hannah said, shaking her head. "I got Freddy this far and I'm not leaving now."

The nurse smiled and she looked much less forbidding. "Doctor said you'd say that, and he'll come to talk to you as soon as he can. That might be a while. He's pretty backed up."

"From the accident out on the highway?"

"They called in everyone from the staff and reserve list. I'm retired, but I came in to handle the intake desk. The big waiting room's packed, but Doctor said you should use the small waiting room at the end of the hall. There's a wall of vending machines near the door if you want something to eat or drink."

Armed with a Diet Coke, Hannah checked out the small waiting room. The hard plastic chairs didn't look appealing so she used the pay phone in the hall to call Delores and tell her that Freddy was at the hospital and Doc Knight was treating him.

"We located Jed," Delores told her, "and the poor boy was beside himself. He said that Freddy was with him all day, but they got separated in the crowd when the fireworks started and he couldn't find him anywhere."

"Is he coming out here?" Hannah asked.

"He's on his way. He said you're a hero for saving Freddy's life, but of course he meant heroine."

The words had no sooner left Delores's mouth than the door to the emergency room opened and Jed rushed in. "Jed's here, Mother. I've got to go. I'll call you back when I know more about Freddy's condition."

"Just a minute. Edna said to tell you it was a tree."

Hannah was about to ask what that meant when she saw Jed's face. "I've got to go, Mother. Jed looks frantic."

Hannah hung up the phone and hurried over to Jed. "It's okay, Jed. Doc Knight's with Freddy right now."

"How is he?"

"I don't know for sure. Let's go sit in the small waiting room. Doc Knight said he'd come and tell us more when he's finished treating Freddy."

Jed followed Hannah to the waiting room and sat down in a chair across from hers. He was still clearly distraught. "I tried to keep an eye on Freddy, but I turned my back for just a second to talk to somebody. When I turned around again, he was nowhere in sight."

"Nobody's blaming you, Jed. These things can happen."

"Yes, but I should have been more careful with him. Sometimes I forget he's retarded, you know? Most of the time he acts almost normal."

Hannah didn't know what to say to calm him down.

"Your sister told me that Freddy was hurt real bad. How did it happen?"

"I don't know."

"Couldn't Freddy tell you?"

"No, he was semiconscious when we found him and he didn't respond to any of my questions. And on the way to the hospital all Freddy did was mumble about how mad you were at him."

Jed sighed. "I wasn't real mad at him. I was just a little aggravated, you know? Freddy kept asking me if he could set off some firecrackers and I told him he couldn't. After about the dozenth time he asked, I got a little fed up. I guess I should have had more patience with him."

"That's hard to do sometimes."

"I know. I'd already explained that fireworks were dangerous and Freddy could burn himself. I said it over and over, every way I could think of, but he just didn't get it."

Hannah decided it was time to take the bull by the horns. "I hate to mention this Jed, but when we loaded Freddy in my truck, he smelled like alcohol. Did he have anything to drink today?"

"No! And I didn't drink either, because I know it's a bad influence on Freddy."

"I'm glad to hear that, but I'm almost positive that Freddy smelled of alcohol. My sister smelled it, too."

Jed was silent for a moment and then he sighed. "I know Freddy didn't have anything when we were together, but maybe somebody gave him a beer or something after we got separated. Do you think he got drunk and hit his head on something?"

"That's certainly possible. We'll know more when Doc Knight comes in to talk to us."

Hannah and Jed waited uneasily and every so often one or the other of them would get up and pace across the tile floor of the waiting room. It was almost impossible to sit in the plastic chairs for long. They were so hard, they gave Hannah aches in places she didn't even know she had.

After about fifteen minutes of pacing and sitting, sitting and pacing, Doc Knight appeared in the doorway. "Hey, Hannah. Are you trying out for the paramedic spot I have open?"

"No. Thanks anyway. This is Freddy's cousin, Jed."

"We've met," Doc Knight said, looking at Jed. "Freddy's stable, but it's very serious."

Jed gulped so loud Hannah could hear him. "But he'll be all right though, won't he?"

"It's too early to tell, but it doesn't look as though his injuries are life threatening. They could have long-lasting results, though. Freddy took a massive blow to the head and I won't be able to assess the extent of inter-cranial damage until the test results are in."

"Does it look like he fell and hit his head?" Jed asked.

Doc Knight shook his head. "Not unless he fell off a tall building head-first. My guess is that someone hit him with a hard object like a tire iron that they wielded with considerable force."

"Freddy couldn't tell you what happened?"

"No, son. He was unconscious when Hannah brought him in. Freddy won't be doing any talking for a while."

"Poor Freddy!" Jed looked extremely distressed. "Can I see him?"

"Come with me."

Hannah followed Jed and Doc Knight down the hospital corridor even though Jed had been the one to ask to see Freddy. They hadn't told her she couldn't come along, so she convinced herself that it was all right. Hannah knew she'd rest easier tonight if she saw Freddy and he looked better than he had when they'd loaded him in the back of her truck.

Doc Knight led them into Freddy's room and Hannah felt the tears well up in her eyes. Freddy, who'd always seemed so full of life and enthusiasm, was perfectly still in his hospital bed. It was a shock seeing him immobile like that and Hannah realized that he looked much older, almost as old as he actually was without the boyish grin and the excited voice that had asked constant and sometimes childish questions.

Freddy was connected by tubes and wires to monitors and other medical equipment, and Hannah was almost glad that he wasn't awake. If Freddy had been conscious, she would have forced herself to be bright and cheerful for his sake and that would have been difficult.

As Hannah moved closer, she noticed what she thought

was a respirator and she turned to Doc Knight. "Freddy can't breathe on his own?"

"Not right now. Shortly after you brought him in, his throat began to swell and it compromised his airway. I gave him antibiotics to reduce the swelling, but they'll take time to work."

Jed looked very concerned. "You mean Freddy could die without that machine?"

"Yes, but it's only a temporary condition. The antibiotics should improve matters by tomorrow morning. Then we can take him off the respirator."

"I'd better stay here tonight." Jed sat down in the chair by Freddy's bed. "If Freddy wakes up in the middle of the night, he'll be scared and he might try to pull that tube out."

Doc Knight shook his head. "We're keeping Freddy heavily sedated and he won't wake up. There's nothing you can do for him now. What you need to do is go home, get some sleep, and come back in the morning. I'll call you if there's any change in his condition."

"Are you sure? I could sleep in this chair and I wouldn't be any trouble."

"I'm sure you wouldn't be, but Freddy's doing just fine and he'll sleep through the night. I need you to be rested for tomorrow when we wake him up. That's when we'll need your help to reassure him."

Jed looked disappointed that he couldn't stay with Freddy, but he nodded. "Whatever you say. You're the doctor."

"If you don't have any more questions, I have to get back to the emergency room. I've got some traffic injuries to treat."

"Sure," Jed said. "Thanks for everything."

After Doc Knight left, Hannah motioned toward the door. "Come on, Jed. Let's go out to the lobby and call my mother. Everybody's waiting to hear about Freddy."

The corridor was quiet as Hannah and Jed walked back to

the lobby. Most of the patients were sleeping, and only two nurses were manning the station that separated the two wings.

"They only have two nurses for all these patients?" Jed sounded worried again.

"Relax, Jed. Doc Knight runs a good hospital. Freddy will get the best of care here."

When they got to the lobby, Hannah placed a call to the cottage and filled Delores and Michelle in on Freddy's condition. Then Jed got on the phone and thanked them again for finding him in the crowd.

"You really should get home, Jed," Hannah said when she'd hung up the phone. "You look tired."

"I am, but I don't think I can sleep. I'm just too worried about Freddy. Do you have time for a cup of coffee in the cafeteria?"

"Sure," Hannah said, even though the last thing she wanted was hospital coffee. Jed obviously needed to talk.

The hospital cafeteria was deserted and Hannah took a table near the window while Jed got them coffee from a vending machine. It was every bit as vile as Hannah had expected and she took small sips, hoping he wouldn't notice that she was drinking very little of it.

"I've been thinking about what Doc Knight said and I'm sure Freddy was in a fight." Jed took a swallow of his coffee without seeming to notice how bad it was. "If I ever catch the guy that did this to him, I'll . . ."

"No, you won't," Hannah interrupted, reaching out to take Jed's arm. "Believe me, Jed, I know exactly how you feel. I'm not a violent person, but I'd be tempted to hammer the person who did this to Freddy. What we both have to remember is that violence is never the answer."

"But I've got to do something! Just seeing him like that . . . it was awful!"

"I know, but the authorities will take care of it. As soon as

Freddy's well enough, Doc Knight will call in a deputy to take his statement. If someone did attack Freddy, they'll be caught and punished."

Jed sighed deeply. "I guess you're right. I just feel so helpless, you know?"

"I know. I've been trying to think of something I could do for Freddy, but there's only one thing that comes to mind."

"What's that?"

"Freddy kept mumbling about the present he had for you and how he had to get it so that you wouldn't be mad at him any longer."

"That sounds like Freddy." Jed sighed again. "He doesn't have much money, but he always wants to buy me things."

"Oh, he didn't buy this. He said it was something you lost and he found in your garbage last week. He told me he had to shine it up for you before he gave it back to you for a present."

"Do you know what it is?"

"I don't have a clue." Hannah shrugged. "Freddy had it in a shoebox, but it was tied up with twine and I didn't look inside. I'm keeping it for him at The Cookie Jar. I'll stop in to get it before I come to the hospital tomorrow morning. We can store it in his hospital room and once Freddy's awake, he can give it to you."

Jed looked amused. "Freddy's always giving me little things that he finds. It's probably an old pair of shoes I got rid of."

"But you're going to be delighted to get it back, whatever it is, aren't you?"

"Absolutely." Jed gave her a grin. "Freddy's a sweet guy and I wouldn't spoil his surprise for anything in the world."

Chapter
Twenty-Nine

Hannah glanced at the clock on the wall as she switched on the lights in her kitchen at The Cookie Jar. It was five minutes past ten—late at night to be mixing up cookie dough. She was closed tomorrow and Sunday so there were no cookies to bake for her customers, but she'd promised to donate some cookies to the Redeemer Lutheran bake sale and she wanted to take Freddy some Molasses Crackles. She'd mix up a batch, let them chill overnight, come in early to bake them, and split them between Reverend Knudson and Freddy.

As Hannah assembled her ingredients, she thought about Freddy and who might have injured him. It was possible that Rhonda's killer was the culprit, especially if Freddy had seen or overheard something that could lead to his arrest. Hannah freely admitted that such a theory was a little far-fetched, but she refused to believe that any of the local residents were to blame. Freddy was well liked around town and everyone knew that he had limitations. It was more likely that someone who wasn't local had attacked Freddy. The fireworks had drawn a big crowd from outside the Lake Eden area and a stranger could be the culprit. In any event, standing at the workstation thinking about it wasn't going give her the answer.

On her way to fetch one of her stainless-steel mixing bowls,

Hannah retrieved the crime-scene photos she'd taken through the basement windows and spread them out at the workstation. While she was mixing the cookie dough, she'd think about Rhonda's murder. She gave the photos a glance as she waited for the butter to melt in the microwave, but she didn't spot anything she hadn't noticed before. The only thing unusual was the strawberry jam on the peach jam shelf. She was almost certain that the three jars of strawberry jam had been set there to replace the three jars of peach jam that had broken on the floor, but why would anyone go to that trouble and not sweep up the broken glass?

Once the butter was melted, Hannah went to fetch the molasses from the pantry. As she took down the jar, she noticed what was stashed behind it and she groaned. It was a large bag of Hershey's Kisses she'd bought for her almond cookies and it was staring her right in the face. She had to hide it quickly before she weakened and opened it. Hannah reached down to grab a sack of pecans and placed them in front of the bag. She kept all of her nuts on the shelf below, but this was just a temporary measure to hide the candy from view. Then she carried the molasses back to the kitchen, picked up her spoon, and set it right back down again as what she'd just done struck her with full force. She'd hidden her Hershey Kisses from view by placing a sack of pecans from a lower shelf in front of them. What if Rhonda's killer had done the same thing? What if he'd hidden something by placing the jars of strawberry jam in front of it?

That theory seemed reasonable and Hannah made a mental note to tell Mike and Bill about it in the morning. Perhaps the murder weapon was hidden there, or some other clue that might help them track down Rhonda's killer. It was certainly worth a look.

Hannah mixed in the molasses and then the sugar, stirring much longer than was necessary. The three jars of strawberry jam had been on the peach jam shelf and Mrs. Voelker's letter had mentioned the peach jam. Hannah set down her spoon and went to retrieve it from her purse. Lisa was sure that the game Speedy had mentioned was the Treasure Hunt game. What if this whole letter was the first clue in a game he wanted Mrs. Voelker to play? Speedy had practically begged her to make peach jam and it was obvious he hadn't known that she was in a wheelchair and her jam-making days were behind her. What if there really was a treasure behind Mrs. Voelker's peach jam? Was it still there?

She thought about that while she grated fresh nutmeg and added the rest of the spices to her bowl. She measured out the baking soda and salt, and stirred everything up. Giving a little shake of her head, Hannah turned back to the letter. One phrase stood out. *The guy next to me is going to find someone to take this letter out and mail it to you.* Take the letter out? Out where? What sort of hospital would refuse to mail a patient's last letter?

A prison hospital! The moment that answer occurred to Hannah, the whole thing made sense. If the dying man had been in prison, all correspondence in or out would have been examined by prison officials and it was obvious that this man hadn't wanted his letter screened.

Hannah thought about that as she beat the eggs and added them to her bowl. Who was Speedy? And why had he been in prison? Edna had remembered the summer he'd spent with Mrs. Voelker, but she hadn't been able to remember his real name. She'd promised to tell Hannah if she remembered, but so far there'd been no word from Edna, unless . . .

Delores had given her a message from Edna, but she hadn't paid much attention to it. Edna had said to tell her that it was a tree. Speedy's name was a type of tree?

Hannah set down the flour canister so hard, a little puff of flour rose up into the air. She paged through her notes, came to the section about the bank robbery, and let out a whoop. One of the bank robbers was David Aspen and an aspen was a tree. This put a whole new spin on things!

The pieces of the puzzle began to align themselves as Hannah measured out the flour. David "Speedy" Aspen had robbed a bank and hidden the money somewhere, perhaps in Mrs. Voelker's basement. Since she'd known him as a child, she would have welcomed him if he'd come to visit. The stolen money couldn't be behind the jam jars. The shelf was shallow and stacks of bills would have taken up more space than that. But the furnace room was old and the walls and floor were dirt. Speedy could have cut a hole in the back of the shelf, dug a cave right into the dirt wall, hidden the money there, and stuck the board back in place. With peach jam on the shelves blocking the cut board from view, no one would ever have found it.

But someone had found it. The money was beginning to surface in the Lake Eden area. Hannah remembered Rhonda's one-way ticket to Zurich as she added flour to her bowl and another piece of the puzzle clicked into place. She'd wondered how Rhonda could afford to stay in Europe and now she knew the answer. Swiss banks had numbered accounts and they were a perfect place to hide the stolen money.

The puzzle was starting to take form now that she had some key pieces. The letter had been in Rhonda's apartment. That meant she'd found it before the night of her death. And if Mrs. Voelker had played the Treasure Hunt game with Speedy, she'd probably played it with Rhonda, too. Rhonda might even have known about the robbery, since the robber was a shirttail relation of hers. Rhonda could have found the letter with her great-aunt's effects, gone down to the basement to check the jam shelf, and realized that the stolen money was stashed in the furnace room wall.

As Hannah added more flour to her bowl, she asked herself another question. If Rhonda had found the letter shortly before she'd bought that one-way ticket, why hadn't she removed the money and taken it back to her apartment? Hannah thought about that as she stirred, and then she remembered what Beatrice Koester had told her about Rhon-

da's apartment. They'd replaced the carpet and repainted it
in June. That meant workmen had been going in and out
while Rhonda had been at work. Rhonda must have decided
that the money would be safer in her great-aunt's basement
where it had been hidden, undiscovered, for years. It was the
reason Rhonda had hesitated about signing the deed. She'd
wanted to make absolutely sure that she could go out to the
house over the weekend to pick up a few mementos.

"A few mementos," Hannah muttered, stirring for all she
was worth. "A fortune in stolen money is more like it!"

Suddenly another piece of the puzzle fell into place. When
Ken Purvis had left Rhonda on Friday night, she must have
decided that it was a perfect time to retrieve the money.
Although Ken had believed that Rhonda was stuck without a
way back to town, Hannah knew that Rhonda had been a re-
sourceful woman. She could have walked to the neighboring
farm to call a taxi, gone out to the road to flag down a passing resident, or stayed overnight and dealt with the problem
in the morning. Rhonda had packed up that money. Hannah
was sure of that. And the killer had caught her in the act of
retrieving it and murdered her for the stolen cash.

Hannah had the motive. It was greed, and greed could be
powerful. Hannah added the rest of the flour to her bowl and
stirred it in, thinking about the money that had surfaced.
Rhonda's killer had it now and he was spending it. One ten-
dollar bill from Lake Eden Neighborhood Drugs had surfaced in her own shop on Wednesday. Someone had shopped
in the drugstore that morning and passed a ten-dollar bill
from the old bank robbery.

"Oh-oh," Hannah groaned, remembering the theory she'd
discarded when she'd discovered that the bank robbers had
never been prisoners at Stillwater. She might have crossed Jed
off her suspect list too soon. He'd been spending a lot of
money lately and he couldn't be making that much doing
handyman work. There was the late-model pickup truck, the
lunches at the café every day, and the expensive hand-

embroidered vest that he'd been wearing at the celebration today.

Hannah tore off a strip of plastic wrap and covered her mixing bowl, smoothing down the edges to make a tight seal. Was Jed Rhonda's killer? Mike had told her that they'd found Jed's cap in the basement. What if he hadn't left it there when he'd replaced the glass in the window? What if he'd dropped it when he'd killed Rhonda?

A likely scenario began to take shape in Hannah's mind. Ken Purvis hadn't seen a car in the driveway when he'd driven up on the night that Rhonda was killed, but that was before Jed had bought the pickup, and he would have been driving Freddy's mother's old car. He'd told Hannah that the starter was defective and he had to park it at the top of the hill. What if Jed had left the car on the shoulder of the road and walked in?

Hannah's mind went into overdrive. If Jed had knocked on the door and gotten no answer, he might have looked in the windows to see if Rhonda was there. And if he'd seen Rhonda in the basement packing up the money, he could have gone inside, killed her, and taken the cash. Jed was strong. He could have dug her grave in the hard-packed dirt floor before Ken Purvis drove up and frightened him away. And in Jed's haste to hide the board that covered the hole in the wall, he could have dropped three peach jam jars and replaced them with the strawberry jam.

Another part of the scenario occurred to Hannah and she gulped. Was Jed the one who'd attacked Freddy and left him for dead under their dock? If Freddy had somehow discovered that Jed had killed Rhonda, he would have told someone. Mrs. Sawyer had taught her son to be a good citizen and Freddy knew that murder was wrong. Had Jed's concern at the hospital tonight been because Freddy was injured? Or had he been concerned that Freddy would recover enough to tell someone that Jed had attacked him and killed Rhonda? Just as soon as she put her cookie dough in the cooler she'd call Mike and tell him her suspicions. If she was right and Jed was the killer, he'd been duping everyone in town, including her!

Preoccupied with this theory, Hannah opened the walk-in cooler and stepped inside to find a convenient place for her bowl of cookie dough. She'd just moved some things around to make room when the door slammed shut and she was plunged into darkness. She grabbed the cord that hung down from the light, flicked it on, and whirled toward the door. It had never banged shut on its own before! She stepped forward to push the inside release, but it was jammed. What was going on!?

As Hannah stood there, trapped inside her cooler, she heard someone rummaging around in her kitchen. It had to be Jed, and unless her theory was full of holes, he was the one who'd shut her in. "Let me out, Jed!" she shouted.

"Sorry, no can do." Jed's voice was faint through the heavy metal door. "You're gonna have to stay there."

Even though Jed's voice was barely audible, Hannah could tell that he was slurring his words. He'd been drinking and that didn't bode well for her. "Come on, Jed. This isn't funny."

"'Course it's not. There's nothing funny about dying and that's what this is all about. Maybe you figured it out and maybe you didn't. I can't take any chances."

A shiver went down Hannah's spine and it had nothing to do with the temperature of the cooler. It would do no good to protest that she hadn't figured anything out, because Jed was standing in her kitchen and he must have spotted the crime-scenes photo and Mrs. Voelker's letter. Still, it was worth a shot and she took it. "I don't know what you're talking about. Just let me out now and you won't get into any trouble over this. I promise I won't say a word about it."

"You think I'm as dumb as Freddy?" Jed's laughter rang out. "I'm plugging up the air vent. When your air runs out, you'll die."

Hannah banged on the door with her fists, then she shouted out, "Why are you doing this, Jed? Are you crazy?"

"Maybe, but that's better than being dumb. Freddy told me about that present you hid for him and he even confessed what it was. But the stubborn retard wouldn't tell me where he hid it. Thanks to your big mouth, I know it's right here."

Hannah's mind flashed on Freddy's still form in the hospital bed and she shivered. "Did you try to kill Freddy?"

" 'Course I did. He was gonna blab, sooner or later. I poured booze over him so it'd look like he was drunk and he fought with someone, but you and your sister got there too quick. You should've let him die in peace. Now I'm going to have to go back to the hospital and finish the job."

"The nurses won't let you near him!" Hannah countered, even though she knew it wasn't true. If Jed turned on the charm and asked to take a peek at his cousin, the nurses would think he was wonderful for caring so much.

"The nurses won't even know I'm there. I unlatched the window before I left. It'll be easy to sneak into Freddy's room right after they check on him at midnight. It was real nice of you to notice that respirator. All I have to do is shut it off and it'll take care of Freddy for good. He's so stupid he doesn't deserve to live anyway."

Hannah saw red. Jed had been living a lie, pretending to like Freddy and freeloading by living in his house. This con man and killer had taken them all in and she wished she had superhuman powers so that she could tear the cooler door off its hinges and break Jed in two like a matchstick.

"You know, you were always pretty nice to me, giving me all those free cookies and stuff. I'm starting to feel real bad about locking you in and leaving you to die. If you tell me where you put that shoebox Freddy gave you, I might just give you a break. I could always unplug that vent and they'll find you in a couple of days. I might even call to tell them where you are. I'm gonna be in a real good mood once I start spending all that cash."

Hannah recognized the ploy for what it was. Jed would kill her whether she told him where the shoebox was, or not. But why not tell him, especially since the box was hidden in the perfect place? Hannah picked up the heaviest thing she could find, the bowl of cookie dough she'd just mixed, and moved close to the door. "If I tell you where it is, you'll let me go?"

"Sure. Where it is?"

"Right here in the cooler," Hannah said, tightening her grip on the metal bowl.

Jed laughed long and hard. "Nice try, but I don't believe you. You're probably holding something heavy right now, getting ready to take a swing at me when I open the door. It'd be nice to have that shoebox and I'll look around some before I leave, but I can get along without it. Nobody around here will guess it belonged to me once you and Freddy are dead."

Hannah pressed her ear to the cooler door and she heard Jed rummaging around in her kitchen, banging cupboard doors. He searched for about five minutes and then she heard the back door open and close behind him.

A shudder ran through Hannah's body, from the top of her head down to the tip of her toes. She was trapped and no one would think to look for her here. Why hadn't she listened to Andrea when she'd urged her to get a cell phone? If she had one, she could call to warn the hospital that Jed was coming to kill Freddy at midnight and she could tell them to send someone to rescue her. But she didn't have a cell phone and even if she had, it was doubtful that she would have carried it into the cooler with her.

Hannah did her best to stay calm and consider her options. There weren't many, but it would take a while for the air to run out and she wasn't dead yet. Banging on the cooler wall wouldn't do any good. It was thick and there was no one around to hear her anyway. Nobody ever came down the alley at night except . . .

Herb Beeseman! Hannah glanced at her watch. It was ten forty-five and Herb made his rounds at eleven o'clock every night. He wouldn't be able to hear her if he just drove down the alley, but if the alarm in Granny's Attic went off, that would get him out of his squad car.

Hannah did her best to concentrate. She had to make the alarm in Granny's Attic go off. It was rigged to trigger every time the power failed and it shared a circuit with her freezer and her cooler. If she could figure out a way to short out that circuit, the alarm would sound and Herb would respond. He'd check Granny's Attic first, but then he'd come into The Cookie Jar. And when he came into her kitchen to check to see that her freezer and cooler were still working, she'd use the metal bowl with the dough she'd just mixed to bang on the cooler door for all she was worth.

How could she short out the circuit? Hannah glanced around her. She couldn't get at any switches, but there was an electrical panel near the floor in the back. She got down on her hands and knees to examine it and started to frown. It was held in place by screws and she didn't have a screwdriver. She spent precious minutes trying to loosen the screws with her fingernails, but the last repairman who'd come to check the cooler had tightened the screws down much too diligently.

Hannah sat down and sighed. What could a person use for a screwdriver if a person didn't have a screwdriver? She'd once used a table knife, much to the dismay of her father who'd caught her doing it, but she didn't have a table knife either. She took a deep breath, let it out again to relax, and that was when she remembered that Rhonda had been stabbed with a knife. Jed had been very anxious to recover that shoebox Freddy had given her and that meant there was something important inside. It had to contain the knife that Jed had used to stab Rhonda!

Hannah stood up to get the shoebox and sat back down to

open it. She was chilled to the bone and her fingers were shaking so hard, she could barely untie the twine. When she lifted the lid and unrolled the old rag that was inside, she let out a cry of pure relief. It was a hunting knife, a long one with a sturdy, wicked-looking blade. She was about to grab it when she realized that the handle was metal and it might have fingerprints on it.

This consideration didn't stop Hannah for long. Her situation was growing more desperate by the minute. She grabbed one of the nonskid mats that lined the cooler shelves and used it for a glove. Then she leaned forward and began to loosen the screws that held the cover of the electrical panel in place.

It took a few minutes, but at last the cover came off and Hannah stared at the array of wires inside. She could pull them loose, but that might not short out the circuit.

Hannah leaned closer to peer inside the panel. There was a caution sticker on one part, a warning to shut off the power before attempting to replace that part and to use properly insulated tools. Hannah glanced down at the metal blade of the knife. The power was on, and the knife blade wasn't insulated. That made two out of two warnings she would ignore and it ought to do the trick. Unfortunately, the handle of the knife was also metal and she could fry. On the other hand, she was going to die anyway and it was worth a shot, especially if she wrapped the knife handle in the nonskid mat again.

Once that was accomplished, Hannah prepared for action. She had to hurry. Herb would be coming down the alley any minute. She took a split second to decide where to plunge the knife and decided to aim for the red sticker that read "Danger." The cooler light would go out when the circuit blew, so she pushed the mixing bowl right up against the cooler door. Then she turned back to the open panel, took a deep breath, and stabbed.

The moment the tip of the knife blade hit the danger sticker, a huge ball of light knocked Hannah flat on her back. Despite the fact that she was seeing stars, Hannah sat up, crawled to the door, and listened. The alarm was going off next door. She'd done it and she was still alive! Now all she had to do was wait for Herb and bang on the cooler door when he came into her kitchen.

It seemed like forever, crouching there in the dark, but at last Hannah heard the back door open and she banged on the cooler door as hard as she could. A second later, she heard a mumbled expletive and then a shout.

"Hannah? Are you in there?"

"Yes!" Hannah shouted back at the top of her lungs.

"The handle's padlocked, but I've got bolt cutters in the cruiser. Just sit tight for a minute."

Just sit tight? Hannah started to giggle with a mixture of relief and anxiety. What else could she do but sit tight? She giggled as she heard Herb cutting off the padlock, and she giggled when she heard him open the door. She was still giggling when he pulled her to her feet and gathered her into his arms. Then she remembered about Freddy and her giggles stopped abruptly.

"What happened, Hannah?"

"Later," Hannah said, taking a huge gulp of welcome air. "Do you have a police radio in your patrol car?"

"Sure."

"Get through to the sheriff's department and tell them to post a deputy in Freddy Sawyer's hospital room. He's going to be murdered at midnight. Tell them not to let anyone but Doc Knight in or out until they hear from me."

"Are you sure?"

"I'm positive. Would a woman who's been locked inside her own cooler by a stone-cold killer lie to you?"

Herb looked as if he wanted to ask a million questions, but he turned on his heel and rushed out to his patrol car to

make the call. By the time he came back in, Hannah had already called the hospital and Doc Knight had promised to
send his biggest orderly to stand guard in Freddy's room until
the deputy arrived. She'd also retrieved the murder weapon
and packed it and the nonskid mat in Freddy's shoebox.

"Now will you tell me what happened?" Herb asked, staring at Hannah with a mixture of alarm and admiration.

"I'll tell you on the way out to the sheriff's station. I know
who killed Rhonda and I need to give them the facts. And I
know who has that old bank robbery money, too."

"And you want me to drive you out there?"

"Rhonda's killer is the one who locked me in my cooler
and plugged up the air vent. I think I'm still a little shaky
from the cold and the lack of oxygen. Not only that, I had to
short out the power with the murder weapon and I got
knocked back against the wall."

"No problem," Herb said, holding the door open for her.

"Good. Mike's not going to be too happy about the murder weapon. I bent it a little when I used it for a screwdriver
and it's got a burn hole in the blade from shorting out the
power. Maybe they can still lift some fingerprints if I didn't
smudge them with the nonskid mat. Are you sure you don't
mind driving me?"

"Anytime, Hannah." Herb shook his head as they went
out the door. "Let me see if I got this straight. You got locked
in the cooler by Rhonda's killer, you used the murder weapon
as a screwdriver and a tool to short out the circuit, you discovered that Freddy was targeted for murder at midnight
tonight, and you know who has the loot from that old bank
robbery?"

"That about sums it up. I'm sorry about pulling you away
from your rounds, Herb. I owe you, big-time."

"Maybe I should listen in at the sheriff's station. Then you
won't have to explain it all twice."

"That's a good idea. I'll tell them I want you with me."

"Okay, then you already paid me back." Herb opened the door of his patrol car for Hannah and helped her in.

"How did I pay you?" Hannah asked, buckling her seat belt and leaning back for the ride.

"I'll be there to see the expression on Mike's face when you explain all this. Believe me, Hannah. You paid me big-time!"

"You look great, Hannah," Norman said as Hannah approached the largest table in the dining room at the Lake Eden Inn.

"Thanks, Norman." Hannah gave him a warm smile and then she turned to Delores and Carrie. "You're here early."

Delores nodded. "I know. I wanted everything to be perfect."

"I'm sure it will be." Hannah pulled out a chair, but her mother shook her head.

"Not there, dear. I want you to sit on Norman's right."

Hannah rolled her eyes, but she took the chair her mother indicated. Delores always liked to arrange the seating at her parties, and she was the one who'd invited them for dinner to celebrate the solving of Rhonda's murder case.

"Aren't these flowers gorgeous?" Delores gestured toward the colorful centerpiece of summer flowers. "Herb Beeseman sent them. They must be for you."

"For me?" Hannah was puzzled.

"Of course. You solved Rhonda's murder. But you really should have brought a gift for Herb. He's the one who rescued you from that cooler."

"I did bring something for Herb," Hannah defended herself. "He's been asking for pineapple cookies for ages and I came up with a new cookie bar recipe. They're called Pineapple Right-Side-Up Bars and they're in Sally's kitchen, along with my pizza cutter."

Norman looked puzzled. "Your pizza cutter?"

"It's something I learned from my college roommate. Cynthia always used a pizza cutter on pans of brownies. It works better than a knife."

"Hi, everybody!" Tracey called out, tugging at Andrea's hand to hurry her along toward the table. She was dressed in a pale blue silk dress with white lace around the sleeves and the hemline. "Look at me. I'm all dressed up for dinner."

"And you look just lovely," Delores said, patting the chair next to her.

"I know. Daddy told me I'm almost as pretty as Mommy. He's coming in a minute with Uncle Mike." Tracey climbed up in the chair next to Delores and grinned at everyone. "Hi, Uncle Norman."

Andrea passed by the back of Hannah's chair on her way around the table, and Hannah pulled her down for a private word. "Tracey's calling everyone uncle again."

"I know. I taught her not to discriminate," Andrea whispered back and then she straightened up to address the whole table. "How many people are coming?"

"Twelve," Delores answered. "All of us, plus Lisa and Herb. And Lonnie is coming with Michelle."

"We're here." Bill came up to the table with Mike. Both of them were wearing their uniforms and they looked very handsome.

"Sit right here, Bill." Delores gestured to a chair next to Andrea. "Mike? Take that place by Hannah."

Hannah maintained her pleasant expression, but she resolved to have a talk with her mother about the seating arrangements for these family gatherings. Her mother always sandwiched her in between Norman and Mike, and she was beginning to feel like peanut butter.

"Did you see Freddy this morning?" Andrea asked her.

"Yes, I did. I drove out to the hospital right after I delivered my cookies for the church bake sale." Hannah gave a small smile. Thanks to the layer of plastic wrap on top of her bowl, her dough had been intact and she'd baked her cookies early this morning. If she didn't tell, no one would ever guess what that batch of Molasses Crackles had been through. "Doc Knight says Freddy's going to make a full recovery. I was there when they took him off the respirator and the first thing he told us was that Jed had attacked him."

"Did he understand why?" Norman asked.

"He did after we explained it. Freddy said he hoped they'd lock Jed up for good so he couldn't hurt anyone else."

"That shouldn't be a problem," Mike said. "We got a full confession. And since we found the stolen money in Jed's truck, the only question now is who gets to prosecute him first, the Feds or us."

"Hi!" Lisa was grinning ear-to-ear as she approached the table with Herb. "I'm sorry we're late. We stopped at the hospital to see Freddy and he wanted to tell us all about his new job."

Herb pulled out a chair for Lisa, then took his place at the table. "Doc Knight found a job for Freddy at the hospital doing maintenance work and taking care of the grounds."

"There's Aunt Michelle!" Tracey said, standing up to wave. "And Uncle Lonnie's with her."

Hannah laughed at the shocked expression on Andrea's face. It was clear her sister was now regretting teaching Tracey indiscriminate use of the term "uncle." It wasn't that Andrea disliked Lonnie, but she'd made it clear that she didn't approve of Michelle dating anyone in law enforcement. She'd explained that it was all right for Hannah since she was older and more independent, but she felt that Michelle should have a boyfriend with a less demanding job.

"Isn't it a beautiful evening?" Lisa asked, looking straight at Hannah and closing one eye in a wink. "I think this is the best night of my life. And there's even a full moon!"

Hannah stared hard at Lisa. Something was definitely

wrong with her partner. Lisa's eyes were sparkling, her face was flushed, and she looked as if she'd been awarded the Nobel Prize, the Miss Universe crown, and an Olympic gold medal all at once. If Hannah hadn't known better, she might have suspected that Lisa was giddy on champagne, but the cork was still in the bottle.

"Are you okay, Lisa?" Hannah asked.

"I've never been more okay in my life!" Lisa gave a little giggle and reached for her water glass.

Hannah blinked. Lisa was holding her water glass awkwardly, with her finger held straight out as if it hurt. She was about to ask how she'd injured her hand and whether Doc Knight had given her pain pills when Andrea let out a gasp.

"Oh, my!" Andrea squealed and rushed over to hug Lisa. "Why didn't you say something sooner? This is just wonderful!"

Hannah regarded her sister with total amazement. Had everyone gone crazy? "What's wonderful?"

"This!" Andrea reached for Lisa's hand and held it aloft. "Lisa and Herb are engaged!"

Hannah laughed long and hard, even though she felt like total fool for not noticing the ring earlier. The champagne was opened, along with a bottle of sparkling apple juice for Tracey to share with Norman, who said that since he was driving, he'd pass on the champagne.

Congratulations flowed for several joyful minutes. Then Delores asked the question that was in everyone's mind. "When is the wedding?"

"On December thirty-first," Herb answered her, with a grin. "Lisa wanted to wait until the busy season was over at The Cookie Jar, but she still wanted me to get the tax break."

Hannah applauded. "Smart girl."

"Can I be in your wedding, Lisa?" Tracey asked. "I always wanted to be a flower girl."

Lisa reached over to give her a hug. "I was just going to

ask you if you'd be my flower girl. You're my first choice. I'd like to make this is a real family wedding."

"What a wonderful idea!" Delores clapped her hands. "Wouldn't it be delightful to make it a double wedding and have a *real* family affair?"

Hannah fumed as her mother turned to smile first at Norman and then at Mike. Delores was getting positively blatant. Silence fell as both men shifted uncomfortably and Hannah knew she had to do something.

"A double wedding would be wonderful," Hannah said, seizing the first idea that popped into her head and running with it, "but I really think that Michelle should finish college before she gets married."

Michelle looked startled for a split second, but then she caught on. "You won't get any argument from me. I want to get my degree before I settle down. That's all right with you, isn't it, Mother?"

"Of course it's all right! But, I didn't mean . . ."

Delores faltered and Hannah almost felt sorry for her . . . almost, but not quite. "I'll come up with a special wedding cookie for you, Lisa. Something spectacular."

"And I'll help you with the wedding," Andrea offered. "I just cleaned out my closet and I found all the plans I used for my wedding. And that reminds me . . . I've got a package in the car for you, Hannah. Remember those summer slacks we bought last year?"

"Oh, yes." Hannah sighed. How could she forget? Those miserable slacks had prompted her diet.

"Well, we must have mixed them up when we took them out of my car. I don't know how, but I ended up with yours."

Hannah's mouth dropped open. "You mean the slacks I have belong to *you?*"

"That's right."

Hannah's head was still reeling when the waitress arrived to take their order. She wasn't overweight. She'd been dieting to try to fit into *Andrea's* slacks!

"Could I take your order?" the waitress asked, pausing by Hannah's chair.

"Just one second," Hannah said, and she turned to Andrea again. "Are you absolutely positive the slacks I have are yours?"

"Of course I am. The pair I wound up with is much too big for me."

Hannah was grinning as she turned back to the waitress. "I'm skipping my salad and entrée tonight. Just bring me the dessert cart and park it right here."

Pineapple Right-Side-Up Cookie Bars

Preheat oven to 350 degrees F.,
with rack in middle position.

(Another recipe with a no-roll crust—don't you just love it?)

2 cups flour *(no need to sift)*
1 cup softened butter *(2 sticks, ½ pound)*
½ cup white sugar
4 beaten eggs *(just whip them up with a fork)*
½ cup white sugar
½ cup frozen concentrated pineapple juice
½ cup drained crushed pineapple *(if you have any left over, freeze it)*
½ teaspoon salt
1 teaspoon baking powder
4 tablespoons flour *(that's ¼ cup—don't bother to sift)*

FIRST STEP: Dump pineapple in a strainer and let it drain while you do this step. Cream butter with sugar and add flour. Mix well. *(You can also do this in a food processor with hard butter cut into chunks and the steel blade.)* Spread mixture out in a greased 9 x 13 inch pan *(that's a standard sheet cake pan)*, and press it down evenly with your hands.

Bake at 350 degrees F. for 15 to 20 minutes. Remove from oven. *(Don't turn off oven!)*

SECOND STEP: Mix eggs with sugar. Add pineapple concentrate, drained pineapple, and mix. Add salt and baking powder and stir it all up. Then add flour and mix thoroughly. *(This will be runny—it'll set in the oven.)*

Pour this mixture on top of the pan you just baked and stick it back into the oven. Bake at 350 degrees F. for another 45–50 minutes. Then remove from oven.

Let cool thoroughly, then sprinkle a little powdered sugar on the top and cut into brownie-sized bars.

(Herb Beeseman loves these—it was the least I could do for him. Mother and Carrie love them too, but they like a double serving with a scoop of vanilla ice cream on top. Marge Beeseman has refused to taste them, probably because she thinks she makes the best Pineapple Upside-Down Cake in the state of Minnesota and she doesn't relish any interference.)

Baking Conversion Chart

These conversions are approximate, but they'll work just fine for Hannah Swensen's recipes.

VOLUME:

U.S.	Metric
½ teaspoon	2 milliliters
1 teaspoon	5 milliliters
1 tablespoon	15 milliliters
¼ cup	50 milliliters
⅓ cup	75 milliliters
½ cup	125 milliliters
¾ cup	175 milliliters
1 cup	¼ liter

WEIGHT:

U.S.	Metric
1 ounce	28 grams
1 pound	454 grams

OVEN TEMPERATURE:

Degrees Fahrenheit	Degrees Centigrade	British (Regulo) Gas Mark
325 degrees F.	165 degrees C.	3
350 degrees F.	175 degrees C.	4
375 degrees F.	190 degrees C.	5

Note: Hannah's rectangular sheet cake pan, 9 inches by 13 inches, is approximately 23 centimeters by 32.5 centimeters.

Index of Recipes

Lemon Meringue Pie — Page 26
Almond Kisses — Page 47
Walnuttoes — Page 69
Cinnamon Crisps — Page 117
Praline Charlottes — Page 168
Mystery Cookies — Page 219
Orange Snaps — Page 240
Cottage Cheese Pancakes — Page 271
Pineapple Right-Side-Up Cookie Bars — Page 321

Thanksgiving has a way of thawing the frostiest hearts in Lake Eden. But that won't be happening for newlywed Hannah Swensen Barton—not after her husband suddenly disappears . . .

Hannah has felt as bitter as November in Minnesota since Ross vanished without a trace and left their marriage in limbo. Still, she throws herself into a baking frenzy for the sake of pumpkin pie and Thanksgiving-themed treats while endless holiday orders pour into The Cookie Jar. Hannah even introduces a raspberry Danish pastry to the menu, and P. K., her husband's assistant at KCOW-TV, will be one of the first to sample it. But instead of taking a bite, P. K., who is driving Ross's car and using his desk at work, is murdered. Was someone plotting against P. K. all along, or did Ross dodge a deadly dose of sweet revenge? Hannah will have to quickly sift through a cornucopia of clues and suspects to stop a killer from bringing another murder to the table. . . .

Please turn the page for an exciting sneak peek of Joanne Fluke's next Hannah Swensen mystery

RASPBERRY DANISH MURDER

coming soon wherever print and e-books are sold!

Chapter Four

Michelle was smiling as she turned to Hannah. They were sitting in front of the giant-screen television, and they'd just watched the commercial that P.K. had made for the Thanksgiving play. "I loved it! How about you?"

"P.K. did a super job. Everyone who saw it is going to come to the play."

"Irma's keeping track of advance ticket sales. I'll check in with her to see if there's a jump in sales tomorrow. The cast really looked good, didn't they?"

"The cast looked really great," Hannah agreed. "I loved those costumes."

"I'm really glad we took the time to do makeup and get into our costumes." Michelle gave a little smile. "At first, I was upset when P.K. suggested it because it takes so much time, but he was right. It looks so much better than seeing the characters in their everyday clothes."

Hannah was about to go to the kitchen to get more coffee when Michelle's cell phone rang. "That's probably P.K. to see if you liked his commercial," she speculated.

"I bet you're right," Michelle said, reaching out for her cell phone. "I'm going to record it to see if he liked his commercial." She answered the call, and almost immediately began to frown.

"What is it?" Hannah asked quickly as a distressed expression crossed Michelle's face.

"It's P.K. There's something wrong, Hannah! Look!"

Hannah glanced at the display and realized that she was watching a video of P.K. driving Ross's car.

"It's real time," Michelle said quickly. "He's got his phone in the dashboard holder Ross has in his car."

"Mic . . . kie," P.K. said, giving a lopsided smile. "How . . . you, girl?"

"He sounds drunk!" Michelle exclaimed.

"Or drugged. Can you ask him if he's okay?"

"Are you okay, P.K.?" Michelle asked.

"Mic . . . kie." P.K. reached up to rub his face. "Pret . . . ty Mic . . . kie. Doan feel goooood."

P.K.'s phone was positioned so that they could see his face and also the driver's side window. As the two sisters watched, the edge of the road appeared to move forward and then recede.

"Tell him to pull over!" Hannah said, grabbing Michelle's arm. "Hurry! He almost went in the ditch!"

"Pull over, P.K.!" Michelle said loudly. "You shouldn't be driving. Pull over right now!"

Hannah moved closer so that she could listen for his response, but there was no response at all. "Please, P.K.," she shouted. "Pull over!"

"It's no use," Michelle told her. "Either he's got our audio off or he's too drunk or stoned to listen to us."

"Noooo," P.K. said, and both sisters could see that his eyes looked vague and unfocused. "Thought I . . . juss hung . . . gry. Ate Rossss . . . hiz . . . desk. Can . . . dees . . . sickkk."

"Pull over!" Hannah shouted again as the car veered toward the center of the road and then lurched back toward the ditch again. "Pull over, P.K.!"

"Please pull over!" Michelle added, the panic clear in her voice.

There was no response to their pleas and Michelle shook her head. "He can't hear us, Hannah."

"You're probably right, but at least he's back on his side of the road again."

"No . . . more . . . can . . . dees," P.K. mumbled, and then his eyelids began to lower. "Got . . . ta get . . . Doc . . . hospit . . . uh . . ."

Both Hannah and Michelle watched in horror as the car weaved from one side of the road to the other, barely missing a county road sign. They had just given sighs of relief when the car began to drift toward the wrong side of the road again.

"Wake up, P.K.!" Michelle called out, leaning close to the phone. "Listen to me! You've got to stay awake!"

Again, there was no response from P.K. The only thing they heard was the sound of the engine growing louder and louder.

"He's stepping on the gas!" Hannah said in horror.

"I know! I can hear it! And he's . . . oh no!"

Michelle's last word was an anguished cry, and Hannah felt as if it had come from her own throat. P.K.'s eyes were closed now, but the car was going faster and faster.

The scene outside the driver's side window appeared to bounce up and down as the pine trees rushed past at breakneck speed. Then there was a loud blaring sound.

"The horn's on!" Michelle identified it. "P.K. must be blowing it for help."

Or he's wedged on the steering wheel, Hannah thought, but of course she didn't say what she was thinking.

"Look!" They watched as the bakery box with the Raspberry Danish that they'd given P.K. that morning flew past the screen as if it had suddenly grown wings.

"He's in the ditch!" Michelle gasped. "And the car's still going!"

Her horrified words were no sooner spoken than the screen on Michelle's cell phone went black.

"His phone shut off, or broke, or something!" Michelle gasped. "We have to do something, Hannah!"

Hannah thought fast. "You said you were going to record the call."

"I did!"

"Can you send that video to Mike's cell phone?"

"I . . . yes, I think so."

"Do it right now. I'll call Mike and tell him it's coming."

While Michelle figured out how to retrieve the video and send it, Hannah placed a call to Mike. Then she ducked into the kitchen to speak to him in private. Michelle was upset enough already. There was no way Hannah wanted her to overhear the conversation she was about to have with Mike.

Luckily, Mike answered on the second ring, and Hannah told him the video was coming. "It looked really bad, Mike, and I recognized a couple of landmarks. I think P.K. went off the road right before Abe Schilling's back pasture, the one where he keeps his bull in the summer. Do you know where that is?"

When Mike had assured her he knew the particular pasture she'd described, Hannah added her final sentences, the ones she hadn't wanted Michelle to overhear. "Hurry out there, Mike. There may be a chance that P.K. is still alive, but . . . I really doubt it."

Before she left the kitchen, Hannah poured the rest of the coffee into a thermos and carried it out to the living room. "Did Mike get the video?" she asked Michelle.

"Yes. He just texted me."

"Good. Now go get your parka and your boots. We're going out there."

"How? We don't know where P.K. went off the road!"

"I recognized some landmarks and I think I know where it happened. Hurry up, Michelle. And don't forget your warm scarf and mittens."

* * *

"Is that the county road sign we saw?" Michelle asked as Hannah drove down the winding road.

"I think so. And if I'm right, we only have a mile or two to go." Hannah slowed for another bend in the road. "Do you hear a siren?"

Michelle lowered her window. "Yes. I hear it, too."

"It's probably Mike."

"Or the paramedics," Michelle added. "I think I hear two sirens now."

When they rounded the next bend, they could see lights in the distance across the expanse of snow. Right after they passed an old yellow and black MINNESOTA BREEDERS ASSOCIATION sign nailed to a tree, Michelle drew in her breath sharply. "I saw that sign on the video," she said, her voice shaking slightly.

"I know." They rounded another curve, and Hannah saw more lights in the distance. "Hang on, Michelle. We're almost there."

"Doc's car," Michelle identified the car that was parked on the side of the road.

"And Mike's cruiser." Hannah pulled past it and parked behind another car that was on the shoulder of the road. "That's Doctor Bob's car. Let's go, Michelle."

As they opened their car doors, two figures materialized through the blowing snow. At first it was impossible to identify them, but as they reached the crest of the ditch, Michelle rushed forward. "Mother?" she called out.

Hannah was right behind her sister. It was obvious that their mother must have been riding with Doc because her car wasn't there.

"Take your mother back to my car, Michelle," Doc said. "I left it running, and the heater is on. Make her take off her wet shoes and wrap her in a blanket. And stay with her until I come back, okay?"

"Of course. But . . ."

"Not now, Michelle," Doc interrupted what was certain to

be a question about P.K. "Just take care of your mother for us. There's nothing you can do to help out here."

Hannah watched as her sister's face crumpled into a mask of sorrow and loss. Michelle had also caught the message behind Doc's words. She slipped an arm around Michelle's shoulders, gave her a comforting squeeze, and leaned close. "I'll take care of everything out here," she said. "You take care of Mother."

Michelle swallowed hard. And then she nodded. "I will," she promised, reaching out to take their mother's arm and leading Delores to Doc's car.

Hannah waited until Michelle and her mother had left, and then she turned to Doc. "Bad?" she asked him.

"Yes. Mike's down there now and he filled me in about the video. What do you want to know?"

"Was P.K. drunk?"

"No."

"Drugged?"

Doc gave a slight nod. "That's my guess. I'll know more after I take your mother home and get back to the hospital. They'll be here to transport him soon."

Hannah asked the question she knew Michelle would have asked. "Was P.K. in pain?"

"That's very doubtful." Doc reached out to pat her shoulder. "I'll know more later, but I'm almost certain he was already gone when he went off the road."

"Did Doctor Bob find him?"

"No. Bob delivered a calf at Karl Schilling's farm. He said it was a breech birth and Karl called him to help. Bob was just driving out when he heard a car horn. As he rounded the bend, he heard the sound of branches breaking and he knew that someone had gone in the ditch."

"So he stopped to help?"

"Of course. And that's when he saw the deer by the side of the road."

"P.K. hit a deer?"

"He sideswiped a deer as the car went into the ditch. Bob was about to climb down in the ditch when your mother and I pulled up. I told him to take care of the deer and I'd take care of anyone who was in the car."

"Is the deer dead?"

"No, just stunned. Nothing broken, no major injuries. Bob thinks it'll be up on its feet in a couple of minutes and hightailing it back into the woods."

Doc rubbed his hands together, and Hannah realized that he was cold in his dress coat and thin leather gloves. "Do you want some hot coffee, Doc? I've got a thermos in my truck."

"I can wait until I get back to the hospital, but I'll bet Mike and Lonnie could use some. If you give me the thermos, I'll take it down there to them."

"I'll take it. I've got on snow boots."

"Not on a bet, Hannah. I know the real reason you want to take that coffee down to Mike and Lonnie."

Hannah did her best to look perfectly clueless. "What do you mean?"

"You want to go down there because it'll give you a chance to pump them for information. Isn't that right?"

Hannah sighed. "You know me too well, Doc."

"That's because I delivered you. I'm the first person you ever saw. And that means I've known you all your life."

Hannah smiled at the predictable line. Doc told all three of the Swensen sisters the very same thing. "How about Mother? Will she be all right if you take her back to the penthouse and go back to the hospital?"

"She'll be fine. You underestimate your mother, Hannah. She's a lot stronger than you think she is."

"But she's had a nasty shock. Except for Doctor Bob, you and Mother were first at the scene, and it must have been . . ." Hannah paused to think of the right word. ". . . an *upsetting* sight."

"It would have been if I hadn't blocked your mother's view. Car accidents are never pretty. The human body is no match for asphalt and metal. Now go get that thermos and I'll take it down to Mike and Lonnie. Then I want you to take Michelle away before my paramedics arrive. She doesn't need to see them take P.K. away."

"But really, Doc," Hannah began to protest.

"Forget it, Hannah." Doc took her by the shoulders and turned her around. "Mike always comes over to your place after something like this happens, and you can pump him for information later."

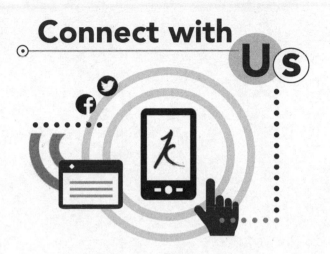